MURDER ON MILLIONAIRES' ROW

MURDER ON MILLIONAIRES' ROW

ERIN LINDSEY

MINOTAUR BOOKS

NEW YORK

MURDER ON MILLIONAIRES' ROW. Copyright © 2018 by Erin Lindsey. All rights reserved. Printed in the United States of America. For information, address St. Martin's Press, 175 Fifth Avenue, New York, N.Y. 10010.

www.minotaurbooks.com

Designed by Omar Chapa

Map designed by Emily Langmade

The Library of Congress Cataloging-in-Publication Data is available upon request.

ISBN 978-1-250-18065-0 (trade paperback)
ISBN 978-1-250-18066-7 (ebook)

Our books may be purchased in bulk for promotional, educational, or business use. Please contact your local bookseller or the Macmillan Corporate and Premium Sales Department at 1-800-221-7945, extension 5442, or by email at MacmillanSpecialMarkets@macmillan.com.

First Edition: October 2018

10 9 8 7 6 5 4 3 2 1

This book is dedicated to the millions of New Yorkers, adoptive and native-born, who make their city the greatest in the world. I heart you.

ACKNOWLEDGMENTS

I am profoundly grateful to the huge cast of academics, journalists, bloggers, podcasters, and other enthusiasts who have so meticulously documented the history of New York over the years. Few cities can be reconstructed with such depth and fidelity; the challenge for the novelist is not where to find the details she needs, but how she can bear to leave any of them out. I'm particularly indebted to Tyler Anbinder's *Five Points*, Edwin G. Burrows and Mike Wallace's *Gotham: A History of New York City to 1898*, and Irving Lewis Allen's *The City in Slang: New York Life and Popular Speech*. Thanks also to New York's wonderful Tenement Museum, and to the Bowery Boys podcast, whose annual Halloween episodes pointed me in the direction of some delightfully obscure and spooky tales.

Finally, special thanks to my editor, April Osborn, to my hard-working agents, Lisa Rodgers and Joshua Bilmes, and to my husband, Don, whose support makes all this possible.

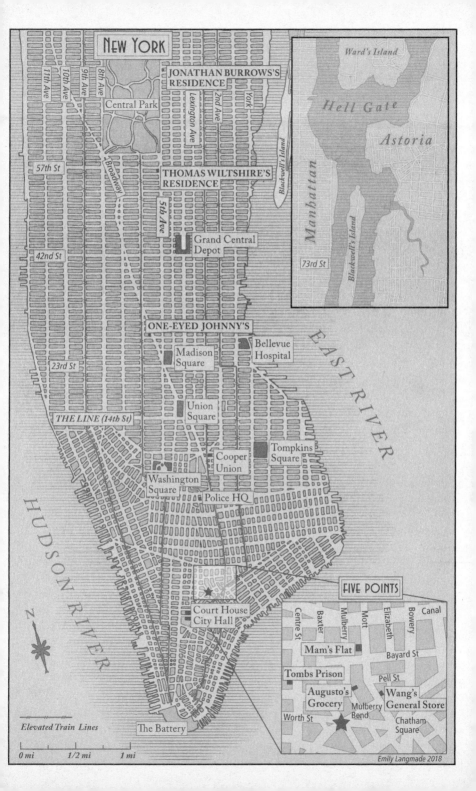

CHAPTER 1

ROSE GALLAGHER OF 55 MOTT STREET—
JUST ANOTHER DAY—CLARA'S ADVICE—
THE FIRST CLUE

s I tell you this story, I'll thank you to remember that I was young and in love. That's not an excuse, but if you're looking to understand what happened on that day in January 1886— what really happened, mind you, not the version you read in *Harper's Weekly* or *The New-York Tribune*—then you ought to have the whole picture. So yes, I was nineteen years old, and yes, I had a blinding crush on my employer, one Mr. Thomas Wiltshire of 726 Fifth Avenue, and those facts together led me to make certain choices in those early hours, choices that might charitably be called *naive*. Some of the actions I took I'm not particularly proud of. But I wouldn't take a one of them back, either—which is saying a lot, considering how near they came to getting me killed.

But I'm getting ahead of myself. I really ought to start at the beginning, which means I should say a little about where I'm from. If you're from around here, then you know that in New York, where you come from is everything. It defines your place in the world—your past, present, even your future if you let it. Why, just your name and address tell a stranger pretty much everything he cares to know about you. Not just *where* you live, but *how*: what parish you belong to, how much money you've got, where your people came from before they were Americans. He can even make a fair guess as to what you do for a living. Your name and address label you a certain *type* of New Yorker, a creature with particular habits and distinctive plumage, not unlike a species of bird. Black-capped chickadee. Northern mockingbird. Italian fruit vendor. Chinese laundryman. So when I say that my name is Rose Gallagher of 55 Mott Street, well, that's a whole story right there, and a common one at that. The story of an Irish girl from Five Points.

What do those words conjure in your head? A photograph of some fair-haired, reedy thing leaning out of a tenement window to hang washing on the line while drunks and ragpickers loiter in the alley below? Well, you wouldn't be far from the mark. But there's more to me than that slip of a girl, just as there's more to Five Points than the vice and violence you read about in the papers. Oh, it's a wretched enough corner of the world, to be sure, but it's home. And it's where I learned that if you don't take care of you and yours, there's nobody else will do it for you.

Which brings me back to the day Mr. Thomas Wiltshire disappeared, and everything I knew in the world went spinning down the drain.

Funny, isn't it, how the days that change your life forever start out like any other? I don't remember much about that morning, except that it was a Sunday and my day off, so I took my mother to church. I'd have spent the afternoon scrubbing Mam's floors and putting dinner on the stove, though I've no recollection of it. My first clear memory of the day is hanging off a strap on the Sixth Avenue el, trying to hold my copy of *Harper's Weekly* steady while the train rattled and swayed beneath me. The el, if you haven't had the pleasure, has all the lumbering grace of a three-legged bull, which makes reading the fine print of *Harper's* a bit of a trick, especially when it's coming on to dark outside. Luckily, I wasn't trying to read the print; I was too busy poring over the illustration on the cover.

It featured Mother Earth seated on her throne at the heart of the world, attended by her children as she greeted the New Year. She looked like a Roman goddess, serene and beautiful, smiling benevolently down at the cherubic 1886. I'd never seen anything so fantastical, so thoroughly exotic. Children of the world clustered around her, African and Indian and Celestial. Skins of lions and tigers beneath her sandaled feet. The volcano looming in the background, the waterfall plunging majestically over a cliff. What wondrous places had the artist traveled that he could capture images like these in such sumptuous detail? I felt a familiar pang of longing, and for a moment I imagined myself standing in a steaming jungle, brushing up against leaves the size of an elephant's ear while I listened to birds shriek and insects sing, the roar of a waterfall in the distance.

Maybe it was longer than a moment, come to think of it, because the next thing I remember it was full dark and I was making my way down the steps of the Fifty-Eighth Street Station in the rain. I must have made a pitiful sight hurrying along the sidewalk with my bonnet pulled low and my precious paper tucked under my arm, because the nighthawks seized on me the moment I turned onto Fifth Avenue, the *clip-clop* of hooves and calls of "Cab, miss?" trailing me down the block.

I burst through the servant's door at Number 726 with my usual grace, stumbling over the umbrella someone had left open to dry in the entryway. I couldn't wait to show Clara the illustration on the cover of *Harper's,* sure she would appreciate it as much as I did. But as I made my way down the hall, I heard a frightful clamor of pots and pans coming from the kitchen, and I drew up short.

Warily, I peered around the doorframe. "Clara?"

My greeting was met with a *crash* of the oven door and a string of language as doesn't bear repeating, the gist of which was this: Clara was having a bad day.

"People starving in this city—*starving*—but that's no bother, just fine, I'll toss away *three hours'* worth of cooking!"

I braved a single step into the kitchen. "What's happened?"

She whirled on me, hand on hip, eyes flared with righteous anger. "Why? I'll tell you *why*. Because His Lordship Sir High-and-Mighty can't be bothered to come home for his dinner! *Again*."

"Oh." I tried to think of a reasonable excuse. "Well, I suppose he's very busy with work."

"I suppose he is. Too busy to send word, even. *So important*."

"Careful," I said, throwing a worried glance at the foot of the servants' staircase. Mrs. Sellers had a way of appearing on those stairs at the most inopportune moments. "*She* might hear you." I didn't need to say who *she* was.

"Don't care if she does," Clara said, but she lowered her voice all the same. She needed her position as much as I, and the housekeeper was always looking for an excuse to get after the both of us, since the only stock of people she cared for less than the Irish were the coloreds. Mrs. Sellers might not have the authority to dismiss us outright, but she could make things difficult with Mr. Wiltshire, and that was cause enough to fear her.

"Did you ask her if we might . . ." I stopped myself short of asking a silly question. Mrs. Sellers never let us keep leftovers. To her way of thinking, that would only encourage Clara to prepare too much food in the hopes of keeping some for herself. It wouldn't occur to her that Clara was too decent, not to mention too proud, to do any such thing.

"So I can listen to her lecture me about how it's practically the same as stealing? No, thank you, ma'am."

"I'm sorry, Clara. It's an awful shame." My gaze slid longingly to the roast beef and potatoes cooling on the stovetop. I couldn't recall the last time I'd had Sunday roast. Easter, probably, some years past.

"Well." Clara surveyed the kitchen, her temper cooling along with her cooking. "Some of it'll keep, and there's always soup to be made. But the nerve of the man, not sending so much as a hint of warning. Uncivilized, is what it is. You'd think a proper Englishman would know better."

"I'm sure he had a good reason."

She gave me a wry look. "You're sure of no such thing, except that Thomas Wiltshire can do no wrong."

I felt my skin warming, so I changed the subject. "Look, I've got something to show you." Drawing her over by the lamp, I smoothed out my copy of *Harper's Weekly*. "What do you think of that?"

Clara squinted. "I hardly know. What is it?"

"Why, it's only the most incredible drawing I've ever seen!"

"Is it now?" She raised her eyebrows. "More incredible than the hot springs of Iceland?"

"Well, I suppose—"

"More incredible than the jaguar fishing in the Amazon? Or the squad of saluting elephants in India?" She made a trunk of her arm, raising it high.

"You're making fun of me."

Looking closer, Clara grunted. "All I see is a white lady with other people's babies in her lap."

"Well, I think it's grand," I said, snatching the paper off the table.

"Oh, don't be like that," she laughed. "I'm only teasing. I think it's fine how you get all lathered up over your magazines."

"I'm not *lathered up*. I'm trying to better myself, is all."

"Better yourself, or escape to the jungle for a spell?"

Escape. It's a strong word, when you think about it. A strong word, and exactly the right one. "And where's the harm in that?" I gestured vaguely at the kitchen. "Is it wrong to want to see more of the world than . . . this?"

"I know, honey."

That was the thing about Clara. She *did* know. She understood me better than anybody, probably because we had so much in common. Clara came from the Tenderloin, which is just about the only part of New York that can give Five Points a run for its money for sheer infamy. She'd seen her share of wickedness and faced more than her share of bigots. Like me, Clara had an ailing mother to take care of. And like me, she dreamed of bigger things—

in her case, marrying her sweetheart, Joseph, and saving enough money to buy a little dairy farm in Westchester.

But if Clara's dream seemed just out of reach, mine was downright unattainable. I wanted more than anything to be a Travel and Adventure writer, or maybe an illustrator. But if being a woman wasn't barrier enough, I was also Irish and poor as a church mouse. The four-story town house at 726 Fifth Avenue was about as close to travel and adventure as I was likely to get in this life.

"I just don't want to see you set yourself up for disappointment," Clara said. "You got to be realistic. Dreams is one thing. Goals is another."

"I know." I rolled up my *Harper's* and stuffed it into the pocket of my overcoat. Forcing a smile, I added, "And right now, my goal is to get some supper in my belly."

"Now that I can help you with." Clara went over to the stove and carved off a slice of the roast, crusty and fragrant, steam rising from it like a chorus of angels. Somehow she'd managed to keep it pink in the center, in spite of it having languished in the oven since late afternoon.

My mouth watered as I watched her load up the plate with golden potatoes and thick, greasy gravy. "What about Mrs. Sellers?"

"I don't see her anywhere, do you?" Clara's smile had just a hint of spite in it. "Now skedaddle. She catches you, we'll both wind up working in the box factory."

I didn't need to be told twice; I grabbed my plate and bounded up the narrow servants' staircase to my room, a little shoebox in the attic where I spent six nights a week.

I sat cross-legged on my bed, hunched over my food like a

savage, licking gravy off my fingers as I paged through *Harper's*. I'd like to tell you that I studied the articles carefully, absorbing worldly details about the Irish question and hostilities in the Balkans, or that I tutted disapprovingly over the latest spiteful cartoons from Thomas Nasty. But I never did care much for politics, and there were no Travel and Adventure stories in this issue to tempt me. So instead I pored over the illustrations, wondering if my own sketches demonstrated enough skill to impress an editor at *Harper's* or *Frank Leslie's*. Reaching for my journal, I let it fall open to its most beloved page: a charcoal sketch of a certain gentleman whose likeness I knew nearly as well as my own. I hope it won't sound boastful if I say that even Mr. Wiltshire's own mother would have called the resemblance striking. Every feature had been lovingly rendered: the pale eyes beneath straight dark brows; the high cheekbones and fine nose; the angular jaw framed by a neatly trimmed beard. It was true in every detail but one: I couldn't seem to capture the *soul* of him, that thoughtful expression that was at once gentle and sharp, reserved and yet curious. The eyes in my sketch were dull and flat, with nothing to suggest the man behind them had any depth at all.

I put the drawing away, resolving to try my hand at reproducing the illustration on the cover of *Harper's*. I'd wait until month's end, and if there was enough money left over after I'd paid Mam's rent, I'd treat myself to a new journal and maybe even some ribbon to fix my bonnet. "There, you see, Clara?" I murmured to myself. "I know the difference between dreams and goals."

I brought my plate back down to the kitchen before heading up the main staircase to prepare Mr. Wiltshire's bedroom for the night. I knocked softly, though I knew he wasn't there, having learned the hard way that it was best to make sure. (That, my friends, is a story all its own, and may have more than a little to do with the origins of my feelings for my employer. If you should find yourself becoming spoony for a young man, seeing the object of your budding affections in nothing but a pair of half-unbuttoned trousers will surely seal your fate.)

But I digress.

Satisfied the room was empty, I set about my chores, winding the clock and trimming the lamps and so forth. I fussed with his fountain pen and his shirt studs and his griffin cuff links, straightening them all *just so*. But it wasn't long until I noticed something out of place. Being meticulously tidy, Mr. Wiltshire was not given to leaving his papers strewn about, so the envelope sitting on his dressing table fairly cried out for my attention. Taking it up, I saw that it was unsealed, so I opened it (yes, I know—you will have many such occasions to exclaim at my behavior) and discovered a pair of tickets to the Metropolitan Opera. Nothing much in that, but two things struck me as unusual. First, the opera in question was by Richard Wagner, and it so happened that I had heard Mr. Wiltshire express a particular dislike for Wagner not two weeks before, over sherry with his good friend Mr. Burrows. Second, the tickets were for the evening of January 2, 1886—in other words, for a performance that had taken place the night before.

I glanced about the room. Had he even come home last night? The bed didn't look to have been slept in, but that didn't tell me much, since Mrs. Sellers would have tidied the room this morning. Taking a quick inventory of his shirt studs, I saw that the mother-of-pearl set was missing. He'd worn those on Saturday, and he never wore the same set two days in a row. No, he definitely hadn't come home. I wondered what sort of urgent matter had arisen to cause my employer to be so detained.

I didn't know it at the time, but *detained* was quite possibly the understatement of the year.

I went to bed feeling troubled. And by the time I woke up, the coppers were already there.

CHAPTER 2

THE COPPERS—CLARA'S COURAGE—ROSE
GALLAGHER AND CLARA FREEMAN,
DETECTIVES

The police arrived at a little after five o'clock on Monday morning, just a few minutes before I was due to rise. Somehow I'd slept through their ringing the bell, so when Mrs. Sellers burst into my little room in the attic to rouse me, it gave me quite a fright. I sat bolt upright, snatching a crucifix from the wall and brandishing it like a dagger. The housekeeper gasped and leapt back. We stared at each other for a spell, me with my makeshift dagger and she with her hand on her breast, both of us wide-eyed.

"*Good Lord.* Is that how you sleep in Five Points? With a knife under your pillow?"

I glanced at the crucifix in my hand. Our Lord and Savior gazed back at me with solemn eyes, silently advising me to hold my tongue.

"Get up," Mrs. Sellers snapped. "The police are here."

"Coppers?" I hopped up and fumbled for my dressing gown. "Why?"

"Don't ask foolish questions, girl, just get downstairs at once. And wake Clara."

Detective Ward and Officer O'Leary of the New York City Police Department were waiting in the parlor, red-eyed and be-whiskered, looking and smelling like they'd just been dragged out of a Bowery saloon—which they probably had. "This everyone?" the detective asked after they'd introduced themselves.

"It is," Mrs. Sellers confirmed. "Being a bachelor, Mr. Wiltshire doesn't require a large household staff."

"No coachman?"

"Mr. Wiltshire prefers to use the livery companies," the house-keeper said, managing to sound only faintly bemused at this eccentric behavior.

Ward grunted and wrote something in his ledger.

"Excuse me," I began, "but what—"

"*Hush*, girl." Mrs. Sellers glared at me.

Ward gestured with a stubby finger. "And when was the last time each of you saw Mr. Wiltshire?" He pronounced it the American way—*Wilt-shy-er*—in spite of having heard Mrs. Sellers say it properly only moments before.

"Saturday morning," said the housekeeper, confirming my suspicions from the night before.

"That go for all of you?" The thick finger waved again. My mother used to say that you could tell a lot about a person by the state of his hands. Detective Ward's hands, with their crusting of dirt and chewed-off fingernails, were telling me that he wasn't a man for details.

"Yes, sir," Clara said. "Saturday morning."

"He left early, before reading the papers," I added, since that was unusual.

Ward grunted and wrote in his ledger.

"Missing since early Saturday morning," said Officer O'Leary, "and here it is Monday."

Missing. The word hit me like a blow to the gut.

"That's a fair point," said the detective. "Why is it none of you ladies thought to report this matter to the police?"

"Thinking to cash in, maybe?" O'Leary grinned and winked. "Make off with a bit of the silver?"

All three of us—Clara, Mrs. Sellers, and I—sucked in a lungful of righteous outrage. In that moment, however fleeting, we were allies, three working women wrongly accused. "We were thinking no such thing," Mrs. Sellers replied, icicles dangling from every word. "I'll have you know that I have been in the Wiltshires' employ for nearly fifteen years, and in that time neither Mr. Thomas nor his late uncle ever had cause to complain about my service, let alone my integrity. My name and reputation are well known in the highest society circles. Ask anyone."

"Oh, that won't be necessary." O'Leary's grin widened. He seemed to find this all very amusing.

"We didn't contact the police because it isn't entirely unusual for Mr. Wiltshire to be absent for long stretches," the housekeeper went on. "Why, only this past spring he was gone for over a week."

What a trying time that had been. You can imagine Clara's fury about the cooking, and Mrs. Sellers had begun to fear that he'd gone back to England, cheating her of two weeks' wages. As for me, I'd just missed him terribly.

Something occurred to me then. "But if none of us reported him missing, who did?"

Detective Ward consulted his ledger. "A Mr. Jonathan R. Burrows of 923 Fifth Avenue."

"Mr. Burrows?" The housekeeper looked puzzled.

"You know the fella, I take it?"

"Of course. The Burrowses are one of the most prominent families in the country. Mr. Jonathan Burrows is an acquaintance of Mr. Wiltshire's."

"His closest acquaintance," I put in, earning myself another glare.

"Would you say this Burrows is the nervous type?"

"Not that I've noticed," Mrs. Sellers said. "Why do you ask?"

"Just trying to work out why my captain saw fit to drag us in before the crack of dawn to ask after some rounder whose own servants don't find anything queer in his absence."

"Oh, I do." The words were out of my mouth before I could stop myself, and suddenly everyone was looking at me.

"That right?" O'Leary narrowed his eyes. "And why's that, love?"

I swallowed hard. Not because I was afraid of the police. I'd grown up in Five Points, after all; if I had a nickel for every time a copper questioned me about some doing or another in the streets—no, the object of my anxiety was the housekeeper. I could feel Mrs. Sellers's eyes burning into me like hot coals. I'd spoken out of turn. There would be consequences. "It's only . . ." I swallowed again. "I noticed something odd last night when I went to prepare Mr. Wiltshire's room."

"And you didn't see fit to inform me?" Mrs. Sellers snapped.

Ward silenced the housekeeper with a wave. "What'd you notice, darlin'?"

"Opera tickets, for Saturday night's performance. A pair of them."

The coppers exchanged a look. "And?"

"Well, Mr. Wiltshire isn't the forgetful sort. He's punctual and organized and very conscientious. If he had an engagement for the opera, he wouldn't have overlooked it."

O'Leary yawned and scratched his stubble. "Maybe he just didn't feel like going. These Champagne Charlies, they don't think twice about wasting money."

"But there were two tickets. What about his companion for the evening?"

"Maybe they both decided not to go. Found themselves a better occupation, if you take my meaning." Ward flashed a leering smile, and both officers chuckled.

I took his meaning all right, and it got my back up. I'd held my tongue when they called him a rounder and a Champagne Charlie, as though he were some kind of frivolous man-about-town, but this was too much. "He's not that sort of person."

O'Leary gave me a knowing smirk. "I'm sure he's the perfect gentleman."

"That's just what he is," I said coldly. "Something must have detained him."

"Or someone," O'Leary said, just to watch me squirm.

I could feel myself blushing, and the wider the policemen grinned, the worse it got. Even Clara was looking at me with something dangerously close to pity. I tried to explain, but all I could do was stammer. "It isn't . . . I'm not . . . *He doesn't even like Wagner!*"

Mrs. Sellers clucked her tongue in disgust. "That's quite enough from you, Rose. Forgive me for letting her prattle on, officers. I'm afraid the girl suffers from a ridiculous infatuation."

"You don't say." Ward slid his ledger into his breast pocket and picked up his hat. They were through with me.

I was near to tears at this point, and might have said something even more ill-considered had Clara not come to my rescue.

"You should listen to Rose," she said, giving the coppers a hard look. "You can make fun all you like, but she knows Mr. Wiltshire better than anybody in this house. If she says he's behaving strangely, you'd best believe it."

"Clara!" Mrs. Sellers stamped her foot as if she'd just caught a terrier relieving itself on the carpet.

"Mr. Burrows was worried," Clara went on fearlessly, "and Rose is worried. That's two people close to Mr. Wiltshire thinking something ain't right. I'd take that serious if I was you."

The detective grunted and donned his hat. "We'll see. Might be I'll be back to talk to you again. Meantime, he turns up, you be sure and let us know."

"I certainly will, officer," Mrs. Sellers said primly, as though she'd been in command of the conversation all along. "I'll show you out."

Clara sighed as she watched them go. "She'll be showing us out next, she has her way."

"Thanks for standing up for me, though I wish you hadn't. You're going to catch it even worse than me."

Clara shrugged. "She can't do anything without Mr. Wiltshire's say-so, and if he really is in trouble, well, I don't suppose you and me will be top of his to-do list. Besides, there's worse things than the box factory." In spite of her words, I could see the worry in her eyes. Our positions in the Wiltshire household were the best either of us could realistically hope to land, and if we lost them, there was a good chance we'd never see their like again. The circle of wealthy families in New York was small; to fall out with any one of them was to be exiled forever from their glittering world.

I sank numbly onto one of Mr. Wiltshire's upholstered chairs. "I can't believe it. Things like this aren't supposed to happen uptown."

"Things like what? For all we know, he's snug as a bug somewhere. There's plenty of innocent explanations—in the eyes of man if not the eyes of the Lord." Clara arched an eyebrow pointedly.

"Not you, too! *He's not that sort.*"

"Rose, honey, you don't know what sort he is. Mending a man's stockings might make you less than a stranger, but don't be mistaking that for intimacy. Have you ever even had a proper conversation?"

"Of course! Just the other day he asked me about Ireland."

"Uh-huh. And you said?"

"That I had no memory of it. We left when I was a baby."

"And then he said?"

"He said . . ." I lowered my gaze, examining my slippered feet. "He said . . . *Is there tea?*"

Clara laughed. When I gave her a wounded look, she put a hand over her mouth. "I'm sorry, I shouldn't . . ." She bit down on her smile. "I'm sorry. It's just . . . look, I know how hard you work to fit in on the Avenue, reading and writing and talking *just so,* but that ain't the same as being one of 'em. You don't know a thing about what goes on in that man's head, or what he does when he walks out that door in the morning."

"What about just now, what you said to the coppers? Why should they listen to me if you won't?"

"I am listening. I'm just saying not to get too lathered up, is all. We don't know what happened, and there's nothing we can do about it anyway, so there's no sense letting it get to you. If he's really missing, the police'll find him."

I snorted. "A girl from your part of town ought to know better."

"A girl from my part of town knows better than to mess with what ain't her business," Clara said soberly, "and so should you."

"What if Mr. Wiltshire needs help? Don't tell me you think it's going to come from that organ grinder and his monkey?"

"And just what do you mean for us to do about it? This ain't one of your Travel and Adventure columns. This is real life, and—"

"The opera tickets," I said, springing to my feet.

Clara eyed me warily. "What about 'em?"

"We should take another look."

"Rose—"

"There are answers in that room, I know it. Some clue about where he went, or who with. I'm going to—"

"What you're going to do, Rose Gallagher, is polish the silver." Mrs. Sellers appeared in the doorway, eyes glittering with malice. "And then you're going to wash the curtains and iron the linens. When you're through with that, you'll beat the rugs and do the mending, and if by some miracle you finish all that before midnight, I'll have thought of a few more chores that need doing. As for you"—she turned to Clara—"Mr. Wiltshire will not look fondly on his servants showing such disrespect for the authorities. I will be withholding your salary until his return, at which point, if I have my way, you will be dismissed."

"But that's not fair!" I cried, painfully aware of how childish it sounded. "Clara and I were only trying to help Mr. Wiltshire!"

"I can assure you that Mr. Wiltshire does not need the help of a *papist* and a *negress*."

Clara drew herself up, seeming suddenly taller than her five-foot-two frame. "Mr. Wiltshire can speak for himself," she said in cool, measured tones. "I don't work for you. If he wants to dismiss me, I'll hear it from him, but until then, I got work to do."

Oh, how I wish I'd looked up to see the expression on the housekeeper's face as Clara flounced out of the room. But I didn't dare.

Mrs. Sellers stood there a moment, quivering in mute rage. Then she barked, "Get on with your chores, girl!"

I bolted up to my room. The sooner I got started, the sooner I could finish—and begin unraveling the mystery. Worried as I was for Mr. Wiltshire, I couldn't help feeling that adventure had found me at last.

I was yet young and foolish enough to relish that.

Miraculously enough, I did finish my chores before midnight. Even more miraculously, Mrs. Sellers had fallen asleep before she could think of something else to stick me with, so I was free to begin my investigations. Clara grumbled and moaned when I roused her from bed, but faithful friend that she was, she donned her dressing gown, wrapped up her braids, and padded downstairs with me, treading carefully so as not to wake the housekeeper. We closed the door to Mr. Wiltshire's room behind us, something I'd never dared to do before, and I couldn't help letting my imagination take flight as I turned the key, picturing myself doing so under very different circumstances. A delicious little shiver skittered down my spine, but I collected myself and got down to business.

"Here they are," I said, drawing the opera tickets from their envelope. "You see? Saturday night."

Clara yawned.

I turned the envelope over in my hand, but there was nothing to hint where it might have come from. "Did he mention anything about his engagements for the evening?" Mr. Wiltshire often dined out on Saturdays, giving Clara the afternoon off.

She shook her head. "But I only saw him in passing, at breakfast. He wasn't at the table long."

"And when I went in to tidy up, I found the *Sun* and the *Tribune* still folded, and the *Times* barely touched. He must have been in an awful rush to leave without reading his papers."

"Didn't look like it to me. When I brought him his breakfast, he was just sitting there staring off into space, winding that fancy watch of his. Looked more thoughtful than rushed."

I'd learned to respect Clara's powers of observation (she'd noticed my feelings for Mr. Wiltshire even before I had), but in this case I was doubtful. "He must have been in a hurry or he wouldn't have left the papers."

"Could be he saw something in the papers that *put* him in a hurry."

"Of course, that must be it! Clara, you're brilliant!"

"*Hush.*" She hooked a thumb at the ceiling, reminding me of the specter of Mrs. Sellers. The housekeeper slept soundly (and snored even more soundly), but after the day we'd had, Clara was right to be cautious.

Lowering my voice, I went on, "Something he read in the papers sent him dashing out the door."

"*Could be.* I'm just guessing."

"But it makes perfect sense." Unfortunately, it also made no difference—not unless we could work out exactly what he'd come across, and my heart sank as I realized that was no longer possible. "I threw the papers away this morning."

"What was left of 'em, anyway." Clara couldn't quite suppress the smug glint in her eye, like a gambler who's just discovered a trump in his hand. Despite her best efforts, she was being drawn in by the mystery.

"What do you mean?"

"I used the papers to wrap up yesterday's dinner. Figured Mr. Wiltshire had no use for the ones he'd already read, so I kept 'em to pack up the roast and such."

I nearly whooped with glee, but at the last moment I remembered the slumbering housekeeper and settled for a silent, manic hug. Clara shook her head, but she was grinning, too, and we fairly flew down to the kitchen in search of what remained of *The New-York Times*.

This, of course, was patently ludicrous. What did we expect to find, and how would we know it when we saw it? We didn't pause to ask ourselves these very reasonable questions. Instead we set ourselves to the task, carefully unwrapping each soggy, stained bit of newsprint and spreading it flat until the entirety of Mr. Wiltshire's Sunday dinner had been stripped naked and every surface of the kitchen papered over.

At which point we were finally struck by the improbability of what we were doing. How were we to know which page, let alone which article, Mr. Wiltshire had seized upon?

Clara sighed. "We could read this all night and be none the wiser."

"Maybe something will leap out at us."

She eyed me doubtfully, but we'd come too far to give up now, so we each hunched over a rumpled square of paper and set to reading.

It was a dull business. MORE SNOW AND COLD WEATHER, read one headline. THE PRISON LABOR PROBLEM, said another. Clara muttered over an article describing the elopement of one Miss Nora Ludlum, "As though it's anybody's business but her own." I could feel my eyelids growing heavy when at length I spied something that didn't belong: a tiny smear of strawberry preserve. Eagerly, I scanned the headlines on the page.

FACTORY FIRE PHOTOGRAPHED. SMALLPOX BROUGHT FROM BOSTON. A NARROW ESCAPE. Grainy images of billowing smoke, a snippet about a family of four wiped out by smallpox, and the outrageous account of a self-styled treasure hunter who claimed to have been attacked by a ghost in the narrows of the East River. Nothing, in short, that could have interested Mr. Wiltshire. "It's no use," I sighed. "We'll never find it."

"It was worth a try. Let's get this put away and hit the straw. Tomorrow's going to be another long day." Stretching, she added, "Besides, this is all so much fuss over nothing, you'll see. Mr. Wiltshire'll be back before you know it, reading his papers and drinking sherry with Mr. Burrows."

"Mr. Burrows!" I snapped my fingers. "Of course!"

Clara groaned and rolled her eyes.

"He reported Mr. Wiltshire missing, even before we noticed anything wrong. Why would he do that? He must know something we don't. Maybe he was expecting to see him, or—"

"Or what, Rose?" Clara snapped, her patience exhausted.

"What good is it standing around here guessing what Mr. Jonathan Burrows knows about this or any other thing?"

"None at all."

She eyed me suspiciously. "Rose . . ."

"Which is why I need you to cover for me tomorrow."

"Cover for you." She gave a brittle laugh and shook her head. "Dear Lord, she's lost her mind. And just how am I supposed to do that?"

"I need to speak with Mr. Burrows. He must know something."

"Supposing he does? He'll tell the police, and they'll—"

"*They'll do nothing*," I cried, too exasperated to keep my voice down. "You heard them, Clara! Champagne Charlie, they called him. Just another swell rounder living the high life, bound to turn up in some fancy hotel or parlor house before long."

"Did it occur to you they might be right?"

"No," I said coldly, "it certainly did not."

Silence stretched between us. Clara sighed. "I'll send you out for groceries early in the morning."

I sagged with gratitude. "I won't be long."

"Best not be, or both of us'll wind up—"

"I know," I said, planting a kiss on her forehead. "The box factory."

CHAPTER 3

MR. JONATHAN BURROWS—TICKING
CLOCKS—HEADED FOR TROUBLE

Morning found me hurrying up Fifth Avenue—or, if not exactly hurrying, doing my best to move along while gawking at the scenery. Even after two years of working for Mr. Wiltshire, I found it impossible to run the gauntlet of Vanderbilts and Joneses and Astors without my head being drawn irresistibly up, up, *up* to gaze upon the limestone palaces lining the wide expanse of Millionaires' Row. If you haven't had the experience, I'm not sure how to describe it to you. Imagine yourself an ant scurrying past a row of towering, elaborately frosted wedding cakes and you'll have something of the idea. New York's elite seemed forever locked in competition for the frilliest cornices, the showiest windows, the stateliest balconies. Follies, my mother used to call them, but if this was folly, it didn't seem to be doing the New York aristocracy any harm.

Mr. Jonathan R. Burrows, youngest son of the great steel baron Frederick R. H. Burrows, lived in a comparatively modest four-story row house across from Central Park. I'd visited it once before on an errand for Mr. Wiltshire and found its smooth brownstone front elegant and inviting, with its handsome bay windows, meticulously pruned boxwoods, and swooping wrought-iron rails. But as I stood at the bottom of the steps on that January morning, shivering with cold, I found nothing inviting in the grim features before me—dark windows staring out from under glowering eaves, the arch of the doorway turned down like a disapproving twist of the mouth. *You have no business here,* that stern visage seemed to say. What would Mr. Burrows think of a lowly maid calling on him in his home? What if he should report me to Mrs. Sellers, or—*horrors*—mention it to Mr. Wiltshire? Which of course he would, I realized with dawning dismay, since they were the closest of friends.

Rose Gallagher, what on earth were you thinking?

But no. Mr. Burrows had always been kind to me. He would understand, surely. After all, I was here under the direst of circumstances.

I convinced myself for exactly the length of time required to ring the bell. At which point I was trapped.

The fellow who answered the door looked like someone's grandfather—the sort who has no use whatsoever for his grandchildren. He scowled first at my bonnet and then at my shoes, and nothing in between pleased him any better. "May I help you?"

"Rose Gallagher to see Mr. Jonathan Burrows, please." And then, in a flash of inspiration: "It's an emergency."

This put the butler in a quandary. I wasn't wearing my maid's uniform, but even so it was plain enough from my humble appearance that I didn't belong in his master's house. On the other hand, I was a young woman in distress, so basic decorum prevented him from casting me out altogether. "Wait here," he said grudgingly, and disappeared inside.

My temporary bravado had worn off by this time, so I was more than a little surprised when the butler reappeared a moment later and said, "Follow me," depositing me in the front parlor with vague assurances that Mr. Burrows would be along presently.

I turned in a small circle, unsure if I should sit or stand. My experience of high society parlors was confined to dusting and sweeping them; what did I know of proper etiquette? I decided it was safest to stay where I was.

I waited. A carriage clock on the mantel ticked primly, an all-too-present reminder of the time racing by. I'd promised Clara that I wouldn't be long, but it had taken nearly half an hour to walk here, and it would be the same going back unless I managed to catch a stage. I glanced anxiously at the clock, and as I did, a glint of gold caught my eye. A gentleman's watch lay on the mantel beside the carriage clock, as though someone had intended to set it and then forgot it.

Curiosity overcame good manners. I picked it up . . . and instantly recognized it as Mr. Wiltshire's. Not only was it a distinctive shade of rose gold, but the monogrammed case confirmed its identity, the initials *T.W.* framed by elaborate scrollwork. I ran my thumb lovingly over the case. Then I opened it, thrilling at the intimacy of the act.

"Rose?"

I started so violently that Mr. Burrows very nearly found me clinging to the ceiling like a spider, an empty Rose-shaped dress pooled on his rug.

"Oh dear, I've given you a fright." Half laughing, half apologetic, Mr. Burrows steered me to a chair. "I'm so sorry. Please, sit. There now, are you all right?"

"I—I'm fine," I stammered, Mr. Wiltshire's watch still clutched damningly in my hand. "You startled me, that's all." Of course, what I really meant was *You caught me snooping.*

"It is you after all. I was racking my brain trying to recall if there was another Rose of my acquaintance. I must say, this is quite a surprise." Mr. Jonathan Burrows regarded me curiously. He was a handsome man, tall and fair, with a ready smile and a mischievous glint in his eye. I'd met him a number of times when he called on Mr. Wiltshire, and he'd always been very warm— even, may I say, a little flirtatious, though I didn't flatter myself to think there was anything in it. Jonathan Burrows was just one of those wealthy young gentlemen accustomed to having the world at his feet, who, like a cat with its prey, takes a languid sort of amusement in trifling with it. "It's not every day a pretty girl lands on my doorstep unannounced," he said. "To what do I owe the pleasure?"

I started to answer, but I felt ridiculous sitting there with Mr. Wiltshire's watch in my hand, so I held it out to him. "I'm sorry, I shouldn't have . . . but I recognized it as Mr. Wiltshire's, and . . ."

"And you're accustomed to picking up after him. I quite understand. He must have left it here the other day. It's lucky you came by—you can return it to him."

"Except I can't, because he isn't at home."

The amused glint vanished from his eye; suddenly, Mr. Burrows

was very serious indeed. "So he hasn't turned up. Blast."
Running a hand over his clean-shaven jaw, he started to pace.
"Where the deuce can he be?"

"I was hoping you might have an idea. That's why I've come."

"I don't understand. Aren't the police involved?"

I felt myself flush, but I answered as frankly as I dared. "I
don't have much confidence in the police, sir."

Mr. Burrows snorted softly. "I daresay you're not alone. But
I'm not sure how I can help."

"Well, sir, if I may ask, when did you last see Mr. Wiltshire?"

"Thursday. He came by in the morning. That must have been
when he left the watch."

"You're sure it was Thursday?"

"Quite sure." Smiling, he added, "After all, I've been over
this with the police already." Which was a gentle way of saying,
This really isn't your place.

I recognized the rebuke, but I wasn't going to let it put me
off, not after I'd come this far. "Of course, forgive me. After all, it
was you who reported Mr. Wiltshire missing."

"Indeed."

"You knew something was wrong before anyone else—but
how?"

"Sorry?"

"Forgive me, I just wondered *how* you knew, since Mr. Wiltshire had only been gone for a short while."

"Why, because he didn't turn up for our engagement on Saturday night. We were meant to have dinner together at the Park
Avenue Hotel."

"Before the opera."

"Pardon?"

"Mr. Wiltshire had opera tickets for Saturday night. I suppose you were planning to go together?"

"That's right. An early dinner on Park Avenue, then the opera. I waited for him at the club, but he never arrived, and that isn't like Wiltshire at all."

There'd been no hesitation, not even a heartbeat, but I knew straightaway something was off. His blue eyes seemed suddenly distant. There was a wariness to him now, a subtle tension in his posture, his too-perfect smile.

You're imagining things, I told myself. *Why would he lie?* And yet his explanation didn't make sense. I might not have known much about New York society etiquette, but it seemed to me that failing to turn up for supper was hardly grounds for involving the police.

I started to say something. Stopped. Mr. Burrows watched me with that wooden smile. "I want to do everything I can to help find him," I said carefully.

"Of course, and I know he'd be touched. But I'm afraid there's little either of us can do except provide the police with whatever information we have, which in my case is regrettably little." He sighed and shook his head. "I simply had a *feeling* that something wasn't right."

"But if you were worried, why not come by the house before going to the police? He might have been there, or at his office."

"I did call at the house, but it was very late. No one came to the door."

An unmistakable edge to his voice now. He *was* lying, I was sure of it. But why? For a moment, all I could do was sit there, confused and a little frightened, at a loss to explain why Mr. Wiltshire's closest friend would lie about what happened to him. I trotted out the only clue I had left, trivial as it was. "The odd thing is, I thought

I heard Mr. Wiltshire say that he didn't care for Wagner. And I
seem to recall that you agreed with him, yet barely a week later—"

"I'm sorry, Rose, what is this about? You seem to think I'm
keeping something from you."

"Are you?" The words tumbled out before I could stop them,
and I blushed again.

A long pause. Mr. Burrows gazed down at me, oddly appraising. Then: "I think you'd better leave."

Blood rushed to my face before draining down to my toes. I
started to tremble; I wasn't sure if I was humiliated or angry or both.
Wordlessly, I sprang to my feet and marched to the door. My hand
was on the doorknob when I paused and, summoning every ounce
of courage I possessed, whirled back around. "You *are* keeping
something from me, though I can't imagine why."

The blue eyes regarded me coolly. "You're mistaken."

"Oh, really?" I brandished the gold watch. "You say you haven't
seen Mr. Wiltshire since Thursday, and you claim not to have noticed that he left his watch behind. So how is it still ticking four
days later?"

He shrugged. "It's a Patek Philippe. The Swiss make miraculous watches."

"You can't seriously expect me to believe that."

"Go home, Rose." His tone was surprisingly gentle. For some
reason, that terrified me.

We stared at each other for another long, tense moment. "I
can help," I said, preposterously.

"Bertram will see you out," he said, and that was that.

I was so flustered by the exchange with Mr. Burrows that I very
nearly forgot to pick up the groceries on my way home. As it was,

Clara clucked and tutted over my hasty selection of vegetables, and she pronounced the chicken fit only for chicken salad with mayonnaise. "Lucky for you the old hag's got one of her headaches today," she said, hitching a thumb to indicate the attic, where Mrs. Sellers cloistered herself whenever one of her "bilious headaches" came on. "She rang for you only once this morning, and I told her you was doing the shopping. Wanted me to send you up there soon as you got back, but it's probably best you wait a while. I'll just say I forgot to pass on the message; that way she'll never know what time you got back."

I nodded distractedly as I tied on my apron, my mind still adrift in Mr. Burrows's parlor.

"He tell you anything useful?" Clara asked, peeling onions for a chicken salad that would most likely end up in the trash. In spite of the crisis, Mrs. Sellers had insisted that we continue on as if nothing were amiss, as befit a proper high society household.

"He lied to me." The words sounded distant to my ears, as if someone else were speaking them.

Clara paused. "What do you mean, lied to you?"

"I asked him about Mr. Wiltshire, and he looked me straight in the eye and lied."

"Now why would he go and do a thing like that?"

I shook my head, at a loss.

"You sure he was lying?"

The bluntness of her question lifted the fog, and suddenly the full meaning of what I was suggesting was laid bare before me, crystal clear in all its ugliness. I was accusing Mr. Jonathan R. Burrows, of the Philadelphia Burrowses, of being a *liar*. "I suppose he can't have, can he?"

"'Course he *could*. Question is, why *would* he?"

"He wouldn't. A gentleman like Mr. Burrows . . ."

Clara *tsk*ed. "What's being rich got to do with it? Rich folks lie as often as poor ones. More, maybe."

I stared at her, scandalized.

"Rose, Rose." She muttered something about champagne bubbles going to my head. Then: "What made you think he was lying?"

"Well, for one thing, he claimed not to have seen Mr. Wiltshire since Thursday, but *look*." I drew his watch from my pocket, dangling the exhibit dramatically before my jury of one.

Clara's eyes widened. "*Put that away!*" she hissed, waving at me as if to shoo a stray cat. "Housekeeper catches you with that, you'll be sent up the river for sure! You wanna spend the rest of your life breaking rocks?"

I tucked the watch out of sight. That wasn't what she meant, of course; I should have put it back in his room straightaway. But I wasn't quite ready to part with my treasure just yet, and even the specter of Sing Sing wasn't enough to bring me to my senses.

"I found it at Mr. Burrows's house, in the parlor. It's *still ticking*, Clara."

"So?"

"So if Mr. Wiltshire hadn't been there since Thursday, the watch would have stopped days ago."

"That it? There's plenty of explanations for that."

"Yes, I'm told the Swiss make miraculous watches," I said irritably. "But what was it doing there in the first place? Weren't you the one who said you saw him winding it on Saturday?"

She paused, thinking back. "Well, I thought so, but maybe I'm remembering wrong. He's always winding that thing."

"Exactly. When have you ever seen him without it?"

"So you're thinking—what? That Mr. Burrows stole it?"

"Don't be ridiculous. He's rich as a Rockefeller."

"So what if he is? Lord Almighty, Rose, we ain't among the angels up here. Fifth Avenue's no different than Five Points or any other place."

I lapsed into a brief silence, stunned by this heresy. New York's belief in the relationship between geography and virtue was practically gospel. For scripture, one had only to consult a map of Manhattan, the grid lines of which seemed to hint at the moral character of their residents. Above Fourteenth Street, the lines were straight, disciplined, reliable—none more so than Fifth Avenue, the undisputed backbone of the city, marching up the center of the island like the hand of a moral compass pointing due north. Below the Line, meanwhile, the streets were crooked and unpredictable, as befit the residents of those blighted lowlands.

But I didn't have time to argue about New York religion. "I can't believe Mr. Burrows would steal a watch, especially from a friend. It looked to me as if Mr. Wiltshire left it there by accident, as though he went to check it against the clock on the mantelpiece and then forgot it."

"Sounds like a man with time on his mind."

"The sort of man who might leave breakfast in a hurry."

"That was on Saturday. So you think . . . ?"

"It would make sense, wouldn't it? What if, after he left here on Saturday morning, Mr. Wiltshire went straight to Mr. Burrows? Maybe he wanted to talk over whatever he'd seen in the *Times*?"

"Lotta ifs and maybes," Clara pointed out. "And it still don't explain why Mr. Burrows would lie about it."

"No," I sighed, "I suppose not."

"Unless he was trying to protect someone."

"Like who?"

"Mr. Wiltshire, say. Maybe he's into some bad business, and Mr. Burrows is trying to keep it under his hat."

Lying to protect a friend's reputation—*that* sounded like something a Fifth Avenue gentleman might do. But I couldn't believe that Mr. Wiltshire, proper Englishman that he was, could be mixed up in anything too terrible.

I was about to say as much when Clara went on, "Or maybe it's you he's trying to protect."

"Me? Why should I need protecting?"

"Because you're sniffing around where you don't belong. If Mr. Wiltshire *is* into some bad business, you could be headed for trouble."

"Worse than the box factory?"

"I mean it, Rose." Clara's brown eyes were earnest. "If you know what's good for you, you'll keep outta this from now on."

We stared at each other for a stretch, and I knew we shared the same thought: When had I ever known what was good for me?

CHAPTER 4

A BUCKET OF LUCK—STAGES, CABS, AND
CARRIAGES—MR. BURROWS GOES
SLUMMING—BAD BUSINESS

The following morning brought a welcome stroke of luck. Mrs. Sellers rang shortly after dawn, and upon entering the dark little cave of her bedroom, I found a pail of sick at her bedside.

Now, I know what you're thinking: How could a bucketful of vomit possibly be lucky? Well, for Clara and me, it signified nothing short of a holiday. Mrs. Sellers would not be leaving the confines of her bedroom for at least another day. I'd learned to classify the housekeeper's headaches according to their symptoms, and vomiting placed it in the severest category, the sort that took two, sometimes three days to clear up. Two to three days of glorious freedom from Mrs. Sellers's relentless harping. Such an event occurred not more than twice a year, and I hope you won't

judge me too harshly if I say that I put it on a par with Easter and
St. Patrick's Day.

I greeted it with special enthusiasm on that Wednesday,
since it freed me to pursue an idea I'd been mulling over all night:
confronting Mr. Burrows.

I'd played the scene out over and over in my mind. I'd arrive
on his doorstep and *demand* to see him, brimming with such righteous determination that even the haughty butler wouldn't dare
deny me. Mr. Burrows would receive me in the parlor, all cheeky
smiles and subterfuge until it became clear that I was not merely
some fragile Fifth Avenue flower to be trifled with as he pleased.
At which point he would tell me everything.

When I put this plan to Clara, she didn't see its merits
straightaway. "That's the dumbest idea you've had yet, Rose
Gallagher," she said, jabbing an oatmeal-coated spoon at me. "And
you know it."

Some part of me *did* know it, but that part had been muzzled
at around two o'clock in the morning. Now, as I stood in the kitchen
with my overcoat on, the loudest sound in my ear was the ticking
of Mr. Wiltshire's watch. Its weight, subtle and persistent, tugged
at the breast pocket of my dress; I fancied I could even feel it beating gently against my rib cage, a constant reminder of the precious
minutes flying past. Mr. Wiltshire had disappeared on Saturday,
and here it was Wednesday. Four days. You didn't have to be a
copper to know what that meant. "I have to do this, Clara. I have
to try. Please."

Grudgingly, Clara ordered me out for groceries again.

I struck out a little before eight o'clock, and for once I didn't
let myself be distracted by the splendor of Fifth Avenue, bowing
my head against the chill and tramping up the street like a horse

with blinders on. I caught a stage just past the Vanderbilt mansion and spent most of the journey rehearsing the speech I planned to give. I don't recall the details of my discourse, but I can assure you it was worthy of a Bathsheba Everdene or even an Elizabeth Bennett. I might not have had the benefit of an expensive education, but I was the daughter of a schoolteacher, and I'd been diligently studying *Harper's* and *Frank Leslie's* for years. I knew words like *vituperate*, and I meant to use them.

I hopped off at Seventy-Second Street, intending to walk the remaining block while I composed the final flourishes of my vituperation, but as I approached the house, I saw to my dismay that Mr. Burrows's brougham waited by the front door. He was on his way out, and if I missed him . . . I hurried my step, but before I could cross the avenue, the coachman twitched the reins and the carriage rattled away.

Gathering up the hem of my dress, I made an absurd and thoroughly undignified attempt to run after it. I can only imagine what Mr. Burrows's elegant neighbors must have thought of the spectacle of a disheveled housemaid chasing after his brougham like a stray dog, hollering and waving as it retreated splendidly down Fifth Avenue.

After about half a block I gave up, breathless and distraught, watching helplessly as my best chance to find Mr. Wiltshire faded into the distance. And then, like the voice of Providence itself:

"Cab, miss?"

"*Yes!*" I whirled to find a hansom cab drawn up at the curb behind me. "That gentleman's carriage," I said, pointing. "Can you follow it?"

The driver eyed the retreating brougham. "If you need me to, miss."

"I do, but discreetly, please. I mustn't be seen. Er, that is . . ." I stumbled, too flustered to come up with a respectable explanation for my request.

But this was New York, after all; the driver just touched the brim of his hat with his riding crop and said, "Discreetly it is, miss. Hop aboard."

We caught up to Mr. Burrows's brougham easily enough. It was a heavier vehicle than the hansom cab, and though pulled by a sleek trotter, it trundled along at a dignified pace. At half past eight on a Wednesday morning, New York traffic was in full flood; we blended in easily with the crowd of carriages, carts, and horses clogging Fifth Avenue. Even so, I huddled up against the tufted upholstery, feeling all too exposed by the cab's open design.

I wasn't sure what I intended to do when we reached our destination (Mr. Burrows's office, I presumed). Officially, my plan was still to confront him, so why had I decided to follow in secret? This was, I suppose, just another of the many flashes of intuition that guided my steps in those early days. And the farther south we went, the more I congratulated myself on my instincts, because it soon became clear that Mr. Burrows wasn't headed for his office after all. Unless, of course, he happened to be employed in a run-down saloon in the Tenderloin.

Seeing the brougham slow, I instructed my driver to pull over, then watched in astonishment as Mr. Jonathan Burrows of the Philadelphia Burrowses, silk hat on head and ivory-handled walking stick in hand, descended beneath the stoop of a cheap hotel into a dive the likes of which even the average Five Pointer would fear to tread.

"Your gentleman friend'd best be careful," the cab driver said, chewing on the nub of a cheap cigar. "Rich fella like him—

they're liable to slip 'im a mickey finn." Pausing, he added, "That's where they put knock-out drops in your grog, so they can—"

"I know what a mickey finn is." Where I came from, tales of crooked barkeeps (invariably Irish) and their hapless victims were practically the stuff of legend. Why, all of Five Points had heard the yarn about old Tom Payne, a bum from Bottle Alley who claimed to have struck it rich at the fights one night only to wake up naked and penniless in a back alley off the Bowery. But would Mr. Burrows have heard the tales? Though you may laugh, it actually occurred to me to rush to the gentleman's rescue. Surely he didn't understand what kind of place he was in? And yet he must have, because he'd sent his carriage on as soon as he'd got out, presumably to avoid it being seen outside a fleabag hotel in the Tenderloin.

"What on earth is he doing?" I murmured.

"You know the place?"

I cast a cold glance through the trapdoor. "I most certainly do not."

The driver gestured with his soggy cigar. "Black-'n-tan saloon, goes by the name of One-Eyed Johnny's. Rough joint."

"So?"

"Just sayin', miss, hunting the elephant's one thing, but there's limits to what you can get away with, least if you wanna keep the clothes on your back."

"I'm sure that's not what he's doing." In truth I was sure of no such thing. It struck me that Mr. Burrows might be just the sort of swell who braved the gutters purely for the thrill of it.

I wasn't sure what to do next, but before I could make up my mind, Mr. Burrows reappeared on the steps, donning his hat with a worried frown.

"That didn't take long," the driver opined around his cigar. I think he was enjoying himself.

Mr. Burrows wandered up the sidewalk, chin tucked into the fur collar of his overcoat, stick rapping the pavement meditatively. It didn't look to me like the countenance of a thrill-seeker. No, whatever had brought him to this part of town, it was obviously a serious matter. Something to do with Mr. Wiltshire, maybe?

Whatever it was, he obviously wasn't through. His brougham waited on the corner, and he climbed aboard and joined the southbound traffic on Broadway.

"Here we go," my cab driver said, with a little more enthusiasm than was seemly.

Downtown we went, following the crooked cant of Broadway, past the dance halls and oyster cellars, past the hock shops and hash houses, our surroundings growing shabbier with each passing block. Soon we joined up with the Bowery, and I looked on incredulously as Mr. Burrows's sleek buckskin pranced through the winter muck, negotiating a delicate path through the menagerie of bootblacks, hot corn girls, patterers, and fortune-tellers. The carriage bore him along like a boat on a river, and he the intrepid explorer forging ever deeper into the wilds of the urban jungle, surrounded by the shrieking calls of the local species. *"Fresh oysters!" "Get your Times here!" "Slaughter in a Pan! Red Mike with a buncha violets!"*

Still the brougham rolled on, and as we neared Canal Street, I found myself rising out of my seat in disbelief. If I was puzzled to find Mr. Burrows slumming in the Tenderloin, imagine my shock when we plunged into the dark heart of Five Points. *This can't have anything to do with Mr. Wiltshire,* I thought. Not here, of all places.

Maybe he's into some bad business, Clara had said, and it had seemed reasonable enough. An investment gone sour, maybe, or a falling-out between partners. Even a gambling debt seemed like a distant possibility, but *this*? The Thomas Wiltshire of my imagination would never set foot in Five Points, let alone sink into its moral quicksand.

It may surprise you that I would take this attitude given that we were barely two blocks from the flat where I was raised. I can only offer it as evidence of how very different I considered us to be, Mr. Wiltshire and me. I got along just fine on these streets, but I'd grown up here. I'd been pickled in the brine of Five Points, and like a factory worker who no longer smells the noxious fumes, or a seamstress whose finger has been hardened against the prick of the needle, I was pretty well immune. Mr. Wiltshire, though—his was surely a much more delicate constitution. I could more easily imagine the Queen of England consorting with the savage tribes of the Amazon.

Or so I thought, but when I saw the languid ease with which Mr. Jonathan Burrows alighted from his carriage and struck out among the natives, I started to wonder.

He sent his coachman on, so I decided to do the same, my cab being much more conspicuous in Chatham Square than on Broadway. I jumped down and scoured my reticule for the fare, which was more than I could easily afford. "Good luck to you, miss," the driver said. "Though if you want my advice, you oughta hop back up here and let me take you home. Whatever your gentleman friend is doing in this part of town, a nice girl like you don't need to see it. Ignorance is bliss, as the saying goes."

My skin grew hot as I realized what the cab driver must think. But after all, could I blame him? "As it happens, I don't want your advice," I said tartly, tossing a few coins into his hand.

I caught up with Mr. Burrows on Mott Street, just south of my mother's flat, and proceeded to follow him through the most colorful circuit of sin Five Points had to offer. If slumming this was, it was of the bravest, most foolhardy sort. He visited every opium den, every gin joint, every dark nook and fetid cranny of Mulberry Bend. He called in at the mission and the Tombs prison. He lingered inside Wang's General Store for at least half an hour. By the time he ascended the steps of the Sixth Avenue el, I felt as if I were through the looking glass, chasing the White Rabbit through a Wonderland that both was and wasn't the familiar world of my childhood. Any moment now, surely, I would wake up in my little room in Mr. Wiltshire's attic wondering what I'd eaten that hadn't agreed with me.

I kept my back to Mr. Burrows on the train, glancing over my shoulder every now and then to keep track of him. I assumed we were both heading home after a long and fruitless day, so I was surprised when he got off at Twenty-Third Street, and, exhausted and confused, I very nearly let him go. But I've never been one to leave a thing unfinished, so I slipped off the train and followed.

I fought my way through the press of bodies on the platform, breaking through just in time to see Mr. Burrows racing up the steps of a magnificent limestone palace on the corner.

To the untrained eye, it looked like a fancy hotel, or maybe a bank. But one glance at the flag thrusting out from its sloping mansard roof and I knew better. I froze instantly, a prickle of dread running down my spine. I hadn't seen that heraldry since my childhood, but I'd never forget it. You wouldn't either, if the mere sight of it inspired your mother to spit and cross the street.

The old Masonic Hall of New York City used to be just a few

blocks from the flat where I grew up, but my mother never passed the place if she could avoid it, and when she couldn't, she made such a great show of crossing herself with elaborate Catholic dread that passersby would stop to look. I never got the full story behind that; all I'd ever managed to find out was that *something* transpired in the fall of 1873 that put the Freemasons at odds with the neighborhood to such an extent that they were run out of Five Points. Which, considering what Five Pointers have put up with over the years, must have been quite *something* indeed. Whatever it was, the Masons were exiled to Twenty-Third Street, consoling themselves by building the grand palace in the shadow of which I now stood.

Through the front doors of which Mr. Burrows had just entered.

He didn't linger. Barely ten minutes later he erupted through the doors, color high, the heels of his oxfords ringing against the stone. He very nearly caught me loitering by the steps; I dropped to the pavement, pretending to tie my laces.

"Burrows. Slow down, my dear fellow, you're making a scene."

I glanced up to see a middle-aged gentleman pursuing Mr. Burrows down the steps, hands raised in a mollifying gesture.

"A scene." Mr. Burrows gave a hollow laugh. "I don't think you quite understand the situation, Roberts."

They paused not three feet from where I cowered in the lee of the steps, tying and retying my laces.

"We mustn't indulge in speculation," said the man called Roberts. "I'm sure he has everything well in hand."

"And I'm sure he hasn't. Thomas Wiltshire has never missed an engagement in his life, and now suddenly he misses two?"

My heart froze in my chest.

"What do you mean, two?"

"Good God, man, have you listened to a word I've said? He made an appointment with Wang for Sunday afternoon. He never arrived."

The older man grunted skeptically. "And you trust Wang's memory? He's chased a few dragons in his day."

"No one saw him, do you understand? Not at Wang's or any other place. I've scoured the city, every supplier I could think of, every informant, anyone I've ever known him to work with. *No one has seen him.*"

"It's a concern, I'll grant you."

"It's a damned mess is what it is!"

"Well, naturally. Did you suppose it would be otherwise? We are talking about murder, after all."

There was a brief stretch of silence. I huddled by the stairs, the word *murder* ringing in my ears like a gunshot.

Roberts sighed. "Look, have you spoken to the police?"

"As much as I dared, for all the good it will do."

"You don't think they're up to the job?"

"Neither do you, or we wouldn't be in this mess in the first place."

"We're doing everything we can, Burrows."

"Which is what, exactly? Why do I get the feeling there's more to this than you're telling me?"

"I'm sure I don't know. I'm as in the dark as you are."

Another pause. Then: "The situation is a good deal more complicated than we thought."

"Pardon?"

"The last words Wiltshire spoke to me on Saturday," Mr. Burrows said. "*The situation is a good deal more complicated than we thought.*"

"What does it mean?"

"The devil if I know. And now he's gone. I tell you, Roberts, with God as my witness, if you've gotten him killed—"

"Come now, you're the one who suggested the arrangement."

"It appears that was my mistake," Mr. Burrows said coldly, and he took the remaining steps two at a time.

CHAPTER 5

DEEP BREATHS—DIMMI TUTTO—
SMELLING LIKE THE DEAD—THE WOMAN
ON THE SIDEWALK

I drifted through the train station as if in a dream, the crowd flowing around me in an anonymous blur. *If you've gotten him killed*, said the voice of Mr. Burrows in my head. *We are talking about murder . . .*

I meant to head back uptown, but instead I found myself on the opposite platform, a decision made without conscious thought. An animal, when startled, will instinctively scurry back to its den. Apparently the same goes for frightened Irish girls, because there I was, scurrying back to Five Points.

I huddled in my seat, hugging myself protectively, lips moving in silent prayer. But the voices pursued me all the way down the tracks, echoes of what I'd overheard playing and replaying like one of Mr. Edison's talking machines. I like to think that if the subject of the argument had been anyone but Thomas Wiltshire, I'd have managed it with a little more grit. As it was, I felt as if a great weight pressed down on my chest. Every lungful of air was an effort. *Heavenly Father, protect us from evil . . .*

The stairs of my mother's building seemed even steeper and more lopsided than usual; I had to grope my way along the wall to steady myself in the dark. The landlord was too cheap to put in gas lighting, leaving his tenants to strike matches on the stairwell or risk tumbling headfirst into the cracked plaster. Ordinarily, I could negotiate these stairs with my eyes closed, but I was still numb with shock—so much so that I didn't even notice the state of Mam's flat when I walked in.

It was my mother's boarder, Pietro, who appeared in the kitchen to greet me. "Ah, Fiora," he said, looking embarrassed. "Sorry, I didn't know you were coming. Here, let me . . ." His lanky form did a quick tour of the kitchen, collecting items of clothing that had been strewn over virtually every surface.

Gradually, my senses began to clear, and I took in the scene. "What is this? It looks like someone's trunk exploded in here."

"Sorry, I just . . . *un momento.*" Pietro tossed an armload on the floor, then hustled into the sitting room to collect another.

"Whose clothes are these?" Not his, obviously. There were dresses and skirts, waistcoats and trousers, everything from children's clothing to a suit that looked fit for an undertaker.

His lilting accent floated back from the sitting room. "Nobody's. Mine."

"What, you're a ragpicker now?" The banality of the conversation washed over me like a warm, soothing bath. It was exactly what I needed in that moment, a refuge from the confusion and fear that had followed me home on the train.

"Ragpicker!" Pietro thrust his dark head through the door-frame. "Please, Fiora. I am a purveyor of fine secondhand clothing."

"Since when?"

"Since yesterday," he said brightly.

I shook my head, maybe even smiled a little. Pietro Avanti (not, I strongly suspect, his real name) had been my mother's boarder for a little over a year, and in that time he'd been a bottle collector, a newspaper wholesaler, a pushcart man, a day laborer, and a lumber thief (though he preferred the term *scavenger*)—and those were just the most recent chapters in a fourteen-year career of curbstone trades going all the way back to his days as a street fiddler at the tender age of six. To say he was adaptable would be putting it politely. So long as he paid his share of the rent, I didn't mind—though in truth it wasn't so much about the money. It was a comfort to have somebody keeping an eye on Mam, and as Pietro was fond of reminding me, *nobody looks after Mama like an Italian boy.*

I glanced over at her bedroom, the only part of the tiny three-room flat boasting its own door. Just now that door stood closed, wooden crucifix hanging slightly askew. On the other side, Mam would be napping on a narrow cot scarcely bigger than a bunk on a steamship. "How is she?" I asked.

"Not a good day," Pietro said. "She spent most of it talking to Nonna."

I sighed. My mother had been talking to my dead granny for years. I hadn't worried about it much back when she'd still been working—so long as she'd had school to fill her day, her evening chitchats with Granny had seemed harmless enough. But when her health started to decline and she quit teaching, Granny be-came her constant companion, and lately it seemed as though she spent more time conversing with her dead mother than anything else. These days, as often as not, I'd come home to find her perched on the edge of her bed, hair disheveled, arguing with the air while the laundry piled up and the dirty dishes sat abandoned on the stove. If it weren't for Pietro's cooking, she'd have starved long ago.

So much for running to Mam for comfort. Just as well, probably—it would only have upset her.

"Rose? *Bella*, what's wrong?" Pietro gave me a worried look. "You're pale as a ghost. What's happened?"

I hesitated. I wasn't sure I could explain what I'd just seen, let alone what I'd overheard. All I really knew for sure was that something terrible was going on and Thomas Wiltshire was at the center of it. I wanted nothing more than to talk it over with Clara, but suddenly I dreaded going back to the house on Fifth Avenue. Even the weight of Mr. Wiltshire's watch in my pocket felt . . . dead.

"Come," Pietro said, motioning me into the sitting room. He tossed an armload of clothing onto his mattress and drew the curtain separating his "bedroom" from the "parlor." Then he dragged a chair from the corner and patted it. "Here. *Dimmi tutto.*"

Tell me everything. But if I did, might it put him, or Mr. Wiltshire, in danger?

"Are you in trouble?" Pietro wore the grave expression of someone who knows all too well what trouble looks like.

"Yes," I said, sinking into the chair. "I think I am." And before I could stop myself, the tale was pouring out of me—every bizarre, horrifying detail, right down to the moment when I very nearly retched on my boots outside the Freemasons' temple on Sixth Avenue. Pietro listened to it all with a bemused frown, but he didn't interrupt, not even when I said the word *murder.* I guess there isn't much you can say that will shock an orphan from Five Points.

When I'd finished, he got up and put the kettle on. He'd lived in an Irish household long enough to know when tea was called for. "So this Mr. Burrows, the friend of your boss—he was looking for him in the neighborhood."

"That's what it sounded like, but I can't imagine why. What could possibly bring a man like Mr. Wiltshire down here?"

"Well, what kind of work does he do?"

"He's a . . ." I trailed off, realizing belatedly that this was the one subject relating to Mr. Wiltshire that I knew almost nothing about. "I'm not sure, actually. He's a businessman of some kind."

"There is business in Five Points." Then, with a wry smile: "Some of it is even legal."

"But is it the sort a wealthy young gentleman might practice?"

"The sort that might get him killed, looks like."

He hadn't meant to be cruel. Pietro knew nothing of my feelings for Mr. Wiltshire; he couldn't have guessed how those words would drive into me like a body blow. I gripped my chair, feeling suddenly dizzy.

Pietro didn't notice; he was too busy pouring the tea. "Maybe he is the lawyer for these men."

I drew a deep breath, forcing myself to think rationally. It *had* sounded as though whatever Mr. Wiltshire was mixed up in, Mr. Burrows and the man called Roberts were part of it. And if he were their lawyer, it would take much of the edge off the word *murder*. Could he be defending one of the Freemasons against a murder charge?

Oh, how I wanted to believe it, but . . . "What about the

suppliers Mr. Burrows mentioned? And the informants? Those don't sound to me like the business associates of a lawyer."

"I'm sorry, Fiora, I don't know." Pietro handed me my tea. "Maybe this argument sounded worse than it was. Maybe Mr. Burrows is a dramatic sort of man."

It reminded me of something the detective had said two days before, when he'd asked if Mr. Burrows was the nervous type. But I'd watched Jonathan Burrows striding through some of the roughest streets in New York with a silk hat and an ivory-handled walking stick. I'd looked him in the eye while he'd lied—smoothly, his smile never wavering—even though he'd obviously been terribly worried underneath. "Actually, he seems awfully composed, all things considered. And then there's the fact . . . Well, look who we're dealing with."

"Who?"

"*Freemasons.*" I said it in a whisper, my eyebrows raised significantly.

Pietro raised his eyebrows back at me. "So?"

"A secret society."

He laughed. "Rose, *bella*, half the men in New York belong to a secret society. It's *obbligatorio* if you want to be fashionable these days."

"Maybe, but this is different. Did you know the Masons were run out of the neighborhood in the seventies?"

"*Sì*, I remember. People used to throw stones at them. I even did it once or twice myself, just for fun. But this is just politics, no?"

I considered that. Paving stones and politics went together like carrots and peas, especially in the Sixth Ward. "But that wouldn't explain why Mam hates them. She's never cared much about that sort of thing."

"Your mama doesn't hate nobody."

"She hates Freemasons. I just don't know why."

"Because they're devil worshipers."

I turned to find Mam standing in the doorway to the kitchen, face pale, hair a fright. She wore only a thin cotton shift; it hung limply from her bony shoulders, one strap drooping nearly to her elbow. Below the hem, her blue-veined calves looked almost translucent. Even her feet were bare.

"Sweet Mary and Joseph!" I sprang from my chair and grabbed my overcoat, sweeping it over her shoulders. "You'll catch your death of cold! Put some slippers on, will you?" In good Fifth Avenue fashion, I pretended to ignore the impropriety of her appearing in front of her boarder in such a state. Besides, I suspected it was nothing Pietro hadn't seen before.

"The Freemasons are devil worshipers," she said again, severely.

"Oh, Mam. That's a bit Catholic, even for you."

"These secret societies, eh?" Pietro said in the playful tone he always took around Mam. "Sprouting up like mushrooms. Everybody has one except the Italians. I am feeling a little left out."

"You have your *padrones*," I said, playing along.

"*Padroni*," he corrected. "Now, those are devil worshipers."

"You two can make light all you like," Mam said, "but you'll do as I say, Rose Gallagher, and keep away from anything to do with Masons. They *are* devil worshipers."

There was no point in arguing with her. My mother was the sort of Catholic who saw wickedness and sin on every corner, and that was *before* she'd started succumbing to dementia. "Never mind that now," I said, bringing her a cup of tea. "This'll warm you up."

As I leaned over to put her teacup on the table, she grabbed the sleeve of my dress and sniffed it.

"Mam!" I twisted away, annoyed. "I washed this dress yesterday. It's perfectly—"

"Where've you been?" Before I could answer, Mam sniffed at the collar of my overcoat, still draped around her shoulders. "You smell like them. Rose, why do you smell like them?"

"*Stop that.* Smell like who?"

She gazed up at me with pale, watery eyes. "The dead."

Silence drifted over the little kitchen.

"You smell just like Granny," my mother said, as matter-of-fact as you please.

I stared at her helplessly, a great sadness welling up inside me. For years now, I'd done everything I could to look after her, and for the most part we'd managed. But *this* . . .

Pietro sprang up from his chair. "Mama, I have a special treat! A gift from Augusto—some nice *salami*. Here, try . . ." Before she could protest, he'd flipped out his pocketknife and sliced off a generous piece of cured sausage. "Maybe this is what you smell, eh? More than enough garlic to wake the dead!"

Mam wrinkled her nose as she took it. "My word. Why would you bring that into the house, Peter?" (Mam insisted that *Peter* was the version preferred by the Lord. If so, He doesn't seem to have mentioned it to the fellows at the Vatican.) "Is it safe to eat?"

"Mama, you hurt my feelings. You will love it, trust me. Just try." Pietro looked over at me and winked.

And just like that, Mam forgot all about dead people and devil worshipers, swept away in that most New York of subjects: national cuisines. "You Italians and your garlic. Is this even cooked?"

"Ah, *sì*. Sort of."

"It'll be havoc with my colon," Mam said mournfully, and took a nibble.

"A little garlic never hurt nobody."

"Never hurt *anybody*, Peter."

He growled good-naturedly. "Always with the grammar lessons. When you gonna give up on me, eh?"

I couldn't help laughing. "Never. She'll keep on you until you speak like a proper English lord." I should know—she'd been badgering me my whole life.

"Language skills are the most important thing you'll ever learn," Mam said, and just for a moment, she sounded like her old self.

Now that she was back on terra firma, I was able to convince my mother to put on some proper clothing and brush her hair. I took advantage of her brief disappearance to thank Pietro, and also to warn him against breathing a word of what I'd told him. "The Masons might not be devil worshipers, but I do believe they're dangerous."

"Powerful men are always dangerous. Promise me you'll be careful, Fiora."

"What do you mean?"

"You're going to keep looking for him, yes? Your boss?"

"I suppose I am," I said, realizing it in that same moment. "I can't just abandon him, especially now that I know for certain he's in real danger." *If you've gotten him killed . . .* I pushed the voice away, shuddering.

"What will you do?"

"I'm not sure. I suppose I'll have to confront Mr. Burrows, and—"

Pietro was already shaking his head. "No, no, that is not the way. Too dangerous."

"Dangerous? But he's Mr. Wiltshire's friend."

"He's a Mason. He will protect their secrets."

I paused uncomfortably. I hadn't really thought about it, but of course Pietro was right. The way Mr. Burrows had strolled through the front doors of the temple, the words that had been exchanged on the steps . . . He must be a Freemason, or at least mixed up with them. And everyone knew what happened to people who exposed Masonic secrets. The disappearance of Mr. William Morgan was another well-known New York legend, and though there were many versions of the tale, they nearly all ended the same way: with the brutal murder of that gentleman. "So you think I should let it go?"

"I didn't say that. It's good to want to protect people, but you must be smart. Try something a little more subtle."

"Such as?"

"Mr. Burrows went into Wang's General Store, yes? They know you in that place. Why not start there? You don't have to tell them you saw Mr. Burrows, only that you are looking for your boss, and you know he had an appointment with Mr. Wang." Pietro shrugged. "Who's to say how you know that? Maybe Mr. Wiltshire told you himself."

"That," I said, "is an excellent idea. Thank you." Impulsively, I threw my arms around him.

He laughed. "Ah, *mia cara*, don't let poor Mama see you hugging an Italian boy. You will give her a stroke."

"I mean it, Pietro, thank you. For everything."

"You're welcome. Now, don't go until you eat something . . ."

I left my mother's flat feeling a little better, and not just because I had a belly full of cured sausage and flaky Italian cheese.

The gas lamps were just beginning to bloom along Mott Street as I headed for Wang's General Store. I shopped there often, Wang's being the most comprehensively stocked establishment this side of Macy's. Aside from the usual American goods and a typical assortment of Chinese ones—jade jewelry and tea sets, silks and sandals—Wang's carried an astonishing array of exotic wares, some of them so mysterious that I couldn't even tell if they were animal, vegetable, or mineral. A visit to Wang's was like strolling through a museum of curiosities. More than once I'd found myself wandering aimlessly among the shelves, trying to guess the purpose of the enigmatic items on display. That was how I'd met Mei. She was about my age and spoke good English, and she'd always been willing to indulge my curiosity about her father's merchandise. Hopefully she'd be just as informative about Mr. Wiltshire.

My breath steamed like a locomotive as I hurried along. It was noticeably colder than when I'd called in at Mam's—near to freezing, judging by the sting of my cheeks and the sharp bite of the air in my nostrils. Small wonder the street was deserted; everyone with any sense had fled inside. Up ahead, the Church of the Transfiguration started to ring out five o'clock.

What happened next is seared forever in my memory. For a long time afterward, the sound of church bells tolling the hour would send a shiver of dread down my spine.

The peal of the bells drew my eyes briefly to the tower, an elegant silhouette against the last wisp of a winter sunset; when they fell back to the street, I noticed a woman loitering on the sidewalk just a little up the way. She hadn't been there a moment ago, I was sure of it. She stood directly in my path, gaze fixed on me so resolutely that I wondered if I should know her. She looked to be a little older than Mam and about the same height, which is to say not very tall. She'd come outside with her apron on, but no overcoat, not even a shawl to protect her from the cold. Even stranger was the look in her eyes—haunted, almost desperate.

I slowed, an uneasy feeling warning me not to get too close. "Are you all right?"

The woman stepped into the muted glow of a streetlamp, and I sucked in a sharp breath. "*Sweet Jesus!*"

Her dress was covered in blood. Not the sort you got from butchering meat, either; there was too much of it, and in all the wrong places. Her collar was soaked through, and her left shoulder. Even at this distance, I could see that her hair was matted with blood, as though she'd taken a hard blow to the skull.

She's hit her head on the pavement, I thought. *Or maybe she's been attacked.* I didn't know what to do. "Just . . . stay right there. Father Francis will know what to do." I started for the church— but the pale woman moved to intercept me. I circled out into the street, but she followed, advancing toward me so determinedly that she didn't even seem to notice the lamppost directly in her path. I shouted a warning—nothing. All I could do was cringe in anticipation of the inevitable collision.

It never came.

The woman strode into the lamppost—and passed through it like it wasn't even there. Or rather, it cleaved through her as though *she* wasn't there.

For half a heartbeat, I stood frozen in disbelief, certain I must have imagined it. Then a layer of frost bristled over the lamppost where she'd touched it, and the hem of her skirt billowed out in the draft of her passing, a wisp of vapor trailing after her like a bridal train.

With a cry of terror, I flew across the street and burst into Wang's General Store, nearly tearing the door off its hinges in my haste. I slammed it shut and braced my back against it. (Yes, I know—what good would that do when I'd just seen her walk straight through a lamppost? You try being accosted in the streets by a dead woman and see how rational you are.)

"Hey, what are you doing? You almost break the door!"

The voice barely registered. Blood roared in my ears, and I was shaking so badly I could hardly breathe. I glanced around wildly for something, *anything*, I could use as a weapon, and spied a gardening trowel on a nearby shelf.

"Rose?" Belatedly, I recognized Mei's voice. "What's wrong?"

"*Ghost.*"

"What?"

"There's a ghost out there!" I didn't stop to think how crazy that sounded; I was too busy trying to keep my heart from bursting out of my chest. I started to reach for the trowel, but then I saw a spade leaning up against the wall. This was clearly an upgrade; I grabbed it two-handed and wheeled back to the door.

Mei emerged from between the shelves, her arms loaded down with inventory. "Ghost? Where?"

"Right outside! Look!"

I lurched toward the window. Mei moved at the same moment and we collided, sending one of her parcels flying. She stooped to retrieve it, but I grabbed her elbow. "Never mind that! Look, she's right—" I pointed, but the street was empty. "She was . . . I saw . . ." I leaned up against the windowpane until my breath fogged the glass, scanning the street from end to end, but there was no sign of her. "She was *right there.*"

Mei hummed skeptically. She seemed more concerned about

the box of salt she'd dropped, which had spilled all over the floor. She scraped at it with her foot as if to sweep it under the doorway, but she did a haphazard job, leaving a thick line of the stuff trailed across the threshold. "Bad luck," she declared, and headed to the back of the store to light some incense.

"She was right there . . ." A hint of doubt crept into my voice, and it might have overtaken me completely if I hadn't glanced at the lamppost: It still glittered with frost, as if gripped in the hand of Winter itself.

I clutched my shovel to my breast and slid to the floor, whispering a prayer against evil and wishing with all my heart that I'd never gotten out of bed that morning.

CHAPTER 6

WANG'S SPECIAL TEA—A SURPRISING
VISITOR—CELESTIAL SECRETS—A
NARROW ESCAPE

At this point, you're probably thinking that I belong in the asylum at Blackwell's Island, or at least that I'd suffered a fit of hysteria. Well, I wouldn't blame you. In truth, sitting there on the floor of Wang's General Store, muttering about Jesus and gripping a gardening implement as if it were a spear, I was more than a little concerned for my own sanity.

"Mei." My voice sounded as if it came from far away. "The lamppost across the street—can you see it?"

She went to the window, moving silently on slippered feet. "I see it."

"Is there still . . . Do you notice anything strange about it?"

"Ice. It must be very cold outside."

Any lingering shred of doubt vanished. I hadn't imagined it, at least not all of it. I squeezed my eyes shut and resumed my silent discourse with the Lord.

I must have stayed like that for a while, because the next thing I knew Mei's small form was crouched beside me and she was offering me a steaming cup of liquid. "Here, drink this."

I took it with shaking hands. An unfamiliar odor pricked at my nose, sweet and faintly cloying. "What is it?"

"Special tea, for calming. My father's recipe."

I eyed the brew uneasily. I didn't want to think too much about what might be in it, surrounded as I was by Mr. Wang's stock of shark fins and chicken feet and tiny shriveled fish. It was a measure of my distress that I drank it anyway.

"Good for when you see ghosts," Mei added, cracking half a smile.

"You don't believe me."

She shrugged. "Chinese revere our ancestors. We believe in spirits, but I have never seen one. Maybe you did, but I think this would be special."

"It didn't feel very special."

"I thought Christian people did not believe in spirits. In Sunday school they told us we should not revere our ancestors, that this was wicked and false."

"You went to Sunday school?"

"For a little while. I thought it would teach me to be American, but . . ." She shrugged self-consciously. "Still Chinese."

"I can relate. I've been here since I was a baby, but to them I'm still Irish, at least in the ways that count."

"Do Irish people believe in spirits?"

I took another sip of the sweet-smelling brew. It did seem to have a calming effect, which meant I could consider Mei's question rationally. "Well, I suppose we're a pretty superstitious lot on the whole. My mother definitely believes in them. Has her entire life."

"Not you?"

"I've never given it much thought, but I guess I'm like you. I've always believed in the idea of ghosts, but if someone tells me they've seen one . . ." *When Mam tells me she's seen one . . .* "That I find harder to believe."

Mei eyed me shrewdly. "What about now?"

"I know what I saw, Mei."

She held my gaze for a long moment, as if debating whether to pursue the matter. It looked like she was about to say something when a voice called out from behind the counter. "Ah-Mei!"

She answered over her shoulder, and Mr. Wang himself appeared from one of the many back rooms. They conversed rapidly in Chinese, and I could tell Mei was relating the story of my ghost sighting. I couldn't help blushing, feeling ridiculous even though I was sure of what I'd seen.

"Bad *qi*," Mr. Wang said inscrutably. He asked his daughter a question, and she pointed, first at the door and then at the pot of incense burning on the counter. Mr. Wang grunted, satisfied.

"Nobody out there now, anyway," Mei said, with another glance out the window. "You should go home, Rose. Get some rest."

"That's a good idea." Suddenly, I felt very sleepy indeed, which I suspected had more than a little to do with Mr. Wang's brew. I accepted Mei's help to stand and dusted off my overcoat. "But before I do, I was wondering if you might help me. I'm looking for Mr. Thomas Wiltshire." I said it as breezily as if I were asking after a particular brand of laundry soap, and in fact it didn't feel much different. Whatever was in that drink, it had soothed my nerves to a degree that would have been alarming if I'd still been capable of feeling alarm. As it was, I punctuated my question with a lazy smile.

Mei glanced at her father. He shook his head; he didn't understand.

"Thomas Wiltshire," I repeated. "He's my employer."

Mei said something in Chinese. Mr. Wang tugged on his mustache reflectively before answering. "He says he does not know the name," Mei translated.

"How strange. I'm sure Mr. Wiltshire mentioned they had an appointment on Sunday."

"What does he look like?" Mei asked.

"About twenty-five years old, slight of build. Well dressed. Dark hair, with a beard. Fine, aristocratic features. He's really very handsome . . ." Dear Lord, I was babbling. With a supreme effort, I managed to shut my gob.

Mei frowned. She said something to her father. His answer was swift and curt. They went back and forth for a moment, their volume rising, until Mr. Wang spun on his heel and plunged past the silk curtain separating the back rooms from the storefront.

"I'm sorry," Mei said. "His memory is not so good, but he does not think he knows this gentleman."

"Mei." Throwing a furtive glance at the curtain, I lowered my voice. "You'd tell me if you knew something, wouldn't you? Because, you see . . ." I swallowed hard, my breath catching a little in spite of the soothing tea. "I think Mr. Wiltshire might be in the most terrible sort of danger."

Mei's gaze fell to the counter. "My father says he does not know this man," she said quietly.

I don't believe him, I wanted to say, but in that moment, the sheer weight of my exhaustion dragged me under, and even that feeble protest seemed beyond my power. All I wanted was to go home and sleep.

I headed to the door, my feet feeling as though they were made of lead. I dreaded the climb up the stairs of the el, dreaded even more the screeching, rattling clamor of the train. I paused at the window to survey the street, but everything looked as it should. Even the frost on the lamppost was gone.

As I reached for the door, my boots scraped loudly beneath me; looking down, I saw that the floor was still covered in salt. "Someone could slip on that," I said, surprised Mei hadn't swept it up yet.

"I know," she said. "Good night, Rose."

I would have overslept the next morning if Clara hadn't rapped on my door, rousing me moments before Mrs. Sellers came looking for me. "She's up and about," Clara said, "so she'll be looking for an account of your doings yesterday. Get your story ready. Best make it a good one, too, 'cause she's in a fine temper. She's been summoned up to the police station, and none too happy about it."

I tried to grasp the significance of this, but my thoughts felt strangely sluggish, as though my brain were wrapped in cheesecloth. The aftereffects of Mr. Wang's brew, most likely. I resolved to avoid accepting unidentified beverages from Chinese grocers in the future. "Have the police found something?"

"No idea. A note came for her last night just before dinner, and that's all I know. What about you? You find something?" Her voice was a shade cooler than usual; she was still cross with me for leaving yesterday.

Where to begin? Out of everything that had happened the day before, what I blurted out was "Mr. Burrows is a Freemason."

"All right," she said with the same disinterested tone Pietro had taken.

"It's not all right. I think Mr. Wiltshire was doing some work for the Masons and something went wrong."

"Like what?"

"Maybe he found out something he shouldn't have. All I know is that I overheard Mr. Burrows talking with another Mason, and the other man didn't seem very concerned for Mr. Wiltshire's welfare. I don't trust him, and I don't think Mr. Burrows does either."

"Yesterday you didn't trust Mr. Burrows."

"I know, but—"

"If you two are through wasting time," a voice interrupted coldly, "perhaps you might consider executing the duties for which you are paid."

Clara drew a deep breath. Calmly, she turned to face the housekeeper. "Last I heard, you was withholding my pay."

Mrs. Sellers scowled, but there wasn't much she could say to that. "I'll be leaving shortly to visit the police station. But first I'll be taking inventory, so I will thank you two to keep out from underfoot." The housekeeper always did inventory the day after a bout of illness, to make sure Clara and I hadn't done any thieving in her absence. "I expect to see you both downstairs momentarily," she concluded before marching off.

"One of these days, so help me Lord . . ." Shaking her head, Clara left me to dress.

I set about my duties in an agitated state, still struggling to process everything that had happened the day before. I felt as if I'd learned so much, and yet so little. And then there was the small matter of the ghost . . .

Mr. Wiltshire's watch dragged at the pocket of my dress, ticking softly.

"Rose." Mrs. Sellers appeared at the threshold of the parlor. "Would you care to explain why there's a Celestial boy on Mr. Wiltshire's doorstep?"

I stared at her in befuddlement, feather duster poised above a Carcel lamp. "Sorry, *who* is on the doorstep?"

"I didn't catch his name," she said tartly, "since I don't speak Chinese and he obviously doesn't speak a word of English. He asked for you. He came to the *front door*, Rose!" This last in a tone of high scandal.

"I can't imagine who it could be."

"I've about reached my limit with you. When Mr. Wiltshire returns—"

"I'm sorry," I said, slipping past her out of the parlor. "I'll take care of it."

There was no one waiting for me at the front door, and I paused, momentarily confused. But of course Mrs. Sellers would never leave a Chinese boy standing on the stoop of Mr. Wiltshire's home in full view of Fifth Avenue. Muttering under my breath, I headed downstairs to the servants' entrance. There I found a boy of about seven, round-faced and rosy-cheeked, peering past me with shy curiosity at the unfamiliar sights within. "I'm Rose Gallagher," I told him, whereupon he thrust a piece of paper into my hand and scampered off.

I started to unfold the paper, but a creak on the stairs warned me of someone approaching, so I stuffed it hastily in my pocket.

"Well?" Mrs. Sellers demanded.

"Oh, it's just . . . er, a note from the Chinese grocer about an order of my mother's." Even as I spoke the lie, I realized it was half true; the note must have come from Wang's General Store.

"You are not to take personal deliveries here, and certainly not at the *front door*. This is your place of employment, not your home."

"Of course," I said distractedly. The words *place of employment* had tweaked my memory, bringing to mind something Pietro had asked me yesterday. "Pardon me, ma'am, but what exactly does Mr. Wiltshire do for a living?"

She frowned. "Why do you ask?"

"Oh, the police questioned me about it," I lied, "while you were fixing the coffee. And I realized I didn't know."

"He's a businessman," she said, and turned to head back up the stairs.

"Yes, ma'am, I know, but—what kind of business?"

A flush colored her cheeks. "The kind that is none of yours, Rose Gallagher."

She doesn't know either, I realized, bemused. What sort of man kept his business dealings so quiet that even his own household staff couldn't say what he did for a living? *The sort who belongs to a secret society,* a voice inside me whispered.

Could I have misjudged Thomas Wiltshire completely?

I hurried up to my little room in the attic, barred the door, and drew the note out of my pocket. The paper smelled faintly of incense. Unfolding it, I read:

> *Dear Rose,*
> *I should not be writing this to you. My father keeps his busi-*
> *ness very private. But you said your friend is in danger and*
> *I believe you because my father's business is very dangerous.*
>   *I have seen this man in my father's store many times.*
> *He comes in the back way where people come for other business*
> *(not store business). He came to see my father on Saturday*
> *afternoon. I did not hear very much but they had a map of*
> *New York and they were pointing at the East River. I heard*
> *my father say yōulíng many times which means specter or*
> *ghost. Last night my father told me that Mr. Wiltshire was*
> *supposed to come back on Sunday but he did not come. Another*
> *man came to look for him yesterday. My father is worried*
> *but as I said he keeps his business very private.*
>   *This is all I know and I am sorry I could not tell you*
> *before. I hope you find him.*
>   *Your friend,*
>   *Ah-Mei*

I went through the note again from start to finish, and then a third time, my heart rate climbing with each reading. The handwriting was impeccable, the English clear, and yet I was sure I must have misunderstood. My mind was still muddled from Mr. Wang's tonic, surely. Like a dream that stitches together a patchwork of unrelated memories, my brain had mingled two disturbing but completely unrelated experiences from the day before.

Hadn't it?

After everything that had happened yesterday, I could no longer doubt that Mr. Wiltshire was involved in dangerous business. Nor could I deny that, whatever they might tell you in Sunday school, ghosts were all too real. But those two facts had nothing to do with each other.

Or did they? I tracked my finger down the letter, singling out one line. "They were pointing at the East River." Saying it aloud sparked something in my memory, and I flew down the stairs, crying Clara's name.

"What in the name of . . ." She stuck her head out of the kitchen. "What's the matter with you, hollering like that? You're lucky the old bat's gone out, or you'd be—"

I grabbed her shoulders, startling her into silence. "The newspaper you kept—those pages from the *Times*. Do you still have them?"

"The paper the food was wrapped in? The food from last *Sunday*?" She wrinkled her nose.

"You threw them away." I groaned, my heart sinking. "Of course you would have."

"What do you need with those? We already looked them over."

"But I think I understand something now that I didn't before. There was a story . . ." I trailed off. I wasn't ready to tell Clara about what had happened on Mott Street. She already thought I was being irrational; bringing ghosts into the picture wasn't likely to reassure her. "There was a story about the East River. I didn't think much of it at the time, but my investigations yesterday lead me to believe—"

"Your investigations." Clara shook her head. "You're a detective now, is that it? Rose, when are you gonna stop playing games?"

I felt myself coloring. "You think this is a game to me? That I'm *enjoying* myself? You know how I feel about . . ." My blush deepened. "You know why I'm doing this."

"Oh, I know all right, but I'm not sure you do."

"What's that supposed to mean?"

"You think you're doing this because you're sweet on Mr. Wiltshire, but that ain't the only reason. This is a big adventure to you. Solve the mystery, save the hero, just like in them dime novels you're always reading. But this ain't a story, Rose. It's real life, and you're gonna get yourself into real trouble."

Her words stung like a slap in the face. "If you had any idea what I've been through these past two days . . ."

She sighed. "I'm not your mama, Rose. You do what you gotta do, but you need to be honest with yourself." She made a weary gesture at the side door to the kitchen. "You'll find your papers out there. Stinks to high heaven, too. *Somebody* forgot to take out the trash. That's what I get for letting you run off playing detective, I guess." So saying, she wiped her hands on her apron and left.

I stood there for a moment, fighting back tears. Clara and I had never argued before, not like this, and it felt as if my best friend had abandoned me. Which just goes to show how thoroughly a person can delude herself. Because of course she was right, though it would take me days to see it, by which point I was in way over my head.

And speaking of being in over my head, digging through three days' worth of garbage is an experience I don't care to recall, let alone relate. Suffice it to say that I found what I was looking for, though not without considerable trauma.

Once again, it was the little smudge of strawberry preserve that caught my eye. The page was soggy and rank but still legible, and I soon found the headline I was looking for.

A NARROW ESCAPE

~

GHOSTLY ASSAULT IN THE EAST RIVER
TREASURE HUNTER NEARLY DROWNED—GHOST OF AN
ENGLISH SEA CAPTAIN BLAMED—VICTIM SAYS HE
WILL RETURN TO THE SCENE FOR PROOF

An alleged ghost accosted a Brooklyn man two days ago in the narrow strait known as Hell Gate. Mr. Peter Arbridge, 22, recounted to a TIMES reporter a harrowing tale of being seized by a spectral sailor from HMS *Hussar*, a frigate of the English Royal Navy that sank on November 23, 1780, while attempting to navigate the treacherous waters between Manhattan and Long Island . . .

For the second time that day, I felt my heart rate climbing. It was impossible to read the account without being thrown back to Mott Street and the pale woman covered in blood. The tale still sounded ridiculous—*an English sea captain?*—but after what had happened yesterday, I could no longer dismiss it out of hand. On top of which, it was somehow connected to Mr. Wiltshire's disappearance, and that meant I had to take it seriously, whether it was true or not.

But how was it connected? I needed to find this Mr. Arbridge,

I decided, and hear the tale for myself. The *Times* story said he meant to return to Hell Gate to search for the ghost, and it gave the name of his vessel, *Goldrush*. That was enough to go on.

I took a bath and changed my dress. I didn't bother asking Clara to cover for me. After yesterday, I was convinced beyond any doubt that something terrible had befallen Mr. Wiltshire, so what did I have to fear from Mrs. Sellers? If I found him, he would surely be grateful, and if I didn't . . .

I opened the drawer of my little desk, seized by a sudden need to look upon his likeness. "Hold on just a little while longer," I whispered to those charcoal eyes. "I'm coming."

CHAPTER 7

MR. PETER ARBRIDGE, TREASURE HUNTER—THE HIDDEN TALENTS OF DETECTIVE WARD—A SWELL MURDER

inding Mr. Peter Arbridge proved to be even easier than I'd hoped, since he was going to rather a lot of trouble to make a spectacle of himself.

The *Times* hadn't printed a photograph of the self-styled treasure hunter, but I knew him the moment I saw him—or rather, the moment I heard him, spewing his gapeseed at passersby like a newsie with too many papers to sell. "See the very spot the *Hussar* sank!" he cried from his perch atop a post on the pier. "Experience the terror for yourself, as reported in *The New-York Times*! Who'll be next to glimpse the ghost of Captain Pole? Will it be you, sir?" The fisherman at whom this was directed laughed and continued on his way. "What about you, miss?" He gestured in my direction. "Step aboard the *Goldrush* and visit the site of the famous sunken treasure?"

I glanced at the vessel in question, a small fishing boat bobbing between the looming hulls of a pair of more seaworthy-looking craft. *What could anyone possibly expect to salvage in a tub like that?* Mr. Arbridge's apparent change of career from treasure hunter to tour operator hinted at the answer. I tried not to judge him too harshly. It could just as easily have been Pietro up there, perched like a seagull on a post, peddling whatever came to hand. You did whatever it took to make a living in New York.

"Whaddya say, miss? Experience the terror for yourself?"

I've experienced more than enough terror in the last twenty-four hours, thank you. Aloud, I said, "I don't think so—but I'd be interested in hearing your tale, Mr. Arbridge."

"How'd you . . . Oh, you read my story in the *Times*!" He grinned, visibly pleased.

"I did indeed, and I'd very much like to hear your version firsthand."

"And I'd be delighted to tell it!" He hopped down from his perch and stuck out a hand. "Nice to meet you, Miss . . . ?"

"Mary Pierce. I'm a reporter with *Harper's Weekly*." The words seemed to speak themselves, and I felt myself smiling that same wooden smile Mr. Burrows had used on me.

Rose Gallagher, what are you doing? There was no need to lie to him. Hadn't he just finished saying how delighted he'd be to tell his story? Clara's words about playing games rang uncomfortably in my ears.

"That so? A lady reporter. Well, now, you don't come across one of them too often. Sure I can't convince you to take the tour?"

"No, thanks. I'm terribly afraid of the water, you see." Heaven help me, the lies were just rolling off my tongue.

"Sorry to hear it." Then, brightening: "But you'd like to put my story in *Harper's*?"

"I would, very much."

His glance flicked over my obviously empty pockets. "You, uh, bring something to write with?"

"I have an excellent memory," I said, wincing inwardly.

"Well, all right then. Where should I start?"

"At the beginning, I suppose. When did all this happen?"

"Last Thursday, just after sunset. I'd been out on the water all day, hoping to find some trace of the wreck."

"The wreck. You mean the *Hussar*?"

He nodded. "You know it?"

"Not really, no."

"British naval ship, twenty-eight guns. She sank out there"— he gestured across the river—"on the far side of Ward's Island during the Revolution. They say she was carrying the Redcoats' payroll. Hundreds of thousands of pounds in gold. Figured what with storms and such, not to mention all that blasting they been doing around Hell Gate, some of that gold musta been pushed in closer to shore. So there I am, trawling around, and that's when I seen him out on the water."

"The ghost."

"Well, I didn't start out thinking that. At first I thought some poor soul was drowning. There was all this arm-waving and carrying on, so I started paddling over. I was hollering at 'em to hang on."

The unsettling resemblance to my own encounter made me a little queasy. Luckily, Mr. Arbridge was too absorbed in his tale to notice.

"So I'm rowing, and I turn around to see how far I got left to go, only there's nobody there. Just . . . vanished. For a minute there, I thought I'd imagined the whole thing. Like maybe I was just tired from a long day, and here it was getting dark . . ."

"I understand." I'd had the same moment of doubt. Any rational person would have.

"And then just . . . *wham*"—he slapped his hands together, startling me—"up outta the water like he's shot from a cannon! Grabs onto the side of the boat and starts thrashing around. I can see his face in the moonlight, and he's like a rabid dog, wild eyes and teeth bared. *Hold on there, fella,* I says, *you're gonna tip us!* And that's just what he does."

"You tipped?"

"Sure did. Straight into the water. Cold enough to blast the air outta my chest. And then he's on me, arms around my neck like this—"

"*Sweet Jesus.*" I crossed myself instinctively.

"—and I'm trying to grab the boat, but it's too slippery and I think, *This is it, I'm done for* . . . And then somehow I manage to get hold of one of the oars and I jab at him with it and he just . . ." Mr. Arbridge spread his hands, fingers fanned. "Gone."

"What do you mean, gone? Disappeared?"

"All I know is one minute he's dragging me under and the next he's gone, and it's just me and my boat. Had a hell of a time flipping her back over. Lucky I didn't freeze to death out there."

"The boat," I said, fighting to keep my voice steady. "It was slippery, you said. Was there ice on the hull? Or maybe frost?"

His eyes widened. "How'd you know? Don't recall as I mentioned that to the fella from the *Times.*"

"Yours isn't the first ghost story I've heard."

"So you believe me, then?"

I did, Lord help me, but where did it get me? "Besides the reporter you spoke with, has anyone else come around asking about this?"

"A few, after the story in the *Times*, but nobody professional. Your story will be the only one, I promise. Other than the first one, I mean."

"The others who came asking . . . Was one of them an Englishman, by any chance?"

"As a matter of fact."

My heart skipped a beat.

Mistaking my reaction for dismay, Mr. Arbridge said, "He with one of the other papers? Didn't tell me if he was. That story's yours rightwise."

"Was he about so tall, finely dressed, maybe a little older than you?"

"Sounds like him."

"What day was this?"

"Saturday." Leaning in conspiratorially, he added, "Didn't much care for him, to tell the truth."

"Oh?"

"Didn't like the way he asked his questions. Where was I *precisely*, what time *precisely*—he used the word *precisely* a lot, like he was trying to catch me out or something. Bit of a know-it-all, too. Told me it couldn't've been Captain Pole I seen." He snorted, incredulous.

"Did he by chance mention any other names to you? A Mr. Jonathan Burrows, for instance, or a Mr. Roberts?"

He shook his head again.

"Did he say where he was going?"

"Not to me," he said, growing impatient. "Is he the competition or not?"

"I . . . I don't think so." I forced myself to smile. "I'm sure it's nothing."

He jammed his hands in his pockets, rocking back on his heels awkwardly. "So . . . a big magazine like *Harper's* . . . Don't suppose there's any money in a story like that?"

"I'm afraid not."

He sighed in disappointment. "Well, maybe there'll be some business behind it, at least. When'll it be out?"

"Oh, soon," I said, feeling guilty all over again. "Thanks for your time, and . . . good luck."

I headed back to the train with my head whirring. Mr. Wiltshire had to be the Englishman in question, but what was his interest in Peter Arbridge and his ghost story? If I was a long way from finding the answer to that, at least I was piecing together a picture of what had happened to Mr. Wiltshire after he'd left home on Saturday.

Whatever he'd been about, it must have had something to do with his business with the Freemasons. The trouble was, I still had no idea what that might be. If only I knew what he did for a living, maybe it would help me figure out the nature of the services he was providing—and what it had to do with murder.

I couldn't ask Mr. Burrows, not now that I knew he was one of them. *Think, Rose. Who else would . . . ?*

I stopped cold. The coppers would know, wouldn't they?

I consulted Mr. Wiltshire's watch. Three o'clock—still plenty of time to get down to the police station on Fifty-Ninth.

Sweeping up the hem of my dress, I broke into a run.

"She's over there, sir," the young officer said, pointing.

Detective Ward didn't bother to hide his irritation, heading toward me in long, ringing strides. "Come to see how we're getting along, have you?" he said, without so much as a how-do-you-do. He didn't offer me a seat, either. Apparently we were going to have this conversation in the middle of the crowded police station.

"What's wrong with that?" I said. "Shouldn't I be concerned?"

"You can be concerned all you like, darlin', so long as you do it someplace else. I got a job to do here, and I've already had to account to you people once today."

It took me a moment to work out who he meant. "Mrs. Sellers? I thought you were the one who called her."

"So did I, but you wouldn't've known it to listen to her. I could barely get a word in edgewise. Felt like I was back in Sunday school facing that shrew of a teacher."

"Oh, really? That doesn't sound at all like the Mrs. Sellers I know."

That earned me an amused snort, at least. "Must be a real treat working for her."

"I don't work for her. I work for Mr. Wiltshire, and I'm very worried about him." I looked the detective straight in the eye as I said it, daring him to make fun.

He couldn't be bothered even with that. "Wish I could help, but we ain't found him yet, so . . ." He started to turn away.

"Just a minute, please. I came here to—"

"Look, we're doing everything we can, but it ain't like this is the only case I'm working. I'm up to my neck in thieving and murdering and suchlike, so quite frankly—"

"Did you say murder?"

"Sure," Ward said impatiently. "Every week. It's a big town, love."

"Were any of them in or around Hell Gate, by any chance?" It was a stab in the dark, but there had to be some connection between the story in the *Times* and Mr. Wiltshire's business with the Masons.

"Come again?"

"The murder victims—recent ones, I mean—were any of them found in the East River?"

"Only half of 'em," he said dryly. "The other half was in the Hudson."

"Or maybe . . . Does the name Peter Arbridge mean anything to you?"

"Not a thing. Should it?"

I almost stamped my foot in frustration. "Look, can you at least tell me what Mr. Wiltshire does for a living?"

Ward growled under his breath. "Christ Almighty, you're all the same!"

I wasn't sure if he meant women or Irish or housemaids, but I supposed it didn't matter.

"I ain't got time to stand here answering whatever question comes into your idea-pot, lady."

"Just answer this one and I'll go. I need to know what he does for a living, and where."

"You mean to tell me you live in the man's house and you don't know what he does for a living?" Ward paused, eyes narrowing. "Well, now. He never told you a thing about his business?" A different quality to his voice now: soft, casual. Too casual.

"I never asked." Feeling suddenly defensive, I added, "We weren't exactly on close personal terms."

"But you know he don't like Wagner." His gaze snagged on mine, sharp as a fishhook.

That's when I knew I'd made a mistake.

I'd dismissed Detective Ward as a buffoon, but I'd been wrong. Lazy he might be, and rude besides, but he was obviously no fool. He'd paid closer attention to our last conversation than I'd thought, and after the fuss I'd made about how well I knew Mr. Wiltshire, here I was admitting ignorance of one of the most basic aspects of his affairs. If that weren't suspicious enough, I'd just finished peppering him with questions about murder.

Oh, Rose, what have you done?

"He's an attorney," Ward said, watching me carefully.

"Yes, of course, that makes sense."

So Pietro had been right after all. But how did Mr. Wang fit into it, or any of the other stops on Mr. Burrows's slumming tour?

"His office is near Wall Street," Ward went on, still watchful. "Locke, Banneker and Associates. Right across from the Equitable Life Building. Ring a bell?"

I didn't trust myself to speak, so I shook my head.

"Well, howdya like that? Almost like he was hiding something."

"I'm sure he wasn't." I was suddenly very aware of the crowded room; it felt as if every pair of eyes were on us.

"Now I got a question for you, same one I had for the housekeeper this morning. Ever hear of a swell called Jacob Crowe?"

"I don't think so."

"You was asking about murders—here's one for you. Ol' Jacob turned up dead last Monday. Funny thing: he belonged to the same club as Jonathan Burrows. City this size, that's quite a coincidence."

Swallowing past a dry throat, I said, "New York may be a big city, but high society is a very small world."

"So they say. Could be if I take another look at that members' list, I'll find some other names I know. Thomas Wiltshire, for example."

Of course he would. Mr. Wiltshire and Mr. Burrows met at the Madison Club several times a week. *I'll bet Roberts is a member, too.* They were all connected—Mr. Burrows, Mr. Roberts, the dead man, the Freemasons . . . and Thomas Wiltshire.

My distress must have shown on my face, because Ward leaned in and said, "Anything you wanna tell me, sweetheart? About Jonathan Burrows, maybe?"

"I don't know what you mean." But that was a lie, and he knew it.

"Maybe Wiltshire got in over his head, eh? Crossed a certain powerful man of his acquaintance, just like poor ol' Jacob?" The detective was so close that I could smell the whiskey on his breath.

I felt ill. I'd come here hoping to put the pieces together, but instead I'd helped Detective Ward put together a picture of his own—one of Jonathan Burrows as a murderer. "You're wrong. It's not like that at all." I'm not sure which of us I was trying to convince.

"You're a good girl, but trust me, these plutes ain't worth protecting. You really think either of them would stick their necks out for you?" He shook his head, as if to say, *Poor, silly thing.*

Maybe it was the condescending look on his face, or the stench of whiskey on his breath. Maybe I'd just reached the end of my emotional tether. All I know is that in that moment, something snapped. I'd had enough of being patronized—by the police, the housekeeper, Mr. Burrows, even my own best friend. I'd had enough of *sweethearts* and *honeys* and *darlin's* and *loves,* and I'd had enough of Detective bloody Ward. "What I am is clever,"

I said coldly, "so you should listen carefully. If you want to look into someone suspicious, his name is Roberts. He's a Freemason. You can find him at the temple on Twenty-Third and Sixth."

The detective frowned. "And what's so suspicious about him?"

"See for yourself. Maybe you can start by asking him if he knows Jacob Crowe. Good day, officer."

I made it all the way out into the street before my knees buckled. I clutched the side of the building, shaking, wondering if I'd just bought Mr. Wiltshire and Mr. Burrows a pair of one-way tickets to Sing Sing. I was so distraught that I didn't even hear the footsteps behind me.

"'Scuse me, miss." The voice belonged to an older man—another detective, from the look of him. "I think we'd better have a talk."

CHAPTER 8

COFFEE WITH A COPPER—AN
UNEXPECTED ALLY—LOCKE, BANNEKER &
ASSOCIATES—BLOOD AND BUTTONS

've said everything I have to say," I told the copper, thrusting my chin out defiantly. "I'm not going to be bullied by you or Detective Ward or anybody else."

"I ain't here to bully you, miss. Thing is, I couldn't help overhearing what you said in there—"

"You and the whole station, thanks to your colleague."

"I'm sorry about that, but . . ." Sighing, he glanced over his shoulder. "Look, would you be willing . . . Do you drink coffee?"

"Coffee?" I echoed stupidly.

"There's a joint around the corner—maybe we could talk there?"

I eyed the detective warily. He was a middle-aged man with prominent ears and sagging, thoughtful eyes. He'd probably been imposing in his youth, but though still tall and broad-shouldered, he was visibly past his prime. Not, in short, the sort of man I typically received invitations from, unless you counted catcalling. "I drink coffee," I told him, which was patently untrue, "but if you're planning on interrogating me about my friends, you needn't bother."

"I'm not planning on interrogating you at all, Miss—?"

"Gallagher."

"Sergeant Chapman," he said, doffing his hat. "I ain't looking to cause you any trouble, I promise. Just hear me out?"

For reasons I can't fully explain, I made a great show of consulting Mr. Wiltshire's gold pocket watch before saying, "All right, but only for a minute," and following him to a lunch joint two blocks away.

"How do you take it?" Chapman said as we sidled up to the counter. "Your coffee?"

"Just black, please," I said, since that's how I took my tea.

"Draw two in the dark," he called to the waiter. "So, Miss Gallagher, let me get straight to the point." There was a grandfatherly growl to his voice, and he had a slow way of speaking, as if to make sure his words didn't get ahead of his thoughts. There was something reassuring about that. "First off, I'm sorry for Ward. He's a good detective, but he's just come to us from the Sixth Precinct, and they do things a little different down in Five Points." Glancing at me, he added, "Could be you know something about that."

This wasn't crack detective work; the boy behind the counter could have guessed it just as easily. My heritage was plain enough from my name, and there's only so many neighborhoods an Irish girl my age was likely to come from. I made sure my expression said as much. I didn't want him thinking I'd be easily impressed—or intimidated.

"He's also . . ." Chapman paused. "Well, he's an experienced officer, but when you been on the job as long as I have, you see a thing or two . . ." He trailed off as the coffee arrived, waiting until the boy behind the counter was well out of earshot before continuing. "Maybe every now and then you even see something that changes the way you look at the world."

I curled my fingers around my coffee while I processed that. The steam rising from the cup smelled wonderful, but I knew that for a cruel trick. Coffee is the one American tradition I simply cannot adopt, no matter how hard I try. It invariably tastes awful; I imagine hot water strained through the dregs of an opium pipe would have a similar flavor. Even so, I made a polite show of sipping at it while I tried to work out what Sergeant Chapman was hinting at. "What sorts of things?"

He studied me a moment before replying. "Do you read the papers, Miss Gallagher?"

"Now and then."

"I'm an avid reader, myself," he said in his unhurried way. "Plenty of us at the precinct are. Helps keep abreast of the local goings-on. Anyways, I come across a story on Saturday in *The New-York Times* that caught my interest. Maybe you saw it? About a treasure hunter in Hell Gate?"

My hands twitched, rattling the coffee cup in its saucer.

Chapman glanced down but didn't comment. "Most people would laugh at a story like that."

There was a stretch of silence. I realized he was waiting for me to respond. He didn't want to go too far out on a limb until he knew what sort of person he was dealing with. I knew just how he felt. I hadn't even been willing to tell Clara about the ghost, and now here I was, on the brink of telling a copper. But there was something in Sergeant Chapman's eyes that made me trust him, at least this far. "I laughed at first," I admitted. "But now I think . . . Well, I spoke to Peter Arbridge myself, and I'm not laughing anymore."

He nodded and took a long draw of his coffee.

"What about you, Sergeant?"

"The same. I'd heard my share of ghost stories on the beat. Far as I was concerned, they was all bull. Till one day, some years back, I had a case changed my mind about that. Sort of thing you'd never believe till you saw it with your own eyes, and then . . . Well, you can never unsee it, can you?"

"No," I said, my voice barely above a whisper. "No, you can't."

"Maybe one day you'll tell me your story and I'll tell you mine. For now, I think we understand each other well enough."

I nodded at my coffee.

"So," he said, "you spoke to the fella from the paper. Not just for curiosity's sake, I'm guessing."

"I thought he might know something about my employer, Mr. Wiltshire. Are you working on his case, too?"

The detective shook his head. "Never heard the name before today. What sorta rub is it?"

"He's been missing since last Saturday."

"Sorry to hear."

"Yes, everyone's *very sorry*," I said bitterly, "but nobody seems to be willing to do a thing about it."

"Sorry about that, too. Whole precinct's pretty tied up with this Jacob Crowe business. Got the mayor breathing down our necks. Not every day a Fifth Avenue swell turns up murdered." Glancing at me out of the corner of his eye, he added, "Sounded like Ward figured your boss was mixed up in that somehow."

I scowled. "He figures a lot of things that aren't true."

"Don't get a bee in your bonnet, Miss Gallagher. Not saying he's right or wrong, I'm just trying to figure how it all fits together."

"That makes two of us," I muttered, daring another sip of my coffee. It tasted like the contents of an ashtray.

"What's your theory?"

"Sorry?"

"You asked Ward a bunch of questions. Talk me through 'em. What're you thinking?" He leaned against the counter, head cocked expectantly.

I couldn't have been more surprised if he'd dropped to one knee and asked me to marry him. In all my encounters with the police, I'd never met one who was the least bit interested in my opinion, let alone my *theory*. Until that moment, I'd have thought myself about as likely to encounter a leprechaun riding a unicorn. "I . . . I'm not sure," I stammered. "I'm just following Mr. Wiltshire's trail as best I can."

"Sensible place to start in a missing person's case. So how does that get you to the fella in the paper?"

"I think Mr. Wiltshire read that story just before he left the house on Saturday morning, and he seemed to be in an awful hurry. So I decided to speak with Mr. Arbridge myself, and sure enough a gentleman matching Mr. Wiltshire's description went to see him last Saturday, asking all sorts of questions about the ghost he saw."

Chapman frowned. "He some sort of enthusiast, your boss?"

"Not that I know of. From what I saw, it seemed to be connected to his business somehow."

"He's an attorney, right?"

"So I'm told, and I think he's working for the Freemasons."

"What makes you say that?"

"A conversation I overheard between someone named Roberts and . . . another man." I decided to leave Mr. Burrows out of it. I'd laid enough suspicion at his doorstep for one day.

"Roberts. Heard you mention the name. What can you tell me about him?"

"Nothing, apart from his being a Freemason. I wondered if Mr. Wiltshire might be defending a Mason against . . . some sort of criminal charges."

Now, a responsible citizen would probably have mentioned having overheard the word *murder,* but I couldn't bring myself to spill everything just yet, not until I was sure it wouldn't send Mr. Wiltshire and his best friend up the river.

Chapman grunted thoughtfully. "Haven't heard of any charges being laid against a Mason, but maybe they're bracing for some. Could be your boss was investigating the crime."

"Investigating? An attorney?"

"Happens sometimes, when they think their client is innocent. Looking for exculpatory evidence, or maybe even the real culprit." Wryly, he added, "Sometimes folks just don't trust the police."

"Imagine," I said, just as wryly.

"Rich family like the Crowes, usually they'd hire themselves some Pinkertons for a job like that, but maybe they hadn't got around to it yet. If your boss was looking into the crime, that might explain what happened to him. He finds out something he shouldn't . . ." Chapman trailed off, looking grim. "Don't explain what none of it has to do with a ghost in the East River, though."

"No, it doesn't."

He straightened and donned his hat. "I'll look into it, provided that don't step on too many toes at the station. Roberts, right?" He took a ledger from his pocket and wrote it down.

I nodded, feeling a rush of relief. "Thank you, Sergeant."

"It's for me to thank you, Miss Gallagher. Sounds like a solid lead. Hopefully it turns up your boss and our murderer both. Now if I can give you a piece of advice . . ."

"Stay out of it?"

"Hard for me to say that. He's obviously important to you or you wouldn't have come this far. But if your boss's disappearance *is* connected to Jacob Crowe's murder, you oughta watch your step. No offense, but anybody willing to murder a high society fella with connections like Crowe's ain't gonna think twice about hurting a working-class girl such as yourself."

"I understand," I said, and I meant it—not that it would change anything. "Thank you for the coffee, Sergeant."

"You're welcome." As he walked away, he added over his shoulder, "Next time, we'll make it tea."

The sun was setting by the time I hopped on the train, but that was just as well. Breaking into a law office, I reasoned, was probably best done after dark.

Finding out where Mr. Wiltshire worked was the one scrap

of success in my otherwise disastrous visit to the Twenty-Eighth Precinct—that, and my conversation with Sergeant Chapman. I could only hope the detective would find something to clear up the cloud of suspicion I'd managed to cast over Mr. Wiltshire and his best friend. In the meantime, I'd have to try to put things right myself, which in my mind meant sneaking into the offices of Locke, Banneker & Associates.

Detective Ward had been helpfully precise in his description of Mr. Wiltshire's workplace, having situated it, in the typical way of New Yorkers, in relation to a landmark. *Across from the Equitable Life Building,* he'd said, which ought to have made matters simple. Except when I got there, I saw no masthead bearing the name of the firm, and none of the passersby I stopped had heard of it. Then I spotted a New York Cab Company livery just down the street. I'd watched Mr. Wiltshire climb into their distinctive yellow carriages every morning for two years. Might one of the drivers recognize a description?

"Sure, I know him," said a young man lounging against the side of his cab. "We call him His Lordship—you know, on account of the accent."

He pointed me to an economical brick structure with nothing much to distinguish it. The front door was unlocked, and inside, I found Locke, Banneker & Associates among the engraved nameplates on the wall. *Must be a small firm,* I thought, a suspicion that was confirmed when I arrived on the third floor and saw the modest-looking door bearing the same name.

A modest-looking door that stood ajar.

I hesitated. Grateful as I was not to have to try my hand at lockpicking, I had no idea how I'd account for my presence to Mr. Wiltshire's business associates. They must know of his disappearance by now, but somehow I doubted that my intrepid tale of amateur police work would impress an office full of lawyers.

Then I noticed something odd. Though the gas lamp on the landing was lit, the office itself was shrouded in darkness. *They've forgotten to lock it,* I thought. *How irresponsible.* I was sure Mr. Wiltshire would disapprove of his clients' private affairs being left to the mercy of anybody that should happen along.

Cautiously, I pushed the door open a little farther. I couldn't see much, but the glow of the gaslight sketched the outlines of a small, barren room. A floorboard groaned under my foot; I froze, but nothing stirred. Satisfied the place was empty, I went inside.

I walked to the center of the room and turned full circle, taken aback by my surroundings. From what I could see, the law offices of Locke, Banneker & Associates consisted entirely of that small, barren rectangle of space, plus a tiny office at the back. The furnishings in the waiting room, if you could even call it that, consisted of two plain wooden chairs and a threadbare rug in dire need of a beating. The smell of dust tickled my nose; I had to pinch it to keep from sneezing. *This can't be it,* I thought. *There must be some mistake.* Surely a gentleman of Mr. Wiltshire's station belonged somewhere a little more . . . impressive? Someplace with plush leather armchairs and engraved Carcel lamps and thick Persian rugs? Someplace with a *desk*?

Small wonder nobody had heard of Locke, Banneker & Associates. Who would be represented by such a firm? Not the Freemasons, surely. Nor a rich man like Mr. Burrows, or Mr. Roberts, or the unfortunate Jacob Crowe. Something was certainly *off* here, and I felt a prickle of unease as I made my way to the little office at the back.

The door creaked as I pushed it open, loud enough to drown out the sound of my gasp.

Papers littered the floor. An inkbottle had been upended on the desk, and the chair lay on its side in a corner. The dim light from the hallway picked out shards of broken glass from the filing cabinets. *Someone's been here. Someone who shouldn't have been . . .*

An arm snaked around my neck, crushing me against the bulk of a man. I tried to cry out, but my lungs wouldn't draw air; I writhed and kicked, clawing ineffectually at the band of hard muscle clamped across my throat.

"Who are ye?" An Irish voice, hard.

I couldn't have answered if I wanted to. I made a choking sound, and when my attacker loosened his grip to let me speak, I twisted under his arm and lunged for the desk. A blinding pain exploded at the back of my skull, sending a flare of white light across my vision. I braced myself against the desk, dazed.

Boot heels rang out on the floorboards behind me. I hauled myself clumsily along the desk, trying to get away, my arm trailing a thick smear of ink. The inkbottle lay a few inches from my fingers.

"I'll ask again—"

I spun and slammed the inkbottle into the side of his head. Glass shattered; the man cried out and stumbled.

He hung back a moment, head bowed, hand clamped against the side of his face. Then he laughed. "I'll say this, darlin', you've got sand." He advanced on me, still laughing, and I heard the *click* of a pistol being cocked.

The room seemed to grow even darker, the shadows threatening to swallow me. Even so, I'll never forget the face that

loomed over me in that moment: long, craggy, with a thick auburn mustache and the hardest eyes I'd ever seen. I grabbed at his
waistcoat, but he batted me away; the last thing I saw was the
butt of his revolver swinging at my temple.

I don't know how long I was out. Something more than a minute
and less than an hour. All I know is that by the time I stirred and
brought a hand to my head, the blood had slowed to a trickle and
it felt as if someone had driven a railroad spike into my skull.

I dragged myself to my feet. It wasn't until I stood propped
against the desk that I thought to be afraid. But as my vision
cleared, I saw that the room was empty; my attacker was gone.

Glass crunched under my shoes. I reached for my handkerchief to stanch the bleeding, and that's when I realized that my
dress had been torn, the breast pocket ripped open at the corner.
Mr. Wiltshire's watch was gone. I gave a strangled cry, patting
myself down and dropping back to the floor to look for it. (I know
what you're thinking: I'd just been attacked and knocked out
cold, and I was worried about a watch? It sounds silly, but the
Patek Philippe had long since ceased to be just a watch to me. It
was a piece of *him*, and if I lost it, it would be as if I'd lost a piece
of him, too.)

As it happened, though, I hadn't lost the watch. It had rolled
under the desk when I fell. Anxiously, I held it up to my ear: still
ticking. The Swiss really do make miraculous watches.

I found something else down there, too: a silver button with
a bit of purple thread still attached to it. I slipped it into my overcoat pocket without really thinking, along with Mr. Wiltshire's
watch.

I took a few minutes to sift through the papers scattered

about the office, but all I found was law books, blank ledgers, and some documents that looked like patent filings—nothing mentioning Jacob Crowe, Peter Arbridge, or the Freemasons. My head throbbed, and I felt nauseous. It would be a trial just making my way to the hack stand. So with a final, rueful glance around the ransacked office, I headed for home.

CHAPTER 9

THE SURLY SEAMSTRESS—DARKENING
THE DOOR—A LUCKY GUESS

"Clara."

She didn't come to the door straightaway, and for a moment I hovered there in the hallway, bleeding, wondering what I should do next. I knew I needed stitches, but I also knew that I would rather spend the rest of my life with a terrible scar than ask for help from Mrs. Sellers.

Happily, I was spared that choice. Clara opened the door, looked me up and down, and nodded, as if this were exactly what she'd expected to find. Which, come to think of it, it probably was. "Well," she said. "Look at you."

"I need—"

"You need a doctor, is what you need."

"I can't afford a Fifth Avenue doctor, and I'm not going all the way back downtown with this." I gestured at the trickle of blood still working its way down the side of my face. "I just need a stitch or two, and you're handy with a needle and thread."

Clara sucked on a tooth, her eyes hard with anger. "All right, then. We'd best get you to the kitchen."

"Thank you. But first . . ." I felt myself coloring. "The cab that brought me home is waiting outside. My reticule was stolen and . . ."

She laughed bitterly. "Help yourself," she said, grabbing her coin purse and tossing it at me.

By the time I'd paid the driver and returned to the kitchen, Clara had assembled a basin of water and washcloths, a little bottle of rubbing alcohol, and a needle and some thread. "What happens when the housekeeper hears us and comes down here?"

"That's the least of my worries right now."

She took a cloth to my temple, shaking her head as she dabbed the blood away. "Quite a mess you got here. I don't even have proper thread for this. For all you know, I'll make it worse."

"I'm sure you'll do fine. Thank you, Clara."

She wasn't in the mood for thank-yous. "Robbed, huh? Big surprise, wandering around at night. Where was it? Five Points?"

"I wasn't robbed," I said wearily. "I mean, I was, but that's not why I was attacked. I was at Mr. Wiltshire's office, and somebody grabbed me. He had a pistol, and . . ." I trailed off, shuddering. Saying it out loud made me realize just how close I'd come to being put in the ground.

Clara paused, cloth suspended halfway between the bowl and my forehead. "A pistol." She shook her head and resumed dabbing. I could see her anger draining away with each wring of the cloth, but I almost preferred it to the look she was giving me now. "Jesus Lord, Rose."

"I know." I felt the prick of tears behind my eyes. "And I would quit, I swear I would, but it's a matter of life and death. I heard Mr. Burrows talking to another man yesterday about a murder, and—"

"*Murder?*" She froze again.

"Mr. Wiltshire is mixed up in it. I don't know how, exactly, but Mr. Burrows was afraid it would get him killed. He might already be . . ." The word disappeared down my throat in a breathy gulp, the tears finally breaking free. "So I went to his office, but when I got there, the place had been turned inside out, and there was a man—"

"*Shh.* Rose, honey, calm down. You're all right now, and I'm sure Mr. Wiltshire is all right, too. We'll figure this out."

I paused, sniffling. "We?"

"Well, you obviously ain't gonna quit, so it seems to me my choices are to help you or let you be, and if this is what comes of letting you be"—she gestured at my bloodied temple—"I don't see the upside."

I nearly sobbed in my relief. "Oh, thank you, Clara!"

"That don't mean I forgive you for putting me in this position. But since I'm in it, why don't you tell me what's going on?" Taking up the needle and thread, she added, "Don't skip the details, neither. Hopefully it'll keep your mind off what I'm doing, 'cause this is gonna hurt like hell."

It did hurt like hell, worse than anything I can recall, but Clara's needlework was as tidy in flesh as it was in fabric, and when she'd finished and I had a glass of cooking sherry in my belly and a slab of cold meat from the icebox against my face, I felt better.

"The murder Mr. Burrows was talking about," she said, "you think it's this Jacob Crowe fella?"

"That's what I was hoping to find out at the law offices, but all I got for my trouble was a smashed head and a silver button."

"What? A button?"

I drew the little silver knob from my pocket and tossed it on the table. "I found it under the desk. I must've torn it loose when I was trying to fend him off."

Clara picked it up. "Purple thread. That's some color for a waistcoat. Did you find what you was looking for?"

I shook my head. "I was only there for a few minutes. It was a strange place, though. Didn't look like much of a law firm, if you ask—"

A knock sounded at the front door. Clara and I frowned at each other. Who could be calling so late in the evening?

I started to get up, but Clara waved me off. "I'll do it. You keep that cold press going."

I did as I was told, holding the slab of cold meat against my head and ruminating. I was so lost in my own thoughts that I didn't hear the approaching footfalls, so when I glanced up to find a man darkening the door of the kitchen, I started violently and sprang to my feet, grabbing the nearest thing to hand and brandishing it like a weapon.

"Well," said Mr. Burrows, "that's the second time in as many days I've startled you out of your skin." Looking me over, he added, "But I think perhaps I understand why. Are you all right, Rose?"

Clara appeared behind him, shrugging helplessly. He must have barged right past her. Hardly appropriate behavior for a high society gentleman, but I'd come to realize that Mr. Burrows wasn't your typical Fifth Avenue swell.

"I'm fine," I told him stiffly.

"Then perhaps you might set the skillet aside for now?"

I glanced at the frying pan in my hand, still cocked threateningly over my shoulder. "Sorry," I muttered, putting it down.

The sight of him brought a confused jumble of emotions—fear, guilt, suspicion, and more than a little anger. Part of me wanted to confide in him like an ally; another part wanted to ring that skillet off his pretty golden head. I did neither, hovering behind my chair with a look that probably wasn't all that welcoming.

"Shall we sit?" Without waiting for a reply, he lowered himself into a chair, arranging his gloves and hat neatly on the table. "Please, Rose, don't just stand there. I feel uncivilized enough as it is, and you look like you could use the rest. And you, Clara. I expect you should hear this, too."

"Should I fetch Mrs. Sellers?" she asked.

"Not unless you'd like to explain a great deal more than I care to."

Clara dragged a chair near to mine—and a notable distance from Mr. Burrows's. The two of us faced him across the table in tense silence.

"First things first," he said, his clear blue eyes settling on mine. "What happened to your head, Rose?"

"I was attacked."

"By whom?"

"I don't know."

He waited for more; when it wasn't forthcoming, he sighed. "This is going to take a very long time if I have to draw you out with questions."

"I'm sorry, is that inconvenient? I wouldn't want you to think I was being deliberately uncooperative."

His mouth quirked just short of a smile. "I deserve that, I suppose. But I'm not sure what I've done to earn your mistrust."

"I hardly know where to begin, Mr. Burrows," I said coldly, well past caring about propriety.

"I do apologize for not having been more transparent," he said, his own voice cooling several degrees, "but if I'd had any notion of how far you meant to take this, I'd have spoken more plainly. I trust you realize by now that our mutual friend Mr. Wiltshire is embroiled in some very dangerous business."

Thanks to you, I nearly retorted, but I held my tongue. I didn't want him to know I'd overheard his conversation with Mr. Roberts. I didn't want him to know anything, I decided, not until I could be sure that Detective Ward was wrong about him.

"Why are you looking at me like that?"

"Like what?" *Like you might be a murderer?*

The silver button sat between us on the table; casually, he picked it up. "Because of what you saw, I suppose, or what you *think* you saw, when you followed me yesterday." He glanced up, meeting my gaze. "What did you imagine you were about, Rose?"

"I don't know what you mean."

He gave me a wry look. "A word to the wise: If you want to be secretive about something, don't do it in the middle of Fifth Avenue. The world has never known a more densely packed collection of busybodies, and they delight in nothing so much as embarrassing their neighbors."

"You'll have to forgive me. I'm obviously not as accustomed to secrecy as you are."

"No," he said flatly, "nor shall you ever be." He was quiet a moment, toying with the button. Then he said, "I came here for your own good. Whether you believe it or not, I'm a friend, to Thomas Wiltshire and to you, and as a friend, I implore you to stop this at once. Thomas would say the same, as should anyone who cares for you." His glance slid meaningfully to Clara. "I know you're only doing what you think is best for Thomas, but unlike you, he has gone into this with his eyes open. He knew the risks, and he chose to take them. I haven't given up on him, nor should you, but please, leave this to me from now on. Will you do that, Rose?"

I scowled and drew little circles on the table.

"Please," he said, dipping his head to catch my eye. "No more following me about. Five Points is a dangerous place, and the Tenderloin, to say nothing of the sorts one finds skulking around derelict gasworks. Though"—his glance shifted to my stitches—"I suppose it's a bit late for that advice. Are you sure you're all right? I can have my physician look at that if you'd like."

"It's fine," I said distractedly, my mind snagging on something. "What do you mean—"

"Rose? Clara?" Mrs. Sellers's voice floated down the servants' staircase. "What's going on? I thought I heard a man's voice . . ." She appeared on the steps and froze in her tracks. "Mr. Burrows!"

"Good evening, Mrs. Sellers." Rising, he dropped the silver button back on the table. "I was just leaving."

"But what are you . . . ?"

"Please excuse the hour, but I came as soon as I heard about poor Rose's frightful ordeal. In Mr. Wiltshire's absence, I felt it was my duty to check in and make sure she was well." Sweeping up his belongings with casual grace, he went on, "Do let me know if you change your mind about the doctor, Rose. Anytime, day or night."

"Ordeal?" Mrs. Sellers echoed blankly.

"Shocking, isn't it?" Mr. Burrows shook his head. "Robbed in broad daylight. What is the city coming to? Good evening, ladies. I'll show myself out." With that, he donned his gray silk hat and was gone.

Mrs. Sellers stood rooted to the spot, staring like a startled cow. Eventually, she blinked her way out of her stupor and said, "Well, are you all right, Rose?"

"I'll be fine, thank you. Only . . . I don't think I'll be able to work tomorrow." Smiling meekly, I added, "I think I ought to follow Mr. Burrows's advice about seeing a doctor, don't you?"

It was a trap, of course; Mrs. Sellers wouldn't dare disagree with a man of Mr. Burrows's pedigree.

"Yes, of course, you should certainly do as Mr. Burrows says."

"Thank you, ma'am," I said sweetly, and smiled at her until she'd disappeared back up the stairs.

We waited until we'd heard the muted sound of Mrs. Sellers's bedroom door shutting. Then Clara said, "What in the hell just happened?"

I shook my head. "He's a very good liar, isn't he?"

"Smooth as a baby's backside. Had more than his share of practice, I'd say."

He'd admitted as much, one of several extraordinary things about the conversation. The one that stuck out most in my mind, though, was this: "What did he mean about a derelict gasworks?"

Clara shrugged. "Probably went there after you lost him yesterday and just assumes you was still tailing him."

"He must mean the Consolidated Gas factory on Twentieth—the one that had that awful spill."

"What would he be doing down there? That place is poison."

"Looking for Mr. Wiltshire, I suppose." I took up the button again, toying with it as Mr. Burrows had done. "I wonder . . ."

"Here we go. Didn't you listen to a word that man said?"

"I'm not quitting, Clara. Nothing Mr. Burrows said changes that. Maybe he's the friend he claims to be, but I don't need his protection."

"You sure about that?" Before I could answer, she held up her hands. "Fine. I am not going over this again. It's too late and I'm too tired. So what're you gonna do?"

"Sleep." Suddenly, it was all I could do to keep my eyes open. "After that, I guess I'm visiting the gasworks."

CHAPTER 10

RECONNOITERING THE GASWORKS—OF
WAISTCOATS AND REVOLVERS—THE MAN
IN THE CHAIR

I don't know what I expected to find at the gasworks. I think some part of me was convinced Mr. Wiltshire was dead, and my way of coping was to go through every motion, no matter how futile, so that when the news came I would at least have the comfort of knowing I'd done everything I could. Either that or my instincts were keener than I gave them credit for. Whatever the reason, Friday morning found me standing across the street from the grim gray compound of the Consolidated Gas Company, huddled under an umbrella and wondering what on earth to do next.

The gates were padlocked, a rusted KEEP OUT sign hanging crookedly above a knot of chains. I might be able to climb the wall, but what for? The compound looked empty. Whoever Mr. Burrows had come here to see was obviously long gone. And Clara was right—the place *was* poison, literally; even two years after the disastrous leak that had shuttered the factory, the fumes felt like sandpaper on the inside of my throat. But I'd come down here in the freezing rain, enduring the stares of my fellow train passengers as I tried to hide Clara's tidy but undeniably grotesque stitches. I wasn't going to give up until I'd at least given the place a once-over.

I approached the gates, giving them an experimental shove. They rattled a little but didn't come apart far enough for me to peek between them. All I could glimpse of the factory was the great hulking cylinders of the gas tanks and the blackened tip of a smokestack jutting into the sky. I walked the length of the block and around the side, but there was nothing to see but wall and more wall. I was about ready to admit defeat when the sound of a heavy tread sent me scurrying like a rat behind a cluster of old barrels; I folded my umbrella away just in time to avoid being seen by a man striding purposefully toward the river. At first I took him for security—who else would be prowling around the perimeter of an abandoned gasworks?—but as he neared my cluster of barrels, I saw that he wasn't wearing a uniform. Instead he wore a flashy overcoat unbuttoned over an even flashier waistcoat . . .

. . . of purple silk.

I couldn't see his face under the umbrella he carried, but his stride had a thuggish rhythm, and as I scanned the full length of his figure I glimpsed the butt of a revolver at his hip.

My breath caught. I clamped a hand over my mouth, sure he must be able to hear it, but he continued past without breaking stride.

It can't be him. It can't be. But there was no mistaking that purple silk.

Frightened as I was, the emotion that gripped me most in that moment was outrage. I would *not* be scared off by some rough in a gaudy waistcoat. I'd grown up with brutes like that loafing on every street corner. And this time, *I* was the one with the element of surprise on my side.

I waited until he'd disappeared around a corner, then waited a little longer for good measure. I wasn't worried about losing him; the smoke from his cheap cigar left a trail almost thick enough to see. When I judged he was well out of range, I came out of hiding and followed.

The wall zigzagged a little near the river, and I flattened myself against it, peering around the corner to make sure the way was clear. I wasn't surprised to find a hole in the brickwork about twenty paces ahead, just large enough for a man. I ducked through as furtively as a kitchen mouse, scampering to the nearest cover and listening for any sign of movement. Nothing. Emerging cautiously from my shadowed corner, I surveyed my surroundings.

The compound was huge, a bleak jumble of buildings covering well over a city block, and I quickly despaired of finding my man. I'd been sure I could follow the cigar smoke, but I'd failed to account for the effluvium of the place, so harsh that it nearly brought tears to my eyes. And now the rain was really coming down, pattering loudly against my overcoat. I scurried to the nearest building, but the door was locked. Cursing a salty streak any Five Pointer would have been proud of, I moved on to the next. This one had a padlock, too, but it had been broken open and lay half buried in the mud. Warily, I nudged my way inside.

I paused on the threshold, letting my eyes adjust. A vast space littered with rusting bits of junk spread out before me. A small office stood in the far corner; that seemed as safe a place as any to warm up while I worked out what to do next. Throwing another quick glance around, I made for it.

I didn't notice the lamplight under the door until it was too late. I stopped so abruptly that my foot scraped against the grimy floor, and I froze, cringing.

"Good," said a voice, "you're here. The lamp is nearly out of oil."

I'd have recognized that voice anywhere, but hearing it speak such familiar words drove it home with a force that nearly made me swoon. With a strangled cry, I lunged at the door.

I burst in to find a small, dimly lit office, at the center of which sat Thomas Wiltshire. He looked up, startled. "What the devil? *Rose?*"

I stood there like a stunned rabbit, struggling to process the sight before me. He sat behind a desk, pencil in hand, papers spread out before him, as if he were merely passing an ordinary day at work. His clothing was disheveled and his beard unkempt, and he was the single most beautiful sight I'd ever laid eyes on.

I wasn't the only one struggling with shock. I can't imagine what must have gone through Mr. Wiltshire's mind when he looked up to find his housemaid standing in the doorway. But he mastered it swiftly. "Quickly, Rose!" He shoved his boot into the desk and sent himself skidding back, and that's when I saw the ropes binding his elbows to the arms of the chair. "They'll be back any moment!"

I started to ask who *they* were—and then I realized what I was looking at. "Sweet Jesus, they've kidnapped you!" I rushed to his side. It was all I could do not to throw my arms around him, but the urgency of the situation cut through even my relief. He wasn't safe, not yet. "I don't have a knife. I'll have to untie you."

"That won't be easy, I'm afraid. They've done a good job of it or I'd have dispensed with their hospitality days ago."

I could feel his eyes on me as I worked, which didn't exactly aid my concentration. The air was thick with unanswered questions, and I sensed he was restraining himself as much as I. Yet he was also remarkably composed under the circumstances. I hoped he could keep it up, at least until we were well clear of this wretched place. "You're handling this very well," I said in the way of a nurse, or a parent comforting a child.

"What a coincidence, I was just about to say the same."

"It's been a strange couple of days." I felt foolish as soon as I'd said it—how could anything I'd gone through compare to what he must have endured?—but when I glanced up, he was looking at me with such a fascinated expression that I felt myself blushing.

"I very much look forward to hearing about it, Rose," he murmured, his gaze lingering on my stitches.

He was right about the knots. Whoever had tied them obviously knew what he was doing, and I struggled to make any headway. Then, in a flash of inspiration, I grabbed my hairpin. It was nothing fancy—just a simple brass pin with a looping head—but its four-inch point was exactly what I needed to slip between the coils and get a bit of leverage. My hair tumbled down in a great mess over my face, but I tossed it back and set to work, jimmying the knot until it was loose enough to let my fingers do the rest. A moment later the rope dropped away from his left arm.

I'd just started in on the right when I heard the toll of heavy footfalls crossing the warehouse. I looked up, my eyes locking with Mr. Wiltshire's in an urgent glance.

There was nowhere to hide. All I could do was grab my umbrella and tuck myself up behind the door while Mr. Wiltshire scuttled his chair forward, concealing his arms beneath the surface of the desk.

"Breakfast, Englishman," said a voice, and a short, stocky man walked in, dropping an old biscuit tin unceremoniously on the desk. "Ye got that finished or what?" Another Irishman—from Sligo, by the sounds of him, just like Mam.

"Or what, I'm afraid," Mr. Wiltshire replied.

"Get on with it, already. Boss is waitin'." He started to turn around.

The room was too small; he'd see me for sure. I did the only thing I could think of: I walloped him over the head with the umbrella.

He grunted, stumbling back into the desk. Mr. Wiltshire lunged and threw his free arm around the man's neck, crying, "*Run!*"

I had no intention of running, but the rough's flailing legs did drive me back—straight into another body. I whirled, leading with the handle of my umbrella, and was rewarded with a *crack* as it met the jaw of the man looming over me. But he'd grabbed hold of me, and we both tumbled backward out into the warehouse. I hit the floor hard, jarring the umbrella from my hands and sending a burst of agony through my bruised skull. I was slow getting to my feet, and when I did, I found myself face-to-face with two very large men—one of whom was all too familiar.

"Well, well," said the Irishman with the auburn mustache,

"here she is again. I like this one. She's got proper pluck. Didn't have the heart to put her down last night." He left his pistol in its holster; he didn't seem to think he needed it. "Look at this, love," he said, gesturing at a row of messy stitches in his cheek. "We match."

Seeing the wound I'd dealt him gave me courage. "Keep away from me."

"Or what?"

I still had my brass hairpin, bent though it was from working at the ropes; I brandished it menacingly. "Or I'll put your eye out."

He laughed, as well he might have. "It'll be a lark watching you try." He advanced on me.

I pivoted, putting my back to the open space of the warehouse. I couldn't hope to outrun them, but at least I could lead them away from Mr. Wiltshire. The little office had gone terribly quiet, but I couldn't let myself think about what that might mean.

The roughs split up, the Irishman blocking the office and his partner standing between me and the far door. I was trapped. "Ready?" the Irishman asked, grinning.

Before I could answer, the Irishman's knees suddenly gave way, and as he fell, the handle of an umbrella delivered a hard blow to his temple, spinning him sideways to the floor. Mr. Wiltshire stepped smoothly over his prone form and came at the other man, clutching my umbrella like a weapon.

The rough's face twisted into a snarl. A knife flashed in his hand. I cried out a warning, but it was too late; the man lunged.

What happened next was almost too fast to follow.

Mr. Wiltshire held his ground, and when the rough came at

him with the knife, he turned the blow aside with the umbrella. Then, in almost the same motion, he brought his improvised staff down on the man's wrist, knocking the knife free. The rough threw a punch, which Mr. Wiltshire sidestepped neatly before hooking the back of the man's neck with the umbrella handle and driving a knee into his face. The thug went down like a sack of potatoes.

I was so focused on the whole deadly dance that I didn't see the third man until it was too late. He came barreling out of the office like a charging bull, bloodied, furious, and wielding a broken chair leg. I shouted a warning, and Mr. Wiltshire turned, but he couldn't get his umbrella up fast enough; the club met his knuckles in a brutal impact. He grunted in pain and stumbled back, but somehow he still managed to block the next swing and follow it with one of his own, a hard blow to his attacker's kneecap. The man buckled, and that was the end of it; Mr. Wiltshire swung again, dropping the thug to the floor.

It was at this point that I thought to go for the gun.

"Ah," said Mr. Wiltshire. "That would have come in handy."

"Sorry," I said numbly.

"Sorry? My word, Rose, you did brilliantly. But I think I'd better have that, if you don't mind." He reached for the gun, and I realized my hands were shaking.

I gave the loathsome thing over, wiping my palms on my overcoat for good measure.

Mr. Wiltshire disappeared inside the office, emerging a moment later with a sheaf of papers tucked under his arm. "We'd better hurry. They won't be out long." Seeing my state, he put a hand on my shoulder. "Are we steady, Rose?"

For a second I just stood there, staring at Thomas Wiltshire as if he were a complete stranger. Which, in a way, he was.

Drawing a breath, I said, "Steady."

"Good girl." He handed me the umbrella and cocked the revolver. "This way," he said, and hustled me across the open floor of the warehouse.

CHAPTER II

HOMECOMING—A CLOSE SHAVE—THE
FIRST DAY OF THE REST OF MY LIFE

We met no one else fleeing the compound, and as we reached the street, Mr. Wiltshire stashed the gun away, jamming it behind the braces at the small of his back. Rain drifted down from the sky in a great gray veil as he popped the umbrella open over my head and handed me the papers he'd taken from the office. Then he struck out into the street—hatless, coatless, wet clothes plastered to his body—in search of a cab. Finding one in the rain was by no means the least miraculous thing he accomplished that morning, and before long we were sitting side by side behind a steaming horse heading up the avenue.

By this point, I'd descended into a fog of shock, and might have stayed like that all the way home had I not felt Mr. Wiltshire shivering beside me.

"Oh!" With a squeak of dismay, I startled to wriggle out of my overcoat. "What a clod I am! You must be freezing! Here—"

"No, no, I couldn't possibly. I'll be all right, thank you." This fine display of gentlemanly behavior was somewhat undermined by the bluish hue of his lips.

"Don't be ridiculous, you're soaked through. You'll catch your death." I draped my coat over his shoulders like a blanket. Then I took a moment to right myself, smoothing my dress and coiling my hair back up to the crown of my head. I sighed ruefully when I saw the state of my poor hairpin, bent beyond recognition, but it would still hold. It was bitterly cold, even in the closed confines of the hack, but I couldn't regret giving my overcoat to Mr. Wiltshire. Already, a little color was coming back to his lips. "When was the last time you had a proper meal?"

He gave a threadbare smile. "Do I look so awful? I suppose I must."

"You look . . ." I trailed off, snared by the pale blue of his eyes. My insides flooded with warmth; all of a sudden, I didn't miss my overcoat anymore. "You look fine," I finished lamely.

"Thanks to you. However did you find me, Rose?"

"I'm . . . not sure, actually. I thought I was retracing Mr. Burrows's steps, but . . ." I trailed off, confused.

"Burrows? He had a part in this, too, then?"

"He's the one who pointed me to the gasworks. Sort of."

Mr. Wiltshire's brow creased in puzzlement. "I don't understand."

That made two of us. "He mentioned it last night when he came by the house, but only in passing. When he saw what happened to me, he warned me to stay away from the gasworks."

"What happened to you—are you referring to your injury?"

He gestured at my stitches. "Did the big Irishman have something to do with that? It sounded as though you two had crossed paths before."

"Last night. He knocked me out cold." Mr. Wiltshire murmured something regretful, but I was too preoccupied to pay much attention. "Mr. Burrows must have known he would be here, and you, too—but how? Unless . . . You don't suppose he was involved in your kidnapping, do you?"

Mr. Wiltshire just smiled at that. "I assure you, Burrows is the staunchest of allies."

"But if he knew where you were being held, why wouldn't he come for you himself?"

"*Hmm.*" Mr. Wiltshire's expression grew vague as he considered that. "He couldn't have known you would find me here, or he would indeed have come himself. And yet how . . . ? Wait." His gaze snapped back into focus. "After you were attacked, did you find any evidence at the scene?"

"Evidence?"

"Something belonging to the Irishman. A handkerchief, say, or a glove, or—"

"A button. I tore it from his waistcoat, but—?"

"Yes, good, and did Mr. Burrows come into contact with the button? Did he pick it up at any point, or even brush against it?"

"I suppose he did, now that you mention it . . ."

"Ah, well," said Mr. Wiltshire, his brow clearing. "That explains it."

I could only stare at him in bewilderment. How did a button explain anything?

"You didn't tell him where it came from, obviously."

"Well, no, but I don't see how any of that matters."

"Mr. Burrows is possessed of an unusual talent. But that is not my story to tell, especially when I am so eager to hear yours."

"I know the feeling," I said, a little more emphatically than I'd meant to. I'd been searching for this man for days, and now here he was, safe and sound and close enough to put my arms around. But instead of being overjoyed, I felt unaccountably foolish, as if the whole world were sharing a joke at my expense.

"I can see that you're frustrated, Rose, and I don't blame you. Let's just wait until we're warm and dry, shall we?"

"But—"

He gestured at the cab driver, and I understood.

"When we get home, then?" I said reluctantly.

"When we get home," he agreed, and burrowed down into my coat.

The rain made a frightful snarl of the traffic, so it was past time for luncheon when we finally arrived. Instinctively, I headed for the servants' door, but a gentle brush at my elbow drew me up short. "This way, Rose," said Mr. Wiltshire, and for the first time, I found myself entering 726 Fifth Avenue through the front door.

Mr. Wiltshire shook out my overcoat and hung it on the rack. Doing so brought him face-to-face with his own reflection in the hallway mirror, and he winced. He looked pale and rumpled, his beard in dire need of a trim, but his eyes were bright and clear. I saw nothing but perfection, even if he bore little resemblance to the tidy figure he usually cut. Running a hand through his damp hair, he said, "Tea?"

"Certainly." I turned to fetch it.

"No, wait, that's not what I, er . . ." For a moment we just stared at each other awkwardly, neither of us quite knowing what the situation called for. Then he gestured down the hall. "We'll go to the kitchen together, shall we?"

I'd have warned Clara if I could have. As it was she was lucky not to lose a finger, because when she looked up to find Mr. Wiltshire descending the servants' staircase, she dropped her meat cleaver midswing; it buried itself in the butcher's block with a heavy *thunk*. Her glance met mine, and my face split into a wide grin, the triumph of the morning's events breaking over me at last.

"Good morning, Clara," Mr. Wiltshire said, as if it were any other Friday.

Clara opened her mouth. Clamped it shut. She watched incredulously as he put the kettle on. Then she blurted, *"Where in the name of all that's holy have you been?"*

Of the three of us, I'm not sure who was most taken aback by this outburst. Clara, probably.

"Sir," she added, tugging the meat cleaver free.

Mr. Wiltshire eyed the big blade warily. "That is . . . a fair question, but the answer is rather too complicated to venture into just now. Suffice it to say that I owe Rose a tremendous debt."

"Mr. Wiltshire? Is that you?" The staircase creaked.

"Good morning, Mrs. Sellers."

The housekeeper appeared on the stairs. Like Clara, she was visibly surprised; unlike Clara, she had no idea just how miraculous his return really was, since I hadn't filled her in on my recent discoveries. She looked him up and down and said, faintly chiding, "We were concerned, sir."

"I do apologize, Mrs. Sellers."

"You might have sent word."

Her tone was almost more than I could bear. *He's been kid-napped and tied to a chair for a week, you horrible harpy!*

Mr. Wiltshire, for his part, just inclined his head and said, "I should have. Please accept my profound regrets."

I looked at him. He looked at me. I looked at Clara. A silent pact was thus made: The housekeeper would be told nothing.

"A business trip came up suddenly." It was the same explanation he'd given last spring when he'd been gone for over a week, and it dawned on me that it had probably been as untrue then as it was now. "A rather trying one, I must say. I am in dire need of a hot bath and a cup of tea."

"Certainly, sir. Rose . . ." Mrs. Sellers took in my disheveled appearance with a disapproving frown, but it would reflect poorly on her to upbraid me in front of Mr. Wiltshire, so she just gestured imperiously at the kettle. "Start with the tea, then draw Mr. Wiltshire a bath."

But before I could move, Mr. Wiltshire said, "Thank you, Mrs. Sellers, but I'm sure poor Rose is at least as cold as I am. She loaned me her overcoat in the rain, you see. Would you mind?"

She blinked. "You want me to do it?" You'd have thought he'd asked her to scrub the privy, so incredulous was her tone.

"If you'd be so good."

Clara fought down a smile. "I'll do one for Rose," she offered sweetly.

"Thank you, Clara. Rose, we'll speak when we've both had a chance to warm our bones." Inclining his head in farewell, Mr. Wiltshire mounted the stairs.

Mrs. Sellers fled after him, I think to avoid the humiliation of meeting our gazes. When she'd gone, Clara said, "I'll take care of the tea. Lord knows I have my questions, but Rose, honey, you look like you been run over by a carriage. Go on upstairs. I'll see you directly." She gave my arm a squeeze. "You did it. You actually did it!"

"I did it," I echoed dazedly, though in truth, I wasn't sure exactly what I'd done.

Hopefully I was about to find out.

Tempting as it was to soak in that blissfully hot bath all afternoon, I allowed myself only a short respite. I wanted to make sure I was ready the moment Mr. Wiltshire sent for me. Questions swirled like embers inside my skull; if I didn't get answers soon, I was going to burst into flames. Clara would have a few questions of her own, but she'd gone out for groceries. After days of restless fidgeting, she'd be looking forward to preparing a proper meal. Mr. Wiltshire would eat well this afternoon.

He found me sitting alone in the kitchen, sipping tea and trying to organize my thoughts. "Ah, there you are."

I sprang to my feet. "How are you feeling, sir?"

"Almost human, thank you. All I need is a shave and I'll be quite restored, but alas." He held up his left hand, and I sucked in a breath. The knuckles were an angry red where they'd been struck by the makeshift club.

"Do you need a doctor?"

"I don't think so. It's really just the finer movements that give me grief. A good night's sleep or two ought to do it. Until then"—he ran his good hand ruefully over his jaw—"I'll have to content myself with looking half a brute, since I can't spare the time to visit the barber."

"I can do it." The words were out of my mouth before I could stop myself, and I blushed furiously, wishing I could take them back. It was an outrageous suggestion.

Or at least it should have been, but such was Mr. Wiltshire's devotion to personal grooming that he merely scratched his stubble and said, "Tempting. Have you ever done it before?"

"Yes, sir." My gaze dropped to my shoes, my face still burning. "My father used to let me shave him sometimes, if I promised to be very careful."

He hummed thoughtfully. "A tad unconventional, perhaps, but I daresay we've crossed that threshold already today. If you're willing . . ."

"Yes, sir," I said, feeling a bit faint.

"Rose . . ." He hesitated, wearing that same awkward expression as before, when I'd been about to fetch his tea. "We are in uncharted waters here, you and I, and I don't suppose either of us is quite sure how best to manage it. But let us at least agree to dispense with *sir* for now. It makes me feel terribly exploitative."

I didn't know quite what to say to that, so I just nodded.

We headed upstairs. Accompanying Mr. Wiltshire to his bedroom gave me a wobble in the knees, but fortunately he was too preoccupied to notice. He assembled his shaving kit, but even gripping the brush was too much for him, so I took over the preparations. At first I was concentrating too intently to think about anything else, making sure everything was just so as I stropped the blade and churned up a good lather. But the closer the moment came, the more my composure started to crumble. My heart rate climbed, my breath coming faster with every circle of the brush. This was a degree of intimacy I'd only ever dreamed of, and it was more terrifying than the trio of roughs at the gasworks.

If the mere thought of touching his face was driving me to near-panic, how on earth was I going to keep my hand steady on the blade? It would be ironic if I'd rescued him from his kidnappers only to open his throat with a razor.

"You look nervous," he said. "Should I be?"

My laugh sounded strained. "It's just been a while, that's all."

"How long is a while?"

"About eight years."

He didn't like the sound of that, I could tell. But he was too much of a gentleman to risk hurting my feelings, so he just flashed a tense smile and said, "Well, I'm sure it will come back to you."

"It will," I said, more for my own benefit than his. "Do you have a sturdy book in here?"

"A book?"

"I used to stand on a chair with my da, but a nice thick book ought to do it for us."

"Yes, of course. Let me see . . ."

So there I stood, perched on *The Collected Works of William Shakespeare*, trying very hard not to tremble as I laid my hand against the side of Thomas Wiltshire's face. His eyes were level with mine, but I didn't dare meet them; it would have undone me. Instead I focused on the outline of his beard, trailing lather along the inside edge where I would begin the shave. "Ready?" I asked, laying the blade against his jaw. His breath ghosted along the inside of my wrist, thrilling the delicate nerves of my skin like a whisper of wind through grass.

"Ready," he said.

I worked in silence, mostly because I didn't trust myself to speak. I had to remind myself just to breathe. My hand rested against his cheek; my face hovered inches from his. If anyone had

walked in, it would certainly have looked like I was about to kiss
him—or kill him. The blood rushing through my veins made me
dangerously light-headed. (To this day, I wonder if he noticed
the glassy look in my eyes. If so, it must have struck terror into his
heart.) But somehow my hand was steady and sure, and gradually
the soft rasp of the razor coaxed my breathing back to a normal
rhythm.

"What happened this morning—" he began.

"Er, maybe you shouldn't."

"Right. Sorry."

I moved on to the other side. The drift of the razor slowed,
and my touch grew feather light. My reluctance vanished; now all
I wanted was to draw this moment out for eternity.

"You're putting me to sleep," he murmured, closing his eyes.
I let my glance roam over those long lashes, yearning to press my
lips to his eyelids.

"You must be exhausted," I said.

"*Mmm.*" His throat thrummed beneath my touch.

It was time to move on to his neck, and that meant I'd have
to unbutton his collar, something I'd pictured myself doing more
times than I care to admit. I lingered over the task, letting my
imagination take flight as one onyx shirt stud after another slipped
through my fingers, exposing another inch of throat. I could have
told him to put his chin up, but instead I indulged myself, threading my fingers through his hair and giving a gentle tug. He tipped
his chin obligingly.

I paused for a moment, overcome. I was in very great danger
here. His hair was luxuriant between my fingers, thick and soft
and damp. His skin smelled of soap and something else, the unmistakable scent of *Thomas Wiltshire*. How often had I brought

something of his—a silk tie, a handkerchief—to my face and inhaled that scent dreamily? And now here he was, eyes closed, head tipped back, my fingers tangled in his hair . . . I had only to move an inch or two to brush his lips with my own.

He would forgive you, a treacherous little voice in my head whispered. *You saved his life.*

I wet my lips with the tip of my tongue. Closed my eyes fleetingly.

I grabbed the soap brush and started lathering his neck.

The razor did its work again. I took as long as I dared to finish, but sooner or later all things must end, and with an inward sigh I released him and dismounted from the volume of Shakespeare. My limbs were as unsteady as if I'd downed a pint of whiskey.

"Thank you, Rose," he said, dabbing his face with a towel. "I do believe that was the most relaxing shave I've ever had."

I'd found it somewhat less relaxing, but it wouldn't do to tell him so. Instead I just smiled and said, "I'm glad. I'll just go wash up. Where shall we . . . ?"

"My study, I think. It should be private enough in there."

I shambled back to my room and threw myself facedown onto the bed, and there I stayed for a good five minutes or more, until I felt fully in control of my faculties. Then I got up, smoothed my dress, and went downstairs to confer with my employer.

CHAPTER 12

REVELATIONS

He was waiting for me in the study. "I'm not quite sure where to begin," he said, pouring himself a glass of sherry. He hoisted the decanter inquiringly, but I shook my head. I wanted to be perfectly lucid for this conversation. "I suppose the first thing I ought to ask is what happened with the Irishman."

"He hit me with the butt of his pistol. Last night, at your office." I managed to say it without blushing, having already resigned myself to the fact that more than a few of my actions were going to raise his eyebrows.

One of them was climbing his forehead already. "My office? How did you come to be there?" Then, in a distracted voice: "For that matter, how did the Irishman? Searching for something to help break the cipher, perhaps."

"Cipher?"

He sighed. "I'm not sure how much I ought to tell you, for your own safety. I know that sounds terribly unfair, but—"

"You're working for the Freemasons. On a murder case."

He paused, visibly taken aback.

"It has something to do with Peter Arbridge," I went on, "though I'm not sure what. Mr. Wang knows, though, doesn't he?"

There was a stretch of silence. Mr. Wiltshire gazed at me with frank astonishment. "You are full of surprises today, Rose."

I tried very hard not to look pleased. "So you see, there's no point in trying to protect me. I know too much already."

"I can vouch for the first part at least," said a voice, and I turned to find Mr. Burrows leaning on the doorframe. "I let myself in, Wiltshire. Hope you don't mind."

"Ah, Burrows. Good." Mr. Wiltshire waved him in. "Sherry?"

"Please."

So much for the study being a private place to talk. I found myself scowling as Mr. Burrows tossed his hat aside and arranged himself on the sofa with an air of perfect insouciance. "Welcome back, dear fellow. I was beginning to think I'd seen the last of you." He was smiling, but there was just enough edge in his voice to convince me that his nonchalance was feigned. He *was* relieved, though for some reason reluctant to show it.

"You had the house under watch, I suppose?" Mr. Wiltshire asked.

"Since this morning. I had a feeling your enterprising housemaid wouldn't be deterred by our little talk last night. My man arrived too late to catch her on the way out, but it appears that's all to the good."

That just made me scowl harder.

"She's been giving me that look for days," Mr. Burrows remarked languidly.

"Yes, well, I think she half suspects you had a hand in my kidnapping."

Mr. Burrows's eyebrows flew up. "Does she now?"

"Excuse me," I said coldly, "I'm *right here*."

"Apologies, Rose," Mr. Wiltshire said. "You're quite right, we're being terribly rude. And after you've been so patient."

I hadn't been remotely patient, and now at last I had a target for my frustration. "I've been giving you *that look*, Mr. Burrows, because you've done nothing but thwart me at every turn. If you'd been more straightforward, I might have found Mr. Wiltshire sooner."

"Found him?" Mr. Burrows glanced at his friend. "Thomas, have you just been rescued by your maid?"

"Indeed I have."

Mr. Burrows laughed. "How wonderful! Was it luck?"

"You have a great deal of nerve, sir."

He just laughed harder. "Obviously not. My mistake."

Mr. Wiltshire regarded me with a sigh. "I'm afraid I don't quite know what to do here."

"I think you'd better tell her, Thomas. She looks fit to explode. Besides"—Mr. Burrows sobered—"she's already paid the price for knowledge she doesn't yet have. Seems only fair to balance the books."

"I know more than you think," I said. "For starters, you're a Freemason."

Mr. Burrows received this accusation with a grave nod. "I am."

"And you?" I glanced at Mr. Wiltshire, fearing his answer.

"No, but I am, as you say, working for them."

"As their lawyer."

He shook his head. "I'm not an attorney, Rose. That's merely a cover. Have you ever heard of the Pinkerton Detective Agency?"

"You're a *Pinkerton*?" On my lips, the word sounded even more accusing than *Freemason*—a fact that didn't go unnoticed.

"Oh, dear," said Mr. Burrows, laughing again. "Safe to say she has."

Of course I had. Where I came from, the only creature more despised than a copper was a Pinkerton agent, owing to their reputation for strikebreaking, union meddling, and sundry other dirty tricks on behalf of the money men. Spy, bodyguard, detective, rough-for-hire—a Pinkerton would do any and all of it so long as the price was right.

"You're disappointed," Mr. Wiltshire said. "Well, I suppose that's understandable, given your background, but I am sorry for it."

"I'm not disappointed," I lied. "I'm just . . . surprised." Though maybe I shouldn't have been. After all, I'd just witnessed him smoothly dispatch three hard-bitten thugs using only my cheap umbrella for a weapon. *No wonder he was so cool under pressure,* I thought. *This is nothing new to him.*

Which made him as big a liar as Jonathan Burrows.

And speaking of that gentleman . . . "Something I don't understand," I said, turning to Mr. Burrows. "Last night, you mentioned a derelict gasworks. Did you know I would find Mr. Wiltshire there?"

"Where? At a gasworks?" He glanced at his friend, puzzled.

"The Consolidated Gas factory on Twentieth," Mr. Wiltshire said. "That's where I was being held. The man who attacked Rose last night was the same one who grabbed me. She managed to get hold of one of his buttons during the struggle."

"Oh, for the love of . . ." Mr. Burrows scowled. "Why didn't you tell me, Rose? I could have brought help! We'd have these bastards in irons by now!"

"Why would I tell you anything after the way you've acted? *Could someone please explain the bloody button?*"

That outburst ought to have earned me a stern reproach, but the two men just exchanged a look. Then, grudgingly, Mr. Burrows said, "Luck."

I clucked my tongue in disgust.

"Not that kind of luck, Rose," Mr. Wiltshire said. "In certain circles, *luck* means something very specific. It's what we call a breed of extraordinary abilities that some people possess. People like Mr. Burrows."

That didn't make a lick of sense to me. "What sort of talent lets you handle a button and guess where its owner has been?"

"Luck," Mr. Burrows said with a shrug. "Of the earth variety, if you want to be specific."

Mr. Wiltshire perched on the sofa beside me, his expression lighting up. "You see, Burrows has the ability to sense the chemical composition of things, down to the elemental level, simply by touching them."

"The elemental level?"

"How shall I explain it? Everything around us—every rock and tree, every animal, even the very air we breathe—is made up of different combinations of the same handful of ingredients."

"Everything physical, at any rate," Mr. Burrows put in.

"Let's not start out too complicated, shall we? This is a lot to take in. Are you with me so far, Rose?"

I wasn't remotely with him, but I nodded anyway.

"Good. Now, Burrows is able to identify each of these ingredients simply by touching them. Were he to pick up this vase, for example, he could tell you exactly where it comes from."

"Baccarat," I said. "In France." I should know; I dusted it three times a week.

Mr. Burrows laughed. "She's got you there, Wiltshire."

"Yes, all right, but that's not what I meant. He can tell *exactly* what minerals the glass is made of. Not only that, but where the sand came from, based on the precise blend of its constituent elements—the silicon, calcium carbonate, and so on—presuming he's encountered it before."

Mr. Burrows *tsk*ed. "And he accuses me of being complicated. Don't bother about the science, Rose, I certainly don't. Think of it like your sense of taste. When something hits your tongue, you can describe the flavor, and draw certain conclusions from there. Some foods you'd know blindfolded, because you come across them all the time. Strawberry jam, say. Others you might not have tasted before, but you can still make a fair guess as to what's in it. So if I gave you a slice of apple pie, even if you'd never had it before, you'd still be able to identify many of the ingredients. Sugar, apples . . . whatever else they put in pies."

"Coal gas is as commonplace as strawberry jam," Mr. Wiltshire said, gesturing at the gas lamp on the wall, "so when Burrows touched the Irishman's button, he recognized it immediately."

"Not just gas, but rotten gas." Mr. Burrows wrinkled his nose. "The thread was positively *pickled* in it. I couldn't for the life of me work out what you were doing poking around a place like that."

"But"—I glanced back and forth between them, still utterly lost—"how is that possible?"

"Luck," Mr. Burrows said again, maddeningly.

"His particular brand of it, at any rate," said Mr. Wiltshire. "*Luck* is simply a generic term for any type of extraordinary ability. There are many different forms of it, all of them hereditary, and they behave like any other family trait: Some offspring inherit it and some do not, and each child born with the trait exhibits it in his own unique way. So while there is always a family resemblance, no two forms of luck are exactly alike."

"They say my great-grandmother could smell gold from a hundred paces," Mr. Burrows said idly. "Put my family in rather good stead in the Carolina gold rush."

"Fascinating, isn't it?" Mr. Wiltshire's eyes were bright and eager, like an inventor explaining his latest creation. "One fellow of our acquaintance has an uncanny mind for patterns. Another can predict a storm weeks ahead of time. Just last month, I met a woman who can perceive entire spectra of light as yet unknown to science, if you can imagine such a thing."

I couldn't, but that didn't bother me too much. When your world is as small as mine, it doesn't take much to go beyond the limits of your experience. I came across wondrous things in *Harper's* and *Frank Leslie's* all the time. But this was something different altogether. "I once read about a man who could make perfect scale models of St. Peter's or Westminster Abbey out of matchsticks," I said, "just by glancing at a photograph."

"Matchstick cathedrals?" Mr. Burrows laughed. "And I thought my talent was useless."

"Every now and then, tales of luck do crop up in the papers," Mr. Wiltshire said, "though the phenomenon is rarely referred to by name."

"But *smelling* gold? I've never heard of anything like that."

"Nor will you, outside of certain highly exclusive circles," Mr. Burrows said. "Families like mine have gone to a great deal of trouble over the centuries to keep it that way."

"Why?"

"Oh, plenty of reasons," he said with a dismissive wave. "In the old days, I imagine it was the fear of being branded a witch. These days we have more modern concerns—being prodded at by doctors for one. Mostly, though, it's because secrecy has proven extremely advantageous for people like me."

"How so?"

He eyed me shrewdly. "Do you play cards at all?"

"Sometimes."

"Then you know that a trump concealed is ten times more powerful than the one your opponent knows you're holding."

"Less of a concern for your family, I should think," Mr. Wiltshire put in. "Secrecy or no, the earth would have surrendered her bounty regardless."

"Perhaps, but gold is one of the rare forms of wealth that can be plucked directly from the ground. Most of the time it has to be plucked from another man's pocket, and most people don't take kindly to that. Nevertheless it's true—my family probably has less to fear from exposure than some others. A modest gift like mine isn't likely to alarm anyone. But some other forms of luck out there . . . What would people make of what Rockefeller can do, or Van den Berg, or even Roosevelt?"

My mouth fell open a little. "You mean those families . . . ?"

"Along with half of Fifth Avenue."

"So luck is very common, then."

"On the contrary," Mr. Wiltshire said, "it's exceedingly rare. Fewer than one percent of people have luck. That's among the general population, of course; among high society, it's closer to twenty percent."

The shock must have shown on my face, because Mr. Burrows shrugged and said, "It's not so surprising, surely? Our gifts may be subtle, but they've been with us for generations. We've had centuries to work out how to use them to our advantage."

So the rich really are different from the rest of us. Generation after generation of luck, advantage piling on advantage . . .

Mr. Burrows gave a wry smile. "That stab of outrage you just felt? *That* is why we keep it secret."

"But how? How do you keep a secret that enormous?"

Hearing the note of hysteria in my voice, Mr. Wiltshire sighed. "I'm afraid the world is a great deal more complicated than most people realize, Rose. There are things we can't explain, things we're told we shouldn't believe in."

"Tell me." The words came out in a whisper. I felt as if I stood on the edge of a precipice; one small step would send me tumbling over, and everything I thought I knew would tumble with me.

"If you're sure that's what you want," Mr. Wiltshire said, "but take care: I daresay life is a good deal simpler not knowing."

This, incidentally, was very good advice, which anyone reading this tale ought to consider. *Ignorance is bliss*, the cab driver had told me, and I guess for some people that's true. If you're one such, well, I'm certainly not going to judge you, but you should probably put this tale aside and forget you ever saw it. Because trust me, you'll never see the world the same way again.

CHAPTER 13

A PARANORMAL PROBLEM—SHADES OF
MURDER—SPECIAL SKILLS

'll let you continue enlightening your new protégé later, Thomas, if you don't mind," Mr. Burrows said. "I have somewhere to be, but before I go, there are a few matters I'd like to get straight. Like who took you captive, for starters."

Mr. Wiltshire shook his head. "I wish I knew. The men I saw were merely hired thugs, working for whom I couldn't say. I'd have trussed one of them up for questioning if I could have, but I'm afraid that was impossible under the circumstances."

"They grabbed you on Saturday, I presume."

"After he spoke with Peter Arbridge," I put in, not wanting to feel left out.

Mr. Burrows frowned. "Who?"

"Do you remember the story in the *Times*," Mr. Wiltshire

said, "the one that brought me to your door on Saturday morning? Peter Arbridge is the young man who gave that account to the newspaper."

"Ah, yes, I remember now. But I still don't understand what that has to do with the case."

That was a very good question, one I'd wanted an answer to for a long time. "Did he know Jacob Crowe?"

Mr. Wiltshire regarded me with the same fascinated expression he'd worn at the gasworks. "You've conducted a thorough investigation, I see."

"I tried to, but there's a lot I don't understand. Where does Peter Arbridge come into it, or for that matter, Mr. Wang?"

"Yes, Thomas." Mr. Burrows leaned forward with interest. "Where *does* Wang come into it? There are cheaper places to procure a medium."

"Not a medium. A witch."

"A witch? Good Lord, what for?"

"That shade, whoever she is, is only part of the picture. Something else is going on here, something much bigger. I can't be certain, but I think we may be dealing with a portal." Raising his eyebrows, Mr. Wiltshire added, "A *leaking* portal, Jonathan."

"What, here in New York?" Mr. Burrows looked startled. "Surely not."

"I asked Wang to find me a witch that could help confirm my hypothesis. Whether he's managed it or not, I don't know."

Mr. Burrows flopped back against the sofa. "*Christ.*"

"I hope to be proven wrong, but the signs are not encouraging. That's the fifth sighting in as many weeks."

"I know. The whole club is abuzz with it."

"And those are just the ones we know about. I daresay there

are more. Regardless, if I'm right about the portal, it would appear to support Rollins's Theory of the Outer Realms."

Mr. Burrows rolled his eyes. "Only you would find a scientific silver lining to a paranormal storm cloud."

"I'll not apologize for intellectual curiosity, Burrows. It does nothing to diminish my dismay at the potential consequences. Either way, it seems clear that poor Jacob Crowe is the least of our worries."

By this time, I had the heels of my hands pressed against my forehead. "Gentlemen . . ."

"Yes, all right," Mr. Burrows said, "the very short version. Shortly after Jacob Crowe's murder, his brother approached his friends at the Madison Club for help—"

"Burrows," Mr. Wiltshire interrupted with a frown. "Discussing general matters is one thing, but as to the details of the investigation, I'm not altogether sure—"

"Don't be such a stick in the mud, Thomas. What harm can it do? Besides, it sounds as if she knows half of it already."

"Be that as it may . . ."

"It will be on my head," Mr. Burrows said with an impatient gesture. "Your professional ethics are intact. Now then, as I was saying, Frederick Crowe believed his brother's murder to be at the hands of a shade—that is, the spirit of a dead person, what you would probably call a ghost—and Freddie was afraid the spirit might mean him harm as well. But that isn't the sort of thing one goes to the police with, so instead he approached a man called Roberts—"

"The Freemason."

Mr. Burrows paused, a smile hitching one corner of his mouth. "Rose, Rose. One day, we shall have to have a meal together, and you can regale me with the details of your morning following me about." I felt myself coloring, but he didn't seem angry, just amused. "Like the Crowe brothers, Roberts is something of an authority on all things paranormal, but even so, he had his doubts about Freddie's theory. So he sought me out."

"Why you?"

"Roberts, like myself, is a man endowed with luck. Men with extraordinary abilities tend to believe in extraordinary things. He thought I might be a good source of advice."

"And you suggested he consult Mr. Wiltshire, because he's a Pinkerton." Something occurred to me then, and I looked sidelong at my employer. "Are you lucky, too?"

"Alas, I have only my wits to rely on."

"That's not what it looked like at the gasworks."

He smiled. "Very well, my wits and a few tricks I picked up in the Far East."

"So you started investigating Jacob Crowe's murder, and when you came across Peter Arbridge's story, the circumstances seemed similar."

"Which led him to Wang's, and after that up to Hell Gate." Mr. Burrows nodded, as if it all made sense now.

"And on my way home, I was kidnapped. There, I believe we're all caught up." Mr. Wiltshire clapped his hands in a gesture of finality.

He obviously wanted to drop the subject, but I had so many more questions. "After you left Peter Arbridge, you were supposed to go to the opera. Did that have something to do with the case?"

"Ah, yes. *Wagner.* I can't honestly say I'm too much aggrieved to have missed that, though I would have liked to hear more from Mr. Crowe."

Mr. Burrows cocked his head. "You arranged to meet Freddie at the opera? That seems an odd place to . . ." He trailed off, eyes narrowing. "I see. A casual setting, is it, to put him at his ease? I take it there's something about his story you don't quite like."

"Maybe he's the one who did it," I said, unable to hide my enthusiasm.

Tasteless, I know. Poor Jacob Crowe was dead, and here I was speculating—baselessly, I might add—on his own brother's involvement in his murder, as if I were guessing the ending of a yellow-backed novel instead of discussing a real person's life. What can I say? The juicier the mystery became, the more I wanted to sink my teeth into it. "Maybe he was afraid you'd found him out, so he had you grabbed."

"Doubtful," Mr. Wiltshire said. "If Frederick Crowe were guilty, he'd be a fool to involve the Pinkerton Agency."

"Then what's your theory?" Mr. Burrows thumped the arm of the sofa. "Come on, man, don't keep us in suspense!"

A knock sounded at the door. Mr. Wiltshire looked relieved.

"Beg your pardon, sir." Clara poked her head in. "The luncheon is ready." If she was surprised to see me in Mr. Wiltshire's study with the men, she didn't show it.

"Ah, good, I must admit I'm famished. Thank you, Clara."

She started to go, but the sight of his hand drew her up short. "What happened?"

"Ugly, isn't it? I'm afraid I took rather a hard blow to the knuckles earlier."

"You oughta to let a doctor take a look at that," Clara said. "One of those fingers could be fractured."

"Oh, I don't think so. Just a nasty bruise," he said, sounding suddenly thoughtful. "By the way, Clara, was it you who stitched up Rose?"

Clara and I exchanged an uncomfortable glance. "I asked her to," I said hastily.

"Tidy work. Where did you get your medical training?" When Clara's eyes widened, he added, "If your word choice hadn't given you away, the quality of the stitching would have."

She shifted on her feet self-consciously. "There was a clinic down the road where I grew up. I used to help out some in exchange for Doc Morris looking in on my mama when she needed it."

"More than *some,* I'd say."

I felt my mouth hanging open a little. As for Mr. Burrows, he just laughed. "Your maid is a detective and your cook a nurse. Really, Wiltshire, you must give me the name of your recruiting agency."

"Have you considered formal training?" Mr. Wiltshire asked. "You seem to have a knack for it."

Clara snorted softly. "I'll have luncheon on the table directly," she said, and disappeared.

"That sounds like a no," Mr. Burrows said, rising. "I'll leave you to it, Thomas."

"You won't stay for a late luncheon? There's a good deal more we should discuss."

"It'll have to wait, I'm afraid. I've a full dance card today." Fetching his hat and stick, he added, "Someone should inform Roberts of your return. Shall I send word?"

"Please do, but hold off mentioning the portal yet. No need to alarm anyone unnecessarily."

"Agreed." Mr. Burrows started toward the door, but not before taking my hand and pressing a kiss to my knuckles. "Miss Gallagher. I look forward to future entanglements."

"I must apologize for Mr. Burrows," Mr. Wiltshire said when his friend had gone. "I'm afraid he's quite incorrigible."

That was one word for it. "I don't understand him. He was so worried about you, but for some reason he's going out of his way to make it look like he wasn't."

"Yes, he's rather adept at concealing his true feelings. I suspect he doesn't even realize he's doing it much of the time. One disadvantage of being lucky, I suppose; you never really let your guard down."

"That sounds like a very tolerable downside."

He smiled. "I daresay." Gesturing at the door, he added, "Shall we? You must be nearly as famished as I."

"You're . . . inviting me to luncheon?"

"Certainly. I don't know about you, Rose, but my curiosity is not remotely satisfied. Besides, it's only prudent that I hear the details of your investigations before resuming my own. It's quite possible that you turned up something I haven't."

In its own way, this was every bit as terrifying a prospect as the shave. But there was nothing for it, so with an awkward smile and a muttering of thanks, I accepted his offer.

CHAPTER 14

SCRATCHING THE SURFACE—A
COCKROACH IN THE SOUP—SHADE AND
SHADOW

M r. Wiltshire listened intently as I related the events of the past five days. The keenness of his gaze unnerved me, so I spent much of the time staring into my soup, dunking bits of fish with my spoon and watching them bob to the surface again. I skipped only a few details, and by the time I'd finished, the soup had gone cold and the winter sun slumped low in the sky.

"It must seem like a very strange thing to do," I said by way of conclusion, "but the police just seemed so . . . disinterested, and I would never have been able to forgive myself if I hadn't done everything I could to help."

"I quite understand. It's terribly frustrating, isn't it, when you're the only one who can read the signs? But you did read them, for which I'm eternally grateful—not to mention impressed. You have a keen eye, Rose."

"I have so many questions," I said. "I know it isn't my right, but . . ."

"But they claw at you, and you must have answers." He sighed. "I know the feeling well. You remind me of myself not so long ago, before I was shown the gears inside the watch. But I meant what I said earlier: that innocence is not lightly parted with."

"And I meant what I said. I don't want to go through life with a veil over my eyes."

"A veil, yes." He leaned forward with sudden intensity. "That's exactly what it is. You deserve to have it torn away, Rose, and I would very much like to be the one to do it—"

I swallowed, feeling unaccountably light-headed.

"—but I worry it would be unethical," he finished, his light dimming as quickly as it had flared. "You're young, and as your employer, it's my duty to protect you."

That got my back up. *His* duty to protect *me*? Had I not just rescued him from mortal peril? "Respectfully, Mr. Wiltshire, I manage just fine on my own."

"Of course, and you've done brilliantly, but you've barely scratched the surface."

"That may be, but I don't see how not knowing what's really out there keeps me safe. The world is the world, isn't it?"

He sighed. "Ignorance certainly brings dangers of its own. More to the point, the choice is yours to make. I could refuse to help, but even were I so inclined, it's clear to me that it would be a futile gesture. You'd simply go elsewhere to learn what you wished to know, and that might lead you down an even more dangerous path."

"So you'll tell me the truth, then? All of it?" I'm not sure what excited me more—the idea that this other, secret world existed or that he would be the one to show it to me.

He started to answer, but just then the door opened to admit Mrs. Sellers with the second course. Clara obviously hadn't told her that I would be joining Mr. Wiltshire for luncheon, because the sight of me drew her up so sharply that she very nearly upset the tray she was carrying, and she paled in horror, as if she'd just discovered a cockroach in his soup. Her glance darted to Mr. Wiltshire, practically begging for an explanation for this outrage, but he just said, "Ah, right on time."

She crossed the room in clipped strides, the heels of her sensible shoes striking out a stern rhythm against the parquet. Setting her silver tray on the sideboard—the one she'd made me polish to a high shine only days ago—the housekeeper proceeded to serve us both. Mortification rose from her like steam from a gravy boat, and I hope you won't think me too petty if I say that it tasted even sweeter than Clara's cooking.

"By the way, Mrs. Sellers," Mr. Wiltshire said, "I have taken the liberty of giving Rose the rest of the day off. She performed a great service for me this morning, and the least I can do is allow her a bit of rest. I do hope you'll forgive my interference. Also, if you wouldn't mind, when we're through with luncheon, please run up to the police station and inform them of my safe return. They can call off the search."

It was all I could do not to snort into my soup. The only thing Detective Ward was searching for was a whiskey bottle.

Still, I wondered what he would make of Mr. Wiltshire's return . . .

My spoon froze halfway to my face. I'd forgotten all about my clumsy questions at the Twenty-Eighth Precinct. "There's something you should know," I said once Mrs. Sellers was safely out of earshot. "I'm afraid the police think Mr. Burrows was involved in Jacob Crowe's murder, and your kidnapping, too."

"Oh?" he said distractedly, his glance cutting between his injured hand and the slices of duck Mrs. Sellers had arrayed artfully on his plate. He seemed more worried about how he'd manage a knife and fork than the possibility that his best friend might be arrested for murder.

"You don't seem very concerned."

"Nor should you be. A man of Jonathan Burrows's stature has little to fear from law enforcement." Gingerly grasping a fork, he went on, "As to your question a moment ago, I will do my best to explain the state of the art, as it were, but you should be aware that much of what we think we know is speculation. For the moment at least, the study of paranormal phenomena remains as much a discipline of philosophy as hard science."

"*Paranormal.* Mr. Burrows used that term, too. I've never heard it before."

"It refers to phenomena that lie beyond ordinary experience and accepted scientific explanation."

"Like ghosts."

"Exactly."

I hesitated. I hadn't yet told him about the bloody woman on Mott Street. I was fairly sure ghosts weren't on Mam's list of approved topics for dinner conversation, but then again, was there ever an elegant time to bring something like that up? "Speaking of ghosts—"

He raised a hand. "Soon, Rose, I promise, but not just yet. I'm knee-deep in a murder investigation. But as soon as my duty to the Freemasons is discharged, we can spend some time in the special vaults of the Astor Library. I'll need to do some research, and what better way to begin your education in the paranormal?"

"That sounds lovely, but . . . How long will that take?"

"I shouldn't think more than a week or two."

A week or two? It might as well have been a year. "What'll I do until then?"

"Why, go on as usual, I suppose."

I nearly choked on my duck. After spending the better part of a week investigating his disappearance—of tailing Mr. Burrows like a bounty hunter, posing as a reporter, fleeing from a ghost, getting walloped over the head by a pistol-wielding rough—was I really supposed to go back to being merely Rose the Maid, dusting his Baccarats and polishing his silver?

Then again, what had *I* expected?

My dismay must have shown, because Mr. Wiltshire frowned and said, "What would you suggest?"

"I could help with the investigation. I know I'm not a professional, but—"

He was already shaking his head. "That is quite impossible, I'm afraid."

"But you said I was resourceful. That I had a keen eye." Oh, how I hated the sound of my voice in that moment. Like a spoiled child.

"And I meant it, but that isn't the point. I have a duty to my client and my employer. I cannot divulge the private details of a case, let alone take on an apprentice, however talented. It would be quite inappropriate."

"Mr. Burrows didn't seem to find a problem in it."

His mouth took a wry twist. "He rarely does, but that does not release me from my obligations. Only Frederick Crowe can do that, or the Pinkerton Agency."

"I see." I set my fork down; suddenly, I wasn't hungry anymore.

He sighed. "I know you're frustrated, Rose, and I'm truly sorry. But I hope you can understand my position."

What did it matter if I understood? I was his *maid*. He didn't have to explain himself to me. He didn't owe me anything except gratitude, and that he'd offered freely. "I'm the one who's sorry," I said. "I got carried away, is all. It's just that after everything that's happened, I thought . . . Well, never mind. It won't happen again, sir."

There was an uncomfortable pause. Several, really. Then he said, "I'm afraid I must ask you to keep the nature of my work and all that you've learned in the matter of Jacob Crowe between us. But if you like . . ." He hesitated, as if casting about for a peace offering. "I'll be heading downtown later, to Wang's General Store. I could give you a lift if you wish to spend some time with your family."

That, I decided, was a grand idea. After everything I'd been through, a little time with Mam would do me good. "Thank you, I would."

"Good." He sounded relieved. "I'll have a livery cab ordered for half five."

I stuffed a few desultory forkfuls of food in my mouth. Then, abruptly, I reached into my breast pocket and yanked out the

Patek Philippe. It was warm in my hand, and heavy, still ticking softly. I felt a gaping hole where it had been, as if something had been torn out by the roots. "Here, this belongs to you."

"Ah, excellent! Where did you find it?"

"In Mr. Burrows's parlor. You must have left it there. I'm sorry I didn't give it to you sooner—I'd forgotten about it."

That was a wretched lie, of course, and I think he sensed it, because his brief smile vanished.

We passed the rest of the meal in silence.

I was dangerously near to tears as I trudged up the servants' staircase to my room. It was more than disappointment. I felt betrayed, though I wasn't sure by whom. The rational part of my mind understood Mr. Wiltshire's position. He was a professional detective, duty bound to provide the best possible service to his clients. I would only get in the way. And there, I suppose, was the sore spot. I'd been so proud of myself, so flush with victory and light-headed with praise, that I'd let myself lose sight of the truth, which was that when all was said and done, I was still just Mr. Wiltshire's housemaid. I'd been fortunate, maybe even clever, but that didn't change the basic facts. *The world is the world, isn't it?* My own words; how bitter they tasted now.

My little room in the attic seemed smaller than ever, as though the walls had crept inward in my absence. Even so, it felt drafty and cold. I could still feel the empty space in my pocket where Mr. Wiltshire's watch had been, and the silence seemed heavier somehow without its constant ticking. Outside my narrow window, the world had gone dark.

I started to light a lamp but instead reached for my shawl. It really *was* cold in there, so much so that I glanced at the window to make sure it was firmly closed, and as I did, something in the mirror caught my eye. Turning toward it, I stiffened in horror.

Frost bristled over the surface of the glass. A thin web at first, growing denser as I watched, until the mirror clouded over in an icy cataract. My breath steamed, and before I could make a sound, a chill unlike anything I've ever known pierced my hide straight down to the bone, stealing the air from my lungs. For a moment I stood paralyzed, every nerve in my body thrumming. My nose pricked; my eyelashes glittered with frost. The cold sank its roots into me as if I were rich soil, branching out into tiny veins of ice . . .

Somehow, I tore myself free and lurched out into the hallway. My lungs still bucked under the shock—I could barely breathe, let alone scream—and I stumbled along using the wall for support. I reached the stairs and made it as far as the first landing before I saw my tormentor. She stood several steps below me, cutting off my escape, her thin frame draped in horror.

The bloody woman.

She looked exactly as she had that night in the street: hollow-eyed and desperate, blood matting her hair and caking the side of her face. Only from this vantage I could see the hideous wound at the crown of her head. The skull was caved in, leaving a gory pulp from which blood still oozed in a thick, dark syrup.

With a cry, I flung myself through the door on the landing, spilling out onto the mezzanine. I had to get to the front door. Had to get out . . .

"Rose?"

Mr. Wiltshire's voice startled me so badly that I flattened myself against the wall with a gasp. I must have looked like a savage creature in that moment, wild with terror; for a moment I didn't even know him.

"Good God, what's the matter?" He leaned out the doorway of his study, glancing about for the source of the trouble.

"*G-g-ghost.*" It was all I could do to push the word from my still-numb lips.

His eyes flared, but he didn't hesitate; he lunged into the hallway, seizing my hand as he passed. "This way!"

We flew down the main staircase. "Clara," I slurred, but he didn't slow, dragging me all the way to the foyer.

But instead of fleeing out into the street, he grabbed his walking stick with his good hand and wheeled back toward the stairs. "Behind me, quickly!"

I stumbled a little in the dark. *I forgot to light the lamps,* I thought, too dazed to remember that I'd been given the evening off. It was cold down here, too, so cold I could actually see my breath.

"Here it comes." Mr. Wiltshire glanced frantically about the room. "The lamps. *Damn.* Rose, grab that mirror. Take it down from the wall and point it over there."

I did as I was told, moving as mechanically as in a dream.

"Now, whatever happens, don't drop it. If you break the mirror, we won't be able to see the spirit, and that will make it very difficult for me to defend us. Understood?"

I didn't understand, not remotely, because as far as I could see the only thing he had to defend us with was a walking stick.

The mirror was heavy and awkward in my hands, but I managed to pivot it around. I'd just finished angling it toward the stairs when the bloody woman appeared in its frame—at which point I very nearly dropped it.

Heaven protect us.

She filled the glass, as terrible in two dimensions as she was in three. But though the reflection placed her at the base of the stairs, I saw no sign of her there. Whatever the mirror was showing us, it was invisible to the naked eye.

"Stay where you are," Mr. Wiltshire called, brandishing his walking stick. "This cane is made of ash. One touch will send you straight back to your point of origin. Nod if you understand me."

The reflection in the mirror shifted. The bloody woman nodded.

"Good. Now, I assume you came here for a purpose other than terrorizing my domestic staff."

The bloody woman opened her mouth, but no sound came. Her figure wilted momentarily in defeat. Then a look of pure despair twisted her features, and she clutched at her hair, just as she'd done that night in the street.

I started to back away, but Mr. Wiltshire put a restraining hand on my arm. "There's no point in trying to speak," he called to the spirit. "We won't be able to hear you, not without the help of a medium."

By this point I was shaking so badly that the mirror rattled in its frame. "She's dangerous," I whispered. "S-she attacked me."

He whirled. "Did she touch you? My God, she did. Rose . . ." He took my face in his hands and peered intently into my eyes. Cursing softly, he threw a look over his shoulder as though debating whether to risk trying to get past the ghost. Then his arm was around me, threading between my waist and the mirror and drawing me flush against his body. "God, you're freezing," he murmured in my ear. "I'm so sorry, I didn't realize . . . Stay close."

As though I was going anywhere.

"Listen to me, spirit." His voice was taut with anger. "I don't believe you have ill intentions, but you must never, ever touch the living, not even for a moment. It can be fatal, do you understand? You could have stopped her heart. As it is, she's half an icicle."

The woman in the mirror fell back, hands flying to her mouth. She shook her head, and when her hands dropped away again, her lips were moving as though in speech. Her eyes locked with mine, pleading.

"As I thought," Mr. Wiltshire said. "You didn't know, did you? I presume you haven't been long in this state?"

The bloody woman shook her head again, still begging my forgiveness with her gaze.

For my part, I didn't know what I felt. Terrified. Confused. Chilled to the bone. Acutely aware of every contour of Thomas Wiltshire's body pressed against mine. "I've seen her before," I managed. "On Mott Street."

I felt him tense in surprise. "When was this?"

"The day I followed Mr. Burrows."

"That can't be a coincidence." To the ghost, he said, "You were attached to one of the Masons, I suppose."

She nodded.

"And now you're following Rose. Well, you can stop that. It's me you want, or rather, we want each other. You're the spirit the Crowe brothers saw, aren't you?"

Another nod.

"We have much to discuss, but we won't get far like this. We'll need a medium. Meet me at Wang's General Store tomorrow night at sunset. You know it? Good. Now, if you don't mind, I think that's quite enough excitement for one evening."

The bloody woman met my eye one final time in the mirror. Then she vanished.

We stood there a moment in silence, Mr. Wiltshire and I,

my breathing ragged against the slow, steady rhythm of his. He was so close that I could feel the Patek Philippe pressed against my back, and when he spoke, his breath thrilled against the nape of my neck. "You're still shaking."

That wasn't all. Every hair on my body was standing straight on end, and never before had they had more reason for it. But the weight of the mirror was becoming too much; I was obliged to abandon his warmth to set it down. "I'll be all right," I said.

"Are you sure?" His pale eyes scanned me with concern. "You feel no lingering cold at all? As if there were a sliver of ice, perhaps, just below the skin?"

"No, nothing like that."

"This is important, Rose. If you feel even a hint of frost—"

"I'm nearly warm again, thank you."

"Good. There's nothing like body heat to banish a chill, except perhaps a hot bath. Are you certain you wouldn't rather—"

"I'm fine, really."

A creak of floorboards sounded, and Clara poked her head out of the dining room. "Everything all right out here? Thought I heard a ruckus."

"Everything's fine, Clara, thank you. Rose and I were just on our way out. Would you be so good as to inform Mrs. Sellers that we've gone? She'll be back from the police station any moment." Consulting his watch, he added, "Look, it's time for our carriage. Let's be off, then, shall we?"

What could I do? With an apologetic glance at Clara, I wriggled into my overcoat and let myself be herded out the door.

CHAPTER 15

THE SPECIAL BRANCH—SALT AND
ASH—AN OVERDUE APOLOGY

Just what kind of Pinkerton are you?" I blurted as the carriage juddered into motion.

He winced. "Please, Rose, the driver . . ."

"Oh, no. I will not be put off a third time. I don't care if he sells his story to *The New York World*. I want answers, and I'd say I've bloody well earned them by now." I still had a touch of the shivers, which gave this little outburst an added edge of hysteria. "What sort of person handles a ghost like that?"

"Like what?"

"You know perfectly well what I mean. Like you've done it a hundred times."

"Nowhere near that many, but it's certainly not my first encounter." Raising an eyebrow, he added, "Nor yours, apparently. You neglected to mention that."

"I tried to, but you cut me off."

"I certainly regret that. I didn't realize your instruction was quite so urgent. I'll do what I can to redress it now. *Sotto voce*," he added, with a meaningful gesture at the window of the carriage. "Ask away."

I wasn't sure where to begin. It was like standing on the threshold of a messy room, trying to decide which bit to tidy up first. "What you did back there—where did you learn that?"

"The Pinkerton Agency. Special branch, to be precise."

"Special branch?"

Reaching into an inner pocket of his jacket, he produced a calling card made of glossy silver paper. Or at least, it looked like a calling card, but when he handed it to me, I saw that it carried no name, nor any lettering at all—just the embossed image of a single human eye. "A small unit dedicated to cases of a paranormal nature. Generally, that means something to do with luck, but we do get our share of shades, ghosts, and so on."

And so on. I shuddered to think what sorts of evils those three little words might include. "I thought luck was supposed to be some great secret."

"Indeed—hence the rather cryptic nature of my card. Only a select few understand what it means. The paranormal community is highly discreet, and the Pinkerton Agency is a key instrument in maintaining that discretion." I must have looked skeptical, because he added, "Consider, Rose: When I told you I was a Pinkerton, you were disappointed. Why?"

I glanced out the window, avoiding his eye. "Because Pinkertons are nothing but a brute squad for the money men."

"My, that is . . . direct." He cleared his throat awkwardly. "Nevertheless, essentially accurate. We are the private security firm most relied upon by the wealthy, and as Mr. Burrows explained earlier, luck and wealth go hand in hand. Many of our nation's most powerful institutions have an inner circle run by individuals endowed with some form of luck. In the case of the Pinkertons, that person is F. Winston Sharpe, my direct superior." Sighing, he added, "Who will be wondering what's become of me."

"Then why didn't he come looking for you?"

"He would have sent someone eventually, but these things take time. He's based in Chicago, you see. For the moment, I'm the only agent of the special branch operating full-time in New York, though I imagine that will change very soon."

I frowned, but on the face of it I was obliged to let F. Winston Sharpe off the hook for now. "When you say *powerful institutions* . . ."

"Government, unions, fraternal organizations, corporations . . . even churches. Where you find power, you will invariably find luck. And where you find luck, there is secrecy and therefore danger. People with luck are not to be trifled with, Rose. That may be the most important advice I could ever give you."

Maybe, but I had more immediate concerns. "That ghost—"

"Shade."

"Pardon?"

"The woman on the stairs was a shade. A damaged spirit, one who can't properly enter the otherworld until she finds a way to repair the damage, usually by redressing some sort of grievance. In this case, she looks to have met a violent end, and my guess is that until the identity of her murderer is brought to light, she will remain as she is, trapped in a sort of anteroom between the worlds."

"When she touched me . . ."

"Yes. In fact, if you'll allow me . . ." He took my face in his hands and peered into my eyes, first one, then the other, just as he'd done in the foyer. "It seems all right, but we should keep an eye on it, if you'll pardon the pun."

"Why? What's wrong with my eyes?"

"Your left pupil is dilated. It happens when you've seen a shade, but the effect is more acute if you've been touched, especially if . . ." He paused, his expression turning grim. "You're fortunate to have survived, Rose. If she'd held on to you a moment longer . . ." He closed his eyes fleetingly. "I would never have been able to forgive myself. As it is, I cannot apologize enough for everything you've been through on my account. I never intended for any of this to happen."

"Of course you didn't. You mustn't blame yourself. I put myself in harm's way, after all."

He started to protest, but I grabbed his hand and gave it a squeeze. A shockingly bold gesture, but it felt right. And I guess he thought so, too, because he squeezed back.

"We're in this together," I said.

Pale eyes met mine. "I suppose we are at that."

For a moment it felt as if we were in a novel, all velvet upholstery and soft *clip-clop* and silver moonlight, and I might have done something even bolder had the carriage not chosen that moment to hit a rut in the pavement, jostling us both.

"Broadway paving," he said dryly.

I glanced out the window, but the glare of the streetlamps was too much for me.

"The dilated pupil," Mr. Wiltshire said. "For a time, it will be more sensitive to light."

"Your eyes look fine."

"Because I didn't see the shade, only her reflection in the mirror."

"I couldn't see her in the foyer either, but she was clear as day on the stairs."

"Shades are only visible by certain sources of light, namely moonlight and flame. Since the lamps weren't lit in the foyer, we were obliged to use the mirror to reveal the spirit."

That explained why I couldn't see her in my bedroom; I hadn't yet lit the lamp. "Who do you think she was?"

"No way of knowing until we secure the help of a medium. She could have died recently or a very long time ago—though from her attire and obvious inexperience, I rather suspect the former."

"When you threatened her with the walking stick, you said something about her point of origin."

"Ah, yes." He turned the cane over in his hands. It was a handsome thing—pale wood polished to a high shine, bone-white handle carved to resemble a griffin—but I couldn't see anything truly special about it. "That's something you should know as a matter of safety. When it comes to spirits, the two most important weapons in your arsenal are salt and ash—by which I mean the wood." He hefted his stick.

"Why?"

"Science has yet to provide an answer, but the spiritual properties of ash trees have been understood since antiquity. Your

Gaelic ancestors, for example, revered it as holy. You've heard of the five legendary guardian trees of Ireland? No? Well, in any case, the closest to a genuine explanation comes to us from the Vikings, who believed the World Tree acted as a sort of conduit between various domains of existence. All we know for certain is that when a spirit comes into contact with ash, it is transported instantly back to the otherworld."

"The otherworld. Do you mean hell?"

"Not in the biblical sense, no." Sighing, he added, "There's just so much to cover. For now I think we ought to focus on what you need to know to keep you safe. So—ash and salt."

Salt. A memory flashed through my mind: Mei Wang kicking salt under the front door of her father's shop. *She knew. The whole time, she knew . . .*

"Ash banishes a spirit, and salt can be used to create a barrier the dead cannot cross. It's helpful to keep some of both within easy reach."

"What, I'm just supposed to walk around with salt in my pockets? For that matter, where am I going to get a piece of ash wood?"

"Keeping a pouch full of salt on your person isn't a bad idea. As to the ash, getting hold of it isn't the problem—it's how you'll carry it. Short of packing a parasol around everywhere you go . . ." He hummed thoughtfully. "Leave it with me. I'll think of something."

I glanced out the window again, squinting this time to protect my oversensitive eye. We were making good time, what with the light evening traffic. Soon, I'd be home with Mam.

Mam who talked to my dead granny. Mam who'd smelled the dead on my dress.

It wasn't until that moment, gazing out the window with one pupil dilated, that I really stopped to think about that. *It can't be real, can it? If Mam was seeing a ghost, it would have killed her by now. Unless* . . . "What's the difference between a shade and a ghost?"

"Yes, good, that's an important distinction. They're both spirits of the dead, but the shade is damaged. Some fragment of it remains bound to the physical world, preventing it from crossing over. Whereas a ghost is a spirit that has crossed over entirely. What we see is only a projection, not unlike a photograph. The image of a thing rather than the thing itself."

"So ghosts can't hurt us."

"Oh, but they can—just not through physical means. The ghost's weapon is madness and suggestion, and they can be remarkably effective at both. Most ghosts appear only to relatives, and they're usually trying to be helpful. Sometimes, though, they have darker designs. Revenge, for example."

"Relatives, you say?" My voice sounded suddenly thin.

The ghost's weapon is madness . . .

"Are you all right, Rose? You've gone quite pale."

"I need your help. I need you to come with me."

"What, now? I'm sorry, but I—"

"*Please.*"

"Yes, of course." He took my hands, meeting my gaze with a worried frown. "Of course, whatever you need."

I forced myself to draw deep, calming breaths. *Don't panic. She's been this way for years; she can wait a few more minutes.* "It's my mother," I said. "She's . . . Well, I think you'd better see for yourself."

In my anxiety, I hadn't really thought through what I was asking. It was only now, alighting from the carriage amid the flotsam of

Five Points tenements, that it hit me: I was about to drag my wealthy, elegant, oh-so-proper gentleman employer into the tattered rookery at 55 Mott Street.

Contrary to what I'd thought, Mr. Wiltshire was obviously no stranger to Five Points. That meant he had a clear enough idea of the sorts of conditions I'd grown up in. But knowing something in theory and coming face-to-face with it are two different things. I could have gone with him into any other building on that street without feeling too awkward, but *this* . . . I was bringing him into my mother's home. A home paid for with wages earned under his roof. Three cramped, dark rooms, the entirety of which would have fit easily into Mr. Wiltshire's kitchen. I wasn't ashamed, exactly, but it did make the difference in our respective situations painfully apparent, like shining a lantern on something best left in the shadows.

Uncomfortable as it was for me, I sensed it was even more so for him. But he did his best to hide it, following me gamely up the crooked little stairs in the dark, trying discreetly to avoid getting soot from the walls on his overcoat. We creaked our way down the hall to Mam's door, where I paused. "Would you mind waiting here a moment?"

"Of course. Take your time."

I opened the door a crack and slithered through, closing it behind me. A lamp glowed in the kitchen, and another in the parlor; there I found Mam in her chair, squinting at the same old novel she'd been reading for months. "Rose," she said, looking up. "This is a surprise. Is it Sunday already?"

I gave her a quick once-over. She looked respectable enough in a faded housedress and shawl, and aside from the line of washing hanging in the kitchen, the flat looked tidy. "It's Friday, Mam. I have the evening off, and . . . well, if you don't mind, I've brought someone to see you. A gentleman."

"A gentleman?" Mam eyed me over the top of her spectacles. "Have you found yourself a young man, Rose?"

"Er, no, it's not like that. It's—"

"You've brought him for Mama, then?" Pietro's head poked out from behind the curtain cordoning off his corner of the room. "Are you trying to make me jealous?"

As usual, I couldn't help smiling back at him. "How are you, Pietro? Sorry to disturb you at this hour."

He shrugged and peeled back the curtain. "It's your flat, Fiora. Besides, I'm Italian. For me it's not even dinnertime. Hey, what happened?" Frowning, he reached for my forehead.

"It's nothing," I said, twitching away.

"What's nothing?" Mam couldn't see my stitches from her angle. "Rose, did you hurt yourself?"

"It's fine, Mam, really. As I was saying, there's a gentleman waiting outside. He's . . . well, I suppose you'd call him an expert in your . . . ah, situation."

"My situation?" Mam looked genuinely perplexed.

"Look, I'll just fetch him, shall I?"

By the time I'd returned with my guest, Mam was on her feet, hands folded primly before her. As for Pietro, he must have decided he was an honorary member of the family, because instead of leaving us to our affairs, he'd pulled up a chair of his own.

The next few seconds were really quite mortifying. Mr. Wiltshire scanned the room with a detective's eye—Pietro's straw mattress in the corner, copy of *Irish American* on the table, lithograph of the Virgin Mary above the mantel—drawing what conclusions, I couldn't say. Meanwhile, the room scanned Mr. Wiltshire.

Pietro's expression went from surprise to wariness to borderline hostility in about five seconds flat. Mam looked more welcoming, but the sight of an obviously wealthy gentleman in her little parlor made her uncomfortable.

All this sizing up took place before I could even make the introductions. "This is Mr. Thomas Wiltshire." The name registered on both of their faces, if a little differently. For Mam, it was relief; for Pietro, it brought a scowl. His glance cut between Mr. Wiltshire and my stitches, drawing some conclusions of his own. "Mr. Wiltshire, this is my mother, Ellen, and her boarder, Pietro."

"A pleasure to meet you both," he said with a courtly nod.

"The pleasure is ours, Mr. Wiltshire," Mam said. "So nice to put a face to the name after all this time. Please, take a seat." Her glance shifted to me, and her smile tightened. "*Rose, dear.*"

"Oh! Of course, pardon me . . . Tea?"

"Not for me, thank you," Mr. Wiltshire said, taking the proffered chair.

I hovered beside him, wringing my hands self-consciously. "Right. Well. I asked Mr. Wiltshire here because, as I was saying before, he's an expert in, ah . . ." Sweet Mary and Joseph, this was awkward, but there was no turning back now. "He knows about ghosts," I finished, lobbing the word like a stick of hot dynamite.

Or so I thought, but if it was dynamite, it fizzled out. Pietro frowned and gave me a look that said, *What are you up to?* As for Mam, she just said, "Does he?"

"Yes, Mrs. Gallagher," he said, "and I gather you have some experience with that yourself."

"My Rose doesn't believe in ghosts," Mam said, turning her watery gaze on me.

"The thing is, Mam," I said quietly, "I think I do now."

Mam frowned, as if she didn't quite know what to do with that. "I smelled them on you," she said severely. "I told you I did."

Mr. Wiltshire narrowed his eyes, but he didn't say anything.

"You did tell me, yes." My voice was barely above a whisper now, choked with guilt. All the times I'd scolded her, patronized her, dismissed her as ill in the head. Dragged her to see the doctor or the priest, or—God forgive me—thought about sending her to Blackwell's Island. And it had been real all along. "She's been seeing them for years now," I told Mr. Wiltshire.

"Not *them*, Rose. Just her. Just your granny."

"Your mother, I take it?" Mr. Wiltshire asked.

Mam eyed him guardedly. "You believe in that sort of thing, do you, Mr. Wiltshire?"

"I certainly do, Mrs. Gallagher. Tell me, how often does she come to you?"

"Oh, now and then."

"Every day." This from Pietro. He was still giving me that look, as if he didn't like where this was going but was prepared to play along. "Sorry, Mama, I know it's hard to remember, but it's every day."

"Do you think so?" Mam looked troubled. "I don't think it's quite that often, Peter, dear."

"Is there a particular time of day she favors?" Mr. Wiltshire asked.

Mam shook her head. "Comes and goes as she pleases."

"And does she look well?"

The question puzzled me at first, but then I thought of the bloody woman. No one who'd laid eyes on that terrible apparition would say she looked *well*, what with the caved-in skull.

"Well enough, I suppose," Mam said. "Pale, of course. Thin, like parchment paper."

"If I may ask, how did she pass?"

"She was very ill. I don't suppose we ever knew exactly what it was, but she'd always been frail, ever since the famine. Why do you ask?"

"Forgive me, I don't mean to pry, but details can be very important in such cases. Just a few more questions, if I may. What sorts of things do you speak about? Does she ever ask anything of you, or make any suggestions about things you ought to do?"

Mam's mouth took a wry turn. "Oh, she gives me plenty of advice, and no mistake. What I should be eating. How I should do my hair. How often I should go to confession. Can't get a moment's peace."

Mr. Wiltshire smiled. "That sounds like a mother."

"I suppose it does at that," Mam said, smiling back.

"Are her visits long?"

"All day, sometimes," Pietro put in.

The reaction was subtle—just a faint compression of the lips—but I could tell Mr. Wiltshire didn't like that answer. "If I may suggest, when next you see her, try to take a nap afterward."

"A nap?" Mam echoed, puzzled. "Why, I suppose I do that most of the time anyway."

"Good. It will help keep your strength up." Rising, he added, "And now I'm afraid I must be off. I have a pressing engagement down the street. It was very nice meeting you both."

I showed him out, holding my peace until we were alone again. "That was fast," I said once we'd reached the street.

He frowned. "I can assure you I covered the necessary. I merely thought to spare your mother a prolonged interrogation."

"I'm sorry, I didn't mean to sound ungrateful. I don't know how these things are done, is all. What do you think?"

"On the face of it, I'm inclined to think your mother's visitations are real."

I wasn't sure how to feel about that. On the one hand, it meant Mam wasn't crazy. But was being haunted by her dead mother any better?

"What if it's not a ghost at all? Could it be a shade?"

"That you needn't fear. Shades only manifest after sunset, whereas your mother sees the spirit at all times of day. It is certainly a ghost, and most likely a benevolent one." Sighing, he added, "But that doesn't mean it isn't dangerous."

I swallowed down a flutter of fear. "Dangerous how?"

"Communing with spirits is extremely taxing on the mind and body, especially for those who don't take appropriate fortifying measures. If the visitations really are a daily occurrence, it will be taking a toll on your mother's health."

"It is. She seems well enough tonight, but . . ."

"But she's not always so lucid." He nodded grimly. "The ghost isn't giving her enough time to recover between visitations."

"What should I do?"

"The first step would be to reason with the ghost, impress upon her the harm she's doing. Ask her to visit less often, and then only in dreams. If that fails, there are more drastic measures we might try, but I'm afraid none of them are very pleasant. Better to reason with her first. Do you think your mother will be willing?"

"All I can do is ask."

He touched my arm briefly in a gesture of support. "Try not

to worry too much. She doesn't seem to be in any immediate danger. We have time."

We. Until that moment, I'd had no idea one little word could be so much comfort.

"I'm sorry," he said, "I'm afraid I really must go. If it were anything less urgent . . ."

"I know." I recalled well enough Mr. Burrows's reaction when he'd mentioned the portal, though I still didn't know what that meant. "Is it . . . Should I be afraid?"

"Not at all."

Yesterday, I would have believed him. Today, I understood that Thomas Wiltshire was capable of hiding just about anything. He was hiding something now, I was sure of it.

But I had more immediate concerns.

I drifted back up the crooked little staircase as if in a dream. *All this time . . .* For years, my mother had been wasting away right under my nose. If only I'd believed her, I might have been able to help. Instead I'd stood by and watched it happen, let it eat away at her body and mind.

I found Mam and Pietro just as I'd left them, exchanging bemused expressions in the parlor. She looked so thin and frail under that blanket . . .

Sinking to my knees beside her chair, I threw my arms around my mother. "I'm sorry, Mam. I'm so sorry."

CHAPTER 16

PLAYING ALONG—ROUGH BUSINESS—THE
BROTHERHOOD OF SEEKERS

D o you think you can ask her that, Mam? For me?"

My mother gave me an exasperated look. "I don't understand you, child. For years now, all I've heard from you—"

"I know, and I'm sorry, but this is important. Granny can
still visit, just in dreams, all right? Please, will you tell her?"

"All right, if it matters that much to you. Can't promise anything, mind. She never listened to a word I said when she was
alive. Don't see why she'd go changing now."

Forcing a smile, I said, "One step at a time."

"Can I go to bed now, or have you more orders for me?"

"Oh, Mam." I helped her tidy up before escorting her to her
room. "I'll most likely be gone by the time you wake up, but I'll
try to come by tomorrow, all right?"

With Mam safely tucked into bed, I went back to the kitchen to fix myself some tea. I wasn't surprised to find Pietro there waiting for me. He leaned against the table, arms folded, looking unhappy. "So, Fiora, where should we begin?"

I flopped into a chair, exhausted. "I don't know if I can, Pietro."

"No? *Va bene*, I'll start. Your boss came back, obviously. He's a doctor, I suppose?"

I hesitated. It was one thing explaining Mr. Wiltshire's presence to Mam. Her dementia, if that was still the word for it, left her all too prone to suggestion. Pietro was another matter. I wasn't sure what I should tell him—or what he would believe. "Not a doctor, exactly, but he knows about these things."

"Rich men think they know about everything."

A typical Five Pointer's sentiment; I left it alone. "It sounded like good advice to me."

"Maybe. Sleep never hurt nobody. But I don't know if playing along with this ghost business is such a good idea, even if you are very convincing."

He thinks you're just humoring her. I couldn't help feeling relieved, even though it meant deceiving him. That sounds awful, I suppose, but how could I tell him the truth? He'd think I was as crazy as my mother. "Whatever it takes to get her to spend less time with Granny."

"I don't like tricking her," he said, as if she were his own mother.

"It's not tricking her, it's . . . using the power of her mind to help her."

"Is that what he says? Your boss?"

"There's that look again. You glared at him like that the entire time he was here."

"Why shouldn't I? He disappears on account of some shady business, and then you go off chasing chickens all over town and end up with an egg on your head for your trouble." He gestured at my stitches. "What happened?"

"It's nothing."

"I'm not stupid, Rose. Two days ago you sat in that chair talking about murder, and now you tell me it's nothing. Don't insult me."

I fidgeted uncomfortably. Pietro was right, I owed him better than this. But Mr. Wiltshire had sworn me to secrecy. "I'm sorry, I don't mean to be slippery. It's just that I don't know half of it myself. I went down to Mr. Wiltshire's office to look for clues, and when I was there a man attacked me."

"Attacked you?"

"He was turning the office upside down looking for something, and I surprised him." I paused, remembering something Mr. Wiltshire had said. *Searching for something to help break the cipher, perhaps.* I'd lost track of that tidbit amid the blizzard of revelations that afternoon. Filing it away for later, I went on, "The important thing is that I found a clue that led me to Mr. Wiltshire. He was being held captive, but he doesn't know by whom."

Pietro scoffed. "So he says. I've never heard of nobody getting nabbed who didn't know exactly why." He started snatching wash off the line, clothespins snapping angrily with each tug. "You need to leave this job. This man is no good."

I started to answer the second part but got snagged on the first. "You make it sound as if you know someone who's been kidnapped. Or who did the kidnapping, maybe?"

He gave me a wry look. "I spend my free time at Augusto's, Fiora."

I took his meaning straightaway. Any Five Pointer would

have. Strictly speaking, Augusto's was a grocery, but like Wang's General Store, it was much more than that. Bank, employment office, gambling house, saloon, and all-around mustering point for the local Italian community, Augusto's was a Mulberry Street institution. It was where Pietro found most of his work and all of his trouble, a good part of both on the wrong side of the law. There could be no better place to hear about shady business—or get mixed up in it.

Something uncomfortable occurred to me then. "Pietro, you haven't . . ."

He scowled. "Of course not! But plenty of people come to Augusto for that sort of thing."

"What sort of thing, exactly?"

"Hire some muscle. Organize a few of the boys to teach somebody a lesson. That's why you nab somebody—to teach him a lesson. That, or because you need something he's got. Either way, he knows why, and it's *always* about money."

"This wasn't about money."

Pietro rolled his eyes. "Whatever it was, it's over now, thanks God, so you should pack up your things and leave that place."

I picked up a pair of trousers and started folding. "You're right about the first bit, though—I think Mr. Wiltshire did have something they needed."

"What does it matter?"

"Because somebody cracked me over the head with a pistol, Pietro, and I'd like to know why."

"A pistol?" He uttered a long, decorative string of Italian curses. "I'll kill him. I'll kill him myself."

Now it was my turn to roll my eyes. "Mr. Wiltshire, or the rough?"

"Both! *Figli di puttana . . .*" He jerked a faded shirt off the line, still swearing under his breath. I couldn't help wondering whether this little display of temper was really about me or just a convenient excuse to vent his contempt for the upper classes. "Did they catch him? The *cazzo* who hit you?"

"No, but he was the same man who nabbed Mr. Wiltshire. A big Irishman. Mr. Wiltshire reckons he was hired muscle, just like you said."

"Of course. Rich men hire other people to do their dirty business."

"Hire them through people like Augusto?" I paused in my folding. An idea was blooming in my mind—and Pietro could see it.

"Oh, no." He raised a finger in a warding gesture. "Don't even think about it."

"Just a few questions. He won't mind if they're coming from you. He's known you for years . . ."

Pietro growled and dug the heels of his hands into his eyes. "*Why*, Rose? Why not just quit that job and find some other place to work? Some nice, quiet house where nobody gets kidnapped?"

Because working as a maid in a nice, quiet house is unspeakably dull. Aloud, I said, "The man who attacked me belongs behind bars. If Augusto or somebody like that can help me find him, I'll have him arrested." *Right after he tells me who hired him.*

Pietro blew out a breath. "You will get me into trouble along with you. Nothing good ever comes of asking favors of Augusto. That man is the devil."

I understood how he felt. It was a man like Augusto who'd tricked Pietro's parents into letting him drag their two young sons across the sea in search of a better life, only to turn the boys into beggars once they arrived in New York. As far as Pietro was concerned, men like Augusto were responsible for the death of his brother and dozens like him. He'd sworn a hundred times over that he'd never set foot in that store again—only to be reminded a hundred times over that an Italian didn't get far in New York without the help of a *padrone*. "You're right," I said. "I'm sure there's another way."

He sighed. "You say the man was Irish?"

"I think they all were. Say, do you suppose there's an Irishman who does the same sort of work as Augusto, acting as go-between for people looking to hire muscle?"

"I'm sure of it, just as there is a German like that, and a Chinese, and a Jew . . ."

"What a relief," I said sourly. "I'd hate to think our people had cornered the market."

"Oh, don't worry, there is plenty of competition."

"Will Augusto know them? The competition?"

"Probably." He shrugged. "We'll see."

"I don't want to be any trouble . . ."

He snorted softly. "Too late for that. But it's a small enough thing. I won't owe him much for it."

"Owe him? Just for answering a couple of questions?"

"Nothing is free in Five Points, Fiora. You know that." I started to protest, but he held up a hand. "It's all right. It's probably time for me to run an errand or two for him anyway. Like paying dues at the club, no?"

That didn't make me feel much better, but he insisted, and I suppose I didn't take a whole lot of convincing. If we could find out who'd hired those roughs, maybe Mr. Wiltshire would let me help with the investigation. And if we couldn't, well . . .

I'd just have to think of something else.

I awoke with a terrible crick in the neck from sleeping on Mam's floor. Even so, I was grateful not to have passed the night in my little room in the attic on Fifth Avenue. The frost would be long gone by now, but the memories wouldn't melt away so easily. And if by some miracle I'd managed to fall asleep, waking up to those familiar surroundings would have left me disoriented, wondering how much of the previous day had been real.

Then again, maybe it would have been better if I'd dismissed it all as a dream, because it would have spared me the unbearable thought of going back to my old life as if everything were normal. As it was, I suffered a terrible pang of envy when I arrived at the house to find Mr. Wiltshire already gone. Barely dawn, and already he was out scouring the city for clues, moving in a world of vibrant color and startling relief while all around me was as dull and flat as a newspaper photograph. I felt as if I finally understood something of the gambler or the opium fiend, craving the rush even though he knows it will only bring him trouble.

Then there was the problem of what to tell Clara. I didn't want to lie to her, but I couldn't tell her everything, either; Mr. Wiltshire had made that very clear.

I gave her as much of the truth as I could. "I found him at the gasworks," I explained over tea and leftover biscuits. "Tied to a chair. They'd been holding him for nearly a week."

"They?" Clara's voice was a low murmur, her fingers curled around her teacup so tightly that her knuckles were pale. We must have looked like quite the pair of gossips, huddled tête-àtête at the kitchen table with our breakfast untouched between us.

"No idea who *they* are," I said. "Something to do with Mr. Wiltshire's work, most likely. We managed to get away, but not without a fight. That's what happened to his knuckles."

"Lord," she said wonderingly. "So he was investigating a murder after all."

"He was, but he doesn't want anyone to know about it. And there's more, so much more, and I wish I could tell you all of it, but—"

She patted my hand. "I appreciate the thought, but the truth is I'm just as happy not sticking my nose where it don't belong. I'm just glad it worked out."

"There's something else."

"I told you, I don't—"

"Not about Mr. Wiltshire. About . . . Clara, I saw a ghost."

There. After the ridiculous jig I'd done last night, I'd decided it was better just to blurt these things out.

Clara was quiet for a spell. "Where?"

"Here, in the house. Last night. Actually it was a shade, but . . . Well, never mind. I saw it in my room and I panicked."

"I guess! Was that the ruckus I heard in the hallway?"

I nodded.

"Mr. Wiltshire was with you. Did you tell him you saw a ghost?" When I nodded again, she said, "He believe you?"

"He did."

"Well, now, that's a surprise."

I could tell she was wondering whether he was just humoring me, so I said, "He believes in lots of things like that." And before I could think better of it, I told her about luck.

In hindsight, it was an incredibly selfish thing to do. Both Mr. Burrows and Mr. Wiltshire had warned me that knowing about luck could be dangerous. In telling Clara, I was potentially putting her at risk, and for what? She could have gone through life without ever knowing and it wouldn't have bothered her a lick—she'd just finished saying as much. I told her because I wanted someone to talk to, which is about the worst reason I can think of to put a friend in danger.

"You sure they wasn't just pulling your leg?" Clara asked with a doubtful frown.

"Mr. Wiltshire isn't the sort."

"No, I suppose not. Anyway, I guess it ain't all that surprising."

For a moment I just stared at her, certain I must have heard wrong. "What do you mean, not surprising?"

She shrugged. "I don't need Mr. Burrows or anybody else to tell me that the world is run by a handful of rich folks. As to how they got rich, well . . . don't see how it matters much how Mr. Burrows's great-granddaddy found his gold, or how John Jacob Astor got his hands on so much land, or any of the rest of it. We always knew it was luck. Just didn't know what kind, is all."

What can I say? If pure, good old-fashioned horse sense was a form of luck, Clara had inherited it in spades.

"I'm not saying I believe all this stuff anyway. Just . . . it wouldn't surprise me, is all."

"Even so, I'd keep it to myself, even from Joseph. These are powerful people, and if they want something kept quiet . . ."

"I figured. So why'd you tell me?"

"I guess because I'm tired of secrets."

Clara looked as if she didn't quite believe that, but she let it be.

"Speaking of which, why didn't you tell me you were a nurse?"

She *tsk*ed. "I'm no more a nurse than you are a detective. I just learned some things from Doc Morris, that's all."

"But you could be, if you wanted to."

"Oh, is that right?" She snorted. "A colored nurse."

"Why not? You wouldn't be the first. There was that woman we read about in *Harper's*, remember? Mary something?"

"Mahoney, and what of it? Can you imagine what she must've gone through?"

I could, at least a little. I'd heard plenty of stories of what it was like for my da when we first arrived in New York, how he struggled to find work on account of his heritage. Things were better now; we Irish were no longer the most despised of the immigrant races. (That honor currently belonged to the Celestials, with the Italians running a close second.) Even so, plenty of people still treated me as though I were less than. There had always been a Mrs. Sellers or two in my life, and I reckoned there always would be.

That went double for Clara, of course. If learning to be a nurse weren't hard enough, being colored on top of it . . . "Still, wouldn't you rather be doing that than . . ." I gestured about the kitchen.

"Why? What's wrong with cooking? It's good honest work, and every dollar saved gets me one step closer to Westchester. Besides, I don't have time for school. You got any idea how complicated that business is, how much to learn? I used to look through Doc Morris's medical books, at the diagrams and such. I tried to memorize as much as I could, but . . ." She shook her head. "It'd take years, not to mention costing a fortune."

"There'd be no Mrs. Sellers."

"There'd be a hundred just like her, believe you me."

That, I figured, had at least as much to do with her reluctance as anything else, but I kept that thought to myself. As hard as my life had been, it couldn't compare to what Clara had endured. For every bigot I'd faced, she'd faced ten more, and they'd treated her ten times worse. She'd carved out a decent place for herself here. Could I really blame her for not wanting to give that up just to put herself through an awful trial?

We were interrupted by the doorbell. I crept to the foot of the stairs to listen, and when Mrs. Sellers answered, I recognized the grandfatherly voice straightaway.

I was already halfway up the stairs when the housekeeper found me. "Rose," she said in her usual chiding tone, "there's a—"

"Yes, thanks," I said, slipping past.

"Morning, Miss Gallagher." Sergeant Chapman made a vague gesture with his hat. "Have a moment?"

I took the liberty of showing him to the parlor, wishing fervently that Mr. Wiltshire were here to see what my efforts had turned up. I felt sure the detective would have something for me, a faith that was not disappointed.

"Your boss got back all right, I hear." Eying my stitches, he added, "I take it you had something to do with that."

I gave him a quick version of the day's events, along with a description of my assailant. "Does he sound familiar?"

"A big Irishman?" Chapman lifted a graying eyebrow. "Sure, he sounds real familiar."

"Too familiar." I sighed. "Well, I figured it couldn't hurt to ask."

"You fended these roughs off by yourself?"

"Mr. Wiltshire helped." I didn't like taking more than my share of the credit, but Mr. Wiltshire wanted his trade kept secret, and I figured a more accurate version of events would raise questions on that score. The gentlemen of Fifth Avenue were not known for their pugilistic prowess.

Chapman narrowed one sleepy eye, but he didn't press the issue. "Found something on your friend Roberts. Probably water under the bridge at this point, what with your boss turning up, but I figured since you're only a couple of blocks from the station, wasn't much trouble to come by."

"I appreciate it. There's still a lot I don't understand, and I'd like some answers about what happened to me."

"Well, I can't give you that, least not yet, but here's what I got. Turns out our friend Roberts has his fingers in more than a few pies. On top of being a Freemason, he's a member of a smaller outfit called the Brotherhood of Seekers."

"How very mysterious sounding."

"Ain't it, though." He shook his head. "These secret society types. Rich fellas acting like a bunch of kids with a clubhouse, you ask me. Anyways, looks like the Crowe brothers are members of this brotherhood, too—or were, in the case of Jacob. So I looked into it some, and it turns out their *sacred mission* involves"—he paused to consult his ledger, holding it out at arm's length and squinting—"psychical research with a view to unmasking the great metaphysical mysteries of our time. So." He snapped the ledger closed. "There you go."

"Metaphysical mysteries?"

"Quite a mouthful, ain't it? Near as I can figure, it means they spend their time researching things we can't explain."

"Ah," I said knowingly. "The paranormal, you mean."

"If you say so. I'm mentioning it because you was looking for a link between the Arbridge kid and the murder. I'm guessing this is it. Sounds to me like a ghost story is just the sort of thing the Crowe brothers and their little secret society would be interested in."

"You think Peter Arbridge might be involved in the murder?"

"Could be. I'll be seeing him next. And I'll want to see your boss, too, when he gets in. I'm guessing he's holding more than a few pieces to this puzzle. You'll tell him that for me?"

I agreed to pass on the message. "Does this mean you're handling the Jacob Crowe case now, instead of Detective Ward?"

"More or less. I got a feeling this thing is more complicated than it looks, so I decided to pull rank. Didn't make myself a friend, but . . ." He shrugged and put his hat back on.

It seemed we were through, so I showed him to the door. "I appreciate you coming by to tell me this, Sergeant. Most people wouldn't have bothered."

"I promised I'd get back to you, and I'm a man of my word." Touching the brim of his hat, he said, "Miss Gallagher," and was gone.

I hovered in the foyer for a few minutes, toying with the lace of my apron and thinking through what Sergeant Chapman had said. That's how I happened to be standing there when my employer burst through the door—looking very grim indeed.

"Mr. Wiltshire!" I took his coat hurriedly. "Is everything all right?"

"I'm afraid not." He paused to brush a lock of hair out of my eyes, checking my pupils in a gesture so reflexively intimate that he scarcely seemed to be aware of it. "Better," he said distractedly, and started to walk away.

"Wait, you can't just . . ." I bit my lip, because of course he *could* just. "Please," I said more calmly, "won't you tell me what's happened?"

"I'm afraid I've just found the body of Mr. Crowe."

"Oh," I said, startled. "I didn't realize it was missing."

"You misunderstand, Rose. It isn't Jacob Crowe I've just found. It's Frederick."

CHAPTER 17

A MURDER OF CROWES—THE CIPHER
MANUSCRIPTS—GLASS HOUSES

News of this grim nature called for tea. I brought a tray up to Mr. Wiltshire's study, where I found him seated at his desk, massaging his bruised knuckles with a faraway look. "Thank you, Rose," he murmured absently.

I set the tray down as soundlessly as I could. "Are you all right?"

"*Mmm?* Oh, fine, thank you."

"You don't seem fine," I said, flushing a little at my own impertinence. A night's sleep had gone a long way to restoring the natural order of things, setting Thomas Wiltshire back up on his pedestal. That left me in a strange sort of limbo, unsure how to behave. Even so, the sight of him in distress was more than I could bear in silence. "Is there anything I can do?"

"Not unless you can turn back time, and even Napoleon didn't have that kind of luck."

I started to ask a question, but it didn't seem like quite the right moment. Instead I said, "I'm sorry about Mr. Crowe."

"So am I. This falls at my feet, and I'm not sure quite how I'll account for myself."

"Don't say that. What could you have done, with everything you've been through this past week?"

"Nothing, and that's just the point. I've lost so much time." He closed his eyes, wilting a little in his chair. "And I'm simply exhausted. My mental faculties aren't what they should be." Then, abruptly, he gave himself a shake and sat up. "Nor is my judgment, apparently. I shouldn't be discussing this."

"You haven't breached any confidences. Your feelings aren't the property of the Pinkerton Agency, are they?"

That earned me a wisp of a smile. "I suppose not."

"Shall I pour you some tea?"

He hesitated, as though I'd asked a very complicated question. "I'll do it, thank you." He reached for the teapot, then paused again, frowning at the tray.

Was there something missing? Just as I was about to start squirming, it dawned on me: He was looking for a second cup, which of course I hadn't brought, since he was alone. *He has no idea how to treat you, either.* Apparently, I wasn't the only one stuck in this strange limbo. To cover the awkwardness, I said, "Sergeant Chapman came to see me."

"Who?"

"The police detective. I thought I mentioned him yesterday. He's handling Jacob Crowe's case now. He's . . . Well, I quite like him. He seems genuinely competent."

"A mixed blessing. Is he the one who believes Mr. Burrows is a suspect?"

"No, but he does believe in ghosts, and maybe other things besides." I added that second part without thinking, and now I paused, wondering for the first time what the detective might know about luck.

Mr. Wiltshire arched an eyebrow. "How exactly did that come up?"

"He overheard me mention Peter Arbridge. He'd seen the story in the *Times,* and I gather he pays attention to that sort of thing. Anyway, he came by to tell me about Mr. Roberts and the Brotherhood of Seekers. He asked me to tell you that he'd like to speak with you, and—"

"I beg your pardon? Back up, please. Mr. Roberts and the what?"

"The Brotherhood of Seekers, I think? Is that not right?"

Mr. Wiltshire's pale eyes hooked on mine, clear and intense. "Take a seat, Rose. I think perhaps you'd better start from the beginning."

I did as he asked, trying my best to recall every detail of my conversation with Sergeant Chapman. "He said he thought the Crowe brothers must have been looking into Peter Arbridge's ghost story on behalf of the Brotherhood. He figured that must have been why you went to see him up at Hell Gate."

Mr. Wiltshire closed his eyes, propping his chin on knitted fingers. "That's it," he murmured. "That's the connection. Rose, I could kiss you."

Color flashed to my cheeks, but luckily his eyes were still closed. "What does it mean?"

"I'm not sure, but this Brotherhood of Seekers appears to

be the hub of it all, the piece that links all the disparate bits together. The shade, the portal, the folios, the Crowe brothers, all of it. Until now, I had nothing more than a suspicion they were connected."

"You didn't know about them? The Seekers, I mean?"

He shook his head. "Not so remarkable in itself—these fraternal organizations do love their intrigue—but the fact that Roberts never mentioned it . . ."

"He knows more than he's saying." I'd worked that much out already. "I'd be willing to bet Mr. Burrows thinks so, too."

"Burrows." His eyes snapped open. "I need to speak with him at once."

"Shall I telephone for him?"

"Mrs. Sellers can do it. I need you here." He swept out of the room, leaving me to gape at his back. Mrs. Sellers never did the telephoning; I wasn't sure she even knew how to operate the thing properly.

Mr. Wiltshire returned shortly, but before he could start peppering me with questions again, I had a few of my own. "You mentioned a cipher yesterday. And a moment ago, something about folios. The papers you took from the gasworks, the ones those men said their boss wanted you to finish . . ."

Mr. Wiltshire smiled ruefully. "You really do pay attention. It makes it frightfully hard to keep things from you."

"Sorry," I said, but of course I wasn't.

"We'd better wait for Burrows. Here, I've brought more teacups. Would you care to join me?" He poured out two steaming cups and handed me one. "How did you sleep last night?" A seemingly casual question, but there was a sharpness to his gaze that made me uneasy.

"All right, considering."

"Good, good."

There was a stretch of silence, broken only by the *clink* of cup on saucer.

"And your mother? How is she?"

"She was still asleep when I left this morning, but she's agreed to ask . . ." I faltered, not sure what to call the ghost. *Granny* didn't feel quite right. "She's agreed to ask the spirit to visit less often, and only in dreams. I guess we'll have to see how it goes. I'd like to stop in later today, if you don't mind."

"Of course. Please give her my regards."

More silence. Just when I thought I would tear my hair out with impatience, a knock sounded and Jonathan Burrows glided into the room.

"That was quick," Mr. Wiltshire said.

"Your housekeeper says she telephoned, but I was already on my way over here. I've just heard about Freddie."

Mr. Wiltshire winced. "Word travels quickly."

"Half the Avenue has heard by now. What the deuce happened?" Mr. Burrows sank into a chair, looking uncharacteristically grave.

"I wish I could tell you."

"The shade?"

"Someone is trying to make it look that way, but no."

"How can you be sure?"

"Among other things, because we've met the shade in question. She was here with us last night."

"What, in the house? Good Lord! Did she attack you?"

"She touched Rose, I'm afraid."

Mr. Burrows swore softly, cutting me a sharp look. "Fragments?"

"No sign of that, thank God."

"Thank God," Mr. Burrows echoed feelingly.

They traded a glance, and for some reason my pulse skipped a few beats.

"You banished it, I hope?"

Mr. Wiltshire shook his head. "I don't think she hurt Rose intentionally. She was just trying to communicate, as I believe she was with the Crowes. We'll know more once we get a medium involved, but I'm quite convinced that whoever killed the Crowe brothers is perfectly human."

"So someone had it in for *both* of the Crowe brothers?" Mr. Burrows hummed thoughtfully. "Something to do with the family business, perhaps, or . . ."

"That's why I asked you here," Mr. Wiltshire said. "Tell me, did you see Roberts yesterday?"

"At the club. I filled him in, as we discussed."

"How did he react?"

"He seemed relieved, I suppose. Why?"

"Have you ever heard of the Brotherhood of Seekers?"

There was a beat of silence. Mr. Burrows's expression didn't change, but I sensed a subtle shift in his bearing—the same one I'd noticed that day in his parlor, when I'd gone to see him about Mr. Wiltshire. Something about him seemed suddenly distant, just as it had in the moments before he'd looked me in the eye and lied.

This time, I didn't give him the chance. "You have, obviously. Please don't deny it."

"Steady on, Rose," Mr. Wiltshire said, frowning. "This isn't an interrogation."

"I'm sorry, it's just that I've been down this road with Mr. Burrows before."

"You have," Mr. Burrows said coolly, his ice-blue eyes meeting mine, "and there were good reasons for my hesitation then, just as there are now." Addressing Mr. Wiltshire, he went on, "Freemasons are not in the habit of telling tales out of school, Thomas. Still less those who happen to be endowed with luck. Where did you hear that name, anyway?"

"From Rose, as it happens."

For the first time, I had the great satisfaction of seeing Mr. Jonathan Burrows thoroughly stunned.

"She had it from the police," Mr. Wiltshire went on, "so it's safe to say school is out."

Mr. Burrows gave me an exasperated look. "I must say, Rose, I'm having decidedly mixed feelings about you at the moment."

It's mutual, Mr. Burrows. I kept that to myself, figuring I'd pushed it enough already.

"I don't know much about them," Mr. Burrows said grudgingly, "except that they're few in number, highly secretive, and thoroughly obsessed with all things paranormal. Most of their members are scientists of one sort or another. They've spent a small fortune on research, I'm told."

"How interesting. Is Tesla a member?"

"Ask him yourself."

"I shall. It sounds as if they're fellows after my own heart, at any rate."

Mr. Burrows hummed a skeptical note but otherwise let that pass. "What's their involvement in this?"

"I've no idea, but I find it curious that Roberts didn't see fit to mention them, given that he and the Crowe brothers are members. That would seem to be pertinent information, wouldn't you agree? What with a shade being blamed for the killing?"

"There's a fair few things Roberts doesn't see fit to mention."

"So it would appear." Mr. Wiltshire crossed one perfectly tailored trouser leg over the other, his expression thoughtful. "The question is, why would he withhold something like that if it could help lead us to Jacob's killer?"

Mr. Burrows shrugged. "There are so many overlapping circles—the Madison Club, the Freemasons, the Seekers, any number of others. I daresay I'm the only Mason in our chapter who isn't involved in at least one other fraternal organization. Maybe Roberts simply didn't think it relevant to list them all."

"Except the Crowes weren't Freemasons," Mr. Wiltshire pointed out, "and only one of those organizations is dedicated to paranormal research. No, I don't think it's merely an oversight. Nor do I think *this* is a coincidence." Opening a drawer, he produced a stack of papers and slid them across the desk.

I leaned forward with interest. "Are these the papers you took from the gasworks?"

"Select pages from a much larger manuscript, from what I can tell. The men who took me captive demanded that I decipher them."

"What are they, Latin?" Mr. Burrows took up a page and peered at it. "Oh, you mean literally."

"Quite literally, yes. A substitution cryptogram, to be precise."

"You cracked it, then?"

Mr. Wiltshire looked a little offended. "Of course. Within the first few hours."

"But you told them you hadn't," I said, remembering the exchange at the gasworks.

"Well, certainly. The moment I translated those pages, I'd have made myself redundant."

It took me a moment to work out what he meant; when I did, my blood ran cold. "They'd have killed you."

"Presumably. So I withheld my findings."

"Which were?" Mr. Burrows prodded.

"As far as I can tell, it's a manual of instruction in the magical arts. Hermetic, mainly, though all the major traditions are covered. Nothing terribly earth-shattering, but the portions I deciphered make reference to an appendix containing a series of more advanced rituals."

"Magical arts," I echoed, glancing between the two men. "Are we talking about luck?"

"Not at all, though the two are sometimes confused." Mr. Wiltshire's expression lit up, just as it had yesterday when he'd explained luck. "Magic is learned, whereas luck is innate. Rather like the difference between study and raw talent, you could say."

"I'm sorry," Mr. Burrows interrupted, "but could we stick to the subject, please? What does this instruction manual have to do with the Crowe brothers?"

"That's what we need to find out. Rose, did your detective friend say anything about these papers, or anything else the Brotherhood of Seekers might be working on?"

"I'm sorry, no. I've already told you everything I can remember. But you think these papers belong to the Seekers?"

"Perhaps, but there's only one way to find out. Burrows, I need the name of every member of that organization you're aware of."

Mr. Burrows scowled. "You know better than to ask that of me."

"I do, and I'm loath to put you in this position, but where else am I to get it if not from you?"

"Maybe if you confronted Mr. Roberts?" I offered.

"He won't tell you anything," said Mr. Burrows. "And if he is involved somehow, asking about the Seekers will only tip your hand." Sighing, he glanced away. "Damn it, Thomas."

"I am sorry. If there were any other way . . ."

Mr. Burrows regarded his friend gravely. "*Whose house is of glass, must not throw stones.* This just isn't done among my set." His mouth twisted somewhere between a grimace and a smile. "Terribly bad form. You'll have me blacklisted from the club if this gets out."

"So you'll help, then?"

"Feldt, Emmerson, and Drake."

"*Edmund* Drake?" Mr. Wiltshire's eyebrows flew up.

"The same. That's all I know, aside from Roberts and the Crowe brothers."

"Thank you. I promise you this information won't go to waste."

"Don't make promises you can't keep," Mr. Burrows said tartly, reaching for his hat.

Mr. Wiltshire shook his friend's hand in farewell. "I'll begin tracking them down immediately. And thanks to you as well, Rose. You've been a tremendous help. Would you mind showing Mr. Burrows out?"

"But I thought . . . Is that all, then?" My cheeks stung in humiliation, a sensation made all the worse by the fact that Mr. Burrows was there to witness it.

"All?" Mr. Wiltshire echoed, puzzled. "I'm not sure I follow."

Mr. Burrows paused in the doorway. "I think what she's asking, Thomas, is why she's just been tossed on her ear."

Mr. Wiltshire frowned. "Please, Burrows, that's hardly helpful. Rose, I'm sorry if I've given you the wrong impression, but my position on the matter hasn't changed. If I've spoken freely just now, it's because I wanted to be sure there weren't any more hidden gems to turn up. You've already provided more than I could have hoped for, and I'm grateful, but—"

"But you don't need the help?" Mr. Burrows put in. "The girl's obviously got a knack for it. Why wouldn't you bring her along?"

Mr. Wiltshire's mouth tightened into a thin line. "Perhaps we might have a word in private, Mr. Burrows?"

I didn't wait to be told; I fled the study, closing the door behind me—and promptly fixing my ear against it.

"Really, Jonathan, this is difficult enough without you making a game of it."

"I'm not making a game of anything. Is it because she's your maid?"

"Among other things."

"Such as? Aside from the obvious fact that she's sharp as a needle and terribly keen besides? She's been chasing this thing for a week, at considerable risk to herself. Don't you think you owe her the chance to see it through? Or are you worried the laundry will pile up?"

"Tell me again this isn't a game to you."

"Amusing, I grant you, but not a game. Look, it's none of my affair, and I'm sorry to have barged in. But if she's been as helpful as you say, I don't see what you have to lose."

"Don't you? I have a professional obligation to my client. On top of which, if the situation is half as grave as I think it is, her life could be at risk."

Mr. Burrows's voice grew serious. "If the situation is half as grave as you think it is, all our lives are at risk. As to the first part, your client was Freddie Crowe, and he's dead. Who's your client now? Roberts? For all you know, he's behind it."

"Technically, my services have been engaged by the Freemasons."

"In that case, on behalf of the Freemasons, you have my leave to involve whomever you choose, so long as it brings you closer to Freddie and Jacob's killer."

"So long as I can keep an eye on Rose, you mean."

"I won't deny that's a useful side benefit. She knows a fair few things that could prove very inconvenient, and I'd like to be sure we can trust her."

There was a long pause. "If anything were to happen to her on my account . . ."

"Anything more, you mean."

"Yes, that's just what I mean! You know perfectly well how bad it could get."

"She's a grown woman, Thomas. Don't be so old-fashioned."

"Old-fashioned." A hollow laugh. "You know me better than that."

"The Thomas Wiltshire I know is curiously reluctant to show himself in this matter. A self-professed man of science—I'd have thought you'd delight in having a protégé."

"It's more complicated than that . . ."

I couldn't risk lingering any longer. Reluctantly, I peeled myself away from the door and headed downstairs to await Mr. Burrows.

He didn't keep me long. Barely five minutes later, he came striding down the hallway wearing his hat, his overcoat, and a very smug grin.

"What happened?" I asked, feeling more than a little foolish.

He just winked and breezed out the door.

Drawing a deep breath, I headed back upstairs. I found Mr. Wiltshire standing at the window, gazing out over Fifth Avenue. "I apologize if I seemed abrupt a moment ago," he said.

"It's for me to be sorry. I shouldn't have jumped to conclusions, especially after you made yourself clear yesterday. As for Mr. Burrows—"

"You needn't apologize for Mr. Burrows. He certainly doesn't apologize for himself."

Smoothing the folds of my apron, I said the words I'd prepared downstairs. "I know you're in a difficult position, and I didn't mean to make it worse. I was disappointed, and I'm not always very good at keeping my thoughts to myself. But I wasn't trying to put pressure on you, I swear. The last thing I want is to be a burden."

"A burden? Good Lord, Rose, you've been the furthest thing from it."

"I'm just saying I know my place, is all."

I knew right away I'd said something wrong. He stiffened and turned back to the window, and there was a stretch of silence. "Tell me something," he said at length. "What is it you want for yourself? For your future, I mean?"

I sensed there was a lot riding on this question, so I thought about it for a long moment before responding. Even so, the best answer I could come up with consisted of only one word: "More."

He nodded slowly. "Well, then, I suppose it's settled." Turning back to me, he said, "I can't promise you more, but I can offer to help you take the first few steps. I think you know they'll be difficult, and possibly a great deal worse. Are you ready for that?"

"I am." I'd been ready my whole life—or so I thought.

"In that case," Mr. Wiltshire said, "we have a very long day ahead of us."

CHAPTER 18

THE DRAGON'S DEN—BAD LUCK—A
DEVIATION IN THE PLAN

Edmund Drake," Mr. Wiltshire said, offering me a hand up into the coach. "Grandson of Sir Ellery Drake of Surrey. They call him the Dragon."

"Because of his surname, I suppose?"

"And because he always gets his way, at least in business. I doubt we'll find him very accommodating." Tapping on the roof with his walking stick, he set the carriage rolling. "Fortunately, you seem to have a good nose for obfuscation, if your assay of Mr. Burrows is any guide. I've a certain aptitude for it myself, so between us we ought to catch any chicanery."

I gave myself an extra moment to digest this flurry of syllables. "Are we expecting, er . . . chicanery?"

"We're going to have to come at our purpose crosswise. The

Brotherhood of Seekers is obviously very good at keeping secrets or I'd have heard of them by now. Even assuming they aren't involved in anything nefarious, I expect he'll be evasive on the subject. And if they are . . ."

"He'll lie outright."

"Presumably."

The rocking of the carriage seemed to help my thoughts fall into place, as if they were marbles rolling about in search of a slot. I had so many questions, but perversely I was more reluctant to ask them than ever. I felt as if I had something to prove now, and I needed to work things out on my own. "The papers those men wanted you to translate . . . If they do belong to the Seekers, that implies they're the ones behind your kidnapping, except . . ."

His eyes fixed on me expectantly. "Except?"

"Well, I don't know much about ciphers, but if cracking it was as simple as you say, it seems to me that kidnapping someone is an awful lot of trouble to go to. Mr. Burrows said the Brotherhood was full of scientists. I'd have thought men like that could work it out on their own."

"Sound reasoning, and a perfect echo of my own thoughts. Something doesn't quite add up there."

"Whoever took you knew you'd be able to crack it, so I guess that means they know what you do for a living. That you're not really a lawyer, I mean."

"So it would appear. Not terribly good news, is it?"

"But it narrows things down, surely? I mean, how many people know the truth about you?"

"Half the Madison Club, I'm afraid," he said ruefully. "The paranormal community is terribly incestuous. You heard what Mr. Burrows said about overlapping circles. I try to be discreet,

but it's challenging." He started to say more, but the carriage began to slow. "Ah, here we are."

"Already?"

"In this line of work, one rarely strays too far from Fifth
Avenue. Now, we don't want to give him anything we don't have
to, so follow my lead and say as little as possible. Ready?"

The carriage door was opened by a footman in bright red
livery, the sort you sometimes see standing outside the Grand
Opera House or some other high society place. Accepting his
help, I stepped down from the carriage onto a small semicircular
drive set back from the avenue. I recognized the property straightaway. Built of the requisite brownstone with the requisite sloping
French roofs, the residence of Mr. Edmund Drake occupied an
entire block opposite Central Park. A butler stood waiting under
the awning, Mr. Wiltshire having sent his card ahead.

It was the grandest building I'd ever set foot in—grander
even than St. Patrick's Cathedral, if the Good Lord will excuse
me for saying so—and I felt awfully self-conscious, even in my
Sunday dress with my best hat. As for Mr. Wiltshire, he looked
perfectly at home, handing over his fur-trimmed overcoat with an
air of such routine you'd have thought he lived in a palace like
this himself, or at least that he'd spent a great deal of time in
them. Which, I realized belatedly, he probably had.

He declined to give the butler his walking stick, though,
which earned him a disdainfully raised eyebrow. Instead he
handed it to me while he removed his gloves. It felt strange in my
hands—lighter than I would have guessed, and curiously *alive*. It
thrummed subtly, as if a breath of wind rustled through ghostly
branches. And when it brushed against the bare skin of my wrist,

a nerve throbbed beneath my rib cage, like a tooth aching with cold. I wasn't sorry to give it back.

The butler ushered us through a series of elaborately decorated drawing rooms, each one seemingly devoted to some sort of theme: Chinese porcelain, medieval suits of armor, stained glass and cherubim. One after another unfolded before us, but there was no time to admire any of it; the butler marched us past like an impatient tour guide at a museum, until at last we were deposited in a sort of parlor, there to await our host.

I say *sort of* because it didn't look like any parlor I'd ever seen. Portraits of stern relatives glowered down at us from left and right. A towering bookshelf brandished row upon row of massive leather-bound tomes, each one boasting a title as ponderous as the volumes themselves. The furnishings were sparse and austere, the woodwork polished to an accusing shine. It was about as inhospitable a space as I'd ever been received in, and I'm including those with straw on the floor.

"My, my," Mr. Wiltshire murmured, taking in our surroundings. "It's all very contrived, isn't it? Even by Fifth Avenue standards."

"Contrived?"

"This room has been meticulously designed to be as intimidating as possible. I daresay there's a second, more welcoming parlor somewhere."

"All those rooms we walked through . . . I couldn't work out what they were for. They didn't seem to be good for anything but looking."

He smiled. "In that case, you've worked out exactly what they're for: to impress you."

"If there's a nicer parlor somewhere, the fact that we've been shown to this one . . ."

"Indeed. I'd say we're in for an even bumpier ride than I thought."

"Do you think he's dangerous?" I asked, gesturing at Mr. Wiltshire's stick. I couldn't think of any reason to keep it close at hand unless he thought he might need it.

He seemed to find that amusing. "I have no reason to think so, but if he were, a walking stick would not be my weapon of choice. I carry a pistol for that sort of thing."

"Oh. I just thought since it's special and all . . ."

"Special?" He considered it with a frown. "Against the dead, perhaps, but against a living man, it's just an ordinary piece of wood."

It certainly hadn't felt ordinary when I'd touched it. I started to say as much, but just then Mr. Edmund Drake entered the room. He was a distinguished-looking fellow, dark-haired and dark-eyed, silver beginning to show at his temples. His clothing was conservative but finely tailored, and he wore a gold tie pin with the same motif as Mr. Wiltshire's cuff links: a griffin with an emerald clasped in its talons. Mr. Burrows had the same tie pin. The emblem of the Madison Club, I figured. All roads seemed to lead back there.

"Wiltshire," Drake said, shaking hands, "this is a pleasant surprise."

There was nothing in his tone to suggest actual pleasure, but Mr. Wiltshire pretended to believe him. "May I present my associate, Miss Gallagher."

I don't suppose I have to tell you how sweet that sounded to my ears.

To Drake, though, it sounded as if someone had unaccountably let an *Irishwoman* into his home—or so I surmised from the faint look of distaste flitting over his features. "Associate, is it? How interesting."

Do you want to know what's really *interesting? I'm actually his housemaid.* I managed to hold my tongue on that remark, for Mr. Wiltshire's sake.

"I take it this is a business call, then?" Drake gestured for us to sit, lowering himself into a creaking leather chair. As he did so, his glance alighted briefly on Mr. Wiltshire's walking stick.

"Unfortunately, yes. You've heard about poor Frederick Crowe, I presume?"

"A terrible tragedy. Though I'm at a loss as to how it brings you to my door."

"I've been engaged to look into the matter."

"So it's true." Drake regarded Mr. Wiltshire with detached curiosity. "I'd heard you might be in the private detective game. Pinkerton, is it? I've dealt with your outfit in the past."

"And how did you find it?"

"A reliable firm. But I'm afraid I still don't see how that brings you here."

"Making my way through the club roll, you could say. As many known associates as I can find."

Drake grunted. "A touch haphazard, isn't it? The Crowes were very well connected socially."

"One has to start somewhere."

"Start?" Drake lifted an eyebrow. "It's been a week or more since Jacob's murder."

"Indeed, but I'm afraid I found myself detained for several days."

If I'd had any warning, I'd have watched Drake closely for his reaction. Instead I was looking at Mr. Wiltshire, and the keenness of his gaze told me that the subject hadn't come up by accident. This was an ambush, cunningly orchestrated, and Drake had walked right into it.

Cunning though it might have been, however, the snare came up empty. Drake just frowned, as though wondering if perhaps he hadn't overestimated the reliability of the Pinkerton Detective Agency. "I suppose we all have responsibilities that keep us busy. With that in mind, why don't we get straight to it. How can I help you, Wiltshire?"

"How well would you say you knew the Crowe brothers?"

"Jacob a little, Freddie not at all, except to say hello."

"When you say a little . . ."

"We dined at the club now and then. We had similar interests."

"What sorts of interests, if I may ask?"

"Botany."

I almost snorted aloud, and Mr. Wiltshire's mouth took a wry turn. Edmund Drake absorbed both of these reactions with a watchful eye.

That's when I understood that we'd walked into a snare of our own. Drake had just taken the measure of what we knew about his association with Jacob Crowe, which was plenty.

Whether Mr. Wiltshire noticed, I couldn't tell. "Is there anyone who distinguishes himself in your memory as a particular friend of Jacob Crowe's? Or an enemy, perhaps? Anyone whom I would be remiss not to interview?"

"Jacob was a studious fellow. He had many acquaintances,

but friends?" Drake shrugged. "As to enemies—why should he have any of those?"

"I couldn't say, but the fact of his murder would seem to suggest that he did."

Drake paused. Once again his gaze fell to Mr. Wiltshire's walking stick. "A striking piece. Ash, is it?"

"Well spotted."

Their eyes met. That's when I understood why Mr. Wiltshire had brought the stick. If ash wood was as important as he'd said, a member of the paranormal community would know it at a glance and recognize its bearer as one of their own. Like a Masonic ring, or a griffin with an emerald in its claws, Mr. Wiltshire's walking stick was a sort of crest. One Drake obviously recognized, which meant he was a member, too.

"In which case," Drake said, "I don't suppose there's much point in subtlety, is there?"

"I beg your pardon?"

Drake leaned forward, leather creaking beneath him. "Thomas," he said silkily, and paused. When he judged he had Mr. Wiltshire's full attention, he went on, "Does this mean it wasn't the shade that killed Jacob?"

My surprise at the question was nothing compared with my astonishment at Mr. Wiltshire's answer. "That's precisely what it means. Whoever killed the Crowe brothers was certainly human."

Follow my lead, he'd said, but I'd understood our plan was to keep our cards close. Now here he was laying them out on the table, right under Edmund Drake's nose.

"Very well," Drake said, "and do you have a suspect?"

"Not as yet."

"There's a reason you sought me out in particular, I imagine?"

Mr. Wiltshire hesitated, frowning.

"Forgive me, that wasn't direct enough, was it?" Drake leaned in still closer. "Thomas, why are you here?"

"Because you're a member of the Brotherhood of Seekers."

Was this his idea of coming at the subject crosswise? I glanced over sharply, but Mr. Wiltshire didn't meet my eye, preferring instead to engage in some sort of staring contest with Drake. I couldn't read his expression.

Drake, for his part, was visibly annoyed. "And just where did you come across that name?"

"Miss Gallagher told me," Mr. Wiltshire said, gesturing casually at me.

I must have looked startled, because Drake smiled and said, "No need to worry. We're all friends here. What's your name, my dear? Your given name, I mean."

I had a sudden, absurd impulse to lie to him. *Mary,* I almost said, the alias I'd given to Peter Arbridge. But Mr. Wiltshire had asked me to follow his lead, so . . . "Rose."

"Rose," Drake said.

His inflection didn't change, but when he spoke my name, it felt as if I were hearing it for the first time. The word seemed to flow around me, thick and sticky, as though I were sinking into a vat of warm honey. A frisson of euphoria sparkled in my veins; suddenly, all I wanted was more of that voice.

"Where did you hear about the Brotherhood of Seekers?" Drake asked me.

"A police officer told me."

"What police officer?"

"Sergeant Chapman of the Twenty-Eighth Precinct."

"What else did he tell you?"

I gave Edmund Drake everything I could recall, down to the last detail.

"And what is his interest in the Brotherhood?"

"I asked him to look into Mr. Roberts, and that's what he found."

"Roberts. Damn. I might have known. Very well, Rose, we're almost through. What other names do you have?"

"Emmerson. Feldt. The Crowe brothers. That's all."

"Nothing incriminating on any of us?"

"Not that I know of."

"Thomas?"

"No," Mr. Wiltshire confirmed, "not as yet."

"Very well, then," Drake said, rising. "I trust that covers it?"

"Admirably, thank you," said Mr. Wiltshire.

They shook hands, and we trailed the butler back through the maze of drawing rooms and out into the street. "That went rather well, I thought," Mr. Wiltshire said as we climbed into the carriage.

"I agree," I said, still riding little waves of euphoria.

All was right with the world until about Sixtieth Street, at which point something occurred to me. "Do you think maybe we said more than we should have?"

Mr. Wiltshire had been quiet for several blocks, and when he looked up his expression was troubled. "Why, what did you tell him? For that matter, what did I tell him?" He shook his head, frowning. "I'm sorry, for some reason I'm having a devil of a time recalling the details of the conversation. Everything feels a bit . . ."

"Foggy."

Our eyes met. In mine, he saw confusion; in his, I saw a dawning dismay. "My God," he whispered.

I could feel the realization creeping up on me, too, like the chill of an approaching shade. Then it hit me. "He drugged us!"

But no—he couldn't have. He hadn't even offered us tea. Then what?

"Luck," Mr. Wiltshire said grimly. "I'd bet my estate on it."

I stared at him, still not quite understanding.

"I'd heard rumors that Drake was lucky, but I had no idea of the extent of it." He shook his head in awe. "That's one of the strongest powers I've ever come across."

"What power? What did he just do to us?"

"Some sort of persuasion, obviously. Almost like hypnosis." He laughed bitterly. "The Dragon indeed. No wonder his business dealings are so successful! It's like a drug or a venom. And so subtle! If you hadn't been here to compare notes, I should never have noticed anything amiss. I'd have put it down to fatigue or distraction or some such." He grimaced, massaging his temples. "I still can't remember what I said. Good Lord, we must have given him everything."

"Luck can do that?" Mr. Burrows's words came back to me then, in perfect clarity: *What would people make of what Rockefeller can do, or Van den Berg or even Roosevelt?* At last I was beginning to truly grasp what he meant. And it was horrifying.

"In theory, luck can do just about anything. And to think—it's weaker now than it's ever been."

"What do you mean?"

"Luck dims a little with each successive generation. The difference is minute from one cohort to the next, but over the centuries, families with luck have seen their powers diminish greatly. A thousand years ago, people with luck must have seemed like gods, or at least powerful sorcerers. One shudders to think what such people might have been capable of."

"No one knows?"

"Tales survive, of course, but it's terribly difficult to separate fact from myth. Was Hercules lucky, or merely legend? What about Merlin, or Gilgamesh, or even Jesus? Impossible to say."

For the first time, I felt genuinely afraid. Until that moment, I suppose I'd thought of luck as some sort of elaborate parlor trick. Impressive—eerie, even—but nothing that would keep me awake at night. But *this* . . . "I don't understand. I mean, I thought I did, but . . . What *is* luck?"

"Some of the greatest minds in history have devoted themselves to that question, and we've still barely scratched the surface."

"But what Drake did to us—you're sure it was luck?"

"It's the most plausible explanation. Regardless, we must consider our position compromised. I doubt we'll get anything from the rest of the Brotherhood now. We'll have to deviate from the plan."

"Deviate how?"

Leaning out the carriage window, Mr. Wiltshire called, "The Tenderloin, please. Twenty-Eighth and Broadway."

The address tweaked something in my memory, but it took me a moment to place it. "One-Eyed Johnny's."

"You're . . . familiar with it?" He looked faintly aghast.

I scowled, every bit as offended as the last time someone had asked me that question. "Only because I followed Mr. Burrows there the other day."

"Did you?" Mr. Wiltshire hummed a thoughtful note. "You'd said he seemed concerned, but I had no idea. I'm touched."

"What could he possibly have been looking for in a place like that?"

"The same thing we're looking for," Mr. Wiltshire said. "A bounty hunter."

CHAPTER 19

THE BLOODHOUND—HARLEM'S HOUSE OF
HAUNTINGS—THE SCENE OF THE CRIME

'm afraid I must warn you," Mr. Wiltshire said as we stepped
out of the brougham, "it is not a pleasant establishment."

　　As though I needed to be told. I'd wandered into my share
of rum shops growing up. Looking for my da, usually, or the husband of a neighbor. I'd even taken a turn or two as a rusher when
I needed some pocket money, though Mam would've had a stroke
if she'd known. (Good Catholic girls did *not* set foot in saloons,
and they certainly didn't run around peddling growlers to any local bum with a few coins to rub together.) Even so, it had been a
long time since I'd seen the inside of a place like this, and I'd never
done so in the company of a high society gentleman. It made the
experience doubly awkward, not unlike our visit to Mam's flat
the night before.

One-Eyed Johnny's smelled like stale beer and a dozen more unpleasant things, but at least it had the virtue of being dark. There were no windows, and the mismatched lamps and candles strewn here and there were barely enough to light a pathway to the bar. It being a Saturday, the place was crowded; Mr. Wiltshire picked his way through the human driftwood with great care, using his walking stick to clear a corridor through the thicker piles of straw. His oxfords fairly glowed in the lamplight, by far the shiniest thing in the room.

"Sir Thomas," said a deep voice, and I looked up to find a big fellow grinning at us from behind the bar. He wore a patch over his left eye; an angry scar ran from the side of his nose to the gleaming crown of his bald black head. The eponymous Johnny, I presumed.

"I wish you wouldn't call me that, Johnny. I'm quite sure I've mentioned that I'm not a knight."

"You English, ain't you? Close enough." Johnny hefted a dark bottle questioningly, but Mr. Wiltshire shook his head. "Who's your friend?"

"This is my associate, Miss Gallagher."

"Pleased to meet you," I said. "Nice joint you got here."

"Five Points girl. I like her already."

I winced inwardly. I'd worked hard to scrub my accent clean, but apparently traces of the slum remained. "Good ear," I said with a weak smile.

"Better than the eye, anyways. Lookin' for Annie, I s'pose?"

"Indeed," Mr. Wiltshire said. "Is she here?"

Johnny gestured with a filthy glass. "She's in a mood, though. Best watch yourself."

"How unusual," Mr. Wiltshire said dryly, grabbing a lamp and heading toward a heap of rags slumped at the end of the bar. As the lamplight drew nearer, the rags resolved themselves into a woman—or at least, a womanlike creature. She was about forty, judging from the lines on her face, though it was hard to tell how much of that was age and how much a lifetime of hard drinking. Her frame, too, showed the ravages of the bottle, and she had a head of hair that might once have been curly but now resembled the dead thistles clinging to the walls at the gasworks. She wore a man's jacket and trousers, and had the nub of a cigar jammed into a corner of her mouth. All in all, she looked like something the cat had coughed up—yet when she reached for her bottle, the light caught a glitter of jewels on her fingers.

"Miss Harris," Mr. Wiltshire said. "It's been a long time."

The woman looked him up and down with a bleary frown. "Thought you was s'posed to be dead."

"Missing."

"Missing is usually dead in your line of work, Pinkerton." She said the word *Pinkerton* much as I'd done yesterday, as if it tasted sour on her tongue.

He glanced over his shoulder, but nobody was paying us the least attention, and besides, it was too loud in there for casual eavesdropping. "How did you hear about my being missing?"

"Not every day Goldilocks Astorbilt descends from on high to ask after ol' Annie. Traipsed all over Five Points looking for me, I hear. Pity he didn't find me. I do so love gazing into those pretty blues."

"You were on the hunt, I take it?"

"If you could call it that. Rat trapping, more like."

"And did you find your quarry?"

"The Bloodhound always finds her quarry, love." Annie flashed a rotten-toothed smile.

"Yes, well, that's what brings us here. I've a job for you, if you're willing."

Annie considered him with a shrewd eye. "Fee's gone up."

"How surprising."

"Sure you can afford it, Pinkerton?"

"You needn't concern yourself with that. Will you come or not?"

"What, now?"

"Immediately. The crime scene is still fresh, but with the police plying their trade as we speak . . ."

Annie made a face. "Coppers'll stink up the whole joint."

"Something like that. We'll wait for you outside, shall we?" He was so eager to be gone from the place that he didn't even wait for her answer, herding me toward the door with a meaningful look.

"That woman is a bounty hunter?" I asked incredulously as we climbed the steps to the sidewalk.

"The best on the eastern seaboard," Mr. Wiltshire said. "Difficult to credit, I know, but Miss Harris is possessed of a particularly potent brand of luck."

"Luck? *Her?*"

"Yes, indeed. She can track a man as easily as a hound tracks a fox—hence her *nom de guerre*. All she needs is a scent. That"—his mouth twisted sourly—"and a great deal of money."

"A scent. In New York."

"It's a wonder, isn't it? Like trying to isolate the sound of a single voice amid a screaming rabble, and yet she manages it. It helps, I think, that she perceives smells as much visually as in the traditional sense."

I tried to imagine what that would be like, but it was quite a stretch. "If her skills are worth so much, what's she doing in there?"

"Heaven knows. With what she charges, she ought to be lounging in the lobby of the Park Avenue Hotel sipping something aged in a barrel."

"She's drinking from barrels, all right—straight from the hose."

"She does enjoy the bottle. Not to mention expensive cigars, games of chance, and a dozen more dangerous vices. But she gets the job done—when you can find her. As often as not, she's passed out in an alley somewhere. Such a waste of her talent." He started to say more, but a shrill voice in the distance caught his attention. "Did you hear that?"

"What, the newsie?" I glanced up the block, where a boy of about ten had just stationed himself with a stack of afternoon papers.

"*Harlem's House of Hauntings! Read the terrifying tale, straight from the coppers themselves!*"

Mr. Wiltshire was striding up the street before the boy had even finished the headline, and by the time he returned with the paper, his mouth was set in a grim line. "Listen to this. *At least three boarders confirm having seen the specters. These persons are not as a rule superstitious, yet each recounts his own blood-curdling tale of visitations in the dark of night.*" Frowning, he added, "It looks as though this isn't the first story they've printed on the subject, either. One wonders how many others I missed while I was being held at the gasworks."

"Is that unusual? Ghost stories in the newspapers, I mean?"

"With such frequency, yes. There's been a rash of them recently, even in the more reputable papers."

"What does it mean?"

He glanced away. "Hopefully we'll learn more when we consult the medium tonight," he said evasively.

Apparently, he'd decided to take a page from Jonathan Burrows's book. "If your being slippery is supposed to spare me worry, you should know it's doing just the opposite."

In reply, he inclined his head subtly; the Bloodhound stood at the bottom of the steps, looking even more frightful by daylight than she had by lamplight. "This your carriage, Pink?"

As though there were likely to be another such conveyance parked outside One-Eyed Johnny's.

"Hurry up, then," she said, hoisting herself into the brougham. "I got a schedule to keep."

The ride uptown was about as comfortable as you'd expect. The brougham is a carriage built for two elegant persons, and perhaps a lapdog. We were two people and a very large Bloodhound in dire need of a bath. Mr. Wiltshire and I rode with our knees tucked into opposite corners of the carriage, Annie wedged between us like a burr. We gave her as much space as the seat allowed, but it wasn't nearly enough—especially when she fell asleep, leaving us to suffer the exhaust from her gaping mouth. When we finally reached the Crowe residence, I flung myself from the carriage with such enthusiasm that I must have seemed distastefully eager to the pair of uniformed coppers flanking the door.

Then again, maybe they took one look at Annie and understood. I wondered how Mr. Wiltshire intended to explain her presence—or for that matter, our own—but he was spared the trouble, for no sooner had he descended from the carriage than the front door opened to reveal the familiar figure of Sergeant Chapman.

"Miss Gallagher. What brings you here?" Then he noticed my companions, and his eyes narrowed. "Well, well. Thomas Wiltshire, I presume? Just the man I was looking for."

"I fully intend to give you a statement, Sergeant," Mr. Wiltshire said, "but I'm afraid now isn't a good time."

Chapman leaned against the doorframe, putting himself directly in our path. "Your convenience ain't really my top priority. And if you're looking to get inside, you'll need my say-so." He lifted his eyebrows, as if to say, *Your move.*

"I've been engaged by the family," Mr. Wiltshire said.

"So I hear. Only I couldn't find any record of Locke, Banneker & Associates with the paper pushers downtown. Small practice, is it?"

Mr. Wiltshire's mouth tightened. He drummed his fingers against the griffin head of his walking stick, eying the two uniformed police officers unhappily. "Inside, perhaps?"

Chapman stood aside and motioned us in.

"I suggest we speak in the parlor," Mr. Wiltshire said. "In the meantime, would you mind terribly if my colleague took a look around?" He gestured at Annie.

Chapman scanned the Bloodhound with an unreadable expression. "Long as she don't touch nothing."

"That should be fine," Mr. Wiltshire said. As for Annie, she just rolled her eyes and wandered off.

"So," Chapman said when the three of us were alone. "Pinkerton, I'm guessing."

Mr. Wiltshire sighed. "Perhaps I ought to just have it printed on my card."

"Thought you was the family attorney at first, but he's in the other room, so . . ." Chapman shrugged. "Not much of a stretch from there. Why the secrecy, anyway?"

"It's a long story, and as you know time is of the essence in these cases. That's why I kept things brief with your colleagues this morning."

"That's putting it mildly. Gave 'em about two words, is what I heard."

"I gave them what I had, which is regrettably little. Hopefully, my colleague will be able to gather something more useful."

"Your colleague." Chapman threw a skeptical glance down the hallway where Annie had retreated. "And what about Miss Gallagher here? How does she come into it?"

"Miss Gallagher is assisting me in my investigation." He didn't elaborate.

Chapman sucked at a tooth, his customary cool giving way to irritation. "Let me explain something here. I'm fully within my rights to bring you in to the station, both of you. So why don't you save us all some trouble and stop giving me the stone wall?"

"What exactly is it that you think I'm not telling you, Sergeant?"

"Let's start with the gasworks. Ward and O'Leary headed down there this morning, on your say-so. What're they gonna find?"

"Very little, I should think. If the men who took me captive have any sense at all, they'll have cleared out the moment Miss Gallagher and I escaped."

"They the ones who did this?" He cocked his head over his shoulder, indicating the crime scene.

"I wish I knew."

Chapman's watery eyes narrowed, and a vein stood out in his forehead, like the fuse on a stick of dynamite.

I figured I'd better step in. "Excuse me, Mr. Wiltshire, may I have a word?" Drawing him aside, I said, "I think we should trust him."

"With what? We have nothing solid."

"But you have a theory."

"To the extent that I do, it's not the sort of thing a police detective is likely to credit."

"He believes in ghosts, doesn't he?"

"So you've said, but . . ."

"Do you trust me?"

He sighed. "It's not a question of—"

"Please, just . . . Do you trust my judgment?"

Pale eyes scanned mine. "I trust your judgment," he said, if a little warily.

"Then follow my lead." Without waiting for a reply, I walked back to Sergeant Chapman. "So it's like this: When Frederick Crowe hired Mr. Wiltshire to look into his brother's murder, he said he thought Jacob had been killed by a shade. That's like a ghost."

"I see." Chapman's gaze flicked to Mr. Wiltshire, as if measuring his reaction to this talk of ghosts. "So when the Arbridge kid gives his story to the papers, you figure maybe there's a connection."

"That's right," Mr. Wiltshire said cautiously.

"And?"

"He may have exaggerated some of the details, but I believe his story to be genuine."

"I got the same impression when I spoke to him this morning," Chapman said.

Mr. Wiltshire seemed to relax a little at that. I wondered if this was the first time he'd met a copper who believed in ghosts. "Even so, I ruled out any direct connection between the incidents. There was nothing paranormal about Mr. Crowe's death—either of them."

"That so?"

"Indeed. For one thing—"

"Uh-uh." Sergeant Chapman crooked his finger. "Show me."

"What, the coroner hasn't arrived yet? Good Lord." Mr. Wiltshire drew out his watch, mildly appalled.

"Busy day." Chapman escorted us from the parlor to the third floor, where we found the Bloodhound poking around outside Frederick Crowe's bedroom. "You should wait out here," the detective told me in his grandfatherly growl. "Not a pleasant sight."

I hadn't come this far to swoon at the sight of a corpse. "I can manage, thank you. I've seen dead bodies before." Drunks and lungers, mostly, but still.

"Your call." Chapman stood aside.

Actually, the sight wasn't all that bad, considering, except that the poor fellow on the floor was certainly dead. He could almost have passed for sleeping were it not for the mottling of his skin where it met the carpet.

"Who pulled the sheet off his face?" Scowling, Chapman leaned out into the hallway. "Thought I told you not to touch nothing?" I didn't catch the Bloodhound's reply, but its brevity suggested it wasn't all that polite.

"So." Mr. Wiltshire approached the body. "Rigor had already set in by the time I arrived, which was shortly before nine o'clock. No marks on the body."

"Smothered, I figure," Chapman said.

"I concur, though the killer has gone to some trouble to make it look as if a shade were involved. For my benefit, presumably, though frankly I'm offended if they thought I'd been taken in by it."

"How do you make it look like . . ." I stopped myself halfway through the question, my gaze falling on a bit of broken glass. Stepping around the bed, I found the remnants of a mirror lying on the floor, just a short reach from Frederick Crowe's outstretched hand.

"Care to explain that?" Chapman wasn't asking me, but I answered all the same.

"To see the shade," I said, squatting. "The killer was trying to make it look like Mr. Crowe grabbed the mirror when he realized a spirit was in the room."

"Shades can't be seen with the naked eye," Mr. Wiltshire explained, "not without aid of a mirror, moonlight, or flame. Crowe would have known that."

"But it's obviously been staged," I said.

Chapman arched an eyebrow. "Because?"

I could feel Mr. Wiltshire's eyes on me. He didn't interject, waiting to hear my answer.

All right, Rose. Here's your chance. Clearing my throat, I said, "He was obviously sleeping when the attack happened. If it wanted to, the shade could have killed him before he even got out of bed." An icy throb in my chest cut me short, and for a fleeting moment I felt it all over again: bone-piercing cold, sinking its roots into me, bristling along my veins in tiny webs of frost . . . I'd barely managed to tear myself free of the bloody woman's grasp, and I'd been awake and alert, with a shade who hadn't really been trying to hurt me. "Even supposing he woke up in time, why didn't he run? Or if he just had to get a glimpse of the shade, why not use those, when they were so much closer to hand?" I pointed at the bedside table, where a box of matches sat beside a lamp.

Mr. Wiltshire smiled down at his shoes and gave a little shake of his head. "Well done, Miss Gallagher. I'd missed that entirely."

"Then how did you—"

He raised his left hand and wriggled his fingers. "Because, like me, Freddie Crowe was left-handed." He gestured at the mirror on the floor, which lay within easy reach—of Crowe's *right* hand. "So you see, Sergeant, it's a fabrication, and not a terribly convincing one. Admittedly, it's difficult to simulate death by freezing, but even so this is a poor effort."

"Freezing, huh?" Chapman sucked on a tooth. "Well, ain't that just goddamn great."

Mr. Wiltshire and I exchanged a look. "What's the matter?" I asked.

"Just seems like a hell of a coincidence how many folks we got freezing to death these last few weeks. That's why the coroner's not here yet—three bodies this morning alone. Two of 'em indigents, but the third . . . just an ordinary fella. No reason he should be turning up frozen, 'specially indoors."

Mr. Wiltshire paled. "I had no idea. There's nothing in the papers."

"A line here and there, maybe, when it's somebody well-to-do, but the papers ain't much interested in that sort of thing. Same goes for the ghost stories. They cover one now and again, but even then it's a drop in the bucket compared to what we been seeing down at the precinct lately. Hardly a day goes by we don't get some hysterical report or another. Most of the fellas laugh it off, but a few of us . . . well, we ain't laughing."

"There was a story just this afternoon in the *World*," Mr. Wiltshire said. "Did you see it?"

Chapman shook his head. "But you can be sure that for every story you find in the papers, there's ten you don't. Folks tend to keep that sorta thing to themselves."

"It's even worse than I thought," Mr. Wiltshire said, half to himself. "So many deaths . . . There must be dozens of shades on the loose, perhaps more."

A grim silence settled over Frederick Crowe's bedroom.

"Got any idea what could cause something like that?" Chapman asked.

"Perhaps, but the more important question is, what can be done to stop it? There, I'm afraid I have no idea. I'll have to consult with my associates."

Chapman didn't look very reassured. "Anything I can do?"

"You can keep looking into Frederick Crowe's murder. It's connected somehow, I'm sure of it."

As if on cue, the Bloodhound appeared in the doorway. "Got a scent," she declared. "Gonna be tough to track, though."

Mr. Wiltshire frowned. "Why is that?"

"Scent's good and masked. His clothes reek of half a dozen stronger things."

"I thought scents appeared to you as colors."

"Just 'cause I can see 'em don't make it easy to tell 'em apart. Like pouring a bunch of different paints into the same bucket: Eventually you just get shit brown. I still got a scent, like I said, but it's soaked in cheap cigars and rotten coal gas."

My hand flew to my mouth.

"Gas, is it?" Chapman grunted. "Speaking of unlikely coin-cidences."

"Ain't no coincidence," Annie said. "Pink here's got the same smell on him. Fainter, on account of him washing up, but it's still there."

Chapman narrowed one eye. "Well, now, maybe we're get-ting somewhere, assuming you're right. Which, by the way, how do you . . ." He held up his hands. "No, you know what? I don't wanna know."

I was barely listening to the exchange. Something had just occurred to me, a thought worrying enough to push everything else aside. "Pietro. Oh, no . . ."

"Your mother's boarder?" Mr. Wiltshire frowned. "What's he got to do with this?"

"I sent him to ask after the Irishman. Oh, God . . ."

"Take it easy, Miss Gallagher," Sergeant Chapman said, his voice extra grandfatherly now. "Where did you send him?"

"Augusto's."

The Bloodhound snorted at that. "Bad idea."

"Yes, *thank you*," I snapped, only too happy to have a target for my distress—not that Annie cared a whit. She just sneered at me, showing a single brown tooth.

"The Italian grocer?" Mr. Wiltshire's frown deepened—and then it cleared. "I see. You thought perhaps he might be able to find out who hired the thugs at the gasworks. Clever." Sighing, he added, "And dangerous."

Stupid, Rose. How could you be so stupid? "I've got to stop him."

Shoving my way past a startled Annie, I ran for the door.

CHAPTER 20

ON THE SIDE OF
CAUTION—AUGUSTO'S—TRUE FEAR

I was halfway down the block by the time the carriage caught up with me. "Get in," Mr. Wiltshire said. "We'll go together."

I didn't slow down, hustling toward the train station with my dress hitched up around my calves. "You don't have time. The Bloodhound—"

"—can manage on her own quite admirably, as can Sergeant Chapman."

"What about what you said in there, about dozens of shades . . ." I stopped myself short, throwing a furtive look at the coachman. "If things are as bad as you say, don't you think you ought to be focusing on that?"

"And I shall." Lowering his voice, he added, "Please, Rose, this is terribly undignified."

Belatedly, I realized what we must look like—me hurrying down the sidewalk with my dress hitched up, Mr. Wiltshire leaning out of a moving carriage, hand extended in supplication. Quite a scene for the Fifth Avenue set. On top of which, here I was running away from the very man I'd spent the past week obsessively pursuing. The irony would have been laughable under other circumstances.

But he was still *Thomas Wiltshire*, so when he said my name again, followed by a gentle "Please," I was powerless to deny him; I took his hand and stepped up into the carriage, furious at the way my whole body thrilled at his touch. How strong could my anxiety for Pietro really be if it was so easily pushed aside, even if only for a moment?

"Why did you run away like that?" Mr. Wiltshire regarded me with a mixture of irritation and concern.

How could I explain it to him? "This is my mistake. I need to be the one to fix it. If anything were to happen to Pietro because of me . . ."

"Try not to worry unduly. Perhaps he hasn't yet acted on your request. And even if he has, I'm sure he understands the risks. He's a neighborhood fellow, isn't he? In my experience, Five Pointers know how to take care of themselves. Present company included."

I wasn't in the mood to be coddled, even by him. "You didn't sound so confident of that earlier, when you were trying to persuade me to stay out of all this."

Something dark passed through his eyes, and he looked away. "Yes, well. The protective instinct is an unreliable thing, isn't it? It doesn't always present itself at the right moment, in the right measure. Perhaps you think me overcautious, but that hasn't always been the case." Softly, he added, "To my lasting grief."

For a moment, I didn't understand. And then I did, and I wanted to kick myself. "You lost someone."

"It was a long time ago," he said, gazing out the window. "But it will be with me to the end of my days, so I trust you'll understand if I prefer to err on the side of caution."

So much fell into place then, and for the first time I knew what it was to experience someone else's pain as your own. I wanted to go to him—to slide down the seat and take his hand, even just touch his shoulder—but I was afraid it would be an intrusion. So I stayed where I was, staring at my lap and hating myself. "I'm sorry," I said. "And I do understand. That's why I have to find Pietro before he puts himself in danger."

"Of course, but that doesn't mean you have to do it alone."

"I just thought, with everything that's going on—"

"But it's all of a piece, isn't it? The men at the gasworks, the murder, the cipher manuscripts . . . As for the outbreak of shades, there is little I can do until I've had a chance to consult Wang's people, not to mention the shade we saw last night. She could prove to be the key to all this."

As always, the mention of the bloody woman sent a throb of cold through my breast. Suppressing a shudder, I said, "How's that?"

"If I'm right, and there is a portal to the otherworld somewhere nearby, the seal has obviously been compromised. Which means the dead are escaping from their domain into ours."

"*God in Heaven.*" For a moment I just sat there, my body rocking limply with the rhythm of the carriage, too stunned even to summon a proper prayer. To my Catholic ears, it sounded disturbingly close to the Book of Revelation. I tried to push that thought aside, reasoning that if we were truly facing the End Times, Mr. Wiltshire would look a little more perturbed.

"Some of the dead, at any rate," he went on. "For now, the phenomenon appears to be confined to shades from the local area, which suggests that they dwell nearest the breach. Hovering in the lobby of the otherworld, if you will."

"How . . . how many are we talking about?"

He shook his head. "No way of knowing. And unless the situation is contained, it could well spread."

"So how do we contain it?" My voice betrayed only a slight tremor. There's a limit, I think, to how much shock a person can experience in twenty-four hours, and I'd reached it. The rest would have to be stored away for later.

"I wish I knew," Mr. Wiltshire said. "This is quite beyond my experience. Hopefully, our friend from last night will be able to tell us more."

The bloody woman. She was no friend of mine. Just the thought of her sent another stab of ice between my ribs.

"But she will only appear after sunset, so there's nothing to be done until then." Checking his watch, he said, "Twenty past three. That gives us a little over an hour. We ought to be able to find Pietro by then."

"We might already be too late. It's like Sergeant Chapman said: Anybody willing to murder a pair of high society brothers won't think twice about hurting somebody like Pietro. If the men from the gasworks hear he's been asking questions . . ."

"Don't do this to yourself," Mr. Wiltshire said gently. "You had no way of knowing the men at the gasworks were murderers."

Maybe not, but I'd known they were dangerous. I'd just been too selfish, too reckless, to let that stop me. I'd put my friend in danger—a friend who just happened to live with my mother.

It will be with me to the end of my days, Mr. Wiltshire had said.

I prayed I wasn't about to learn firsthand what that felt like.

"You're sure he'll be here?" Mr. Wiltshire asked, eying the red-and-green awning of Augusto's.

"Unless he's working. Saturdays can go either way with him." I tried to peer around the lettering on the window, but it was a waste of time; I couldn't see much of anything. If I wanted to find Pietro, I'd have to go inside. "No point in both of us going. That would only draw attention."

"Then perhaps I ought to be the one to—"

"This is my mess, Mr. Wiltshire. I need to clean it up." I like to think I'd have felt that way even if I wasn't so eager to prove myself. As it was, I wanted Mr. Wiltshire to know that I was the sort of person who took care of her own problems.

"As you wish," he said, though he didn't look happy about it. "Shall we meet at Wang's?"

"Give me ten minutes," I said, and began to squeeze my way through the usual crowd of loafers under the awning.

An even bigger crowd awaited me inside, women of all ages jostling and chatting amiably as they stocked up for dinner. Augusto's wasn't a specialist like Luigi's or the *salumeria* up the block, but he boasted the cheapest olive oil on Mulberry Street, as well as an assortment of cheeses from his native Bologna that apparently couldn't be had anywhere else in New York. I got this from Pietro, of course, who never tired of banging on about the superiority of Italian cuisine. Even so, I had a strong suspicion that the lion's share of Augusto's profits were not dairy based.

A heady fragrance of garlic accompanied me to the back, where, to my great relief, I immediately spied Pietro among the collection of young men drinking and laughing at the counter. His eyes widened when he saw me, and he moved quickly to intercept me. "Fiora, what are you doing here? Is your mama all right?"

"I haven't seen her since this morning, but I think so." Throwing a quick look around, I lowered my voice. "We need to talk. Someplace private."

"There is no place private in here, that's for sure."

"Back at the flat, then? Just for a moment."

"What's going on?"

"Not here," I said, putting a hand on his arm. "Please?"

"Pietro," called a deep voice, "*Chi è questa bella signorina?*"

Pietro's glance went over my shoulder, and his smile grew strained. "Augusto. This is my landlady's daughter, Rose." His brown eyes shifted back to me, and they held a clear message: *Careful.*

Summoning my most charming smile, I turned.

I'm not sure what I expected to find, but the short, stocky man standing behind me wasn't it. Jovial and leathery, with wild salt-and-pepper eyebrows that seemed to be searching for a means of escape, he looked like somebody's eccentric uncle. "Augusto, I've heard so much about you."

"Have you?" The wild eyebrows climbed a fraction. "Good things, I hope?"

"Why, I can hardly drag Pietro away from here, he loves it so much."

"Why drag him at all? Join us! We have the best wines in New York, direct from Italy. I will open a bottle just for you. A nice Chianti, *sì?*"

"What a lovely offer," I said, grinning for all I was worth. "But I'll have to take you up on it another time. I need Pietro to come home with me for a moment, if you all can spare him."

I probably should have chosen my words more carefully. A burst of laughter went up from the counter, followed by a series of jibes that you didn't need to speak Italian to get the gist of. I didn't mind so much for myself—there's nothing quite like an outbreak of deadly spirits wandering the streets to put things in perspective—but poor Pietro flushed to the tops of his ears. He shot something irritable over his shoulder, but that only earned him another round of ridicule.

Augusto, though, wasn't laughing; he was too busy staring at the stitches on the side of my forehead. "What happened to you?"

"Oh, it's nothing. Just a little accident."

"An accident." He cocked his head, one eye narrowed shrewdly. "This does not by chance have something to do with what Pietro asked me this morning? About some Irishmen?"

My heart fluttered uneasily, but I forced myself not to look at Pietro. "I'm sorry, I don't know what you mean."

He didn't buy that for a moment. "These are delicate questions. I ask myself, why does young Pietro want to know about these things? Maybe he has a grudge, *sì*? Now I think maybe I understand." Dark eyes shifted to Pietro, and he said something in Italian. Pietro didn't answer, but his uneasy expression said plenty.

The conversation was slipping out of control. I'd just pulled up in Mr. Wiltshire's hired brougham, an awfully conspicuous means of getting around in Five Points. It wouldn't take much for Augusto to start putting the pieces together, and that could be very bad for Pietro. I needed to throw him off the scent, fast.

I brought a hand to my temple, leaving it there long enough for everyone to see how it trembled. "They came out of nowhere," I said in a quavering whisper. "I thought they were going to . . ." Swallowing, I finished, "It could have been worse."

Augusto's eyes hardened. All of a sudden, he didn't look so harmless. "Where? In the street?"

"In the gashouse district." Then, borrowing a little flourish from Mr. Burrows: "In broad daylight, if you can imagine. One of them had a pistol, and he . . ." I paused to let a few tears brim in my eyes. It wasn't hard to do. After everything I'd been through over the past twenty-four hours, it was a miracle I'd only broken down once already.

Augusto scowled, and the young men at the counter exchanged dark glances. *There,* I thought. Now Pietro had a good reason for asking after a bunch of Irish roughs. Even so, if word got around that he had a grudge against them, no matter the reason, he could still be in trouble. I needed to make it clear that *I* was the one looking for them.

"I asked for Pietro's help because . . ." *Think, Rose . . .* "Because they stole my granny's brooch, and . . ." Suddenly I was weeping openly, stammering out the lie between gulps of air. "It's the only pretty thing I ever had. My mam brought it all the way from Sligo. Even through the famine, the family never parted with it, and . . ." I buried my face in my hands, sobbing now.

It wasn't just an act. Though the story was pure hocus-pocus, the feelings were all too real. The events of the past week had left me more fragile than I'd realized. I'd been keeping a tight rein on my emotions, but now that I'd loosened my grip, I was in danger of losing it entirely.

"Don't cry, Fiora." Pietro put his arms around me, and as he gathered me close, he whispered, "What are you doing?"

Augusto made an imperious gesture, and a moment later somebody pressed a glass of something into my hands. I tossed it back without even looking at it, wincing as it blazed a trail down my throat. "I'm sorry," I said, composing myself with a genuine effort. "I didn't mean to fall apart like that."

The aging *padrone* considered me with a thoughtful look. "I tell you what. I look into this for you, quietly."

"Oh, I don't want any trouble. I should never have asked Pietro to bring it up. I was just so upset."

"It's all right, *signorina*. No trouble."

"Are you sure?" I dabbed at my eyes with a handkerchief. "These are dangerous men, and I would hate for it to come back on Pietro, or you."

"You don't worry about it. Augusto can take care of himself. And his people," he added, inclining his head at Pietro.

The relief in my expression was perfectly genuine.

Sensing an opening, Pietro put his arm around me again and said, "Come, Fiora, I take you home."

"*Sì*, take her home," Augusto said. "Get some rest, *signorina*."

"Thank you so much, Augusto." I let myself be led out of the store.

"*Porca Madonna*," Pietro blurted when we reached the sidewalk. "What was *that*? Are you planning to join the theater?"

"Honestly, I'm not even sure where that came from."

He shook his head, rubbing his bare hands in the chill. "Do me a favor, Fiora. Next time you need me, send a boy inside."

"I'm sorry. I suppose I made quite a scene."

"It's not that. I don't want you anywhere near Augusto. I told you, he's dangerous." He started to say more, but just then we rounded the corner onto Mott Street, and he drew up short. "What is *he* doing here?"

Mr. Wiltshire loitered outside Wang's General Store, head bowed, tapping his walking stick absently. He was so deep in thought that he didn't even look up at the sound of his name; I had to touch his arm to get his attention. "Ah, good," he said, "you've found Pietro. All is well, I trust?"

"As well as can be," Pietro said coldly, "considering you keep putting Rose in danger."

I frowned. "Pietro, please, that's unfair."

"Not entirely," Mr. Wiltshire said. "I had my misgivings about leaving you alone in that place."

"But you did it anyway," Pietro said. "I guess that's what you call being a gentleman, eh?"

Heat flashed to my cheeks. "*That's enough.* You're being terribly rude, and not only to Mr. Wiltshire. I'm not a child."

"No, you're not a child. And what you did in there"—Pietro gestured back at the Italian grocery—"was not a game. If Augusto finds out you lied to him, we are both of us in a lot of trouble."

"I said those things to protect you. I should never have asked you to get involved, but now that you are, I needed to say something that would take the focus off you and put it back on me where it belongs."

"Trust me, you don't want the focus of a man like Augusto."

Mr. Wiltshire sighed. "What's done is done. All we can do now is wait to see what it brings."

"We?" Pietro snorted but otherwise left that alone. "It's freezing out here, Fiora. We should go."

"Er, there's something I need to take care of first. I'll meet you later?"

"Ah, *sì, va bene*," he said caustically. With a final cold glance at Mr. Wiltshire, he headed up the street.

"I'm sorry about that," I said when Pietro was out of earshot. "I don't know what's got into him."

"Don't worry, I quite understand. It's natural for a young man to be protective of his sweetheart."

"*S-sweetheart?*" I blushed all over again. "I'm not . . . He's not . . . It isn't like that between us."

"Oh? My mistake. It seemed as if . . . Well, he obviously cares for you a great deal."

"Maybe, but not in *that* way."

"It's none of my affair. Please forgive me for bringing it up."

I could tell he didn't believe me, and that got under my skin. "I promise you he doesn't. I would have noticed."

Mr. Wiltshire smiled at that. "Even the best detective can be woefully blind about such things."

"Oh, really, do you think so?" I scowled and looked away. "Are we going inside or not?" It really was freezing out here, even under my heavy wool overcoat.

"In a moment. I'd like to hear about what happened at Augusto's, if you don't mind."

"Well, I doubt Mam would be proud. I danced for the king and demanded the head of John the Baptist on a silver platter."

Mr. Wiltshire didn't know quite what to make of that. "You, er . . . seduced him?"

"The next best thing. I cried." Sighing, I added, "It was all I could come up with on the spur of the moment. Augusto noticed my stitches and made the connection straightaway. He could easily have traced it back to you, and that would have been very bad for Pietro. So I did my best to distract him."

"By appealing to his chivalry."

"That's one word for it. I don't much fancy playing the damsel in distress, but at least it worked. Pietro's safely in the background now. On top of which, Augusto offered to look into it, so we may get our information after all."

"You did the right thing. Not every disguise we adopt can be entirely to our liking."

That made me feel a little better. "I wonder if Augusto will come up with anything."

"It certainly helps to have a second iron in the fire. I have no doubt Miss Harris will track down the Irishman eventually, but it's his employer we really want, and that could be more difficult. Augusto may prove to be a valuable resource. You really have done very well, Rose."

Muttering a shy thanks, I glanced up at the sinking sun. "What time is it? I guess we'd better—" The words were cut off in a mangled cry. A stab of cold doubled me over, seizing every muscle in my body.

"Rose!" Mr. Wiltshire caught me as I buckled. "Are you all right?"

Another stab, as if an icicle had been driven between my ribs. I gasped, filling my lungs with just enough air to say, "*Shade.*"

"Impossible." He clamped my face between his hands, scanning my pupils urgently. "It's not yet sunset, a shade couldn't . . . No." A look of pure horror came into his eyes. "*No, no, no . . .*" Sweeping me up into his arms, he reeled back and kicked open the door of the Chinese grocery. "*Wang!*"

There was a great commotion around me, people dashing

about and shouting in at least three languages. I barely registered any of it, writhing in a futile attempt to dislodge the phantom blade of ice in my chest.

"Be still," Mr. Wiltshire whispered, clutching me against him. "I know it hurts, but you must be still, or you could drive the fragment deeper."

"*It burns.*"

"I know." Then, in that same broken whisper: "I'm sorry. Oh, Rose, I'm so sorry . . ."

And for the first time in my life, I knew true fear.

CHAPTER 21

FRAGMENTS OF THE DEAD—THE MAN
FROM CHICAGO—A RARE MEDIUM

She will be awake soon."

A familiar voice, though for a moment I couldn't place it. I tried to raise my head, even just open my eyes, but the effort was too much. I felt as if I were suspended in that moment between sleep and waking, when your mind is slowly becoming alert but your body refuses to budge.

"You should drink this." Mei Wang, speaking gently to someone nearby.

"Thank you, but no." The low murmur of Mr. Wiltshire's voice sounded from just below my head. That, and the prickle of straw beneath me, told me that I was lying on some kind of cot. How much time had passed? I didn't even remember blacking out.

"Shall I get you a chair? The floor is not clean."

"I'm fine, thank you."

"Sir—"

"You're very kind, Miss Wang, but truly, you needn't fuss over me."

A sigh, followed by the sound of Mei's slippered feet retreating. Then silence. It was so quiet that I could hear Mr. Wiltshire's watch ticking softly. I tried again to stir, but my body still refused to obey.

At length, another set of footsteps entered the room, and someone asked a question in Chinese. "No, thank you," Mr. Wiltshire said. "Your daughter already offered. I'm afraid I couldn't stomach it just now." Then, very quietly, "You saved her life, Wang. I'm eternally grateful."

Mr. Wang said something in reply.

"I don't know." Mr. Wiltshire's voice sounded strangely muffled, as if his head were bowed. "God help me, I've no idea."

Mr. Wang answered in Chinese. Back and forth they went, and though only one side of the conversation was in English, I followed it well enough.

"Of course it's my fault. She wouldn't be caught up in any of this if it weren't for me . . . Yes, but for how long? A day or two, perhaps three if she's lucky. I've wired Chicago, but even if Jackson takes the first train out, he'll never get here in time . . . No, I don't think she'd thank us for that. If anyone's to inform her mother, it should be Miss Gallagher herself. Or me, if she's unable . . . It's not only that, Wang. My every instinct warned me not to involve her, and yet I did it anyway."

Mei's voice interrupted them, murmuring something to her father. "He's asking for you, Mr. Wiltshire," she added in English.

He hesitated. "I should be here when she wakes. She'll be frightened and confused."

"I will stay with her. We know each other."

"I'm not sure if—"

"I will take care of her, I promise."

Mr. Wiltshire sighed. "Very well. I'll be back as soon as I can. If she wakes, tell her . . ." Another sigh. "Tell her whatever you think best."

Time passed. I managed to wiggle my toes, and then my fingers, but Mei didn't notice. She sang softly to herself in Chinese, a sad, beautiful melody that sent my thoughts abroad to a tiny village framed by mist-cloaked green mountains, where a young girl sang of lost love.

Eventually, I managed to pry my eyelids apart. Seeing me stir, Mei leaned in close. "Rose, it's Mei. You are in my father's store. Can you understand?"

At first, all I could manage was "*Mmm*." It felt like my vocal cords were lashed together, my tongue glued to the roof of my mouth. But as the minutes passed, my throat seemed to clear, and my head, too. "Why can't I sit up?"

"My father gave you special tea to keep you from moving. It's wearing off now. You will sit up in a moment. Don't rush."

I took her advice, lying back and letting my thoughts order themselves. Awareness was creeping back in, but that came at a price; as the fog receded, fear took its place, clear and hard-edged as a blade of ice. "I could hear you talking."

Mei smiled—the sad, indulgent sort of smile you bestow on a sick person. "You speak Chinese?"

"Mr. Wiltshire does."

"Some."

"He seemed to understand it well enough. And I understood him." Swallowing, I said, "Mei, am I going to die?"

She glanced away. "Mr. Wiltshire is very upset. He said some things maybe he should not."

"Please tell me the truth. I need to know."

There was a long pause. Mei continued to avoid my eye. "You are very sick. Most people with this sickness . . . do not survive."

"What sickness? What's wrong with me?"

"It's better if Mr. Wiltshire explains. My English . . ."

"It's the shade, isn't it? The one who touched me?"

Mei's head drooped. She nodded.

"*Jesus.*" I didn't think even Mam would judge me for taking His name in vain under the circumstances.

Mam . . . Who would take care of her now?

Tears pricked behind my eyes, but I squeezed them shut. If I let myself go now I might never recover, and I would be damned if I spent my last hours in this world wailing and gnashing my teeth. Besides, I thought I'd heard a word of hope, however faint. "Mr. Wiltshire said something about Chicago. That's where the Pinkerton Detective Agency is based, isn't it?"

"He sent a telegram. There is a man there, he says, maybe he can help you. That is all I know."

With Mei's help, I managed to sit up and prop my back against the wall. From the look of things, we were somewhere among the warren of Mr. Wang's back rooms, the hidden reaches of which I'd only guessed at before. Muffled voices and the creak of floorboards reached us through the walls, and a sweet floral scent drifted down the hall, suggesting we weren't the building's only occupants.

"Fan tan today," Mei said apologetically. "Noisy sometimes."

"How long was I out?"

"Not long. Half hour, maybe."

"Mr. Wiltshire says your father saved my life. What did he do?"

"He gave you medicine."

"Let me guess. Special tea."

Mei smiled at that, something closer to the real thing this time. "My father has many special teas."

I was beginning to understand that, and a lot else besides. "Mei, what is this place? Not just a store, obviously."

She sighed. "I'm sorry I could not tell you before. My father keeps his business—"

"Very private, I know. You said so in your letter. Thank you for that, by the way. I don't know that I'd have found Mr. Wiltshire without it."

"Something of a mixed blessing, I'd say." I looked up to find Mr. Wiltshire hovering in the doorway, his posture as grim and stiff as if he stood before St. Peter himself, awaiting judgment.

The remark would have made me angry if I'd had the energy. As it was, it just hurt. "If you think saying something like that is going to make me feel better, you couldn't be more wrong."

"Forgive me, you're right of course. Miss Wang, would you mind terribly if I spoke to Miss Gallagher alone?"

Mei looked to me; when I nodded, she gave my hand a squeeze and left.

"May I sit?"

"On a chair, or would you prefer the floor?"

"Ah." He glanced away awkwardly. "You've been awake for some time, obviously. How long?"

"I'm not sure. The first thing I remember is Mei offering you tea." Sensing what was coming, I added, "And the last thing I remember before that is you apologizing, so please, let's not cover that ground again. I'd rather focus on what happens now."

He closed his eyes fleetingly, overcome. With what emotion, I couldn't tell. His fingers twitched at his sides, as though he were battling some raw impulse. "As to that, I hardly know what to tell you. I will of course do everything I can, but your situation is beyond my power to resolve. I've wired my superiors in Chicago. I'm hopeful they'll send someone who can help."

"But it will take him at least two days to get here, and you're afraid I don't have that kind of time."

He forced himself to meet my eye. "The fact is, I don't know. But yes—that is my fear."

A wave of dizziness came over me. I gripped the edge of the cot to steady myself.

"Rose—" He started toward me.

"Just give me a moment, please."

In the silence that followed, the muffled laughter of the fan tan players buffeted me like a cold wind, cruelly indifferent. *Show some respect*, I wanted to scream through the walls. *Don't you know I'm going to die?*

But no. I wasn't going to die, not just like that. There was still hope. "The man from Chicago—he's a doctor?"

"His name is Jackson, and he's a witch."

"A witch?" That set me back a step. "What exactly is wrong with me?" I kept my gaze trained on the floor. The smooth tenor of Mr. Wiltshire's voice was a comfort, but the haunted look in his eyes was not helping my composure one bit.

As though sensing this, he gave his answer in carefully measured tones. "You recall what I told you about shades being damaged? Their spirits retain some physical link to the mortal world, but it's extremely brittle. Like slate, or a thin layer of ice. The slightest stress can cause it to fracture."

"Stress . . ."

"Coming into contact with a physical object, for example. Or a living person. When the shade touched you, she left a fragment of herself behind. A very small one or you would already be . . ." He faltered. "Small enough that you exhibited none of the symptoms. Your pupils were returning to normal, and . . ." He trailed off again, and when I looked up, he was shaking his head. "Stop making excuses for yourself, Thomas. Better to say that if the signs were there, I missed them."

"What sorts of signs?"

"Nightmares. Shivers, or in severe cases, seizures. I've heard it described as a splinter of ice embedded in the flesh. It comes and goes, flaring if the shade is near. Sometimes the mere memory of the shade is enough to trigger it."

Nightmares. That was why he'd asked how I'd slept. And shivers . . . "I've felt them, I think. A shudder in my breast when we talked about the bloody woman. I thought it was just nerves. But what happened to me outside . . ."

"It was the shade. She was waiting for me outside the store, as I asked her to. The sun still hadn't set, so she was unable to manifest, but even so, her presence caused the fragment embedded in your flesh to resonate. It's buried somewhere deep inside you, slowly working its way toward your heart."

"My heart?" Instinctively, my hand went to my breast.

"The source of your life. The fragment is a piece of death, and like a magnet, it is inherently drawn to its polar opposite. It's making its way through your chest cavity even now, one millimeter at a time. That's why Wang immobilized you. We were afraid you'd drive the fragment deeper. When it flares, you see, it's like a hot knife, and . . . Well. I suppose it doesn't matter. Wang gave you a potion to settle the fragment, but it's no more than a balm over a bullet wound. Unless the bullet itself is removed . . ."

"How do we do that? Surgery?"

"If only it were that simple. The fragment is not a physical thing, strictly speaking, so it cannot be extracted by physical means. As far as I know, there are only two ways to remove it. The first is to destroy the shade. I've only encountered one person who could do that—years ago, in Japan. The second is to restore the fragment to the shade. That requires powerful magic."

"Hence your message to Chicago."

He nodded. "I believe Jackson can help us, but . . ." There was no point in finishing the thought. We both knew how it ended.

"If Mr. Wang can make a special tea that settles the fragment, maybe he can make one that slows it down even more. To buy us some time until Mr. Jackson gets here."

But of course it couldn't be that easy. "Wang is a talented apothecary, but the best he can do is keep the fragment from resonating. That will help prevent another acute episode, but the fragment will continue burrowing deeper until it reaches your heart."

"What about your walking stick? Ash banishes spirits, you said."

"If it were to come into direct contact with the fragment, perhaps, but . . ." He winced. "It's buried too deep, and merely touching your skin with it . . . I've no idea what that might do to you."

"I do," I said, realizing at last what had happened at Drake's. "You handed me your stick this morning, remember? It felt strange in my hands, like it was alive. And when my skin brushed against it . . ." I shuddered, but this time it really was nerves. "I wish I'd said something."

"So do I. We might have spared you a great deal of pain. Though as to the larger problem, it wouldn't have mattered. I'd have been as powerless then as I am now. The fragment has obviously made you sensitive to the spiritual properties of ash, but experimenting with that would probably do more harm than good, and would be extremely unpleasant besides."

"Still, it's hope." Slim, maybe, but that didn't mean it wasn't worth clinging to. After all, what was the alternative? Wallowing in despair wasn't going to get me anywhere, and as for prayer . . . well, the Lord helps those who help themselves, or so they say.

I slid down off the cot and was surprised to find myself steady—so much so that for a brief moment I wondered if Mr. Wiltshire might be mistaken and there was nothing wrong with me at all. "I feel fine."

"I'm glad to hear it," he said with a weak smile. "But I'm afraid you're not fine, Miss Gallagher."

Miss Gallagher. I knew it for a sign of respect, but it still felt cold and impersonal. "I liked it better when you called me Rose."

"That feels like a privilege I no longer deserve."

"To you, maybe. To me it feels like distance, and that's the last thing I want from you right now."

There was more in that remark than I'd intended—a lot more. Whether he registered it or not I couldn't say, but he gave me the best possible reply. "In that case, I think you'd better call me Thomas."

"Thomas." The name melted on my tongue. For two years it had been nigh-on sacred to me, spoken rarely and almost always privately. To say it now, with those pale eyes fixed on me . . . It was all I could do not to repeat it over and over, but I'm fairly sure even he couldn't have missed the subtext then.

Subtext or no, the intimacy of the moment wasn't lost on him, and he dared something even bolder, taking me by the shoulders and meeting my gaze steadily. "I'm in awe of your courage, Rose. If you can show such mettle, then I can do no less. We will find a way."

It was in that moment, I think, that I truly understood what it was to be in love. If I'd had any sense at all, the timing would have struck me as tragic, but I was young enough yet that the concept of my own mortality hadn't truly sunk in. Which meant I could savor the tiny flecks of green in Thomas Wiltshire's eyes, the warmth of his hands on my shoulders, and most of all, the lingering sweetness of his name on my tongue. To say it was a solace would be an understatement—but of course it ended all too soon. Mr. Wang came bustling in, taking us both by surprise. His dark eyes shifted between us, absorbing the scene, but his tone was all business.

"He's ready, then? Good." Mr. Wiltshire—*Thomas*—turned back to me and gave my shoulders another squeeze. "I'll be back as soon as we're through with the shade."

"She's still here?"

"On the far side of the store, waiting for the medium to prepare. I'll be able to speak to her properly now."

"Good, I'm coming."

He blinked. "Why would you want . . . ? Rose, I don't think you quite understand. Proximity to the shade is what caused you to collapse. *In great pain*," he added, in case I needed the reminder.

"You said Mr. Wang's special tea kept the fragment from resonating."

"Temporarily, yes, but who's to say—"

"Safe," Mr. Wang interrupted. "For now."

Thomas frowned. "Are you certain?"

"Certain," Mr. Wang said, looking a little smug. "Strong tea."

"That's settled, then," I said.

"I know you think you feel well, but—"

"Are you going to tell me how I feel?" I said impatiently. "Or how I ought to go about trying to save myself? That shade might be able to tell us something that will help me. It's my decision, *Thomas*."

I'm guessing he regretted according me that privilege just then.

"I know you're trying to help me," I went on, "and I'm grateful. But I have to help myself, too, and that means I have to keep looking for answers."

I expected more of a fight, but he just sighed. "I can't disagree with you there, though I hope you feel you can rely on me. It's not necessary for you to put yourself directly in the path of the shade. But"—he held up his hands to forestall another protest—"since you're determined, may I at least suggest that you approach slowly. Give yourself time to judge whether the fragment is reacting to the spirit's presence."

"That sounds like a fine plan."

"And I think it would be wise to have some of that potion on hand, just in case. You needn't look so offended, Wang, it's just a precaution. Now, Rose, will you follow me, please?"

Grudgingly, Mr. Wang went off to prepare more of his special tea, leaving us to wend our way through the labyrinth of back rooms. They extended much farther into the alley than I'd realized. It looked as though there was a cellar, too, not to mention a second floor—all of it built to the usual Five Points standard, which is to say that it listed like a drunkard and looked fit to blow over in a stiff wind.

Everybody knew about the opium and the gambling, even the coppers. But as far as I knew, Mr. Wang didn't run a brothel, or anything else that might account for the size of the place. "Mr. Wiltshire . . . Thomas," I amended, blushing, "what exactly goes on here?"

"Anything and everything. Wang is a singularly gifted apothecary, and he's also known for having the most comprehensive stock of rare magical items this side of the Atlantic. That's given him an unparalleled network in the paranormal community, and he's managed to turn that into a lucrative business. For a fee, Wang puts people like me in touch with the resources we require. If I need a medium or a witch or someone with a very particular skill set, chances are Wang knows just the right person— or how to find him. And if I need a discreet space in which to work . . ." He gestured at a set of double doors covered in peeling gold paint. "The medium should be ready for us. I must warn you, however, he's a touch . . . theatrical." So saying, he knocked.

"You may enter," said a voice.

We found Mei waiting inside, along with one of the most extraordinary-looking persons I'd ever encountered. "Mr. Smith," said Thomas, and I almost laughed aloud at the irony. "May I introduce Miss Gallagher, of whom we were speaking earlier. She has expressed a desire to participate in the session. Do you see a problem?"

Mr. Smith looked me up and down, which I figured gave me

leave to do the same. It didn't take long, since he was approximately the height of a twelve-year-old, and had the soft complexion to match. That wasn't the extraordinary part, though. No, that distinction belonged to his hair, which I'm not sure quite how to describe except to say that it resembled meringue: white on the bottom, golden at the tips, and whipped into improbably stiff peaks. "*Hmm,*" he said, not flatteringly. Then, without the slightest warning, he pressed a hand flat to my chest, right between my breasts. I gasped and flinched away, but he just tutted impatiently and did it again. Thankfully, it was over before the rest of us could even recover from our astonishment. "The fragment is stable," the little man declared. "There shouldn't be a problem."

"*How dare you?*" I spluttered, blushing furiously.

"That was bloody out of order," Thomas snapped, his own color high, and Mei added her two cents in Chinese.

"My friends," the medium said, drawing himself up to his full five feet, "I am a professional. You would not react thus with a physician, would you?"

"I would if he touched me without asking! You're lucky you didn't end up with a knee in your bits!" I might have said worse if Mei hadn't burst out laughing.

"Good Lord," the medium said, flushing to the roots of his confectionary hair. "Born on the Bowery, this one."

"Let us recalibrate, shall we?" Thomas said. "Now, Smith, do you have everything you require?"

"Everything except the shade," the medium replied sullenly.

On cue, Mr. Wang appeared, bearing a steaming pot of tea. He said something to Mei, and she nodded, gesturing at a table laden with various items. I recognized salt, incense, and a length of wood that looked a little like a spear—ash, presumably—along with a host of other less familiar implements. Mr. Wang grunted in satisfaction and said something else; I recognized the word *yōulíng* from Mei's letter.

Specter.

"It's time," Thomas said. "Are you sure about this, Rose?"

Swallowing down a thick knot of fear, I said, "I'm sure."

"Very well. Let's begin."

CHAPTER 22

SHADES IN THE DARK—MRS. MATILDA
MEYER—HELL GATE—THE RIBBON
OF LIGHT

I stood at the far end of the corridor, willing my racing pulse to slow. Mr. Wang had promised I'd be fine, and the medium had agreed. The special tea was ready just in case, and Thomas would have his ash walking stick *in extremis,* as he'd put it. I wasn't in any real danger, or so I tried to tell myself. But I couldn't keep my knees from wobbling as I started down the hall toward the room with the peeling gold doors, approaching slowly as Thomas had suggested, and when I felt the first throb of cold behind my ribs, I very nearly turned and fled.

But my situation was too dire to let myself give in to fear. The fragment in my breast was going to kill me if I didn't find a way to stop it, and the damaged spirit behind those doors might be able to help. So I gritted my teeth and kept walking.

I opened the doors hesitantly, unsure what I would find. I smelled incense, and for a moment all I could see was smoke swirling in the shadows. Gradually, my eyes adjusted to the gloom and I took in the scene. Thomas, Mei, and Mr. Smith sat cross-legged on the floor, arranged in a triangle. Mr. Wang stood at the back of the room near the table, where a pot of incense burned. He had a box of matches in his hand. When he lit one, I knew, the shade would appear.

"Stand back with Mr. Wang, my dear," the medium instructed.

Thomas met my gaze. "Are we steady, Rose?"

"Steady."

"Good," said Mr. Smith. "The lamp, Mr. Wang, if you please."

Mr. Wang gave me a reassuring nod. Then he struck a match.

The bloody woman flared into view at the center of the triangle. I fell back a step at the sight of her—bloodstained clothing, hair matted with gore, eyes as desperate and haunted as the first time I'd seen her. She was looking right at me, and the force of that stare sent a stab of cold through my flesh. Mr. Wang approached the triangle warily, keeping one eye on the shade as he lit a series of candles arranged in a circle on the floor. They hissed to life, sending up thick ropes of fragrant smoke that formed a sort of boundary outside the triangle. By their glow, I saw that Thomas's walking stick lay beside him, within easy reach. That made me feel a little better.

"Spirit," the medium intoned gravely, "I am Archibald Smith, medium between the worlds." He paused, as though to give his audience time to absorb this pronouncement. "I shall speak for you this night. Were you whole, I would accord you use of my corporeal form, but in your current state that would be fatal to me. Be assured, however, that I can hear your voice perfectly well, and I swear to repeat faithfully all that you say, in your exact words. In exchange, I ask only that you do not attempt to touch any of the living, nor step outside the smoke barrier. Be warned: If you fail to heed this directive, you will be summarily banished. Do you agree to these terms?"

The bloody woman tore her eyes away from me briefly, her lips moving as though in speech.

"She agrees," Mr. Smith said. "These are the last words I shall speak as Archibald Smith. From henceforth, I speak for the spirit. Wiltshire, the floor is yours."

"Thank you." Thomas looked perfectly calm, as if this were nothing new to him—which, I supposed, it wasn't. "I'm grateful that you kept our engagement, spirit. We have much to discuss. First, I believe introductions are in order. My name is Thomas Wiltshire. To my left is Miss Ah-Mei Wang, and at the back of the room is her father, Wang Jianguo. Miss Rose Gallagher you have already met."

"Rose."

The voice was Mr. Smith's, but I'd watched the bloody woman shape my name with her lips, and it sent another shudder down my spine.

"Forgive me, Rose. I never meant to cause you injury. I didn't know."

I nodded stiffly. What else could I do?

"Please, spirit," Thomas said, "tell us your name."

"My name . . ." The bloody woman closed her eyes in grief. "My name is Matilda." It was unnerving, hearing her words spoken in a man's deep tones—the more so because Mr. Smith was doing his best to convey the emotions as well as the words. His voice quavered now, as though speaking the spirit's name were painful to him. "I whisper it to myself every day, or I shall certainly forget it. I forget so much already."

Thomas nodded. "Regrettably, that is the way of it when a spirit is trapped in the mortal world. The longer you remain here, the worse it will become."

"Why am I trapped?"

"That is what we must ascertain. Your injuries . . . They would seem to suggest that you died by violence."

The bloody woman—*Matilda,* I corrected myself—raised a hand to the gruesome wound on her head. "My husband."

"I see," Thomas said. "I'm sorry."

"I always knew he would get carried away one day. I should have left him years ago." She paused, her expression twisting in anguish. "But I was so afraid, and then our son died and Charles lost all our money and the drinking got worse . . ." Mr. Smith's voice climbed in pitch. "I'm afraid he'll hurt my other children, too. Please, you have to help me. I have to find my children. I have to make sure they're safe—"

An icy throb seized my chest, and I sucked in a breath, stumbling back against the table.

Thomas stirred, but Mei stopped him with a sharp gesture. "No, you must not! If you disturb the barrier—"

"You make it worse," Mr. Wang growled, pressing a cup of hot tea into my hands. I gulped it down, not caring that it scorched my throat.

Thomas grimaced but stayed where he was. "Calm yourself, Matilda. You're hurting her!"

"How?" The bloody woman's gaze darted between Thomas and me. She didn't understand.

"When you touched Rose yesterday, you left behind a fragment of your spirit, like a splinter embedded in her flesh. It's reacting to your emotions."

Mr. Wang put a hand on my shoulder. "Better?"

"Yes." I took a few deep breaths just to be sure, but it was as if the tea had melted the shard of ice inside me, at least for now. "Better, thank you."

Thomas didn't look convinced. "Perhaps you ought to—"

"I'll be fine. Keep going."

The bloody woman wrung her hands anxiously before her. "What do you mean, a fragment of my spirit?" Mr. Smith's voice conveyed fear, frustration, and most of all bafflement. "How is that possible?"

When she said that, I felt cold all over again—the sort that couldn't be banished by any tea, no matter how special. *So much for the shade being able to help me.* She couldn't even understand how she'd hurt me in the first place.

Thomas's shoulders sagged, and I knew he'd had the same thought. "You can't sense it, then? The fragment?"

"I can feel a connection, but . . ." The spirit shook her head, looking so lost that I couldn't help pitying her, in spite of everything. "I don't understand any of this."

That made two of us.

"Perhaps we should focus on what you do know," Thomas said. "I take it from what you've said that your husband was abusive, and you're afraid for your children now that you're gone." When Matilda nodded, he went on, "That's most likely what caused your spirit to fracture—the force of that anxiety. Until it's resolved, you will remain a shade."

"Can you help me?"

"Perhaps, but your situation is more complicated than a typical case. Your fate is now tied to Rose's. The damage to your spirit cannot be repaired until you are intact, and that means removing the fragment."

"Then remove it."

"Yes, we're working on that," Thomas said curtly. "In the meantime—what else can you tell me about your circumstances? Surname, time of death, residence, and so on?"

"Meyer. We used to live on Seventy-Fifth Street, but they've moved on now, and I don't know where. That's why I can't find my children."

Behind me, Mr. Wang was taking notes, scratching out the details in spidery Chinese characters.

"Very well," Thomas said, "we'll check with the police. Now, I know it's very difficult for you to measure the passage of time, but can you estimate how long ago you died?"

Matilda Meyer considered that. "More than a year. Less than five, I think. Beyond that . . ." She shook her head; the medium mimicked the gesture. "But most of that time was spent in the drawing room."

"I beg your pardon?"

"That's how I think of the dark place, where the broken ones gather."

"The outer realm, you mean." Thomas hummed thoughtfully. "An apt description. I presume you've attempted to forge deeper into the otherworld?"

"I can't cross the bridge. None of us can."

"No—not until the damage is repaired and you become an ordinary ghost. Then you will be able to cross into the next domain, the place of the dead."

"Is that Heaven?"

"Alas, no. It is merely another drawing room. It is a very long way to the heart of the otherworld, with a great many bridges to cross."

The shade regarded him with terrible sadness. "Then where is Heaven?"

"I wish I could tell you. I cannot say what lies at the center of the otherworld. No living man can, nor even the dead. The fae, perhaps, but they have been gone for a great many centuries."

Fae? I hadn't heard that word since I was a child listening to Da's bedtime stories. I longed to ask some questions of my own, but I sensed it would be a mistake. Besides, it seemed that every time Thomas Wiltshire answered one question, it raised five new ones.

"You say most of your time has been spent in the drawing room," he went on. "What drew you out into the mortal realm? Some sort of spell, I presume?"

"I couldn't say what it was. I saw a ribbon of light and I followed it. Many of us did. It showed us the way out."

"But you weren't pulled by some force, or pushed?"

"We just walked out through a small crack in the door. At first I was too afraid to go, but so many of the others were leaving . . ." Mr. Smith's voice grew unsteady, a crease appearing between his brows. The medium didn't like what he was hearing.

Neither did Mr. Wang. He made a low noise in his throat, tugging fretfully at his mustache.

"This crack in the door," Thomas said, "where does it lead?"

"The bottom of the East River."

I'm not sure how I knew. Maybe it was the memory of Peter Arbridge, or maybe the fragment of the dead woman buried inside me whispered to me somehow. But I knew. "Hell Gate," I murmured, and Matilda Meyer looked at me.

"Yes, Hell Gate. We walked out of the dark place and straight into the water."

"Are you certain?" Thomas's tone was crisp with tension. "We need the precise location."

"I'm certain. I've been there before, just after I died. It's where my body was dumped. We all came from that place, in one way or another, those of us who saw the ribbon of light."

"Mrs. Meyer." Thomas closed his eyes and knitted his fingers, almost as if in prayer. "I cannot emphasize enough how vital this is. When you say you all came from that place, what exactly do you mean? Is that where you died?"

"No. How can I describe it? It's the place where our spirits left our bodies. When I died, I tried to let go straightaway. All I wanted was to close my eyes and get to Heaven, but I couldn't. It was as if I were snagged on something and couldn't get free. It took me a long time to leave my body behind."

"Yes." Thomas's eyes were still closed, his expression so grim that it chilled my blood. "Something still bound you to the mortal realm, and you had to tear yourself free to travel to the otherworld. That is the moment you fractured your spirit and became a shade. From what you're saying, it sounds as though the other spirits who have been drawn to the breach also became shades in or around Hell Gate."

"If you say so. I understand so little of what is happening to me."

"How many of you are there?"

"Outside, only a few dozen. But there are many more crowded inside the doorway, and the crowd gets bigger each day. More and more of us are being drawn there by the ribbon of light. There are . . . *Dear God*." Mr. Smith's eyes flew open, the blood draining from his rosy cheeks. "Wiltshire, this can't be right. If this is true—"

"Please, Smith, for God's sake! How many?"

With a visible effort, the medium composed himself. "Thousands," he said, his words the spirit's once again. "Too many to squeeze through all at once, but they're trying."

"You have no idea what's holding the door open, or where the ribbon of light came from?"

"No, but I followed it to Jacob Crowe."

In the ensuing silence, Thomas Wiltshire nodded slowly. "I see," he said. "I see now."

I didn't see, not at all, but the ashen faces around me told me to be afraid.

"I thought Jacob Crowe could help me," Mrs. Meyer said. "I thought he had summoned me for a reason. But when he saw me, he was so frightened . . ." The spirit sagged, grief creasing her features once again. "I didn't know what to do."

"You didn't hurt him? Even by mistake?" When she shook her head, Thomas asked, "Can you tell us who killed him?"

"I'm sorry, I don't know. I tried to speak with him two nights in a row, and both times he sent me away, with one of those." She leveled an accusing finger at Thomas's walking stick. "The third night, I arrived to find him dead in his study. That was when his brother saw me. He banished me to the river, too. Please don't send me back there, sir. The bottom of the river is a gloomy place, and it takes so long to make my way out . . ."

"I will do what I can to help you, Mrs. Meyer, but you must be patient. There is a crisis looming over this city, and I must do my best to attend to it. In the meantime, if it's not too much to ask, please remain close to Mr. Smith, in case I need to contact you."

"Shouldn't I stay close to you?"

"I'm afraid I'll need you to steer well clear of Miss Gallagher for the foreseeable future, and that means steering clear of me. In any case, I shan't be able to hear you without Mr. Smith's help."

"I see." The spirit looked downcast, but she said, "If that is what you think best."

"In that case, I believe we're through here, unless Miss Gallagher or Mr. Wang . . . ?" Mr. Wang shook his head, and I did the same. It was clear to me that Matilda Meyer was in no position to help me, which meant we had nothing to say to each other. "Very well. Thank you, Mrs. Meyer. Until next time."

Bowing her head, the spirit vanished.

A brief silence followed in her wake. Then Mr. Wang said, "We have trouble."

"Trouble!" The medium gave a brittle laugh. "You have a gift for understatement, my friend. This is nothing short of a catastrophe! Not only do we have a compromised portal on our hands, someone or something is actively drawing shades out through the breach with this . . . ribbon of light. Who would do such a thing? And for God's sake, *why*?"

"Sounds like magic," Mei said.

"Yes, but what kind?" Rising with the aid of his stick, Thomas took a meditative turn about the room. "I've never come across anything like it before. Wang? No, I thought not. But at least now we know where it came from. Jacob Crowe was obviously meddling with forces beyond his capacity to control. I knew him, and I don't believe he would deliberately put the entire city at risk." Mr. Wang interrupted with a question, and Thomas nodded. "I've an idea about that, too. Do you recall the ciphered pages I showed you last night?"

Mr. Wang frowned, and his reply sounded skeptical.

"You're right, those spells aren't anywhere near on the order of power required for something like this. But the pages I translated made reference to a series of appendices containing instructions for more potent magic. Perhaps Jacob Crowe had access to the full set of manuscripts."

"That sounds like a good deal of speculation to me," Mr. Smith declared, unhelpfully.

Thomas ignored him. "I need that witch, Wang, and fast. And remember—it can't be just any alchemist. We need a virtuoso. Will you give it your full attention?"

Mr. Wang nodded, and Mei added, "I can send word out to the mystic community as well. Maybe someone has heard of these manuscripts."

"Thank you, Miss Wang, but please be careful. Whoever is behind this has already murdered two men, not to mention holding me captive for nearly a week. Speak only to those you know you can trust. I'll do the same, starting with Burrows and a handful of others at the Madison Club. And I'll need the use of your telegraph again, Wang. Chicago must be informed."

"Chicago." Mr. Smith snorted. "What can the Pinkertons do about any of this?"

Thomas regarded him coolly. "The special branch of the Pinkerton Detective Agency has thwarted two presidential assassinations, secured the skystones, and averted a second war with Mexico. I'd say we've earned the benefit of the doubt."

By this point I'd recovered enough of my wits to start asking questions. "I'm not sure I understand. You're saying that someone created a doorway to the otherworld at the bottom of the East River?"

"The doorway already existed," Thomas said. "There are many such places in the world, but virtually all of them are sealed and have been for centuries—so long, in fact, that most of their locations have long since passed from record. I had no idea there was one in New York." Shaking his head wonderingly, he added, "I thought the name *Hell Gate* referred to the perils of the strait as a shipping lane, but apparently it was once quite literal. Probably a translation from the original Lenape name for it."

"So it's been here all along, but no one realized it because it was sealed. Except now it isn't, because Jacob Crowe accidentally broke it open with magic."

"No." Mr. Wang shook his head. "Too much magic."

"I'm inclined to agree," Thomas said. "To my knowledge, only great natural calamities—earthquakes, volcanoes, and so on—have succeeded in rupturing portals. I've never heard of magic doing so."

"But aren't they sealed with magic?"

"Nothing quite so impressive, I'm afraid."

"Rocks," supplied Mr. Wang.

I blinked. "What do you mean, *rocks?*"

Holding his hands a couple of feet apart, Mr. Wang said, "Big rocks."

"Just a minute. You're telling me that the gates separating the dead from the living are sealed with—"

"Monoliths, to be precise," Thomas said. "Or islands. In one case, an exceedingly large pyramid. Moved there by magic, yes—but not sealed with magic, strictly speaking."

"Islands," I said, something tweaking in my memory. "Islands like Flood Rock?"

"*Ahh*," Thomas closed his eyes briefly. "The explosion last October. You're perfectly brilliant, Rose. That must be it."

"Flood Rock?" Mr. Smith echoed. "Forgive me, I'm not from the area—I've never heard of such a place."

"It was a small island in the middle of the strait," Thomas explained.

"*Was*." Mr. Smith arched an eyebrow. "How does an island cease to exist?"

"The army blew it up," I said. "Last October, to clear the way for ships."

"Flood Rock was the seal," Thomas murmured, as if to himself, "and when they blasted it to clear the strait . . ."

"So we have the army to thank for our woes." Mr. Smith gave another humorless laugh. "How typical."

"The army and three hundred thousand pounds of explosives." Sighing, Thomas added, "Not that it matters. What matters is that the portal has been breached, and it lies in an incredibly dangerous location. The surrounding islands—Randall's, Ward's, Hart—fortresses of human misery all, full of potter's fields, asylums, hospitals, prisons . . ."

"The mother lode of broken souls," Mr. Smith said, shuddering.

Thousands of them, Matilda Meyer had said, the spirits of people who'd died in the most horrible ways imaginable, all of them following the ribbon of light. The thought was too terrifying to contemplate, so I took a page from Clara's book and focused on the practical. "How do we stop it?"

"*We?*" The miniature meringue peaks of Mr. Smith's eyebrows climbed in astonishment. "My dear girl, you have a fragment of a dead woman embedded in your body. You ought to go home and be with your family."

"Thank you for your concern, Mr. Smith, but if I have to wait for help from Chicago, I might as well keep busy while I do it. And if I'm going to die, I'd rather not spend my last days contemplating my own doom, especially when I could be helping make sure the same fate doesn't befall my friends and family."

Mr. Wang grunted approvingly. "*Tā shì zhànshì.*"

Thomas's pale eyes settled on mine, and there was something in them I couldn't name. "*Shì.*"

"My father praises your courage," Mei said.

"I wish I could say it's courage. The truth is, I just don't want to think about it."

"I don't blame you, my girl," Mr. Smith said. "I don't want to think about any of this. A breached portal, shades running riot all over the city . . . It's positively apocalyptic."

"Then perhaps you ought to spend your time in prayer," Thomas said, fetching his hat from Mr. Wang's table. "As for the rest of us, we have work to do."

CHAPTER 23

OUT OF THE FRYING PAN—INTO THE DRAGON FIRE

Thomas was suddenly in a great hurry to be away, and I wasn't sorry for it. I'd meant what I said about not wanting to think too much. I knew that if I let myself dwell on what I'd heard over the past hour, let alone the past twenty-four, I would come quite undone. Better to focus on how I could help make things right. So we lingered just long enough for Thomas to send his telegram and Mr. Wang to supply me with a small pouch of tea leaves in case of emergency, and then we were on our way.

"Where to now?" I asked, handling Mr. Wang's broken front door gingerly.

"Home, I think. I'd like to take another look at those pages the Irishmen had me translate, in case there's a clue I missed. I could use a second pair of eyes, but if you need to check in on your mother, I quite understand."

Mam. I'd promised to pass by, but I didn't think I could face her right now. I was frightened enough without looking my mother in the eye and telling her I was dying. And there was no way of keeping it from her, not if I went over there; she'd take one look at me and know something was wrong. "I'd rather not," I said, glancing away.

I think Thomas understood, because he didn't press the issue. "Half seven," he said, consulting his watch. "Time yet to make some progress."

We arrived at Number 726 to find the house in near darkness, the lamps turned low for the evening. "Straight to the study, then?" Thomas asked as he helped me out of my coat.

"I ought to check in with Clara. I left her pretty abruptly this morning. Shall I bring up some tea?"

"That would be splendid," he said before heading up the stairs.

The kitchen was quiet when I got there, the mouth-watering aroma of another wasted dinner lingering in the air. Clara had already gone up for the evening, and as I stood there debating whether to disturb her, I heard a noise in the hallway. I stuck my head out to look but no one was there. The sound seemed to be coming from the little office under the stairs, the private warren where Mrs. Sellers kept her ledgers, as well as the expensive wines, under lock and key. The door was ajar, and I could hear a rustling of papers and the soft groan of drawers being opened and closed.

I had no desire to cross paths with the housekeeper, so I

turned to go. But then I heard the *thump* of something heavy hitting the floor.

I paused. "Mrs. Sellers?"

Silence.

Clara's umbrella sat propped against the wall just behind me. Taking it up, I crept toward the door of the little office.

"Mrs. Sellers?"

Still no answer. Standing back a pace, I pushed the door open with the umbrella and peered inside. I couldn't see anyone, so I took another step—and got a face full of door as someone slammed it into me, sending me stumbling back against the wall. A man's form reared up out of the shadows. Strong hands seized me by the scruff of the neck, forcing me up against the wall and twisting the umbrella from my grasp.

I'm not sure what my attacker intended to do but I didn't give him the chance. I drove the heel of my boot into his shin and shoved myself off the wall with all my strength, breaking his grip and fleeing for the kitchen. He grabbed at me, tearing my dress; I made it as far as the stairs before he was on me again, and this time he took a fistful of hair and clamped a hand over my mouth, muffling my scream.

"Quiet, bitch. Hold still or I'll—"

Whang.

A hard blow sent him staggering. I nearly went down with him, but at the last moment I managed to grab the handrail. The man wasn't so lucky; he hit the floor hard, giving his skull a second thump. Whirling, I found Clara standing over him with a cast-iron skillet, her arm cocked back threateningly. "Don't you move," she told the intruder, "or so help me Lord, I will flatten your head like a pancake."

His reply was a long, drawn-out groan.

A flurry of footsteps on the stairs signaled the arrival of Mrs. Sellers. The housekeeper took in the scene with a gasp, her hand flying to her breast as though her heart might quit right then and there. "Dear God! Clara Freeman, what have you done?"

Clara ignored her, still brandishing the skillet at the figure on the floor. "I mean it. You stay put now."

"When Mr. Wiltshire sees this—"

"Thomas!" I shoved past the startled housekeeper and took the bottom three steps in a single bound. "*Thomas, come quickly!*"

"Thomas?" Mrs. Sellers echoed incredulously, looking even more horrified than when she'd entered the kitchen to find a half-conscious stranger on the floor.

He must have been halfway down the stairs already, because he appeared on the landing only moments later. "Rose, are you all right?"

"I'm fine. There's a man—"

"Yes, I know, he's been in my study." Thomas swept into the kitchen, touching my shoulder as he passed—a gesture that did not go unnoticed by the housekeeper. "Is anyone hurt?"

"Just him." Clara pointed with her frying pan. "That's gonna need stitches."

"Well done, Clara." Thomas circled around the prone intruder, tilting his head to get a better look. "Do you recognize him, Rose?"

"No."

"Nor I. He wasn't at the gasworks."

By this time the man had recovered enough to roll onto his back. He touched his head gingerly, wincing.

"Who sent you?" Thomas demanded.

The rough eyed him balefully but didn't answer.

In a single smooth motion, Thomas whipped out a derringer and clicked back the hammer. "Speak quickly, please. Miss Gallagher and I have had an extremely trying day, and I promise you my current temperament is not to your advantage."

"I got nothing to say to you, Pinkerton."

Well, you can imagine the look on Mrs. Sellers's face now. As for Clara, she cut him a sidelong glance but otherwise held her peace.

"Suit yourself. Mrs. Sellers, kindly fetch Sergeant Chapman at the police station. If he's not on duty, see to it that they send for him. Rose, we'll need something to bind this one. A curtain tie ought to do the trick. Clara, I'll need a knife. Something small, I think, for fine work." Only one of us hesitated. "*Now*, Mrs. Sellers, if you please." He could have asked her to telephone instead, but I think he wanted to get rid of her, and I wasn't sorry.

"So," Clara said as we tied the bleeding man to a chair, "this is how you all spend your time, is it?"

"It's been quite a day."

Thomas lowered himself to eye level with the rough. "Now, I'll ask you again, whose man are you?"

"I told you, I got—"

"—nothing to say. Yes, I did hear you, but I wondered if perhaps you'd rethought your position, given the circumstances."

"Think I'm afraid of you? You ain't gonna carve me up, Englishman." Brave words, but his tone didn't quite live up to them, and his gaze kept sliding to the paring knife in Clara's hand.

"You're right, that's a trifle extreme. I did, however, think you might be interested in learning about those papers you came here to steal." Reaching into the man's jacket, Thomas pulled out the ciphered pages he'd shown me this morning. The rough must have taken them from the study. "Did he tell you what they are, the man who sent you? Genuinely fascinating. The magic in these pages can do all sorts of things. For example, do you see these runes here? Inscribing this one into your flesh supposedly makes your bones as brittle as a dry twig. This one here inflames the nervous system, so that even a breath of wind feels like fire against your skin. You'll be off to the Tombs in a few minutes, and both of these strike me as inconvenient afflictions to have in prison."

The man sneered. "You believe in that stuff, Pinkerton?"

"Your employer does, or he wouldn't have sent you to steal these pages. Myself, I'm a man of science, which means I'm terribly fond of experiments. Clara, shall we put those talented hands of yours to good use?"

Bluff or no, this was asking a lot of poor Clara—or so I thought, but she played right along. "Seeing how he was fixing to do worse to Rose here, it would be my particular pleasure."

I can't help wondering if the man would have reacted the same way if it had been me holding the knife. As it was, he took one look at Clara and said, "Drake."

"*Edmund* Drake?" I made a disgusted sound. "Doesn't that just figure."

Clara eyed me askance. "Sounds like you know the man."

"Oh, we know him, all right. He hypnotized us this morning. Sort of."

Thomas didn't react straightaway, but I could see the gears turning in his head. "We would have to take precautions this time," he said at length.

"This time? You can't mean for us to go back there?"

"We need answers. Drake didn't know about my kidnapping—I'd bet my estate on it. So how did he know about the pages?"

"You gonna let me go?" the rough interjected. "I told you what you wanted to know."

"My dear fellow, didn't you hear me? You're off to prison." Turning to Clara, Thomas said, "Rose and I haven't time to give a statement. We won't leave you alone with this lout, but once the police arrive we'll make a discreet exit through the downstairs door. That will leave you to speak with the sergeant, and I'd appreciate it if you kept Drake's name out of it for now. Are you comfortable with that?"

Clara scowled at the both of us. "All right, but I expect a full accounting when you get back."

"I thought you said you didn't want to know," I reminded her.

"That was before Mr. Wiltshire asked me to carve up a white man with a paring knife. If he's a Pinkerton, that means trouble follows him wherever he goes. I need this job, but I don't need it that bad. Before I decide whether I'm staying, I'd like to know what I'm in for."

"That's fair," Thomas said. "Now, in the meantime, are you sure you'll be all right with the police?"

"Oh, don't you worry about that."

"Splendid. Rose, I'll meet you at the door. There's something I have to fetch first."

Clara watched him go, still wearing a scowl. "Pinkerton. Well, well. Looks like you got your adventure after all. Is it everything you hoped?"

She already knew the answer to that or she wouldn't have

asked, but I don't think she was quite prepared for the force of my reaction. I flinched visibly, and for a moment I couldn't even speak, teetering on the brink of tears. "Please, Clara, I don't think I can handle *I told you so* right now."

Her scowl melted away, replaced by a look of genuine concern. "I'm sorry, I didn't mean to—"

"Let's talk about it later, all right?"

Thomas returned, and we waited by the servants' door until the creak of floorboards overhead signaled the arrival of the coppers. Then we slipped out into the night like a pair of thieves, skulking along Fifth Avenue for a full block before hailing a cab.

Twenty minutes later we arrived at the Dragon's den.

"Here," Thomas said, pressing a derringer into my hand. "Just in case."

So far, my weapons had included a crucifix, a shovel, an ink-bottle, an umbrella, and a hairpin, so this was a definite improvement. On the other hand . . . "Don't you have something with a little more kick?"

"A Colt .45, perhaps?"

He was being sarcastic, but that's exactly what I had in mind. "What happened to the gun we took off the Irishman at the gas factory?"

"Tucked away safely in my office. We have all the firepower we need right here."

I wasn't so sure about that. "You wouldn't get any respect in my neighborhood with one of these," I said, brandishing the little one-shot pistol.

"Perhaps not, but in my estimation, Burrows has the right of it: A weapon concealed is far more powerful than one your opponent knows about."

When he put it that way, I saw the sense in it. The derringer fit easily into the pocket of my dress, and it was light enough that I had no fear of being able to handle it. But I still felt ill at ease contemplating another encounter with Edmund Drake. "We can't let him use our names," I said.

"Sorry?"

"That power of his . . . It seems to rely on his using our Christian names."

"Is that so? I hadn't noticed."

"That's because he did it to you first. You were already under his spell by the time he did it again. But I heard everything he said to you, and he even repeated your name when it seemed as if you might not answer him."

"Well spotted. Hopefully that will give us some measure of protection. If he says either of our names, the other must intervene immediately."

So armed, we were as prepared as we could possibly be to confront the Dragon.

Which was not very prepared at all.

CHAPTER 24

THE DRAGON'S
HOARD—DR. LIVINGSTONE, I
PRESUME—AN UNLIKELY ALLIANCE

The butler made no effort to hide his umbrage when he answered the door, but after duly consulting with his master, he led us back to the unwelcoming parlor. There, Drake awaited us. "Wiltshire," he said. "And Miss Gallagher. Again."

"I do apologize for the hour," Thomas said, "but I'm afraid we couldn't get away any sooner. I had a deuce of a time getting your man to answer my questions, and the police were slower to arrive than one would have liked."

Drake didn't even bother to deny it. He just snorted, his mouth twisting sourly. "It is so hard to find good help these days, don't you agree?"

"Actually, no. I appear to be particularly blessed in that regard, though I daresay at least two of my staff are contemplating a career change. Shall we sit? I have a few more questions, if I might."

Drake gave an impatient growl and said, "Thomas."

He'd scarcely finished lingering over the S before I had the derringer cocked and pointed at his chest. "Don't."

Warily, he raised his hands. "You catch on quickly, Miss Gallagher."

"You're not the first to say so."

"And if I simply spoke your name as well?"

"You tell me. How fast does your little magic spell work? Faster than a bullet, do you think?" It was immensely satisfying to be able to vent just a little of my anger. In fact, if I wasn't careful, my anger might not be the only thing that got vented this evening.

Maybe Drake sensed it, because he didn't put up much of a fight. "You are released," he said, with a dismissive gesture in Thomas's direction.

Thomas didn't react right away. It wasn't until he saw my gun that he even realized anything was amiss, at which point he stiffened and started to reach for his own pistol.

"Don't worry," I said, "nothing happened. Not for lack of trying, mind you."

"Your associate is rather quick on the trigger," Drake said, eying me coldly. "Then again, I suppose I oughtn't be surprised. The Irish are a notoriously violent race."

"I'm not entirely sure insulting her is the best strategy under the circumstances," Thomas said.

"Then perhaps you could convince her to point that instrument elsewhere."

"Why would I want to do that? You did just send a hired thug to burgle my home, after all."

"You cannot steal that which already belongs to you. Those papers are my property, Wiltshire, and if you know what's good for you, not to mention the rest of this city, you'll give them back."

"How did you know I had the papers?"

"I didn't, until this very moment. It was a guess, and apparently a good one. You were first on the scene of Frederick Crowe's murder, after all. My man on the force found no sign of the folios, so it stood to reason that either you had them or the killer did."

Thomas frowned. "Why should they have been at Freddie's house at all?"

"Because he stole them from me, you imbecile. He or his brother. Roberts must have tipped them off. I was a fool to trust him."

"Stolen, is it?" Thomas's eyes narrowed. "When was this?"

"Nearly a month ago, from the strongbox in my study."

"If you thought I had them, why not simply ask me to return them?"

"My dear fellow, we barely know each other. How am I to know what you want them for?"

"I don't want them," Thomas said irritably. "And as it happens, I have only a few pages anyway."

"Maybe we could talk about how they came to be in your possession at all," I interrupted. I still had my gun trained on Drake; I didn't trust this man any farther than I could spit. "You say he didn't know about your kidnapping, but I'm not so sure."

Drake frowned. "Your what?"

Damn. Thomas was right—Drake obviously hadn't known.

Which meant we were no closer to figuring out who'd taken him captive, unless . . . "Roberts. It must have been."

Thomas shook his head. "Roberts is the one who hired me in the first place. Why would he have done that if he were the killer?"

"I beg your pardon," Drake said, "but what's all this about a kidnapping? When did this happen?"

"You'll recall, perhaps, that I mentioned being detained these past few days? I meant that quite literally. As to why, it was in order to decipher these." Thomas tugged the folded pages just far enough out of his jacket that Drake was sure to recognize them.

"Decipher them?" Drake's frown deepened.

"I know, it's a simple cryptogram, and yet my kidnapper was apparently incapable of breaking it."

Drake grunted. "The bulk of the folios are simple, I grant you, but the annexes are another matter. The more sensitive the material, the more sophisticated the cipher becomes. It took me several weeks to work out the final chapters. But I did, eventually, and Jacob Crowe could have done the same, given enough time. Why should he resort to kidnapping?"

"Jacob Crowe couldn't have been behind my kidnapping. He was murdered before I was taken captive, and Freddie within hours of my release. As for Roberts, he was the one who hired me to find Jacob's killer, as I've just said. Clearly, there's another party involved."

Drake swore under his breath. "It just keeps getting worse. Look, will you give the folios back or not?"

"I told you, I haven't got them. Just these few pages, and harmless ones at that. I suspect the idea was to test my skills before moving on to something more sensitive. That way, if I didn't prove out, he hadn't put his more precious materials at risk."

"They didn't sound so harmless to me," I said, recalling the threats he'd made to Drake's man.

"Fabrication," Thomas said with a wave. "Those so-called runes were merely Hebrew letters. The special vaults of the Astor Library contain more dangerous material than this." As if to emphasize the point, he tossed the pages on the table beside Drake. "What I want to know is, what's in the rest of those folios?"

"If you have to ask, Wiltshire, you're not much of a detective."

"Dangerous magic."

"The most dangerous I've ever come across. I had them from an old friend in London. He's been taken ill, and feared they would fall into the wrong hands once he passed."

"And now they have," I said, "thanks to you."

Drake scowled. "My only mistake was trusting Roberts." Coldly, he added, "Not that I have to explain myself to you."

"Actually," Thomas said, "I rather think you do. This city stands on the brink of calamity. Perhaps more than one, if those manuscripts are as dangerous as you say. They must be recovered and the portal sealed. That means we ought to work together."

Drake glanced between us, visibly turning the prospect over in his mind. "Very well," he said, "if only to encourage your associate to stop pointing that blighted gun at me."

Reluctantly, I lowered the weapon. "If I feel so much as a hint of your luck . . ."

"Yes, yes." Drake sank into a chair, an irritable gesture inviting us to do the same. "What exactly do you want to know?"

Thomas crossed his legs, the high polish of his oxfords glinting in the lamplight. "You say the manuscripts came from London. Who authored them, and for what purpose?"

"No idea. All I can tell you is that whoever drafted them was very knowledgeable indeed. Much of the text is, as you say, harmless. But the annexes . . . that's another story. They contain all manner of highly delicate spells, including one that claims to allow the living to enter the otherworld."

"Good Lord. Whatever for?"

"I can't speak to the intentions of the author, but in Jacob's case, his interest was of a scientific nature. He was intoxicated by the idea of exploring and cataloguing the otherworld. A would-be paranormal Dr. Livingstone, if you will."

Something sparked in Thomas's eyes, a glimmer of that same fervor he'd shown when he'd explained luck to me. "I can understand that. It would be fascinating, wouldn't it? To shine the light of modern science on the great spiritual questions of humanity?"

Drake snorted softly. "You sound just like him."

"I take it you didn't share his enthusiasm."

"Doors work both ways, Wiltshire. Or have you forgotten our recent outbreak of shades? And that's not even the worst of it. That spell I mentioned purports to act as a kind of magical rope, the sort a mountain climber might use to cross a particularly treacherous patch."

"The ribbon of light," I murmured.

Drake frowned again, but before he could ask, Thomas said, "Go on."

"According to the manuscripts, clinging to that rope would enable a man not only to enter the otherworld but to cross the bridges separating its various realms. Think on that for a moment, Wiltshire. A rope that allows free passage between the realms of the otherworld. Perhaps all the way to the kingdoms of the fae, or even beyond."

Thomas paled. "Is that possible?"

"Who knows? As you said, the light of modern science has never been shined there. What do we really know for sure?"

Much as I'd have liked to avoid flaunting my ignorance in front of Drake, I had to ask. "These fae you're talking about . . . Do you mean . . . fairies?"

"Some have called them that," Thomas said, "though it's meant in the Germanic sense rather than the British one."

"Meaning?"

"Meaning they're not pointy-eared sprites," Drake said impatiently. "They're immortal creatures of immense power, and more dangerous than anything that's walked the earth since they vanished."

"Vanished."

"The fae once lived among us," Thomas explained. "Every mythical tradition mentions them in some form or another. The Greeks and Mesopotamians called them demigods. To the Norse, they were elves. The Arabians call them djinn. Even the biblical notion of angels and demons may have its roots in mortal interactions with the fae."

"Good Lord, Wiltshire, you're as bad as Crowe. The point is, they're long gone. They retreated to their respective kingdoms and sealed the portals behind them. They didn't want to be found, and I imagine they'd take it badly if someone went looking for them. Especially if that someone left a magical rope lying around that allowed shades and ghosts and God knows what else to wander freely about the otherworld, creating chaos. Those realms are kept separate for a reason. To each his place. Man wasn't meant to go poking around the otherworld, and he certainly wasn't meant to unlock all the cages and let the entire zoo run riot."

"And that's what you think Jacob Crowe meant to do?" Thomas asked.

"I speak of the potential consequences of his actions. As to his intentions, all I can say for certain is that he wanted to explore the otherworld. He spoke of it incessantly to anyone who would listen. That's probably why Roberts told him about my folios." Darkly, he added, "Which makes him just as great a fool as the Crowes."

"Wasn't that the whole idea behind your little secret society?" I pointed out. "Unmasking the great metaphysical mysteries, or some such?"

"I joined the Brotherhood of Seekers to keep an eye on men like Jacob Crowe. The pursuit of knowledge is well and good, but there are limits—or at least there ought to be."

"So." Thomas bowed his head, fingers knitted below his chin in thought. "You mention the manuscripts to Roberts, and he mentions them to Jacob Crowe. Crowe steals the manuscripts, probably with the help of his brother, if not Roberts. They begin experimenting with the spells they find there, inadvertently drawing out Matilda Meyer and at least a dozen other shades from the breach at Hell Gate."

"So that's where it is." Drake shook his head. "God help us."

"You knew about the breached portal?" I glared at him accusingly.

"How does that indict me, Miss Gallagher? I read the papers—as did the Crowes, obviously. The matter is clear to those of us who know what to look for. To Jacob, it would have presented an irresistible opportunity."

Thomas ignored us both, continuing to talk it through. "Matilda Meyer appears to Jacob. Two days later, he turns up dead, but not by her hand."

"Maybe someone found out what he was doing," I said, "and decided to stop him."

Drake grunted. "I can certainly understand that. I might have done it myself had I realized he'd finally found a way to implement his disastrous little schemes." He said it plain as you please, as if it were perfectly ordinary for a man to contemplate murdering his friend.

"Or maybe he lost his nerve," I went on, taking a page from Thomas's book and ignoring Drake, "and someone killed him for *that*."

"Interesting." Thomas pressed the steeple of his fingers to his lips. "If Jacob was as frightened by Mrs. Meyer as she claims, he must not have foreseen the consequences of his actions. Once he did, one would certainly hope that he'd begin having doubts. And if he shared them with his brother . . ."

"He'd start having doubts, too," I said, "especially once Jacob turned up dead."

"A collaborator," Thomas said, speaking with more energy now, "someone who didn't want to drop the experiments. But no . . ." He sighed, fading back into his seat. "That doesn't make sense. I don't care how passionate you are about science, you don't kill purely for the sake of knowledge. Not unless there's something concrete to gain by it, and who gains from risking his life in the otherworld?"

"Dr. Livingstone gained plenty from risking his life in Africa," I pointed out. "Anybody who's ever read *Harper's Weekly* knows his name."

"David Livingstone died of malaria in the middle of no-where."

"Maybe, but he died famous. Men kill for less."

"She's right, Wiltshire. On top of which, there are plenty of other ways a clever entrepreneur might profit. You know what mediums charge to traffic with the dead. Imagine that on an industrial scale. Or perhaps our mysterious collaborator is more ambitious still. If he believes that magical rope can guide him to the fae . . . Well, I hardly need explain how that prospect might appear attractive to some."

"But not to you?" I asked sarcastically.

"As I said, the fae have made it abundantly clear that they don't wish to be found. Ignoring those wishes could put countless lives at risk."

"Forgive me, Mr. Drake, but you don't exactly strike me as the sort who frets about the greater good."

"Very well, I'll give you another reason. Luck originated with the fae, and since they left this world it's steadily withered away. Even so, I've done very well by such talents as I possess. I have no wish to see that advantage eroded by the sudden reappearance of beings a thousand times more powerful."

I stared at him. "Just to be sure I understand, your main concern with unleashing a race of all-powerful, possibly very angry immortal beings on our world is that you wouldn't be *special* anymore?"

He shrugged. "You asked, Miss Gallagher. I'm simply being honest."

As I sat there staring at Edmund Drake—with his fancy suit and his emerald tie pin and that unapologetic look on his face—I felt something akin to Pietro's contempt for the rich. Not all of them, maybe, but those endowed with luck. People who, through a simple accident of birth, had the whole world at their feet, and had the nerve to think it *belonged* there. Who deceived everyone around them in an effort to make sure it *stayed* there. When I thought of how hard I'd worked to make a place for myself among their glittering set—learning to speak, act, maybe even think differently—well, I didn't just feel deceived. I felt cheated.

That is why we keep it secret, Mr. Burrows had said. At last, I truly understood.

"Putting all that aside," Thomas said, "I suspect we're giving our killer too much credit. A man who lacks the patience to crack a cipher hardly strikes me as the sort who would harbor ambitions of that scale."

"His ambitions don't matter," Drake said. "As I said, it's the potential consequences of his actions that signify, and those are nothing short of catastrophic. Miss Gallagher mentioned a ribbon of light a moment ago. If Jacob Crowe or one of his collaborators cast that spell, it has already begun. The shades will keep coming. Dozens will become hundreds, then thousands. And if the rope reaches even deeper into the otherworld, who knows what else might climb out?"

I didn't care to think about that, so I stuck to the practical. "I don't see how speculating helps us any. Seems to me we ought to be speaking with Mr. Roberts."

"Leave him to me," Drake said. "Roberts trusts me. I ought to be able to catch him unawares. I'll have the truth from him—in its entirety."

Thomas looked uncomfortable; I don't think he much liked the idea of using Drake's power to our advantage, even indirectly. For that matter, neither did I. "Can't we just talk to him?

What you did to us this morning . . . Have you got any idea what that feels like? It's—"

"A violation," Drake said matter-of-factly. "But physically harmless and wholly effective. Whatever you may think of me, Miss Gallagher, or what I can do, we haven't the luxury of fretting over it now. The stakes are too high."

"At least let us try a more . . . *conventional* interview first," Thomas said. "If we fail, you can stop by later and try your luck, as it were."

Drake frowned. "You'll only put him on his guard."

"There's no reason for him to suspect that the three of us are working together, and besides, all you have to do is get him alone and he'll be powerless against you. Surely you can manage that?" Thomas arched an eyebrow.

Drake took that as a challenge—just as Thomas knew he would. "I'll do my part, Wiltshire. You just make sure you don't ruffle his feathers so badly that he won't even agree to see me."

"Good. Now can you think of anyone else who might be involved?"

Drake shook his head. "I'll look into the other members of the Brotherhood, but I doubt any of them had a hand in this. These men are scientists and scholars. Every one of them would have been able to crack that cipher, given enough time. Whoever kidnapped you is obviously in a great hurry. As should you be, because if he does succeed in translating those folios, he'll have powerful spells at his disposal, some of which could be turned upon you."

"What sorts of spells?"

"I couldn't give you details. I only glanced over the contents, and I'm no witch. What I can say is that the more complicated spells seem to be some form of necromancy."

"That stands to reason," Thomas said. "If one planned to explore the otherworld, one would need to be confident of being able to interact safely with the dead. Having a few spells up one's sleeve would only be prudent."

"Perhaps, but it also means our killer would have still more dangerous toys to play with. We *must* recover those folios, Wiltshire."

"Thomas . . ." I swallowed past a suddenly dry throat. "When you say *interact safely with the dead* . . . Might one of those spells . . . ?"

He understood straightaway. "Yes," he said, leaning forward eagerly, "yes, why not? If these spells are so rare and powerful, perhaps one of them might do the job!"

"What job?" Drake scowled; he didn't like being left out. "What are you talking about?"

I'm not sure why I answered him. I still didn't trust this man, and the last thing I wanted was to look weak in front of him. But the words fell from my lips before I could stop them. "I have a fragment embedded in my chest. A shade—the same one Jacob Crowe saw."

Drake absorbed this news with a grim expression. "I am sorry to hear that, Miss Gallagher. Very sorry indeed."

I wanted Edmund Drake's sympathy about as much as I wanted cholera, but manners were manners, so I forced myself to say, "Thank you."

"But there is hope," Thomas said, meeting my gaze and holding it firmly. "With or without these manuscripts, there is hope."

Whether he truly believed that I don't know, but I loved him for saying it.

"In that case, Wiltshire, it sounds as if you haven't a moment to lose."

It was a dismissal, but neither of us minded; we were only too happy to be out of there. We left with a list of names and a promise to keep each other informed of any new developments.

"What now?" I asked as we stepped into the carriage.

"It's late."

"But Drake's right. We've got so little time, and unless we recover the folios, what chance do we have of righting any of this? That magical rope is a lit fuse on a stick of dynamite, to say nothing of the other spells . . ."

"I don't deny the situation is grave, but driving ourselves to exhaustion isn't going to help."

As soon as he said the word, I could see it in his features: the gray circles under his eyes, the sag of his shoulders beneath his overcoat. So much had happened to me over the past twenty-four hours that I'd all but forgotten about what had happened to *him*. He'd had only a single night's sleep since his week-long ordeal at the gasworks. "I'm sorry. Of course you need to rest."

"We both do. We have another full day ahead of us tomorrow, and after that—"

"After that, I'll most likely be dead."

I hadn't meant to say it aloud.

"Don't." He grabbed my hand, looking stricken. "Don't give up now, Rose, not after you've shown such courage. We *will* find a way."

I nodded numbly, listening to the *tick-tock* of the horse's hooves as it dragged us down Fifth Avenue.

CHAPTER 25

THE SOCIETY FOR PSYCHICAL RESEARCH—
THE MYSTERIOUS MR. S—TUB OF BLOOD

The coppers were gone by the time we got back to 726 Fifth Avenue—or at least, most of them were. As we hung up our overcoats, I noticed a battered old hat and threadbare scarf on the bench, and a moment later our grim silence was interrupted by a familiar, grandfatherly voice.

"Making a few after-dinner calls?" Sergeant Chapman lounged against the doorframe of the parlor. "Dodging police statements is becoming a bad habit for you two."

"I do apologize, Sergeant," Thomas said wearily, "but we had a lead that needed chasing. I know you appreciate how delicate the timing of these things can be."

Chapman snorted. "You must think I'm a pretty soft mark, Wiltshire." When Thomas started to object, the detective raised a hand and said, "Save it. I didn't hang around to lecture you about civic duty. I think you'll wanna see this." He produced an envelope from his jacket pocket.

Thomas took it with a frown, turning it over to reveal a postmark from Boston. "What is it?"

"Take a look. Came for Jacob Crowe this morning, just after you left."

"Did it indeed?" Thomas ushered us into the parlor and held the letter under the lamplight.

"*American Society for Psychical Research,*" I read over his shoulder.

"Quite a new outfit, I believe. Modeled after the one in London."

"Read on," Chapman said.

Dear Mr. Crowe,

I was delighted to receive your letter. It is always a great pleasure to connect with other persons dedicated to scientific investigation of paranormal phenomena. And thank you for your kind words about my lecture at Harvard University. I am glad you enjoyed it. You ought to have introduced yourself! Any friend of Roberts is a friend of mine.

As to the specifics of your letter, I am certainly intrigued! However did you come by these manuscripts? Are you certain they are genuine? I am flattered that you would seek my advice, but as I have not heard mention of these folios before, I cannot offer an opinion as to the nature of the spells contained therein—their origin, purpose, or probable effects. That being said, I would certainly welcome the opportunity to examine the materials in question. In the meantime, in view of your concerns, further experimentation strikes me as imprudent, particularly since you are not, in your own words, "proficient in the magical arts." Moreover, if your suspicions are correct and the mysterious "Mr. S" has designs other than those of a purely scientific nature, you may unwittingly be contributing to an agenda of which you would not yourself approve. (I presume your reluctance to name "Mr. S" stems from a concern that I may expose him to censure, but you need not fear on that score. It is not my place to do so, particularly since you say you are not certain of your suspicions.)

At the very least, if I may be so bold, I would suggest that you share your misgivings with trusted members of your Brotherhood. They would be better placed than I to advise on this matter, particularly if any of them is acquainted with "Mr. S" and can offer an informed opinion as to his character. In this regard, may I commend our mutual friend Roberts to you. It seems clear from the contents of your letter that you have not, as yet, consulted him. I must confess that I find this curious, and cannot help but wonder if it signals a concern that Roberts might disapprove of some aspect of this enterprise. If that is the case, sir, I must warn you that anything arousing Roberts's disapprobation would be likely to inspire similar sentiments on my part, as I know him to be a man of sound judgment. I do not mean for this to sound harsh; I hope rather that it moves you to seek his counsel, which should be valued at least as highly as my own.

I regret I cannot offer more, but as a man of science, I am not disposed to speculation. However, I would very much welcome the continuation of our correspondence, in the hopes that I am able to be more helpful in future.

Yours very sincerely,
Edwin Marshall

"So," Chapman said when we'd finished reading. "Got any ideas about the mysterious Mr. S?"

Thomas sighed. "I'm afraid not. And it would appear that our plans to interview Roberts may not prove as fruitful as we'd hoped. The contents of this letter would seem to suggest that he isn't party to the conspiracy, at least directly."

Chapman looked thoughtful. "Unless Roberts and Mr. S are the same person, and Crowe was just using an alias to keep his correspondent from guessing."

The thought had occurred to me, too, but it didn't feel right. "If Jacob Crowe didn't trust Roberts, it seems to me this Mr. Marshall is about the last person he'd write to for advice."

"Agreed," said Thomas. "It's clear from this letter that Crowe and Marshall weren't previously acquainted. If Crowe were going to reach out to a stranger, why choose one who just happens to be a longtime friend of the man you suspect? No, were I to hazard a guess, I'd say that Crowe chose his correspondent precisely because he *did* trust Roberts, but didn't dare consult him directly. Telling Roberts the truth would have meant unmasking himself as a thief, so he did the next best thing, writing to another expert whose opinion Roberts valued."

"Wouldn't that get back to Roberts eventually?" Chapman asked.

"Perhaps, but by then Crowe would have had time to consider the best course of action."

"Which he did," I said, "and it got him killed. He decided to drop the experiments, and Mr. S didn't like that."

"In other words," Thomas said, "our theory has been sound in all the particulars save one: the involvement of Roberts."

"Which means our best lead just went up in smoke." The words tasted like ash on my tongue.

"I wouldn't go that far. Roberts may yet hold some clue as to the identity of Mr. S." Thomas started to say more but was interrupted by the doorbell. Frowning, he went to answer it, returning a moment later with an unsealed letter. "It's from Miss Harris."

"The Bloodhound?" Frankly, I was a little surprised she was even literate.

He scanned the scrap of paper, and as he read, the exhaustion seemed to melt away from his features. "She's found the Irishman and his gang. The lot of them are drinking at the Tub of Blood right now. I say, that's quick work, even for her."

"Tub of Blood?" Chapman made a face. "Half the saloons below the Line go by that name. She give you something more specific?"

"On the Bowery, just north of Canal. She's waiting outside, keeping an eye on them." He snatched his overcoat from the rack. "I have to go."

"Hold up there, chief. This fella's wanted for murder. We'll be doing this properly. Just let me use your phone and I'll call the station."

Thomas looked aghast at the idea. "We haven't the time, and even if we did, involving the police would only make a mess of things."

"Glad to hear you have such faith in law enforcement, Wiltshire."

"Sergeant, please. I know you'd prefer to do things by the book, but there's too much at stake. This isn't merely a murder investigation. Those men may be our only link to finding their employer, and he, in turn, may hold the key to ending the scourge of shades afflicting this city. How many bodies today?"

Chapman sucked at a tooth and glanced away. "Unexplained deaths . . . half a dozen."

"Half a dozen deaths in a single day. If you would spare others that fate, please, let me handle this."

"Look, I don't deny we got problems in the department, but doing things by the book is what separates me from the crooked ones."

"What separates you from your colleagues is competence."

Chapman scowled. "If you think insulting my fellow officers is gonna convince me—"

"Can't you see I'm trying to avoid a bloodbath?"

"*Stop.*" I stepped between them, literally. "Mr. Wiltshire is right, Sergeant. These are dangerous men. You show up at that saloon with a bunch of coppers . . . Well, I think we all know what'll happen." I could see Chapman was about to object, so I went on hastily, "But you're right, too—the police ought to be involved. So maybe we can compromise. You come along and help us make sure we take our man alive."

"*We?*" He flicked an eyebrow. "You're not suggesting you oughta come along, too?"

"No, I'm not *suggesting* it, I'm telling you. Both of you," I added, shooting Thomas a warning look. "I have more at stake here than you know, Sergeant, and I'm not about to be left out just because I'm a woman."

Thomas and Chapman eyed each other for a long moment, silently transmitting manly thoughts. I could guess what they were, but I didn't care. Chapman would have to handcuff me to the front door if he wanted to leave me behind. As for Thomas, I think he'd finally learned that there was no point trying to put me off.

Chapman sighed and looked away, shaking his head in irritation.

"It would be good to have you there, Sergeant," Thomas said. "I could use a man of your experience."

Man. Experience. At least one of those words was aimed at me, but I let it alone. We'd come a long way in twenty-four hours, Thomas and I; by this time tomorrow, I figured our working relationship would be good and broken in.

If I lived that long.

"All right," Chapman said, "but so help me, Wiltshire, if our man slips away because of this . . ."

"If our man slips away, we have much more to fear than a botched murder investigation." So saying, Thomas grabbed his hat.

"What in the hell took you so long?" the Bloodhound hissed from the shadows. "And what's *he* doing here?"

I counted it a strange sort of victory that Annie didn't seem to have any objection to my presence—just the copper's.

"We need all the help we can get," Thomas said, his words half lost amid the babble of revelers lining the street. "Now, are you certain he's in there?"

"Him or his gang, or both."

Thomas frowned. "You were paid to find the murderer, not his accomplices."

"Like I said, it's damned tough tracking that scent. Fact is, I only found it 'cause of the rotten gas, and there's at least three of 'em in there reek of it. How do I know who's who?"

"I should have given you a physical description." Irritably, Thomas added, "And you should have asked for one."

"Never needed one before." Annie shrugged. "Reckon there's a first time for everything."

"All right," Chapman said, "let's do this. You armed, Wiltshire?"

Thomas nodded, drawing his trusty derringer from the silk lining of his jacket. Chapman eyed the little pistol with a frown, drawing his own weapon—a Colt .45, naturally. The Bloodhound reached into the waistband of her men's trousers and pulled out a big army revolver.

I gave Thomas a sour look.

"Pinkerton with a muff pistol," the Bloodhound said with a shake of her head. "Now I seen everything."

Our strange foursome hurried across the Bowery, guns tucked away once more as we weaved through the crowd. My pulse should have been pounding in my ears, but instead I felt curiously calm as I hefted my own lacy little pistol inside my pocket. In a few minutes, I might have cause to fire this gun, something I'd never done before. Maybe even to kill a man, if things got out of hand. That ought to have terrified me, but for some reason I just couldn't call up the fear. I guess when you've got a fragment of a dead woman working its way toward your heart, it's hard for anything else to compete.

"I'll head around back," Annie said, "in case any of 'em tries to make a run for it."

"Remember," Thomas said, "this is a live bounty. If he dies . . ."

"Don't you fret, Pinkerton. Comes to that, I'll take me a leg shot." She flashed a rotten-toothed smile and ducked around the side of the building.

"Here's what I'm thinking," Chapman said. "After what happened at the gasworks, these fellas'll see you coming a mile off. So what say I head in there first, get the lay of things. I'll sidle up to the nearest Irish accent and we can take it from there."

"That sounds eminently sensible," Thomas said.

"The ringleader has auburn hair," I told the detective, "and he's big. Well over six feet. Flashy dresser, too, like a Bowery Boy."

With a brisk nod, Chapman shouldered his way through the door.

Thomas drew out his Patek Philippe (an instrument not much smaller than the derringer, incidentally) and we waited a full five minutes before following the detective.

It was a scene straight out of a dime novel—or a Sunday morning sermon. The place was packed to the rafters, roughs and gamblers and stargazers mingling with rheumy-eyed old men who looked like they were ready for the potter's field. The piano was out of tune, the laughter shrill and gritty, the air so thick with cheap cigars that it brought tears to my eyes. It was, in short, a living ode to the sporting life, the kind you're always hearing about but rarely see in the flesh. And sweet Mary and Joseph, was there flesh—not just of the female variety. A few of the men had taken off their shirts, presumably getting ready for a boxing match. Most gin joints cover the floorboards in sawdust to help sop up the beer, but I had a feeling that wasn't all that got spilled in here. The Tub of Blood had probably earned its name a dozen times over.

"And here I thought One-Eyed Johnny's was bad," I muttered as we elbowed our way through the mob. "Annie'll be right at home, anyway."

"Sorry?" Thomas couldn't hear a word above the clamoring piano.

"Never mind."

He'd had the good sense to leave his fur-collared overcoat behind, and he took his tall hat off now, tossing it onto a table as he passed. He didn't exactly blend in, but at least he didn't stand out quite as much. As for me, a few of the patrons might wonder at the presence of a woman who obviously wasn't a stargazer, but I doubted I'd attract anything more than idle curiosity.

We found Chapman near the bar. Scanning the patrons nearest him, I tensed in instant recognition. The short, stocky man from Sligo—the one who'd brought Thomas his lunch at the gasworks—hovered near the detective's elbow, along with the man who'd attacked us with a knife. The big auburn-haired fellow was nowhere to be seen.

Thomas leaned in close to my ear. "I recognize three of them. You?"

I raised two fingers.

"The third man, the one you haven't had the pleasure of meeting—he's the chap with the ridiculous side-whiskers. No sign of the ginger, though."

I shook my head. "I'll make my way over and signal to Chapman. You stay back—they'll recognize you straightaway."

Thomas pursed his lips in displeasure, but he nodded.

I drew out my hairpin—still mangled from its work on Thomas's bonds—and let my hair fall down about my face, partially hiding my features. Thomas watched me in silence. Just as I was about to turn away, he reached for me, brushing my forehead as he took a lock of hair between his fingers. He paused for a moment as if he might say something. Then, gently, he arranged the hair over my stitches.

I don't know if it was the look in his eyes or something else entirely, but suddenly I felt very nervous indeed. But it was too late to back out now. Squaring my shoulders, I started off through the crowd.

Chapman spotted me from a way off. Slowly, deliberately, I cut a glance at the short man from Sligo. Then, bringing a hand to my forehead as if to brush hair from my eyes, I raised three fingers, drawing them conspicuously down the side of my face to indicate side-whiskers. In reply, Chapman cocked his head subtly at the remaining man, the one in the bowler hat. I confirmed it with a nod, then watched as Chapman reached into his jacket to rest a hand on the butt of his revolver.

I sidled up to the bar at right angles from Chapman and the Irishmen, giving myself a good line of sight.

A few moments later Thomas appeared, moving fast through the crowd. He came up behind Sligo and pressed his gun to the back of the short man's head, and before his comrades could even react, Chapman had Bowler Hat by the scruff of the neck, revolver jammed into his ribs. Figuring that was my cue, I drew my own gun and leveled it across the corner of the bar at Side-whiskers.

The floor around us cleared awfully quickly after that, the saloon's patrons retreating to a safe distance to watch the drama unfold. Most of the chatter died down, though the piano player went on stomping on the keys, oblivious.

Bowler had a gun of his own stashed in his jacket; Chapman grabbed it and pointed it at the barman. "Hands where I can see 'em. No need to make this your concern."

The barman eyed him darkly but complied, raising his hands up from under the bar where he'd been reaching for whatever weapon helped him keep order in the Tub of Blood.

Thomas patted his man down and found another gun, plus a knife concealed in the man's belt. "Here, Miss Gallagher," he said, sliding the revolver down the bar toward me. "Perhaps that will suit your tastes better."

I picked up the Colt .45—and very nearly dropped it, surprised by its weight. It was all I could do to hold the thing steady with one hand while I cocked the hammer, but I didn't dare lose face now. "Thanks," I said stoutly, "it does."

Chapman frisked Bowler, then Side-whiskers. More guns and knives on the bar; he had the barman toss them into an ash-can. By this point, the music had finally gone silent, so his next words were clear to everyone in the saloon: "Who gets the cuffs?"

"How about you use 'em on yourself, copper?"

Thomas stiffened, but before he could turn the auburn-haired Irishman had the barrel of a revolver pressed against the base of his skull.

Where in the hell did he come from? Not that it mattered; he'd got the drop on us somehow, and now the tables had most definitely turned.

"I'll have your iron on the floor," he said, "all of you."

Chapman narrowed one sleepy eye. "Seems to me we got a standoff here. You got one of ours, we got three of yours. Advantage to us, I'd say."

"You sure about that, copper? What makes you think you know who's who? Could be five of me lads in here, or ten. Maybe this saloon belongs to one of me mates."

"Or maybe," Sligo put in, "there's a fair few in here who

fancy the idea of having a go at a copper and a Pinkerton, just for the hell of it."

The first threat was probably bluster, but the second rang true. I couldn't help glancing nervously at the crowd, wondering how many had been thinking just that.

"I'll have a go!" cried a slurring voice, and a wreck of a woman lurched through the onlookers. She made it as far as the edge of the crowd before blundering drunkenly into the corner of a table and tumbling to the floor, landing in a heap in the middle of the standoff.

Thomas moved.

Liquid as a dance step, he twisted and threw the big Irishman over his hip, planting him flat on his back even as he wrenched the man's wrist, forcing him to drop the gun. Before Sligo could turn to help, the Bloodhound had her Colt pointed at his chest, grinning up at him from the floor with her rotten smile. As for Chapman, he'd clocked his man in the skull with the butt of his revolver, sending him staggering. That left the detective free to deal with Side-whiskers, since I was too far away to do anything but shoot the man down.

Unfortunately, we all forgot about the barman, and before anyone could react he had a shotgun racked and leveled across the bar at Sergeant Chapman.

That's when things turned into a real bag of nails.

Quicker than you could say *rough neighborhood*, pistols and knives were everywhere. The crowd was nervous now; what had started out as a good show was turning into something uglier. So far nobody looked to be choosing sides, but I'd witnessed enough street brawls to know that could change in a heartbeat. As for the barman, I think he intended to chase the lot of us out of his saloon, but he never got the chance. Side-whiskers must have liked his odds now that Chapman was staring down the barrel of a shotgun, because he threw an elbow into the detective's ribs and made a grab for his gun.

A split second later the auburn-haired Irishman drew a knife and slashed it across the back of Thomas's leg. Thomas buckled, sending Sligo sprawling; the Bloodhound mistook the sudden movement for an attack and fired. She'd aimed low, but the short man had lost his balance and took the bullet full in the chest. He collapsed right on top of her. Thomas went for the fallen gun, but the auburn-haired man was faster, hauling him down and using his bulk to pin Thomas's slender form to the floor.

Shouts from the crowd now, people scattering. A bystander tried to wrestle Side-whiskers away from Chapman, but all he managed to do was knock the detective off balance. Still weapon-less, Side-whiskers lunged for a bottle of whiskey on the bar—startling the barman and ending up with a gutful of buckshot for his troubles. Bowler fared no better; he got tangled up with the helpful bystander and took a bowie knife in the belly. As for me, I'd nearly reached Thomas by the time Annie righted herself. She kicked the auburn-haired Irishman in the ribs and rolled him off Thomas. But the big man recovered quickly, and while Annie helped Thomas to his feet, the Irishman grabbed the fallen Colt and cocked the hammer.

I had a heartbeat to react, maybe less. I fired.

The bullet struck the Irishman in the thigh. He bucked on the floor, howling and clutching at his leg. Thomas snatched up the fallen gun, but he needn't have bothered; the thug wasn't going to be any more trouble. I might not have had Clara's medical train-ing, but I knew straightaway something was wrong. Blood pumped from the wound in great gushes, soaking the Irishman's trousers.

"Damn!" Thomas dropped to the man's side. "Quickly, Annie, your belt!"

"He needs a doctor," Chapman said, his words barely audible above the howls of pain. "I'll find a cab . . ." Meanwhile, Annie kept a wary eye on the saloon's patrons, in case anyone was still feeling jumpy.

The Irishman's screams were fading by the time Thomas drew the tourniquet tight. "Stay with me!" He slapped the big man's cheek. "I want a name! *Whose man are you?*"

But it was no use; the rough's eyelids fluttered and his head lolled. He wouldn't be answering questions anytime soon, and maybe not ever again.

Chapman found a cab, and a pair of stout patrons helped to hoist the wounded man up. All I could do was watch as they hauled the Irishman away. He was limp, bleeding, on the brink of death.

I've killed him, I thought numbly. And for good measure, I'd killed our case as well.

CHAPTER 26

HAND OF FATE—THE EMERALD ISLE—A KISS GOOD-BYE

Chapman climbed into the cab with the Irishman, but not before extracting a promise from Thomas to wait for the police. *No more dodging statements,* he'd said, and Thomas had just nodded, his gaze fixed on the unconscious figure slumped in the seat.

"I'm so sorry," I said miserably as the cab juddered away.

"You've nothing to be sorry for, Rose. You saved my life, again, and even had the presence of mind to take a leg shot. It's terribly bad fortune the bullet struck an artery, that's all."

Terribly bad fortune. That was one way of putting it. To me, it felt as if the hand of Fate had grabbed the blade of ice in my breast and given it a twist, just for spite.

Thomas tied a handkerchief around his slashed leg, and we

waited for the police. The crowd around us continued to grow. Half the saloon had followed us out into the street, and there's nothing like a mob to draw an even bigger mob. The Bowery was always good for a spectacle, especially on a Saturday night, and even if you were too late to catch the show, there was usually a good yarn to be had from the audience. I recognized one or two of the faces from the neighborhood, since we were only a few blocks away from Mam's flat. I wondered if it would get back to her that I'd been mixed up in a shoot-out in a Bowery saloon. For some reason, that almost made me laugh.

Annie reappeared, smelling of fresh whiskey. "Well, Pink, I done my part. Sorry your man took one in the pipes, but that ain't on my books."

Thomas gave her a sour look. "Don't worry, your reputation is intact."

"Reputation is everything in my line of work," the Bloodhound said, without a lick of irony.

"The Pinkerton Agency will see to the remainder of your payment."

She nodded, satisfied. "Good luck to you, then. Till next time." Doffing an imaginary hat, she tottered off down the road.

"She'll disappear for at least a week, I expect," Thomas said as he watched her go. "That's usually how long it takes her to drink away a bounty."

She'll still outlive me, most likely. I kept the dark thought to myself.

The coppers showed up, and we gave them a quick accounting of what had happened. We may have varnished things a little, casting the incident as a police operation with the support of the Pinkerton Detective Agency, but the coppers didn't seem much interested in the details anyway. To their way of thinking, four murder suspects had been dealt with, one of whom would be taken into custody if he lived, and that was good enough for them. They took Thomas's card in case they needed to follow up, and that was that.

By this point it was well after midnight. The longest day of my life was officially over. As for Thomas, he looked fit to collapse. "You need rest," I told him.

Alas, it was not to be.

"Rose," said a familiar voice, and I whirled in surprise.

"Pietro? What are you doing here?"

He stepped out from the crowd, scanning the scene warily. "Ricardo fetched me. He recognized you from Augusto's this afternoon, said you were in trouble."

"I'm not. That is, I was, but—"

"I watched you talking to the coppers. Word is they killed some Irishmen in there." His dark-eyed gaze slid to Thomas, and he added, "With a Pinkerton." For a moment I feared a rehashing of the argument outside Wang's, but Pietro had bigger worries. "After what happened this afternoon, Ricardo will have gone straight to Augusto with this news."

I tell you, that just about undid me. *Dear Lord in Heaven, is it too much to ask for one lucky break? Just one?* "What do you think he'll do?"

"I don't know, but after you left the store this afternoon, he went straight to work looking for the Irishmen who attacked you, and he didn't get back until suppertime. He's not a fool, Fiora. He will know these are the same men."

"Very well," Thomas said, "then we take the news to him ourselves. We explain that in a rare flash of police brilliance, the men who robbed Miss Gallagher were tracked to this location. One of the officers came to the house to inform her of the impending raid, and as her employer, I felt it my duty to come along. A gunfight ensued, *et cetera*."

Pietro listened with a wary frown. "And the Pinkerton?"

"Rumor. A bounty hunter who happened to be drinking at the Tub of Blood got involved, but as far as we know, she wasn't employed by the Pinkerton Detective Agency."

Pietro's glance cut between us. He didn't look convinced.

"Unless you've another suggestion?" Thomas said.

"No, I don't have another suggestion," Pietro returned coldly. "But if you want to do this, we should do it now, before the rumors get out of hand."

I groaned. "It's after midnight. Won't he have gone to bed?"

"No."

"How can you be sure?"

"Because he's Italian. Are we going or not?"

I didn't really understand what he meant until we hit Mulberry Street. Past midnight on a Saturday, yet lamplight glowed in many a window, and the scent of supper still lingered in the air. Augusto's, meanwhile, was in full swing. The king himself held court at the back of the store, pouring out little glasses of dark liquor for his subjects. The *padrone*'s wild eyebrows climbed at the sight of us, and he waved us over. "Come, *signorina*. Have a *digestivo*. I think you need it, yes?" He poured out three more glasses and handed them to us. "And who is your friend?"

"This is my employer, Mr. Wiltshire. Sir, this is Augusto, whom I was telling you about."

Thomas nodded politely. "A pleasure to meet you, sir. I'm very much obliged for your kindness to my . . . er . . . housemaid."

"Your *er* housemaid." Crinkles of amusement fringed Augusto's eyes. Definitely no fool, though I suspect the conclusions he was drawing just then were slightly off the mark. "And what brings you to our neighborhood, Mr. Wiltshire?"

I jumped in before Thomas could answer. "He's been such a gentleman," I said, and proceeded to recount the story we'd rehearsed. "It was simply terrifying. Mr. Wiltshire was even wounded trying to protect me." I gestured at the bloodied handkerchief tied around Thomas's calf. "I owe that bounty hunter a great debt, wherever she is."

Augusto regarded me with shrewd eyes. "You didn't tell me you had gone to the police with this."

"I'm sorry, I suppose I thought it went without saying. I started shouting for the police the moment those bandits were out of sight. A patrolman came running straightaway, but it was too late. It honestly never occurred to me that they'd find the culprits."

"They so rarely do," Thomas agreed. "I could hardly credit it when they came to my door."

"Well, it's over now, thanks God," Pietro said. "Those bastards got what they deserved."

Augusto grunted and sipped his liqueur.

I did the same; it was bitter enough to make me wince. "I'm so grateful for your help, Augusto. By the way, did you manage to find out who they were?"

I thought poor Pietro was going to choke on his *digestivo*. As for Thomas, he merely glanced at me, but I read the warning clearly enough: *Don't push it.*

"It's only, I still don't have my granny's brooch . . ."

"I found a man who knows them," Augusto said, sounding

more than a little smug. "They call themselves the East River Gang. This man I know, he says the whole Gashouse District belongs to them, so if somebody rob you there, it must have been one of theirs. We can go to see him tomorrow, if you like, to look for your grandmother's brooch. He runs a hockshop on Canal Street, and the East River boys sell him things now and then. I looked over his wares, and he has many brooches, but you never told me how yours looks, so I can't say if he has it or not." His eyes crinkled again, and he added, "I even saw a pin that made me think of you, *signorina*. An emerald pin for the lady from the Emerald Isle. A tie pin, though, so maybe not quite right for you." He laughed and sipped his drink.

"Sorry," Thomas put in, "did you say an emerald tie pin?"

"*Sì*. Very handsome. I would have bought it if I could afford it, but I think maybe you can." Augusto's glance flicked meaningfully over Thomas's fine clothing, and his smile was not altogether friendly.

"Actually, I think I may have one just like it. Was it this design, by any chance?" Thomas flashed his cuff links: the golden griffin with the emerald in its talons.

Augusto's eyes narrowed. "Exactly like that. How strange."

"Why, it's the crest of the Madison Club," Thomas said brightly, as if delighted by the discovery. "Every member has that very pin! Myself, I rarely wear it—a bit flashy for my tastes—but the cuff links suit me well. It sounds as if one of our members has fallen on hard times."

"Or maybe he *died*," Pietro said with an exasperated glare. His meaning was clear: Keep talking and maybe we would, too.

"Possible. We have many elderly members." Thomas paused,

grimacing in pain. "In any case, I think we'd better be off, Rose. It's late, and I daresay this leg of mine needs stitches."

Glancing down, I saw that it was only half a lie; the hand-kerchief was soaked through. "We may have to walk a few blocks before we find a nighthawk. Will you be all right?"

"I'll manage."

We downed our *digestivi*, made our farewells, and headed back out to the street. Pietro came to see us off, and when we were safely out of earshot, he rounded on Thomas. "What were you thinking, showing him those cuff links? You might be a very good liar, but that was a stupid risk to take."

"I needed to be certain."

"What for? So a man from the same club hocked his tie pin, what does that prove?"

"Nothing. It does, however, strongly suggest that whoever hired the East River Gang is a member of the Madison Club."

"We might have guessed that anyway," I pointed out. It hadn't taken me long to realize that when it came to matters of luck and the paranormal, all roads led to the Madison Club.

"Perhaps, but the circumstances of the pin's discovery tell us more still. The Madison Club is highly exclusive, its membership invariably wealthy. Why, the annual dues alone . . ." He trailed off awkwardly. Clearing his throat, he went on, "The point is, members of the Madison Club are not given to pawning their belongings, especially items as prestigious and recognizable as a membership pin. It suggests the pin's owner has fallen on very hard times indeed. And *there* is the real clue."

Now I understood. "Mr. S, who belongs to the Madison Club, is having money troubles."

"A highly specific profile, wouldn't you agree? Even if Mr. S is an alias, his financial situation winnows down the list of suspects considerably."

"Unless it's a coincidence and the pin doesn't belong to Mr. S at all."

"Too much of a coincidence to credit, surely. No, I'll wager that pin was used to purchase the services of a certain Irish gang."

Pietro followed this exchange with a sullen look. "So what now? You go to the police?"

"We go home," Thomas said, passing a weary hand over his eyes. "And we regroup in the morning. Shall we, Miss Gallagher?"

I hugged Pietro in farewell. "Thank you for everything you've done. Give Mam a kiss for me. I'll see you both . . ." I faltered, my throat closing over the words. "I'll see you soon."

We caught a cab on the Bowery and headed back uptown. Thomas was waning fast, but there was still a faint gleam in his eye. "We're nearly there," he murmured. "We've nearly got him. We'll have our hands on those manuscripts soon, and all this will be behind us."

All this. I wondered if that included the fragment of Matilda Meyer embedded in my breast.

Then Thomas glanced at me—a fleeting, haunted look—and I knew that it did. And I also knew that he only half believed it.

Anxious to change the subject, I gestured at his bandaged leg. "That really does need stitches. We ought to wake Clara when we get home."

He winced. "We've imposed on her enough for one night, don't you think?"

"You need to be in fighting shape. It'll be a long day tomorrow."

I wasn't about to take no for an answer, so when we arrived

at 726, I bounded up the servants' staircase and woke poor Clara. She was about as happy as you'd imagine, swearing into her pillow and muttering the whole way down the stairs, but she did the job, neat and steady as a surgeon, while Thomas perched awkwardly with his knee balanced on a chair.

"So," she said as she snipped the final knot, "you all planning on making a habit of this?"

Thomas surveyed her work approvingly. "One of us ought to."

She rolled her eyes. "Listen, just because you're my boss—"

"I'm not trying to tell you how to live your life, Clara. It's merely my belief that people ought to do what makes them happy."

"What makes you think I'm not happy cooking?"

"On the contrary, I think your enjoyment shows plainly in the quality of the dishes you turn out. I'm merely applying the same observation to your stitching. I'm not insensible to the difficulties you would face, but you strike me as more than strong enough to overcome them if it's something you genuinely love."

Clara didn't look appeased. "And you love this, do you?" She gestured at the pile of bloody bandages.

"Not every aspect of it, obviously. But on the whole, yes, I find my vocation satisfying."

"Uh-huh. And how about you, Rose? You fancy living the rest of your life like this?"

God help me, I did, even if the rest of my life were to be measured in hours instead of years. Which probably means I belong in the asylum on Blackwell's Island, but there it is. Even with the shadow of my own death hanging over me, the prospect of going back to a life of drudgery, of being merely *Rose the Maid*, was too awful to contemplate.

Clara saw it in my eyes, and she shook her head. "I'm going to bed."

"As should we all," Thomas said, rising. "You have my profound thanks, Clara, and my apologies for waking you. And Rose . . ." He paused, as though unsure how to finish that sentence.

Which was just as well, because whatever he planned to say, I wasn't in any shape to hear it. "Good night, Mr. Wiltshire. I'll see you in the morning."

That night I dreamed of the bloody woman. But it wasn't until the following morning that the real nightmare began.

I woke a little before dawn. On any other Sunday, I'd be putting on my best dress and heading downtown to take Mam to church. Belatedly, it occurred to me that I hadn't told Pietro I wouldn't be coming; Mam might still be expecting me. The thought of her perched on the end of her narrow bed, bonnet in lap, waiting for a daughter who might never arrive was so gut-wrenching that I nearly burst into tears. I remembered how long she'd waited for my da before finally accepting the truth. *He'll be along, Rose, dear. Just a few more days, you'll see.* It had seemed as if that winter would never end, and in some ways it hadn't; my father had never come home, and no one had ever explained why. Who would explain it to Mam if I didn't come home?

Clara was still out doing the shopping when I reached the kitchen, so I went up to the dining room, where I found Thomas flapping restlessly through *The New York Herald*. He stood when I entered the room, as if I were a proper lady instead of his maid. "How are you feeling?"

"All right, I suppose." That was a lie. It might have been my imagination, but it felt as if something cold pressed against my heart, like a blade held to the throat—but it would do no good to tell him so. He knew perfectly well I was running out of time, and there was nothing he could do about it. "Clara's gone out for groceries. I'm sure she'll be back directly. Shall I bring tea in the meantime?"

"Thank you. You'll have some, of course? I daresay both of us are going to need a lot of tea to get through the day."

A soft knock sounded; Mrs. Sellers came in. "I apologize for the interruption," she said, her tone as stiff as her posture, "but there's a gentleman at the door. I'm afraid he wouldn't give his name."

"I see. Thank you, Mrs. Sellers." Thomas donned his jacket and headed for the front door, leaving behind an awkward silence. The housekeeper glared at me, her mouth a thin line of disapproval.

"Mrs. Sellers, I know these past few days have been—"

"Don't concern yourself, *Miss Gallagher*," she said coldly, and disappeared.

I lingered in the dining room, torn between fetching the promised tea and following Thomas to the front door. The matter was settled when I heard the unmistakable lilt of an Irish accent, followed by "*Give me one good reason why I shouldn't shoot you down where you stand.*"

Cursing under my breath, I grabbed the nearest weapon to hand: a fire iron from the hearth. So armed, I flew out into the hall to find Thomas leveling his derringer at a bearded stranger in a bowler hat.

"You could do that," the stranger replied coolly, "if you didn't get your fill of gunplay last night. But it'd have unfortunate consequences for your cook."

The sound of my gasp drew the Irishman's gaze over Thomas's shoulder. "Ah, here she is, the Irish girl I've been hearing so much about. We'd have preferred to grab her instead, but that turned out to be a bit tricky, what with the two of you being joined at the hips." He sneered, in case either of us had missed the innuendo.

Blood roared in my ears. I advanced on the stranger, brandishing the fire iron. "What have you done with Clara?"

"Stay back," Thomas said. "It's me they want."

"What do you mean?"

The Irishman's glance met mine. "It's simple, love. Your boss here comes with me and translates the papers, nice and quiet and cooperative, and the cook goes free. He refuses, or calls the coppers, or pulls that trigger . . ." He shrugged.

"*Clara* goes free," I said. "And what about Thomas?"

"Well, now, that's up to him."

Thomas snorted. "I rather doubt that."

The stranger just shrugged again. "Not my decision. Makes you feel any better, boss did his best to get on without you, but whatever fish he was hoping to snag on the other end of that line, that ain't what's biting. Got a few unwelcome guests about. So here we are."

My knuckles went white against the fire iron, as if I were throttling it. I wanted to hurt this man so badly I could taste it, a metallic bite on my tongue.

"It seems I have no choice," Thomas said, lowering his gun.

"Thomas, no!" I grabbed his arm. "You can't—"

"I'll come with you," he told the stranger, "but I need a moment alone with Miss Gallagher. Wait by the carriage."

"Do you think I'm stupid, Englishman?"

"Eavesdrop if you must," Thomas said coldly, "but at least

have the decency to accord us the *illusion* of privacy while we say our farewells."

The Irishman dropped back a single pace and folded his arms.

Thomas turned to me. "Rose—"

"You can't," I said again, fighting back tears. "They'll kill you."

"They'll certainly kill Clara if I don't. This is my fault. I have to do everything I can to fix it."

"But—"

"Listen." Laying a hand against my cheek, he leaned in close, as though comforting a distraught lover. "Listen to me carefully, Rose. What I said last night—I meant every word."

I gazed back at him vacantly . . . and then I understood. He was sending a ciphered message of his own, under cover of a lover's words. *What I said last night . . .*

"About the emerald," he prompted, his thumb drifting along my cheekbone.

"Yes, the emerald. I remember." *There is the real clue*, he'd said. The tie pin would lead us to Mr. S.

"You'll have it soon. We've narrowed it down already. Now all you have to do is pick it out. Burrows will help you."

I heard the message all too clearly, and it terrified me. He was counting on *me* to work out the identity of his kidnapper. To come to his rescue, and Clara's. "But what if I can't . . . find one I like? There's so little time."

Cupping my chin in his hand, he leaned in closer. "You found me once," he murmured. "You can do it again."

The Irishman growled impatiently. "I haven't got all day. Just kiss her and be done with it."

Thomas obliged, brushing my lips with his. "Burrows," he whispered, his mouth barely grazing mine. "No police."

To this day I wonder if, had he known of my feelings, he would have imposed upon them so cruelly. As it was, I had all I could do to hold it together. I stood there mute and shaking, my insides buffeted by waves of emotion I couldn't name, let alone give voice to.

"I'll do everything I can to protect Clara, I swear it."

I believed him, and that was the problem. Any way I looked at it, I couldn't see an outcome that didn't involve one of the people I cared about most in this world ending up dead. Even if I managed to work out the identity of the kidnapper, there was no guarantee it would lead me to Thomas and Clara in time to help them—or myself.

It was in that moment, I think, that the reality of my own situation truly sank in. *I could die.* Nor were his prospects of survival any better. In all likelihood, we would never see each other again. "Thomas . . ."

I love you.

The words were on my lips, but I didn't dare speak them. I couldn't add to his burden now.

His pale eyes held mine for a heartbeat longer. "Good-bye, Rose."

"Remember," the Irishman called as they climbed into the carriage, "you try following us, the cook dies. You call the coppers, she dies."

He twitched the reins, and they were gone.

I stood trembling in the doorway for a solid minute, maybe two. Then I grabbed my overcoat, Mr. Wang's special tea, and my Colt .45, and I hailed a cab.

CHAPTER 27

TIE PIN IN A HAYSTACK—FISHING FOR
PHANTOMS—GOOD NEWS

M r. Burrows listened to my tale in silence, his expression keen
but composed, only the tension of his posture betraying any
emotion. I spared him the details, but even so there was a lot
to get through, and I couldn't help marveling at how much had
happened since I'd seen him last, barely twenty-four hours ago.
Maybe that explained why I felt as if I'd aged a decade since then.

When I'd finished, Mr. Burrows sprang from his seat and
started to pace. "The Irishman gave no clue as to where he might
have taken them?"

"The carriage was headed up Fifth Avenue, but beyond
that . . ." I shook my head. "The East River Gang used to make its
headquarters in the old Consolidated Gas factory, but they'll have
cleared out by now, what with the police poking around. Our best

hope is working out the identity of the man Jacob Crowe mentioned in his letter. Mr. Wiltshire thought you would be able to help with that." I could still feel the thrill of Thomas's lips as he'd whispered that advice—hand cupping my chin, mouth warm against mine. For how long had I dreamed of his kiss? To have the moment finally arrive—but only as subterfuge, in what might very well have been our last moments together . . . It tasted more of cruelty than joy.

"Whoever he is, he's a ruthless bastard," Mr. Burrows growled. "Kidnapping, murder, and for what? To translate a bunch of papers?"

"Papers that may hold the key to entering the otherworld, not to mention a host of other powerful spells. Mr. Wiltshire and Mr. Drake were both adamant that we recover those folios."

"Recover them? We ought to destroy them!"

"We can't, at least not yet. They might be able to help me . . ." I trailed off awkwardly.

"Help you how?"

"There's something else. I didn't mention it before because I didn't want you to worry. I won't slow you down, I promise."

"Why should you slow me down?"

"The shade . . . when she touched me . . ."

"Oh, no. Oh, Rose." He sank back down onto the sofa. "A fragment?"

I looked away. I couldn't face the pity I saw in his eyes. "But there's hope. Mr. Jackson is on his way from Chicago, and Mr. Wiltshire thinks the folios might contain something that could help me. Anyway I feel fine, at least for now. I won't be distracted by it."

"Good God, Rose, you'd be superhuman if you weren't."

Clearing my throat, I continued. "In any case, it seems to me we have two possible paths to Mr. Wiltshire and Clara: Mr. S and the Bloodhound."

Mr. Burrows sighed. "I doubt Annie will be an option. She usually disappears after a job, crawling into some horrid little den or another until she's drunk her bounty dry. We can always ask, but . . . I don't suppose One-Eyed Johnny's will have a telephone, will they? I'll send my coachman down." He rang a bell and, after a hurried conversation with his butler, dispatched the coachman on his errand. "Now, as to the identity of Mr. S, it's not quite a needle in a haystack, but it's not obvious, either. Let me see . . . There's Sanford, but as far as I know, his finances have recovered from the crash. Sturgeon? No, he's in France for the winter. Summers, but he's rich as Croesus . . ."

And so on, dismissing each name as soon as they occurred to him. He tried telephoning Mr. Roberts and even Edmund Drake, but they were both at church. "I'm sorry," he said at length, "I'm afraid I'm thoroughly confounded. We could head down to the club and ask for the members' roll, but I'm quite sure I've exhausted all the S's. It must be an alias."

At which point I made a rather emphatic remark that doesn't bear repeating. Suffice it to say that it qualifies as one of the more colorful examples of Five Points vernacular. Mr. Burrows observed this lapse without comment, which I took as a sign that he was just as upset as I.

I racked my brain for a moment. "Maybe we're coming at this backward. Instead of trying to think of a Mr. S who's broke, what if we focused on the broke part first? Mr. Wiltshire seemed to think it very strange that a member of the Madison Club would be obliged to hock his tie pin."

"Quite shocking, in fact. Even in '84, such behavior would have been extreme—but that's just the problem. A man in such embarrassing circumstances isn't likely to telegraph his situation too widely."

"Weren't you the one who told me that Fifth Avenue loved nothing better than gossip? Surely *somebody* knows?"

His eyes lit up. "Of course, I know exactly whom to call! She ought to be at home, the old goat. Too fat to go much of anywhere these days . . ." He stalked out of the parlor, and a few minutes later, his familiar merry tones floated down the hallway, punctuated by the occasional burst of laughter. To listen to him, you'd think nothing whatever was amiss. I envied him that talent just now. I'd done my best to pack my fear down into the pit of my stomach, but I could still feel it churning away like a supper that didn't quite agree with me. Nearly an hour had passed since Thomas had climbed into the Irishman's carriage. I could feel the time ticking by as surely as if I still had his watch tucked into my breast pocket. My hand went to my mouth, fingertips drifting across my lips. *You should have told him. You might never get another chance . . .*

Mr. Burrows returned, his expression smooth as marble. He walked over to the mantel, picked up an engraved Carcel lamp, and hurled it against the wall. Glass exploded, and the heavy base met the floor with a desultory *thunk,* sending a pool of oil spreading over the parquet. "Please forgive the outburst," Mr. Burrows said, straightening his waistcoat, "but my telephone conversation was a trifle discouraging."

"What happened?"

He sighed, throwing himself onto the sofa. "Old Mrs. Phipps didn't disappoint. Once I mentioned the Madison Club, she had

Mr. S picked out straightaway. You were right, it was an alias. For Mr. Danforth Essex, of Barber, Essex and North. Do you know it?" When I shook my head, he went on, "A Wall Street firm of some repute. At least until recently, when Mr. Barber disappeared with rather a lot of his clients' money. That left Essex and North in a tricky spot. Completely ruined, in point of fact. Assets seized, possible charges pending. I'm a fool not to have worked it out, except that I was so distracted by the damned initial."

"*S*," I murmured. "Essex. You're sure it's him?"

"Quite sure. I've seen him in Jacob and Freddie's company more than once."

"Why, but isn't that good news? Now that we know who he is, we can find him and—"

"That's just it. We can't. In good high society fashion, Essex has fled in the face of scandal, hoping to hide away until the storm passes. No one has heard from him in days. I suspect he's in the country somewhere, but that doesn't narrow it down much. It would be one thing if we could go to the police—"

"We don't dare. If Essex finds out—"

"He'll kill Thomas and Clara. Yes, you made that clear—hence my outburst." He gestured at the lamp. "Immensely satisfying, by the way. Would you care to have a go with the other one? Not much point in keeping only one of a pair."

The sick feeling in my belly reared up, like a pot coming to a boil. At last we knew who was behind everything—the murders, the kidnappings, the stolen folios, all of it—and it didn't do us a lick of good. We had no idea how to find Essex or where he'd taken Thomas and Clara. We didn't know how to seal the portal or cut the magical rope or . . .

I paused.

"Now there's a look I recognize." Mr. Burrows leaned forward eagerly. "I've seen it on Wiltshire's face a dozen times. Tell me."

"Something the Irishman said. *Whatever fish he was hoping to catch on that line,* or something to that effect. He mentioned unwanted guests, which I took to mean shades."

"So?"

"When we spoke to Matilda Meyer, she said she'd followed the ribbon of light to Jacob Crowe. If Essex has been fiddling with that spell, might she be able to follow it to him, too?"

Mr. Burrows was on his feet before I'd even finished speaking. "Rose Gallagher, when this thing is done, if Wiltshire doesn't marry you on the spot, I'll have him committed. Get your coat."

"Rose?" Mei Wang came out from behind the counter, visibly surprised to see me. "Are you all right? Where is Mr. Wiltshire?"

Before I could answer, Mr. Wang came flying out of the back rooms, waving his arms frantically as though trying to shoo a stray hog. "Go away! Not safe!"

"I know, but—"

Mr. Smith appeared from behind the silk curtain. "I say, Wang, what's all this—"

The medium's presence struck me like a tuning fork. I doubled over, ears ringing, body thrumming. White light flared in my vision; every beat of my heart sent ripples of cold pulsing out from my core. The pain was unbearable, and I very nearly blacked out, but somehow I managed to pull the little pouch of tea leaves out of my pocket. Mei grabbed a pot of green tea from behind the counter and tossed the contents of my pouch inside, and a moment later I had a cup of hot liquid to my lips. I gulped it down—

only to throw it back up again. My chest grew tight. I could hardly swallow, hardly breathe for the panic.

If it hadn't been for Mei, I don't think I would have made it.

She steered me away from the others and sat me on the floor, like a mother comforting a squalling child. "Breathe," she murmured. "It's only pain. Your body still works. You can breathe." Putting her arms around me, she sang softly in my ear. Dimly, I recognized the song from yesterday.

Breathe, Rose. The voice in my head was Mam's. *Just breathe.* Gradually, I managed to drag a little more air into my lungs.

"Now drink." Mei held the cup to my lips.

This time I managed to hold it down, and a moment later, the fragment subsided. The ringing in my ears faded, leaving only the soft, sweet sound of Mei's singing. I'm not sure if it was the lullaby or Mei's arms around me or the lingering sound of Mam's voice in my head, but it was all I could do in that moment not to cry like a baby.

"It's my fault." Mr. Burrows's voice sounded strangely distant, though he stood only a few feet away. "I shouldn't have brought her. I didn't realize the shade was still in the store."

"And I didn't realize Miss Gallagher was out here," Mr. Smith said, "or I'd have stayed in the back. Will she be all right, Wang?"

"For now." Mr. Wang sounded angry, and when I looked up he was scowling at me like a furious father. He said something in Chinese, then made a sharp gesture at Mei, instructing her to translate.

"My father says you are . . ." She paused, looking embarrassed.

"Stupid?"

"Careless."

"Close enough." I struggled to my feet, leaning heavily on Mr. Burrows. "I'm sorry for scaring everyone, but I didn't have much choice. Mr. Burrows, maybe you could . . . ?"

"Of course."

Propping myself against the counter, I downed two more cups of special tea while Mr. Burrows explained the situation. By the time he was through, I felt a little stronger. "Believe me, Mr. Wang, I wouldn't be here if I could have avoided it, but Matilda Meyer may be our only hope of finding Mr. Wiltshire and Clara." Glancing uncomfortably at Mr. Smith, I asked, "Is she . . . ?"

"Right here." The medium gestured at the empty air beside him. "That's why the fragment resonated as strongly as it did. She cannot physically manifest until sunset, but she can see and hear us well enough. And I can hear her."

"Can you ask her . . . Does she still see the ribbon of light?"

Mr. Smith tilted his head, listening. "Not here. She would have to return to Hell Gate."

"Is she willing?" Mr. Burrows asked, looking only slightly flustered at the idea that he stood mere feet from a shade.

Another pause. Mr. Smith nodded gravely. "She is. But it will take time."

Desperation arced through me, as bright and cold as a flaring fragment. "Time is the one thing we don't have."

"We can only do so much, my dear," the little man said. "If it makes you feel any better, Mrs. Meyer has already put herself to the task. She is gone."

A gray silence settled over the store, broken only by the low groan of wind through the hastily boarded front door. Then

Mr. Wang clapped his hands, saying something in a businesslike tone.

"My father asks that you join him in the back," Mei said. "There is some good news, at least."

"Thank God for that," Mr. Burrows muttered, and we trailed the Wangs through the warren of back rooms.

CHAPTER 28

HENNY WEBER, WITCH—A VERY OLD
DEBATE—DEATH IS NOT THE
END—ZHÀNSHÌ

The good news turned out to be a witch.

She didn't *look* like a witch—or so I thought at the time, my expectations having been molded by storybook tales of wizened old crones and black cats. Plump, golden-haired and ruddy-cheeked, with deep dimples and sparkling blue eyes, she looked more like somebody's favorite auntie, the kind who's always baking cookies and slipping you peppermints when your mam's not looking. "Henny Vayber," she said in a thick German accent, shaking my hand. "Pleased to meet you." She gave me a little embossed card. It read HENNY WEBER, WITCH.

"Mrs. Weber is an alchemist," Mei said.

"Best in America," Mr. Wang added.

"Oh, dear." Mrs. Weber flushed with pleasure. "I don't

know about that, but I have learned a trick or two in my long years." Her long years couldn't have added up to much more than forty, I reckoned, but it was hard to be sure with such a cherubic face.

"I'm sorry," I said, "I'm afraid I don't know what an alchemist is."

When Henny Weber smiled, her eyes all but disappeared behind the rosy apples of her cheeks. "It is nearly the same as a chemist," she said, gesturing at a collection of glass bottles and vials arrayed on a nearby table. "It starts with the science of mixing things together. Then, with a bit of luck and a lot of magic, I can bend the laws of nature just enough"—she held her thumb and forefinger half an inch apart—"to do some very interesting things." She laughed merrily, as if she'd told a joke.

"Luck *and* magic?" I glanced at Mr. Burrows, confused. "I thought those were two different things."

"They are. Let me see, how shall I explain it? Do you attend the opera at all?"

"Why, of course. I have my very own box right next to the Duke of Buckingham." I gave him a flat look, in case he'd missed the sarcasm.

"Yes, well." He cleared his throat awkwardly. "I imagine it's the same for any type of music. That is to say, there are those with raw talent who can simply pick up an instrument for the first time and create beautiful music, even if it's not very complicated. And there are those who, through studious application and practice, learn to play proficiently, but without any real . . ." He paused, searching for the right word.

"Soul," Henny Weber supplied.

"Exactly. *Soul.* That intangible thing that transforms a sequence of notes into something genuinely moving. The true virtuoso has both of these things: craft *and* talent."

"So magic is craft and luck is talent?"

"That's right." Mr. Burrows looked very pleased with himself for explaining it so efficiently. "One needn't be endowed with luck to learn magic, but the most gifted witches generally are."

Mr. Wang said something in a tinder-dry tone, which Mei diplomatically translated as "My father disagrees. And respectfully, so do I. My mother was not lucky, but she was a very powerful witch."

"Yes, well." Mr. Burrows inclined his head in polite acknowledgment. "It's a very old debate. But the important question is, can you seal the portal, Mrs. Weber?"

"I hope so. I specialize in opening and sealing things, which is why Mr. Wang sent for me all the way from Lancaster. I have never tried something as big as this, but the same basic principles apply, which means the right alkahest should do the trick. The hard part is getting it into place. The portal is at the bottom of the East River, after all."

I had no idea what an *alkahest* was, but Mr. Burrows and the Wangs looked hopeful, so I chose to follow their lead. I desperately needed a little hope just then.

"Even so," Mrs. Weber went on, "the seal will be imperfect, which means we must dispel the ribbon of light. Otherwise, spirits will still find their way out."

"Matilda Meyer seeks out the ribbon of light as we speak," Mr. Smith said. "Hopefully, she will be able to follow it to the caster, and we can stop him and recover the folios."

"And save Mr. Wiltshire and Clara," I added with a frown.

The medium gave a little bow of acknowledgment. "Of course your friends are our chief concern. All I meant is that once they're safe and we have the manuscripts in our possession, we can finally put an end to this madness."

Something occurred to me then, another branch of hope blossoming in my breast. "Mrs. Weber—"

"Henny, please."

"Henny. Once we have the cipher manuscripts, will you be able to cast any spell you find there?"

Mr. Burrows understood straightaway. "I think what Miss Gallagher is asking is whether you might be able to use the folios to remove the fragment embedded in her body."

"Ah." Henny's kindly expression clouded over, and I had my answer. "I didn't realize you were the girl with the fragment. I'm so sorry, my dear, but I have no skill with necromancy. Unless there is an alchemical formula that somehow helps . . . but I have never heard of such a thing."

"Take heart, child," Mr. Smith said, putting a hand on my arm. "Death is not the end."

I stared at him in mute horror. It may surprise you, but it hadn't occurred to me until that moment to wonder what would happen to me after I died. It was hard enough to grapple with the idea of my own demise; the thought that I might soon join the ranks of those restless spirits wandering the otherworld was just too terrible to entertain. Would I become a ghost like Granny, or—I shuddered—a shade like Matilda Meyer?

Mr. Burrows hastily changed the subject. "How long before we know whether the shade will be able to follow the spell?"

"Her name is Matilda," the medium said tartly, "and she will return as soon as she's able, but I wouldn't expect her for several hours."

"What the devil are we supposed to do until then?"

"Wait," Mr. Wang said. "Drink tea."

I was in dire need of something warm in my belly just now. "Tea sounds wonderful," I said, "and hopefully Mrs. Meyer won't take too long."

"You'll want to be well clear of this place before she returns," Mr. Smith said.

"I'm not going anywhere."

The medium frowned. "That fragment becomes more dangerous with each passing hour, and when the sun sets and Mrs. Meyer manifests physically, the effect will be magnified many times over. I don't care how much of that special brew you drink, you're flirting with disaster."

"I'm not flirting with it, Mr. Smith, I'm facing it head-on, and it's not as if I have much choice. I made a promise to Mr. Wiltshire. He needs me, and so does Clara."

Mr. Wang muttered something to himself; I recognized some of the same words he'd used yesterday. "*Zhànshì*," I said, looking at Mei. "What does it mean?"

"It means *warrior,*" she said with a smile.

I blushed. I didn't feel like a warrior. I felt like a frightened little girl who'd bitten off far more than she could chew, but there was no turning back now. Clara and Mr. Wiltshire needed help, and since we couldn't involve the police, that left the people in this room: a medium, a witch, an apothecary, two young women, and a Fifth Avenue gentleman. Not exactly an army. Of the lot of us, I suspected only Henny Weber would be any use in a fight.

As it turned out, I was wrong about that, and a good many other things besides.

Matilda Meyer returned just after sunset.

I felt her presence an instant before she materialized, in the now-familiar stab of cold in my breast. This time I was ready for it, downing a cup of special tea before panic could take over and rob me of my senses. I drank a second one for good measure, but even then, a subtle *thrum* lingered, like the vibrations from a passing train. *It's not working like before,* I realized grimly. I brushed the thought aside. There was nothing I could do about it anyway.

"I followed the ribbon of light," Matilda reported through the medium. "It leads to a house on the Hudson. I can show you the way."

"Mr. Wiltshire?" I asked, my breath clouding in the chill of her presence. "And Clara?"

"I saw them. They seem well enough, at least for now."

"Then we haven't any time to lose," Mr. Burrows said, grabbing his hat. "I've got the four-in-hand waiting outside. Who's coming?"

"Everyone is coming," Henny Weber replied cheerfully. "Why shouldn't we?"

Mr. Burrows hesitated. "We're grateful for the help, of course, but . . ."

"Whom would you leave behind?" the medium asked, gesturing at our little group. "You need Mrs. Meyer to show you the way, which means you need me. But her presence is dangerous for Miss Gallagher, so you ought to have Mr. Wang on hand, just in case. That leaves Mrs. Weber and Miss Wang, and I daresay you'll find a pair of witches rather useful."

"A *pair* of witches?" I looked at Mei in astonishment.

She shrugged self-consciously. "I am not a proper witch, but my mother taught me some things."

"Well, then," Mr. Burrows said, "that settles it. It'll be a trifle cramped, but we'll manage. Er, Mrs. Meyer, would you mind terribly riding in the boot?"

"I'll do what I must," the shade replied. "Shall I vanish as well?"

Mr. Burrows's smile grew strained. "If it's all the same to you, I'd prefer to know where you are."

I didn't blame him one bit.

It was slow going at first, the coachman having to negotiate a four-horse team through the cluttered streets of downtown. But the farther north we ventured, the more our path opened up, and by the time we reached Central Park, we were thundering along at a pace I would ordinarily have found alarming.

"It's just north of here," Mr. Smith reported. "Among the summer estates on the cliffs overlooking the river."

"Not his own property, then," Mr. Burrows said. "Essex's summer house is halfway to Albany."

"I suppose that makes sense," I said, "if he's trying to hide from the world. But how did Matilda get all the way up here?"

Mr. Smith shrugged. "Why, she took the train, of course."

That's right: the shade of a dead woman, whose very touch could be fatal, rode a passenger train from one end of Manhattan to another, as if she were taking a leisurely Sunday trip. Not a comforting thought, is it?

But I had bigger worries just then. "What will we do when we get there?"

"Mrs. Meyer had a good look at the property," Mr. Smith

said. "Apparently Clara and Wiltshire are being held separately, on the first and second floors, respectively."

That meant we'd have to split up. The idea didn't much appeal.

"How many men are guarding them?" Mei asked.

"Mrs. Meyer saw five, plus Essex, but there may be more. She doesn't know if they're armed."

"We'll have to assume so," Mr. Burrows said. Patting his breast pocket, he added, "Fortunately, so are we."

"I pray it won't come to that," I said, feeling a pang of regret as I thought back to the Tub of Blood. I might not have been the best sort of Catholic, but *Thou shalt not kill* was one Commandment I took very seriously indeed.

"We'll do our best to bring this to an end without bloodshed," Mr. Burrows said, "but I wouldn't set my hopes too high. Essex has proven how far he's willing to go to get what he wants."

Mr. Burrows was right, I knew. Essex wouldn't go down without a fight.

So a fight was just what we'd give him.

CHAPTER 29

THE HOUSE ON THE HUDSON—JARS AND
CROCKS AND LITTLE VIALS—A SHADE TOO
MANY—THE WHITE KNIFE

The carriage drew to a halt at the bottom of a long, S-shaped drive that wound up through the darkness. We couldn't see much from this vantage, but the moonlight picked out a cluster of turrets not unlike those of a castle, giving the impression of a vast, sprawling estate at the top of the rise. To our left, the Hudson River was a canyon of shadow.

We descended from the carriage, each of us shouldering a small pack of supplies. I'd learned from my experience at the gasworks and the Tub of Blood, and this time I meant to be prepared. We each had a knife, a length of rope, and some strips of clean cloth to use as bandages. I'd even packed a needle and thread, just in case. As for Henny Weber and the Wangs, they'd brought along a host of mysterious things—jars and crocks and little vials sealed with wax—whose purpose I couldn't begin to guess at. No doubt I'd find out soon enough.

Sneaking through the woods was easy, but slipping inside the house undetected would be another matter. "Someone's guarding the door," I whispered, pointing. A man reclined in a chair on the porch, smoking. "He'll have a gun stashed under that sheepskin, I suppose."

"Perhaps one of the other doors?" Mr. Burrows suggested.

I had a fleeting vision of the five of us creeping about the grounds in search of another door, an image so absurd I almost laughed. "We'll be spotted for sure."

"I can help." Shrugging out of her pack, Mei retrieved an earthenware crock and sniffed it, as if to verify its contents. Satisfied, she whispered something to her father, and before we could even ask what she was up to, she'd slipped away through the trees, moving so quietly that I soon lost track of her in the shadows.

For a minute or two, all was still. We huddled among the pines, shivering. Then something sailed through the air, and a moment later the dry *clink* of broken pottery brought the guard's head snapping around. He sprang from his chair and started toward the trees, but he didn't get far. A strange mist curled up from the pavement under the portico, hissing. The guard drew up short. He started to back away from the mist, but his legs buckled beneath him, and he went down hard. Mr. Wang darted out of his hiding place and grabbed the unconscious man by the ankles, dragging him off into the bushes.

Cautiously, the rest of us crept out of hiding. Mei met us with a shy smile. "Magic?" I whispered.

"Chemistry."

"Very interesting!" Henny declared, patting Mei's shoulder approvingly. "You must tell me what's in it sometime!"

"A pity we don't know what's on the other side of that door," Mr. Burrows said. "Our sleeping friend could be one of a pair."

"Mrs. Meyer can help with that," said Mr. Smith. Already, the spirit was gliding toward the door, passing through it as effortlessly as she had passed through the lamppost that night on Mott Street. "The foyer is clear," Mr. Smith reported upon her return, "but it looks as though the door is locked."

"Can't she unlock it?" I asked.

Mr. Smith shook his head. "Some shades are able, with proper instruction, to manipulate physical objects, but Mrs. Meyer has not yet mastered the technique."

"That's all right," Henny said. "I have a spell that does interesting things to solid objects." She laughed, loudly enough that I threw a worried glance at the house.

Henny, I decided, had an interesting definition of *interesting*.

The witch rummaged through her pack and produced a glass jar filled with ruby-red liquid. And when I say *ruby red*, I mean it quite literally: The liquid glittered subtly, as though someone had melted a ruby into a molten state. More rummaging, and this time Henny came up with a paintbrush. "Wait here," she said, and tottered up to the front doors. She dipped her brush into the jar and painted the outline of a rectangle on the right-hand door, standing on her tiptoes to reach the top, grunting as she crouched to complete the bottom edge. Then she laid a dimpled hand against the door and closed her eyes, concentrating.

At first, nothing happened. She might as well have dipped her paintbrush in water for all the effect it seemed to have. Then Henny leaned in and blew on the wet paint, and it flared to life as if she breathed on fading embers. A glowing rectangle seared itself into the wood, and the door began to smoke as though it might go up in flames at any moment. And then it *was* smoke, wavering and insubstantial, offering a clear view of what lay behind.

Henny waved us forward urgently. "Hurry, it won't last!"

Mei reached the door first and didn't hesitate, ducking headlong through the red smoke and disappearing inside. Mr. Wang followed, and the others, until I found myself alone out there, eyes wide and heart pounding, frozen with fear and astonishment. I'm not sure how long I might have stood there had Mr. Burrows not reached back and grabbed my wrist, dragging me through the smoke, but the next thing I knew I was standing in the foyer along with the others, watching incredulously as the glow faded and the door congealed into ordinary wood once again.

Henny Weber grinned. "Interesting, no? It doesn't work on stone, but it's perfect for wood."

I had so many questions, but now wasn't the time. "We need to get out of sight."

"This way." Mr. Smith pointed. "There's a drawing room through here."

We closed the door behind us and paused to listen, but the only sound was our breathing. We'd made it undetected, at least so far.

"All right," Mr. Burrows whispered, "this is it. Does anyone wish to stay behind? This room seems like as good a place as any to wait it out."

Nobody spoke up, and I felt a pang of affection for each and every one of them.

A webbing of frost crawled across the far wall. Matilda Meyer appeared, lips moving animatedly. "Mrs. Meyer has verified the location of our friends," the medium reported. "There's only one guard on Clara, but Mr. Wiltshire has three attendants, one of whom appears to be the master of the house."

"Essex." The name tasted foul on my tongue.

"There's more," Mr. Smith said. "They're all armed, and not just with guns. Every one of them has a baton of ash wood on his person. Our host has been having a spot of trouble with shades, it seems. Mrs. Meyer thinks there could be half a dozen or more on the property, lured here by the ribbon of light."

"Fool," Mr. Burrows muttered. "Meddling with supernatural forces he can't control."

"That's why he needs Thomas," I said bitterly. "So he can work out how to use those spells properly instead of blundering about."

"Be that as it may," said the medium, "it makes things rather more difficult for us. Especially for Mrs. Meyer: One touch of that ash wood will send her straight back to Hell Gate."

"What we need is a diversion," Mr. Burrows said. "Here's what I propose . . ."

It was a simple enough strategy: The Wangs would find Clara and get her to safety while the rest of us focused on Thomas, since he was under heavier guard. Matilda would provide the diversion, luring the guards into the hallway, where the rest of our little rescue party would be lying in wait. The others would keep the guards busy while I freed Thomas.

That was the plan, anyway.

"You'll find Clara in a sitting room at the end of the hall," Mr. Smith told the Wangs. "As for Wiltshire, he's in a study upstairs. Mrs. Meyer will show us the way."

We took the servants' staircase, figuring there was less chance of being discovered. I couldn't help wincing as we creaked our way up the steps, sure that the whole house must be able to hear it, but we made it to the second floor unmolested. The study where Thomas was being held had two doors, one at either end of the hall; we split into pairs to make sure both were covered. Mr. Burrows and Mr. Smith concealed themselves just around the corner at the far end while Henny and I crouched behind a sideboard. Matilda, meanwhile, stationed herself just outside the door at Mr. Burrows's end of the study.

This is it, I thought, swallowing down a queasy feeling. *Please, God, let this work.* One small mistake, even a moment's hesitation, could cost Thomas his life.

Cocking the hammer of my Colt, I gave Matilda a sharp nod. Then I watched, breath caught in my throat, as she drifted through the door.

Muffled shouts came from inside the study. Footfalls thumped along the floor. Matilda reappeared, hovering just outside the door until it swung open, spilling bodies into the hallway.

I couldn't tell how many guards she'd managed to lure away, but I didn't dare wait to find out. Darting out of my hiding place, I slipped quietly through the rear door of the study.

A moment's hesitation and I would have been spotted; as it was, I barely managed to duck behind a wingback chair before a well-dressed man at the far end of the study glanced in my direction. I froze, heart hammering in my chest, but there was no reaction. He hadn't seen me.

"Another one." Thomas's voice, wryly amused. Peering around the chair, I saw him seated behind an ornate desk at the far end of the room, papers spread out before him in a scene very similar to the one I'd found at the gasworks. "It's Grand Central Depot for the dead in here. Really, Essex, didn't your mother ever teach you not to leave your toys lying about?"

Essex. The man responsible for all of it—the murders, Thomas and Clara's kidnapping, the shades running loose all over New York. My finger twitched on the trigger of my Colt.

"Mock if you like, Wiltshire, but those things are as likely to kill you as the rest of us."

"Perhaps, but I console myself with the notion that they'll get you first. There would be such poetic justice in it, don't you agree?"

"Justice." Essex gave a derisive snort.

"Of course, forgive me. A man like you wouldn't believe in justice, would he?"

"If by a man like me you mean a realist, then no. The world doesn't work that way."

"So the world can be damned, is that it?" Thomas had seen Matilda, which would have alerted him to our presence. Now he was trying to distract his captor.

"Good Lord, Wiltshire, are you always this dramatic? You make it sound as if I'm some sort of anarchist. I'm simply willing to do whatever is necessary to get back on my feet, like any good businessman."

"Don't give me that. Barber's chicanery is barely two weeks old. You and the Crowes have been at this for nearly a month."

"Barber's thieving left me little choice but to seek remedy where I may. But you're right, I recognized the business potential of this venture long ago."

"*Business potential.*" Thomas's voice dripped with scorn.

"Have you even stopped to consider the commercial value of

what lies beyond that portal? Loved ones, lost secrets, curiosities beyond our wildest imaginations . . ."

"Deadly spirits, immortal beings . . ."

"No great enterprise comes without sacrifice. How many men have died building the railroads?"

"Forgive me, but I don't see the analogy."

Essex *tsk*ed. "I can see I'm wasting my time. Just get back to work and maybe you'll come out of this alive."

Now it was Thomas's turn to snort. "You must think I'm a fool."

Cautiously, I dared another peek around the chair. It was just the three of us in the study. Matilda had succeeded in luring the other two guards away; Mr. Burrows and the others were presumably dealing with them right now. But that didn't make things easy. They were on the far side of the room, and Essex had a gun. I could take a shot at him, but what if I missed? If I could just get a little closer . . .

"If I thought you were a fool, Wiltshire, you wouldn't be here. Then again, perhaps you're not as clever as I was led to believe. What the deuce is taking so long, anyway?"

"This cipher is inordinately complex," Thomas said, sounding genuinely irritated. "If you're in such a hurry, why not simply consult the folio's rightful owner?"

"Drake?" Essex laughed humorlessly. "Do you have any idea what that man is capable of?"

"I've recently become acquainted with his abilities, yes."

"Then you understand perfectly well why he isn't an option. Believe me, if I saw a more expedient means of translating these manuscripts, I wouldn't have gone to all this trouble. But I need a competent cryptologist familiar with magic, and I'm afraid those don't grow on trees. Moreover, as you can see, my need has grown rather urgent of late. If we don't get this spell under control . . . Well, it's like an industrial leak, isn't it? All these shades running rampant—positively toxic. So in a way, we're both on the same side, at least for now."

"In a way," Thomas said dryly, and I heard a rustle of pages as he went back to work.

My time was up. I'd have to take my chances with the gun. Mouthing a silent prayer, I eased back the hammer.

Whether God heard me or not I couldn't say, but just then a *crash* sounded in the hallway. Essex turned at the sound, and I saw my chance. Uncoiling from my crouch, I fired.

But the Colt .45 was too much gun for me. The bullet went well wide, splintering the wainscoting behind Essex. He whirled and fired back, but he wasn't much of a shot either; a picture frame cartwheeled off the table beside me. I squeezed off another round, two-handed this time, and managed at least to graze his arm. Essex howled and staggered for the door, and before I could cock the hammer again, he fled.

I dove back out into the hallway—and found myself face-to-face with a new threat, a man barreling toward me with a murderous expression. Except it wasn't a man, because each step he took sent a glitter of frost radiating out from his footfalls.

A shade. Not *our* shade.

I took a shot at him—which was perfectly pointless and nearly cost poor Mr. Smith his life. The medium scrambled for cover, while the shade didn't even break stride. I stumbled back, gun still leveled uselessly at the spirit. My heart clutched like an icy fist, and not just from fear; I could feel the fragment humming to life inside me. My muscles seized, knees locking beneath me, and I hit the floor hard. The shade was nearly on top of me now, reaching for me with blue-black hands . . .

The shade went rigid. In the same instant, a wooden pole pierced him like a spear, passing through his body and clattering to the floor behind me. The shade vanished like smoke in the wind. Behind him, Thomas straightened from his throw.

My heart started pumping again, but I could still feel the fragment burning inside me. I grabbed the flask of special tea in my breast pocket and drank greedily, and the icy burn subsided.

"Rose." Thomas helped me to stand, and without thinking, I threw my arms around him. He returned the embrace warmly. "I knew you'd come," he murmured, his voice honey in my ear. "Are you all right?"

"No time for that!" Mr. Smith waved frantically at the far end of the hall. "The way is clear, but who knows for how long? This house is teeming with shades!"

"The folios," Thomas said. "We don't dare leave them behind . . ." He ducked back into the study.

"Where are the others?" I asked the medium.

"Leading our hosts on a merry chase. There were more of Essex's men just in there, playing billiards, so Burrows and Henny split up and led them in opposite directions. That's when the shades started showing up. I managed to convince the first one to leave me alone, but this fellow"—he gestured at the wooden pole Thomas had thrown—"was too far gone."

"In that case, we'd better take this." I started to retrieve the ash pole—and then thought better of it, remembering what had happened when I'd touched Thomas's walking stick. "On second thought . . ."

Thomas reappeared, a leather satchel slung over his shoulder. "Clara?" he asked, stooping to retrieve the ash pole.

"Outside, I hope, with the Wangs."

"As should we be," Mr. Smith said. "This way!"

We made it as far as the staircase before running into one of Essex's men. He raised his gun, but Thomas was quicker, cracking the wooden pole over the man's wrist and forcing him to drop his weapon. They struggled. Then Henny Weber burst through a door on the landing and bowled straight into the man, shoving him bodily into the wall. She pinned him there just long enough to tuck a little vial into his breast pocket and slam her palm into his chest, breaking the glass.

"I'm sorry, young man," she said, laying a hand against the wall behind him, "but we don't have time for this." And as the rest of us watched in astonishment, the man tumbled backward through the wall as if it weren't even there, only to have Henny snatch her hand away and return the wall to a solid state, trapping the man within.

"Er," said Thomas, "I beg your pardon, but who—?"

But we didn't have time for introductions either, so I grabbed his hand and we took the rest of the stairs two at a time.

We'd nearly made it to the front door when I heard the *click* of a revolver being cocked. Three of Essex's men materialized from the shadows, guns leveled at us. "I'll take that," one of them said, snatching the Colt from my hands; I recognized the bearded man from that morning. "Where's Essex?" he demanded.

"Fled," I told him, "like the coward he is."

"That's a lie."

"It's not, actually," Thomas said. "Feel free to search the

house, though you ought to be careful. There are a fair few angry spirits about."

The roughs exchanged looks. "That's it," said one. "I'm through."

"And me," said another. "Not getting paid near enough for this shite."

"Fine," said the bearded man, "we'll go. But this lot have seen our faces, so we take care of 'em first."

"Right." And suddenly there was a revolver against Thomas's head, the hammer clicking back, but before I could even cry out, the bearded man batted the gun away.

"Not here, eejit." He gestured at the narrow hallway. "Want his brains all over you? We'll do it outside."

They marched us out into the cold night and forced us to our knees. Henny had tears in her eyes, and Mr. Smith's lips moved, as though in prayer. As for Thomas, he met my gaze and held it as if trying to transmit some silent message, though what it was, I couldn't say.

I lifted my gaze to the moon, cold and bright between the clouds. It looked changed to me somehow, as though I were seeing it through new eyes. For a few days, everything had been different. Even in that moment, kneeling in the wet grass with a gun pointed at my head, I knew that for a gift. *Heavenly Father*, I prayed, *please watch over Mam* . . .

A crackle sounded from the trees. I felt a pang of fear, thinking it must be Clara and the Wangs. Then Matilda Meyer erupted from the pines, hands outstretched, face twisted in wrath. The roughs whirled. Guns went off. Thomas spun on the grass, sweeping one man's legs out from under him and diving for his gun. But before he could reach it the bearded man cracked a wooden pole over the back of his head, dropping him like a sack of flour.

Things happened even faster after that.

Henny made a grab for her pack but met the same fate as Thomas, taking a hard blow across her shoulders and slumping to the ground. The bearded man swung at Matilda, forcing her to leap back even as another rough came around to flank her. I scrabbled in the grass for something, *anything*, to use as a weapon, but I couldn't even find a rock on that well-tended lawn. All I could do was look on helplessly as Matilda was surrounded. Then Mr. Smith got to his feet, pointed at the roughs, and said, "Them," and a figure stepped out of the shadows and grabbed one of the roughs by the scruff of the neck. For half a heartbeat, I wondered who the newcomer was; then a throb of cold pulsed through my body, and I understood.

The rough couldn't even scream. His whole body went rigid, face contorting in a rictus of terror. The shade held on to him for a moment more, until Mr. Smith said, "That's enough, I think," and the spirit let go, watching dispassionately as the rough crumpled to the ground.

Another shadowy figure emerged from the trees, and another. The shades formed a ring around us but didn't attack. They seemed to be taking orders from Mr. Smith.

Mediums, it turns out, can be quite handy in a fight. Provided you're surrounded by dead people, of course.

I'm not sure the East River Gang fully understood what was going on. They didn't know Mr. Smith, after all, or what he was capable of. But they certainly knew a mob of shades when they saw one, and they panicked. Most of them scattered, but a few started attacking blindly, including the bearded man. He lunged at Matilda, sweeping the ash pole through her middle as if she were made of smoke. An instant later she vanished—and I started screaming.

I fell to my knees, clutching the sides of my head in torment. The fragment was resonating so powerfully that I could actually hear it, a high-pitched whine fit to shatter my skull. There was movement all around me, friend and foe shouting and running, and suddenly Mr. Wang was at my side, but I knew instinctively that no amount of special tea would save me this time.

"They're getting away!" someone cried.

"Let them!"

Faces and voices blurred together; it was all I could do to make out words.

"What's happening? What's wrong with her?" Clara—*that* voice I would know anywhere.

"The fragment. When the ash touched Matilda . . . My God, it must be tearing her up inside!"

Not tearing. Nothing so crude as that. This was searing, incandescent agony. It was just as Thomas had said: a hot knife, and any moment now it would slide into my heart. I knew because I could feel exactly where it was, its precise shape and size, as if it were being branded onto my insides.

Mr. Wang pressed a flask of tea into my hands but there was no time; I had the strength for one thought and one alone. "Clara." It came out as little more than a sob. "Clara, I need your help."

She fell to her knees in front of me. "What can I do? Tell me what to do, Rose!"

I forced the words out in tortured gasps. "I need . . . you . . . to stab me."

She reeled back in shock.

"With that." I gestured at an ash pole lying in the grass.

"What do you mean, stab you?" She threw a terrified look at the others. "What does she mean?"

"I think I understand," Mei said. "If the wood touches the fragment inside her, it may banish it."

"No . . ." Thomas's voice, distant and groggy. He struggled to sit, one hand clamped against the back of his head. "Don't. Too dangerous . . ."

I started to argue, but another stab of pain turned my words into a scream. *No time. There's no time . . .*

I wasn't the only one who thought so. Mr. Wang grabbed the ash pole and smashed it over the garden wall, shattering it. He took one of the pieces and carved off a few hasty chunks with a pocketknife, then thrust the makeshift dagger at Clara. She took it with a numb expression.

"It's here." I clutched at my chest. "Right here, up against my heart. *It burns . . .*"

Tears streamed down Clara's face. "I'm not a doctor."

"You studied. You know where to do it."

"I'll kill you! I'll puncture a lung, or tear a hole in your chest cavity, or . . ."

Henny gave a little cry. "I can help with that! I can seal the wound! It's my specialty, sealing things."

Clara shook her head, staring at the wooden knife in her hand. "I can't. Rose, I can't . . ."

I wanted to reassure her, to tell her I had faith in her, but I could only grind my teeth against the screams.

"No choice!" Mr. Wang gripped her shoulder urgently. "If you do not, she dies!"

Clara tore my dress open. Cold fingers flitted over my bare

skin, and she started whispering to herself. "Heart, lungs, liver . . ." Laying her hand against my left breast, she started measuring finger widths. "One, two . . ."

She pressed the tip of the wooden blade against my chest. Then she froze, shoulders heaving with panic.

"*Clara, please.*"

She pushed. I screamed until I could scream no more, and everything went black.

CHAPTER 30

AFTERMATH—A SHARPE SET OF
QUESTIONS—THE PLAN

The first few seconds after I woke were profoundly disorienting. I was in a strange bed, yet the room was somehow familiar. Gradually, it dawned on me that I was in a guest room in the house on Fifth Avenue, but I couldn't quite recall which one. My mind felt sluggish, and as for my body . . . I couldn't feel the fragment anymore, but in its place was a throbbing pain, and when I stirred I felt the tug of a bandage on my chest.

"I'm sorry we couldn't put you in your own bed, but the doctor needed space to work."

The sound of that well-loved voice lifted the fog, at least partially. "Mr. Wiltshire?"

"Thomas," he said, appearing at my bedside. "Remember?"

"I don't, actually. I mean, I remember that part, but . . . How did I get here?"

"In a carriage. You were unconscious but stable, thanks to Clara and Mrs. Weber."

"Is everyone—"

"Whole and accounted for, among our friends at least. Essex escaped." A flicker of anger crossed Thomas's face. "That reckoning will have to wait for another day, it seems." He helped me to sit and poured a strong-smelling drink from a teapot at my bedside table. "From Wang. It will help you recuperate."

I'd had more than enough special tea for one lifetime, but it seemed rude to refuse, so I took a few swallows. Thomas sank into a chair at my bedside, watching me through asymmetrical pupils. I must have had the same strangely unbalanced look. We all must have. *Battle scars,* I thought, though thankfully not permanent ones. "The fragment?"

"Gone." Thomas's mouth curved just short of a smile, and there was a warm, glassy look in his eye that I couldn't quite read. "Banished back to the otherworld, along with the rest of Matilda Meyer. Not only did you save yourself, you managed to make an important scientific discovery in the bargain, one that could help save lives in future. You truly are the most resourceful person I've ever met."

That was one word for it. *Reckless* was another. Or *mad.* "Poor Clara, she must be furious with me."

"I'm sure she isn't."

He didn't know Clara like I did. Still, her wrath was a small price to pay for having my death sentence lifted. "I had no choice. The way the fragment was resonating . . ." I shuddered at the memory. "What exactly happened?"

"I wish I could tell you, but in truth we're not sure. There's so much we don't yet understand about such things. As nearly as I can work out, when Mrs. Meyer was banished back to the otherworld, it was like a fishing line going taut, dragging at the fragment embedded in your flesh. I can't imagine the pain you must have experienced."

No, you can't. I was suddenly eager to change the subject. "What about you—are you all right? You took quite a blow."

He raised a hand to the back of his head, wincing. "I've been better, but the doctor says I needn't be concerned."

"And the portal?"

"There is work yet to do on that front, I'm afraid. Mrs. Weber is confident that her alkahest will work, but we still have no idea how we're to place it at the site of the breach. As for the ribbon of light, we can't dispel it until we understand its nature, which means we must first crack the cipher used in the manuscripts."

"*Hmm,*" I said. "We could ask Drake for help, I suppose, but frankly—"

"Please, don't worry yourself. I have all the assistance I require. You need only rest and regain your strength."

I frowned. "You ought to know me better than that by now. After everything I've been through to get to this point, I'm not about to quit."

He sighed. "Rose—"

"I'll take things easy, I promise."

"The doctor prescribed a week's bed rest."

"I won't tell him if you don't."

"Good Lord, you're as bad as Burrows. Who's been asking after you, by the way. He's expressed a desire to visit when you're feeling up to it, as has Mei Wang. Which reminds me—shall I contact your mother?"

Mam. I wasn't ready to tell her about all this. I wasn't sure I ever would be. "I sent her a note yesterday while we were waiting around at Wang's, saying that I was feeling under the weather."

"I can stop by this afternoon if you'd like. It will give me a chance to check up on her, see how things are getting along with her own mother. I'll tell her you're feeling better but not quite up to heading downtown just yet."

"Thank you."

"It's the very least I can do," he said, taking my hand and giving it a squeeze. "You saved my life yet again, and Clara's. I can never fully express my gratitude."

Gazing into those pale eyes, I could think of any number of ways he could express his gratitude, but of course nothing like that would occur to him.

Then again, the look he was giving me now, so full of warmth . . . The way his thumb drifted absently across the backs of my knuckles . . .

"Thomas." I swallowed a nervous lump in my throat. "What happened yesterday morning on the stoop . . ."

"Ah. Yes." He straightened awkwardly, his hand slipping away. "Please accept my apologies. I hope you know I would never have presumed upon you that way had I not been compelled by the circumstances. It shan't happen again, you have my word."

The wound just below my heart gave a little twinge, as if in answer. But really, what else had I expected? "Of course," I said, forcing a smile. "Think nothing of it."

Rising, he consulted his watch. "I'll leave you to rest."

That, I decided, was a grand idea; all of a sudden, I felt completely, shatteringly exhausted.

Thomas closed the curtains, and I promptly fell asleep.

I woke to an empty room. Gingerly, I rolled out of bed and drew open the curtains to find the winter sun slung low in the sky. Fresh clothes had been laid out on the window seat, and a pitcher of water stood beside the washbasin, still warm. There was even a spray of roses on the dressing table, courtesy of Mr. Jonathan Burrows (from Klunder, naturally). Lifting a corner of the bandage on my chest, I found a bright pink scar, still tender to the touch. It hurt to twist or bend—to draw air, really—but it wasn't as bad as I might have guessed, all things considered. Pronouncing myself fit for duty, I set out to find Thomas.

Lamplight spilled under the door of his study. *Good,* I thought, *he hasn't left without me.* But the voice answering my knock wasn't his, and when I opened the door, I found a pair of strangers poring over a familiar set of manuscripts. "Oh," I said, "excuse me. I didn't realize Mr. Wiltshire had company."

The men stood, as if I were the lady of the house. One was a tall, splendidly dressed colored man, the other a stout, balding white man with a mustache and exuberant side-whiskers. "Ah," said the latter, "this must be the infamous Miss Gallagher. Wiltshire said we might have the pleasure of your company. Tell me, have you any facility with cryptography? We're having a devil of a time."

"Speak for yourself," the other man said. "I do believe I'll have it cracked soon."

My gaze shifted between them, my hand still on the doorknob. "I'm sorry, you seem to have me at a disadvantage."

"Of course," said the stout man, "do forgive me. F. Winston

Sharpe, at your service." He handed me a calling card—the same as Thomas's, silver with a single staring eye. Except this one had his name printed across it, and beneath that, in bold letters, CHIEF OF DETECTIVES. "And this is my associate, Mr. Jackson."

"Jackson? The witch?"

The tall man inclined his head. "I prefer warlock, but yes, I am he."

"Pleased to meet you both. And deeply indebted to you, Mr. Jackson. I'm sorry you had to come all this way on my account."

"Not at all. I was glad to hear you no longer required my assistance."

F. Winston Sharpe gestured for me to sit. "Please, my dear, you must be terribly uncomfortable, what with your injuries."

I lowered myself carefully onto the sofa opposite the two men. "Is Mr. Wiltshire here?"

"He'll be back presently," Mr. Sharpe said, eying me with a gaze that lived up to his name. "So this is the young woman we've heard so much about. I must say, I was expecting someone a little more . . . formidable. You're just a wisp of a girl, aren't you?"

"I beg your pardon?"

"Sleuthing takes all types, to be sure, but still." He looked me up and down. "Gallagher. Irish, isn't it? And you're from *Five Points*?" His brows came together disapprovingly.

I glanced at Mr. Jackson, but if he was surprised by his superior's atrocious manners, he didn't show it. He was too busy making notes in the margins of Drake's folios.

"You don't know a thing about me, sir," I said coldly, "and you're very rude."

"I've been called worse."

"I don't find that in the least difficult to believe," I said, springing to my feet. "If you'll excuse me . . ."

Mr. Jackson stood, but Mr. Sharpe stayed where he was, still fixing me with that strangely appraising look. "*Extraordinary*, he called you. *Remarkable*. Wiltshire isn't given to superlatives, and yet . . ."

"And yet what? Do you suppose you can take the measure of a person just at a glance?" Out of the corner of my eye, I thought I saw Mr. Jackson smile.

"People take the measure of each other at a glance every day, my dear. Especially in New York."

"I hardly need you to tell me that. I've been dealing with it my whole life. I just expected more from a detective."

"Tell me, why did you take it upon yourself to go looking for Wiltshire when he disappeared? Why not just leave it to the police?"

It took a supreme act of willpower not to blush. "Because I knew I could find him."

"That's not much of an explanation."

"It's more of an explanation than you're owed." I spun on my heel, fixing to flounce out of the room in righteous indignation.

"Please, Miss Gallagher, don't go." I turned back to find F. Winston Sharpe on his feet. "Forgive me. I've been a detective for so long, I've forgotten that not every conversation is an interrogation."

His manner hadn't seemed reflexive to me. In fact, it seemed like he'd gone out of his way to insult me. I started to say as much, but just then Thomas arrived. He still had his overcoat on and carried a long roll of paper tucked under his arm. "Ah, Rose. How are you feeling?"

"Well enough," I said coolly.

"Miss Gallagher and I were just becoming acquainted," Mr. Sharpe added with a most peculiar smile.

Thomas's glance cut between us, but he kept his questions to himself. "Our associates await us in the parlor. Shall we?" He gestured behind him, and Messrs. Sharpe and Jackson filed past.

"Is Clara here?" I asked him on the way out.

"No, thankfully. It took some doing, but I convinced her to take a couple of days off. She seems all right, but our nerves are sometimes more delicate than we think. As are our bodies," he added, raising an eyebrow pointedly.

"I'm fine," I said in a tone that made it clear I considered the matter closed.

We arrived in the parlor to find Henny Weber and Mr. Smith waiting. The kindly witch exclaimed when she saw me, embracing me delicately in her dimpled arms. "I'm so glad to see you well, my friend! It was a very hard night, wasn't it?"

"Thank you for the part you played in that. My being well, I mean."

"I'm not much of an alchemist if I cannot seal a wound, eh? I have bigger things to seal these days, that's for sure!" She laughed merrily, as though the task before her were no more consequential than a challenging bit of baking.

Thomas made the introductions, though in one case at least, they didn't seem to be necessary.

"I am a great admirer of yours, Mr. Jackson," Henny said, shaking his hand.

"You're very kind. I'm familiar with your work as well. Pennsylvania, isn't it?"

"Perhaps we could save the pleasantries for later," Mr. Sharpe said, lowering himself into a chair. "We have a great deal to discuss. Let's begin with the portal, shall we?"

Thomas unfurled a large map of New York and smoothed it on the coffee table. "We believe the site of the breach to be here," he said, tapping a finger on a spot between Ward's Island and Astoria. "The tiny island you see here, known as Flood Rock, was obliterated this past autumn in a controlled explosion. Shortly thereafter, shades began appearing in greater numbers in the city. These facts, combined with what we know from Matilda Meyer, lead us to believe that Flood Rock was the seal. When the army destroyed it, they breached the portal."

Mr. Sharpe grunted thoughtfully. "When you say *breached* . . ."

"Not catastrophically, thank heavens, or the entire city would be swarming with shades by now. Just enough, according to Mrs. Meyer, to permit a slow, steady leak."

"Urged on by the ribbon of light," Mr. Jackson put in.

"Precisely. That spell appears to create a direct line between the caster and the portal. Jacob Crowe hoped to use it to enter the otherworld, but instead he found himself on the business end of a fishing pole, inadvertently drawing out shade after shade."

"And you tracked these shades to a house on the Hudson," Mr. Sharpe said.

The question had been put to Thomas, but it was Mr. Smith who answered. "Say rather that the shades did the tracking. Miss Gallagher here had the rather brilliant suggestion of asking Matilda Meyer to follow the ribbon of light to its caster."

"Did she?" Sharpe's dark eyes shifted to mine. "How unconventional."

"Indeed," said Mr. Smith. "Most of us regard shades as merely a threat, but they are human spirits with desires and agency, just like the living. Many people forget that, but fortunately Miss Gallagher did not."

"Fortunate indeed," Thomas echoed distractedly, his gaze suddenly far away.

Mr. Sharpe tapped a thick finger on the map. "Assuming you're right and the breach is here, how do you propose to seal it?"

"That is where I come in," Henny Weber said. "I will use my strongest alkahest." She drew a flask from her satchel and gave it a little shake.

I eyed the flask dubiously. Made of unvarnished pottery and stoppered with wax, it couldn't have held more than half a pint of liquid. I couldn't see how something so humble could seal a crack in the pavement, let alone a portal to the otherworld.

Judging from his expression, F. Winston Sharpe had similar misgivings. "How does it work?"

"By itself, it doesn't, but when you smash it against this one"—she drew out a second, identical flask—"something very interesting happens. When the liquids combine, a powerful solution is formed, one that dissolves anything it touches. It will begin to melt the matter around the portal. Then, when the water starts rushing into the breach, the solution will be diluted, the breach will harden back into stone, and then"—she smashed her palms together—"sealed! Like cauterizing a wound, no?"

"I would be very curious to know what's in it," Mr. Jackson said, "if you don't mind my asking."

Henny smiled. "We shall trade recipes. We're not in the same line, but I think we could learn interesting things from each other."

"I've no doubt. This alkahest sounds quite remarkable. But

are you sure it will be enough? If adding water dilutes it as quickly as you say, it may harden before the portal is completely closed."

"That's true. The seal will certainly be imperfect, which is why we must dispel the ribbon of light."

"And quickly," Mr. Smith put in. "From what we saw at the house on the Hudson, spirits are drawn to that spell like moths to a flame. So long as it remains active, even the tiniest of cracks in the seal will be dangerous."

"Well, Jackson?" Mr. Sharpe demanded. "Can you manage it?"

The warlock frowned, his pride evidently piqued. "If a trio of amateurs can manipulate that spell, I daresay I'll manage. It's merely a question of decrypting the cipher, and the sooner we're finished here, the sooner I can get back to it."

"Fine, fine," said Mr. Sharpe, "so we've a plan. There's just one tiny difficulty: How do you propose to place the alkahest at the site of the breach if it's at the bottom of the East River?"

"That," Henny sighed, "is the problem."

Our little group traded dejected glances—all except Thomas, who still wore a faraway look. "Actually," he said, "I think perhaps Miss Gallagher has given us the answer."

All eyes swiveled to me, but I just stood there, blinking in astonishment. I'd been no more than a mute witness to the conversation. How could I have answered anything?

"What Mr. Smith said a moment ago is perfectly true," Thomas went on. "We so rarely think of shades as human beings. It frankly never would have occurred to me to ask Matilda Meyer for anything more than information. But it occurred to Miss Gallagher, perhaps because she's new to all this. She saw Mrs. Meyer not merely as a problem to be solved, but as an ally with a valuable contribution to make."

"Is there a point here, Wiltshire?"

"The point, Mr. Sharpe, is that I believe Matilda Meyer may yet have a part to play in this. None of us here can hold his breath indefinitely, nor resist the powerful currents of the river . . ."

". . . but Mrs. Meyer can," Mr. Smith finished, nodding. "I see. Very clever, sir. Very clever indeed."

"The credit properly belongs to Miss Gallagher. As I said, it would never have occurred to me had she not led by example."

"Do you think she'll be willing?" Mr. Sharpe asked.

Personally, I had no doubt Matilda would be willing. But would she be able? "I thought she couldn't manipulate physical objects. Isn't that what you said last night, Mr. Smith?"

"More precisely, I said that she had not yet mastered the technique. But with proper instruction, she ought to be able to do so. I could teach her, given a little time."

"Time is rather precious at the moment," Mr. Sharpe said.

"Jackson and I still need a few hours to decrypt that cipher," Thomas pointed out.

"And I must procure some waterproof pouches to carry the liquids in," Henny added.

"Well, then." Mr. Sharpe hauled himself to his feet. "Let us get to it, my friends. As for you, Miss Gallagher, I suggest you get some rest. It sounds as if tomorrow will be a rather big day."

CHAPTER 31

BATTLE SCARS—NECROMANCY AND ALCHEMY—AURORA GOTHAMIS

The following afternoon found the same collection of people assembled in the same room, only this time we were ready for action.

"It was clear from the outset that we were dealing with a poly-alphabetic substitution cipher," Thomas was saying as I brought in the tea. "A devilishly tricky one, too. It wasn't until we referred back to Alberti's work from the fifteenth century that we—"

"Yes, all right, Wiltshire." F. Winston Sharpe cut him off with a wave. "My brain hurts already. The point is, you've cracked it."

"We have," Thomas said, looking a little hurt.

"And I was right," Mr. Jackson added. "The spell Jacob Crowe was meddling with is relatively simple. Ingenious, in fact, when you consider—"

"Excellent," Mr. Sharpe said. "And you're confident you can dispel it?"

"I didn't even have to make a trip to Wang's. I have everything I need right here." Mr. Jackson patted his black leather satchel, which looked a lot like a doctor's bag.

"And what about you, Mrs. Weber? Were you able to procure a waterproof receptacle?"

"An oilskin," she confirmed with a nod. "Mrs. Meyer has only to mix the two solutions and the alkahest will be complete."

"She ought to be able to manage that," Mr. Smith said. "We spent most of last night reviewing various techniques for manipulating physical objects. It was slow going at first, but by dawn she was able to lace up a pair of shoes without any trouble."

"Well then," said Mr. Sharpe, "it sounds as if everything is in place."

"Everything except the sun," Henny said with a laugh. "We will have to wait until it sets."

"Not long now," Thomas said, consulting his Patek Philippe. "We should get going if we're to reach the docks by dusk. Mrs. Meyer will meet us there, I presume?"

"Indeed," said Mr. Smith, "nor will she be alone. I watched half a dozen spirits climb out of the river last night, following the ribbon of light. So long as the spell remains active, they will keep coming."

Mr. Sharpe grunted and tugged on his mustache. "Will they give us any trouble?"

"I doubt it. They've only just stepped into the mortal world, some of them for the first time in centuries. Most of them will be far too disoriented to worry about us."

"We needn't be concerned in any case," Mr. Jackson said. "I

have more than enough spells at my command to keep them at bay."

"Always good to have a necromancer about," Mr. Smith said, which is a phrase you don't hear often.

We piled into an oversized carriage and headed uptown.

"How are Mrs. Meyer's spirits?" Thomas asked as we rattled our way up Fifth Avenue.

"Low," Mr. Smith admitted. "She's awfully tired of being banished back to the portal, poor thing. Are you going to be able to help her, Wiltshire? She deserves her rest."

"I promised to try. We'll have to help all of them, I suppose, or banish them, if they're too far gone."

"Condemning a human soul to an eternity of agonized wandering is not lightly done," Mr. Jackson put in. "I hope we'll consider that a last resort."

"Agreed," said Mr. Sharpe, "but we'll need to do whatever is necessary. Grace is counting on the Agency to resolve this matter as quickly as possible."

Grace? My mouth fell open a little. "The mayor knows about all this?"

"Why, of course. For a while there, things were looking quite grim, weren't they? I expect I'd have had the president himself shouting down the telephone if things hadn't turned a corner when they did."

The mayor knows. The president knows. Not for the first time, I felt as if the whole world had been sharing a secret at my expense.

It was nearly dark by the time we reached our destination: the same modest cluster of graying piers where I'd posed as a reporter from *Harper's* and interviewed Peter Arbridge. A mere four days ago, yet it might as well have been a lifetime.

"We can watch from here," Thomas said, gesturing at the end of the pier.

Mr. Sharpe gazed out over the river with a frown. "Where exactly is it? Will we be able to see around Ward's Island?"

Henny giggled, as if the question were ridiculous. "You will see, don't worry."

I started to ask a question of my own, but the words were stolen from my lips. A familiar shiver rippled through my body, and I went rigid with terror. "She's here," I whispered. "*Thomas, I can still feel her.*"

Matilda Meyer appeared under the moonlight.

"That shouldn't be." Thomas gripped my shoulders; I saw my own fear reflected in his eyes. "Are you in pain? Is the fragment still—"

"Wiltshire, please." Mr. Jackson steered him aside. "May I?" When I nodded, he tugged off his glove, unfastened the top buttons of my overcoat, and rested the flat of his hand against my chest. "The fragment is gone," he declared after a moment. "All of it."

I let out the breath I'd been holding.

"You're certain?" Thomas demanded.

"I'm certain. What Miss Gallagher experienced was merely an aftereffect of her ordeal. It has passed already, has it not?"

Merely didn't feel like quite the right word, but the rest was true enough; I nodded.

"I've heard of this before," Mr. Smith said. "On the rare occasions when someone survives a fragment, it is possible that they will forever more be sensitive to the presence of shades. Not unlike myself, actually."

More battle scars, I thought. Only this one was permanent.

Thomas seemed to have a similar thought, judging from the look of quiet regret in his eyes. "Does it hurt?" he murmured, taking my shoulders again.

"Not really. It's not like before. I don't know how to describe it. Like a chill, or a tuning fork being struck."

"You're certain you're all right?"

"I'm certain."

He stayed where he was, hands on my shoulders, pale eyes locked on mine, and for a few heartbeats it felt as if we were the only two people on the pier. But of course we weren't, and gradually I realized that everyone was staring at us, even Matilda Meyer.

There is nothing quite like the gray stare of a dead woman to throw cold water on your romantic moment, let me tell you.

Matilda's lips moved. "No," Mr. Smith said, "I'm afraid she still can't hear you. But if you've something to say, I would be happy to relate it."

The shade advanced on me, fingers knotted anxiously before her.

"Rose," the medium said, "I can't tell you how sorry I am, for everything. Mr. Smith told me what happened after I was banished, how you nearly . . . I would never have been able to forgive myself."

For the first time, I was able to look her straight in the eye when I answered. "You have nothing to apologize for. It wasn't your fault. And it's over now." But no, I realized, that wasn't quite true—it wasn't over for Matilda. She was still a shade. Still a mother terrified for her children. "When this is done I'll help Mr. Wiltshire in any way I can. Whatever it takes, I promise."

She bowed her head briefly, and when she looked up again, there was a tear working its way down her cheek. That's how I learned that the dead can still weep.

"All right," Mr. Sharpe interrupted, "this is all very touching, but we'd better get on with it. I imagine it will take some time for Mrs. Meyer to reach the site of the breach."

Mr. Smith nodded. "The current will have no effect on Mrs. Meyer herself, but it will drag at the pouches she's carrying." To Matilda, he added, "This will greatly test our lessons, my dear. Are you sure you can manage?"

By way of answer, Matilda picked up a bit of rope lying on the pier and bound it about her waist. Not only did she successfully manipulate the knot, the makeshift belt hung about her hips as though she were an ordinary, perfectly solid woman.

"An apt pupil," Mr. Smith said, beaming proudly.

Henny deposited her satchel on the pier. "There is a waterproof oilskin in the bag. One flask is in there, the other in a separate pouch, here. When you reach the site of the breach, all you have to do is put both flasks in the oilskin pouch and smash them."

"She won't be harmed?" Mr. Smith asked.

The witch shook her head. "She is not a physical being, so the alkahest will have no effect on her. But once the portal is sealed, if she is banished once again, she will not be able to return without the help of a necromancer."

"Well then," said Mr. Smith, "I suppose I'll have to help her stay out of trouble until Wiltshire finds a way to make her whole."

Matilda stood over the satchel, staring at it with a look of fierce concentration. She picked it up, hefted it a few times, and shouldered it. Then she turned and walked off the end of the pier,

plunging into the water without so much as a splash. A thin sheet
of ice bristled over the surface, only to break apart in the current.

"Well," said Thomas, "that's that, I suppose. Let's hope this
works."

"It will work," Henny said.

"In the meantime . . ." Mr. Jackson started emptying the
contents of his doctor's bag. Nothing fancy to look at—I'd seen
more exotic items on the shelves at Wang's General Store—but he
manipulated them gingerly, as though any one of them might explode if it wasn't handled *just so*.

Henny hovered over him, curious. "Is that sawdust?"

"*Mmm*. Ash."

"And incense paste. Very interesting . . ."

Between their two kneeling bodies, the rest of us couldn't
see much. There was a *hiss* and a flare of light, not unlike a match
being struck, and a moment later the warlock unfolded himself
from his crouch and declared, "It's done."

"That's it?" Frankly, I was a little disappointed. "Just like
that, the ribbon of light . . . ?"

"Dispelled." Mr. Jackson smiled. "What were you expecting,
Miss Gallagher? Thunderclouds, perhaps? Lightning crackling
from my fingertips?"

"Oh, don't make fun," Henny said. "She's new at this."

"Forgive me, you're right, of course. Actually, I sometimes
wish my art were a bit showier, but most necromancy is invisible,
at least to mortal eyes. I can assure you that what I just did looked
rather more impressive to any shades nearby."

"And I can assure you," Henny said, tottering back up the
pier, "in a while you will wish that alchemy was a little less showy."

Thomas winced. "Exactly how much attention will we be drawing to ourselves this evening?"

"A lot," said the witch.

As it turned out, that was something of an understatement, because about three hours later New York was treated to a spectacle the likes of which it probably hadn't witnessed since the ancient days of the fae.

At first it looked like the ebbing of the tide: a modest, if rapid, receding of the water. But as the river drew away from the shore, I felt a rumble beneath my feet like the tremor of a distant earthquake. And then the pier bucked beneath us, pitching the lot of us to the boards, and a wall of water erupted into the sky. It hung there for a split second, dark and shivering, before collapsing with a *roar*, soaking us in mist.

All of us sat frozen in various poses of disarray.

"Well," said Thomas, "you were certainly right about a show."

"That wasn't the show." Pointing a plump finger, Henny said, "*There* is the show."

Another wall rose up out of the water, but this time it was made of light: a great undulating sheet in every color of the rainbow, indigo and green and deep cobalt blue. It reached as high as the stars, as wide as the span of Hell Gate itself, spreading over New York City like the wings of an angel.

It was the most beautiful thing I'd ever seen.

CHAPTER 32

THE OFFICIAL STORY—A COLD CASE—THE JADE ROSE—NEW RESPONSIBILITIES

urora borealis? You have got to be kidding me!" I stared incredulously at the page, but the words failed to rearrange themselves under my glare; the article continued stubbornly to insist that the undulating wall of light over the East River had been a particularly dazzling display of the Northern Lights. In *New York City*.

Mr. Burrows laughed, turning over a page of the *Herald*. "God bless the papers. Like a pack of starved dogs, aren't they? They'll gobble up any scrap of garbage you feed them."

Thomas frowned into his morning tea. "I'm not sure I can share your delight in that, Burrows. We'll come to rue it one day, I think."

"Maybe, but for now it's deucedly handy. You can set the sky

afire with magic before the whole of New York, but a few calls
from F. Winston Sharpe, and *voilà*." Mr. Burrows turned his paper around, brandishing the headline across the breakfast table.
"Aurora borealis."

"And a nighttime explosion courtesy of the Army Corps of
Engineers," I added, "which the fine gentlemen at *The New York
World* report as if it had no connection whatsoever to the mysterious appearance of the Northern Lights a matter of seconds later,
in exactly the same spot." I shook my head in disgust. "To think I
actually wanted to be one of them."

"An army engineer?" Mr. Burrows inquired idly, sipping his
coffee.

"A reporter, obviously."

"You'd make a very capable one," Thomas said, thumbing a
page of the *Times*.

"Thank you, I think."

Clara poked her head into the dining room. "Sorry to disturb, but there's a policeman at the door."

Thomas sighed. "I suppose it was too much to hope that we
might actually have some peace and quiet this morning."

Mr. Burrows glanced up from his paper. "Good morning,
Clara. Does Wiltshire have you answering the door as well as
baking these delectable scones? Where's Mrs. Sellers?"

"Ah," said Thomas, "didn't I tell you? Mrs. Sellers resigned
yesterday."

"Resigned?" Mr. Burrows raised his eyebrows. "Oh, dear."

"Yes, I'm afraid the past two weeks have been a bit much for
her. She had a hard enough time coping with Rose's new role in
the household, but Clara getting in on the fun was more than she
could take."

"More than a lot of us could take," Clara muttered.

"And so," Thomas went on, "speaking of new roles, Clara will be taking on greater responsibilities from now on."

I glanced at her in surprise. "You didn't tell me that."

She shrugged. "I could use the pay rise."

"To put toward nursing school, perhaps," Thomas said, keeping his gaze trained carefully on his paper.

Clara clucked her tongue impatiently. "That's enough of that, now. Advice is one thing, but now you're just being pushy. I said I'd think about it and I will. Let that be the end of it."

"Fair enough." Thomas rose and buttoned his jacket. "Rose, you're welcome to stay and finish your breakfast, but I suspect the police officer at my door is a mutual friend."

"No, I'll come. Excuse us, Mr. Burrows."

"Not at all. Have you finished with the *World*?"

As Thomas predicted, the copper at the door was Sergeant Chapman, looking even more bedraggled than the last time we'd seen him. "Wiltshire. Miss Gallagher."

"Good morning, Sergeant. Would you care to come inside?"

The detective shook his head. "Got a busy morning. Just thought you might like to know that your friend from the East River Gang pulled through, barely."

I offered a silent prayer of thanks. I hadn't much cared for the notion that I'd killed a man, whatever sort of person he might have been.

"Seems almost losing his leg made him reconsider his position with the man upstairs, so he was feeling talkative yesterday. Gave up his boss and everything. Fella by the name of Danforth Essex—you know him?" His tone was casual, but I'd spent enough time around Sergeant Chapman to recognize a pointed question when I heard one.

So had Thomas, apparently. "Yes, Sergeant, we know him, and yes, we'd already worked out that he was our mysterious Mr. S. Or rather, Miss Gallagher had."

Chapman grunted. "Gave us an address, too. Turns out it matches the location of a shoot-out three nights ago, up in Astorbilt country. Know anything about that?"

Thomas sighed. "Would you like to take our statements now or later?"

"That's what I thought." Chapman sucked a tooth, regarding us both as if we were badly behaved children. "The statements'll have to wait, though. I'm headed for the Tombs. They got Essex locked up down there."

"In a jail cell?" I actually clapped my hands in delight. "Where did they find him?"

"He didn't get far after the shoot-out. Neighbors spotted him lurking in the woods and called the police. He spent the past two nights in the Tombs, but our friends down in the Sixth only saw fit to inform me this morning. Hopefully his memory's no worse for wear, 'cause I got more than a few questions."

"I have a few questions for him myself, Sergeant, if you don't mind," Thomas said.

"Don't see why not, once we're done with him. I'll be bringing your friend Roberts in, too."

"Sensible, though I doubt you'll get much from him. Roberts was just a bystander in all this."

"Anyways," Chapman said, "I'll let you know when I'm ready for that statement. Meantime, I looked into that thing you asked about." Taking out his ledger, he read, "Mrs. Matilda Meyer, forty-five, body discovered floating in Long Island Sound on January 2, 1884, by the lighthouse keeper on North Brother Island. Coroner initially suspected foul play but changed his mind. Ruled an accident, case closed."

"The coroner was right the first time, I'm afraid," Thomas said.

"You got evidence of that?"

"Not at present, but I intend to get it."

"Two years later?" Chapman grunted. "Good luck to you."

"Yes, thank you, Sergeant," Thomas said tartly. "What else can you tell me?"

Thomas copied down the rest of the information, and we sent the good sergeant on his way with a promise that we'd head down to the Tombs later to give our statements.

"Perhaps it would be a good time for you to stop by your mother's," Thomas said when Chapman had gone.

I sighed inwardly. I'd put it off for as long as I could, but I'd have to face Mam eventually. I still wasn't sure how much I ought to tell her. Part of me wanted to confess everything, to curl up in my mother's arms and have her comfort me like a little girl. But I didn't know where to begin, and anyway, I wasn't sure her delicate health could take it.

As though reading my thoughts, Thomas said, "She's your mother, Rose. Whatever you decide, she'll love you all the same."

Which of course was true, but that didn't make the decision any easier.

I helped Clara clear up breakfast, and she changed the bandage over my scar, applying some fresh ointment that made it feel a little better. "Ain't that somethin'," she marveled, running a finger gingerly over the wound. "You'd think it was weeks old already. Who needs stitches when you got magic?"

"I don't know about that. I'd take your stitches any day."

She eyed me askance. "Don't you polish my shoes, girl. I'm still mad at you."

"You have every right to be. I'm sorry you got dragged into all this."

"And what about you? Now that you've seen what all comes of *adventure,* you still got the taste for it?"

I thought about that for a long moment before answering. "I don't know about adventure, but I'm not sorry I learned about this"—I gestured vaguely around us—"other world. The real world, I guess I should say."

"Magic, ghosts, special powers . . ." Clara shook her head. "Next thing you know he'll be telling us the Easter Bunny is real."

We finished tidying up, and on my way out Clara handed me a paper bag soaked through with butter spots. "Are these—?" I peered inside and found a treasure trove of leftover scones.

"No sense letting 'em get hard."

"Mam will love these! But are you sure—?"

"New leftover policy," Clara said, smug as a cat licking cream off its whiskers. "Courtesy of the new lady in charge."

I grinned back at her. Loath as I was to go back to being Rose the Maid, answering to Clara instead of Mrs. Sellers took some of the sting out of it.

Later that morning, Thomas and I headed down to Five Points. There was a nasty bite to the air, and I found myself wondering if Mam had enough coal to heat the flat. Funny, isn't it, how quickly things settle back into the mundane? The night before, I'd been huddled on a pier on the East River watching magical lights shimmer in the sky, and now here I was worrying about coal and iron stoves. Life goes on, I suppose.

We arrived at Wang's to find it bustling as usual. Mei was up to her ears in customers, but she extracted herself for long enough to give me a quick hug. "I'm so glad you're feeling better," she said. And then, of course, she pressed a pouch of dry tea into my hands.

"Let me guess—your father's recipe?"

"My recipe," she said with a smile. Turning to Thomas, she added, "The item you ordered is ready. The red lacquer box on the counter." Then we heard the sound of pottery breaking somewhere, and Mei shouldered past me, scolding someone roundly in Chinese.

"Ah," said Thomas, "look, there's Jackson." His fellow Pinkerton was examining some of Mr. Wang's wares; as we approached, he sniffed at what looked like a jar of dried mushrooms.

"Morning, Wiltshire. Miss Gallagher." He hefted the jar of mushrooms, shaking his head in admiration. "How does Wang manage it? I've been after these for six months."

"Some sort of spell component?" I asked, peering at them warily.

"Not that I know of, but they're quite wonderful in soup."

"If you're so enamored of the local shops," Thomas said, "perhaps you ought to consider relocating to New York."

"So I can molder away in that horrible hovel you call an office? No, thank you. Speaking of which, I spoke to Sharpe, and he approves of your suggestion. Thinks it's a tremendous idea, in fact. He also asked me to tell you that your services have been requested in Colorado, so we'd best be quick rounding up those shades."

"In that case, we ought to get started. Shall we?" Thomas gestured at the silk curtain separating the store from the back rooms. On our way past the counter, he paused and picked up the red lacquer box. "You go on ahead, Jackson. I just need a moment with Miss Gallagher."

"Is Matilda back there?" I folded my arms against a sudden shiver. "I think I can sense her."

Thomas nodded. "We won't be able to see her until after dark, of course, but we can still communicate with her through Mr. Smith. In any case, it seems like an appropriate moment to give you this." He handed me the red lacquer box.

"You're giving me a gift?"

"Call it a replacement, rather. Open it."

The box creaked open to reveal the most magnificent hairpin I'd ever seen. Six inches long and bone white, it was topped with a beautifully carved jade rose. My breath caught in my throat; for a moment I couldn't even speak. "It's exquisite," I managed eventually. "Is this . . . ash?"

"Magically treated by Mrs. Weber, for added strength. I promised I'd think of something, didn't I? Not quite as easy to use as a walking stick, but you can carry it with you wherever you go without attracting notice, and it wouldn't be the first time you've brandished a hairpin as a weapon. I felt terrible when I saw the state of yours after you used it to free me, so this seemed an elegant solution."

Elegant. It was so much more than that. For a moment I was quite overcome, and I very nearly threw my arms around him. I caught myself just in time, arresting my momentum so abruptly that I swayed a little on my feet.

"Are you all right?" He put a steadying hand on my elbow.

"Fine. I'm just . . ." I swallowed, fighting down a blush. "Thank you, is all."

"You're very welcome. It's the least I can do after everything you've done for me. In fact . . ." His grip tightened on my elbow, but then he hesitated, his pale gaze doing a quick tour of the crowded room. "No, not here. We'll discuss it later."

We found Mr. Wang and Mr. Smith waiting in the back. I hugged them both, which embarrassed them, but I didn't care. I was in a wonderful mood, and I meant to share it—that is, until we got down to the grim business at hand.

Thomas spoke to Matilda Meyer as if she were any other client of the Pinkerton Detective Agency, updating her on the particulars he'd managed to dig up with the help of Sergeant Chapman. "I'm sorry I don't have more for you at the moment, but at least you know your children are safe."

"I can't tell you what a relief that is," she said. "Thank you, Mr. Wiltshire."

There was a brief, hopeful pause. Then Mr. Smith sighed in disappointment. "She's still here, alas."

"I was afraid of that," Thomas said. "It would appear that until your husband is brought to justice, you will remain a shade. I'm so very sorry, Mrs. Meyer."

"It's all right," the medium said on her behalf. "I was prepared for that. Anyway, it's not as bad as it was, now that I have someone to talk to." At which point we were treated to the bizarre sight of the medium acknowledging himself with a nod.

"I'll keep searching for evidence," Thomas said. "For as long as it takes."

"Thank you," the medium said, and a moment later: "She has left us."

"Right," said Mr. Jackson, "shall we discuss our plans for the rest of them?"

Our plans. That didn't include me, I supposed. "I'll leave you to it, then. It's time for me to head home."

Past time, I thought as I headed up Mott Street. I wondered if Mam would be angry with me. Pietro certainly would, but there was nothing I could do about that.

As it turned out, though, I needn't have worried; when I apologized for not turning up for church, Mam just creased her brow and said, "Oh, didn't you?" She didn't remember any of it, not even the note I'd sent from Wang's telling her that I felt ill. That settled it, of course. There was no way I could burden her with everything that had happened to me over the past two weeks. It would only upset and confuse her, and she'd just forget it all anyway. So we drank tea and ate Clara's scones with strawberry jam, and when Pietro came home later that afternoon, we both pretended nothing had changed.

At least until Mam headed off for her nap. As soon as we were alone, Pietro said, "So. Feeling better, are we?"

"Much better, thank you. Mam seems to be as well. She told me Granny hasn't visited since she asked her to stay away. Is that true?"

"I haven't heard her talking to herself lately, anyway. It seems all right for now."

"Listen, Pietro, I'm—"

He cut me off with a weary gesture. "Just tell me this: Is it over, whatever it was?"

"I think so."

"Thanks God. And what happens now?"

"I really don't know."

"Are you staying with him, your boss? I don't like him, Rose."

"Oh, really? I hadn't noticed." I fiddled with one of Mam's doilies, avoiding Pietro's eye. Of course, what I really wanted to avoid was his question, to which I had no answer. "What about you? Are things all right with Augusto?"

"For now. He has me working on a few projects. Nothing illegal, don't worry." Sourly, he added, "For now."

"I guess *for now* is the best we can hope for sometimes."

"Especially in New York," Pietro agreed.

A knock sounded at the door. Answering it, I found Thomas, looking grave. "I'm sorry to interrupt, but I'm afraid our appointment at the Tombs has been moved up a few hours."

"Oh?"

He glanced over my shoulder. "Good afternoon, Pietro. I'm afraid I have to steal Miss Gallagher away again."

I half expected another storm, but Pietro just shrugged. "I have to get back to Augusto's anyway. Don't forget your coat, Fiora."

Thomas's carriage was waiting for us outside. "What's going on?"

"Danforth Essex has just been found hanged in his cell."

"*What?*" Catholic or no, I couldn't bring myself to feel sorry for Essex, but it was certainly shocking. "Why would he do that?"

"I haven't the faintest idea."

"Maybe after everything that happened with his Wall Street firm, he just couldn't take it anymore. Or maybe . . ." I trailed off, remembering something. "Edmund Drake mentioned that he had a man on the police force, didn't he?"

Thomas frowned. "Are you suggesting that Drake had Essex killed?"

"Maybe. Or maybe he didn't even need to. Suppose all he had to do was visit Essex in prison and use his luck?"

"His powers of suggestion are strong, I'll grant you, but there's no evidence they extend that far. On top of which, why bother? Essex doesn't have his folios anymore."

"You heard what he said about Jacob Crowe. If he was willing to murder his own friend to stop him experimenting with the otherworld, why would he hesitate to do the same to someone else?"

Thomas mulled that over. "I still think it's a stretch, but your instincts have proven themselves time and again. If you *are* right, that would make Drake one of the most dangerous men in America."

"Should we tell Chapman?"

"Without a lick of evidence? No, that would be unfair, not to mention unwise. It does make me think twice about returning the manuscripts to him, however."

"At least Essex got what was coming to him."

Thomas arched an eyebrow. "I prefer a more legal brand of justice, myself."

"In that case, maybe you should have become a police officer instead of a Pinkerton."

"Touché." Thomas took out his watch. "One thirty. We'd better get on. But before we do, Rose, there's something I'd like to ask you." His gaze fell, and he shifted on his feet, suddenly awkward. "We've been through a great deal these past few days, you and I, and it's given me cause to reevaluate the nature of our relationship."

Could it be? My heart started thudding in my breast.

"The last thing I wish to do is pressure you, but I've given it a great deal of thought, and I think perhaps . . ." He glanced up, his eyes searching mine as if for signs of encouragement. "I think perhaps I need you. What I'm getting at is . . . Would you be willing to join the Pinkerton Detective Agency?"

I stared.

"I've spoken to Sharpe, and he was very impressed with you. And as I say, I need you. *We* need you. There's a desperate shortage of Agency assets in New York, and as a native, you know this city better than an outsider ever could." Mistaking my stunned silence for reluctance, he went on, "I know you have your reservations about the Agency, but I think you'll find the special branch different. We have a number of female agents, so you wouldn't be alone. And I think we make a tremendous team, you and I."

Finding my voice at last, I said, "I agree, but, Thomas . . ."

I almost told him then, I really did. The words were on the tip of my tongue. But Thomas Wiltshire had just laid at my feet the one thing I wanted even more. I didn't dare put it at risk, not even for him.

"I'm sorry to catch you off guard like this. I ought to have found a better way to ask."

"It's not that. I'm flattered, and grateful. I'm just . . ." *Terrified.* "A bit overwhelmed."

"But you'll consider it?"

Get ahold of yourself, Rose. Drawing myself up a little straighter, I said, "I don't need to consider it. I would be very pleased to work alongside you."

His pale eyes lit up brighter than one of Mr. Edison's lamps. "Excellent. In that case, you'd better have some of these." He handed me a little book of calling cards—silver, with a single staring eye. Hopping up onto the step of the carriage, he said, "Shall we?"

I hesitated, still reeling. Could I really do this? Become like him and Mr. Jackson and Henny Weber and the others? *You know this city better than an outsider ever could.* A few days ago, I would have agreed with that. But the city Thomas knew wasn't the New York I'd grown up in—or rather, it wasn't the New York I'd *thought* I grew up in. "This world you move in . . . There's so much I don't know. So much I don't understand."

Thomas smiled and held out his hand. "Come, then. Let me show you."

AUTHOR'S NOTE

The section of New York's East River known as Hell Gate is just about the perfect setting for a work of fiction. It's been the backdrop of fierce battles, shipwrecks, murders, Nazi conspiracies, hauntings, and sundry other bizarre and notable incidents throughout New York history, only a handful of which are mentioned in this novel. The immediate vicinity was also populated with some of nineteenth-century America's most chilling locales, including quarantine hospitals, potter's fields, and the infamous insane asylum on Blackwell's Island (now Roosevelt Island).

Undoubtedly the most dramatic moment in the strait's history was the annihilation of Flood Rock on October 10, 1885. The explosion shattered windows from midtown Manhattan to the Upper East Side and was heard as far away as Princeton, New

Jersey. *The New-York Times* breathlessly described the spectacle as a "momentary but magnificent display of upheaved waters" in which a "solid wall of water [hung] trembling in mid-air." It was the single largest controlled explosion ever undertaken, and remained so until testing began for the atomic bomb decades later. The incident reportedly served as the inspiration for the climax of Bram Stoker's *The Lair of the White Worm*—and, of course, this story.

Another real-world locale to inspire this novel was Wo Kee's General Store, which stood at 34 Mott Street in the heart of Chinese Five Points and served as the blueprint for Wang's General Store. Mr. Wang himself borrowed his entrepreneurial spirit (and his mustache) from the real-life Wo Kee, though I suspect the similarities end there.

The character of Matilda Meyer is loosely based upon an unfortunate New Yorker whose body was discovered floating in Long Island Sound just north of Hell Gate in January 1884. While the coroner originally suspected foul play, he eventually concluded that Mrs. Meyer met with an unfortunate accident. I have no reason to believe this to be anything other than the case; the version of her story presented here is purely a work of fiction.

Sergeant Chapman is *very* loosely based on one Officer Chapman (given name unknown), who, according to a trio of articles in the archives of *The New York Times*, investigated a series of hauntings at 131 West Fourteenth Street in June of 1881.

The Cipher Manuscripts, a collection of sixty folios containing a syllabus of instruction in magic, were brought to light by Wynn Westcott in London in 1886, though their true origins are in dispute. They formed the founding scripture of the Hermetic Order of the Golden Dawn, an offshoot of Masonic Rosicrucian tradition that still exists today. The manuscripts were a compendium of known "magical traditions," though some claimed they also contained information on how to contact the "secret chiefs"—supernatural beings of immense power.

HMS *Hussar*, a twenty-eight-gun frigate of the British Royal Navy, sank in Hell Gate on November 23, 1780, reportedly carrying up to £960,000 in bullion. For the next century and a half, treasure hunters scoured the East River in hopes of salvaging the gold, rumored to be worth anywhere between $2 million and $576 million. Somewhat less romantically, historians have since concluded that the *Hussar*'s remains probably lie beneath a landfill in the Bronx.

The American Society for Psychical Research was founded in 1885 by a group of scholars in Boston and still exists today. According to their website, their mission is to "explore extraordinary or as yet unexplained phenomena that have been called psychic or paranormal, and their implications for our understanding of consciousness, the universe and the nature of existence." Their modern headquarters can be found on West Seventy-Third Street in New York.

The cover of *Harper's Weekly* that so enchanted Rose is a faithful description of the actual illustration from January 2, 1886. Readers interested in admiring it for themselves can find it on the web courtesy of the Hathi Trust Digital Library.

The supper-stained headlines Rose and Clara peruse in chapter II are actual headlines drawn from the archives of *The New York Times*—with the exception of the story of Mr. Peter Arbridge, which is entirely fictional. Two of the articles referenced in this author's note appear in abbreviated form on the following pages. I hope you find them as enlightening and entertaining as I did.

Brooklyn, NY

October 2016

The New York Times
June 18, 1881

TWO SPECTRAL LODGERS

GHOSTS IN A FOURTEENTH-STREET BOARDING HOUSE—BOARDERS FRIGHTENED AWAY AND SERVANTS IN TERROR—WHAT PERSONS WHO HAVE SEEN THE PHANTOMS SAY

Two alleged ghosts have been engaged in the unholy business of making day and night alike hideous for some time past in the house at No. 131 West Fourteenth-street. During the past year the house has been occupied by Mrs. Mary Carr, a widow lady, as a boarding house, and at times it has been completely filled. The ghosts, however, have played sad havoc with Mrs. Carr's business of late, and her boarders have been gradually leaving her as the fact dawned on their minds that the house was haunted.

Those who have seen the unearthly visitors all agree in their descriptions of their personal characteristics, so that it may be set down as certain that only two ghosts have taken up their abode up to this time in the Fourteenth-street house. The man is described as tall and slightly stooping, with English side whiskers, mustache, and very large black eyes, which strike terror to all upon whom they are turned. The woman is a maiden lady, who seems to have just passed the age of 20, and her face, though beautiful, is disfigured by marks which would seem to indicate a life of dissipation. Both the ghosts differ from those with which we have been familiar from childhood in that they seem to be restricted to no hours in the regulation of their appearances. They are apparently permitted to roam at will in the apartments of the house whenever it suits their convenience, whether it be high noon or at the solemn hour of midnight, the latter time being that usually affected by the ghost species.

On Tuesday night the male ghost created such an excitement that the facts of the mystery could no longer be kept from all the inmates of the house. On that night the chamber-maid retired at about 10 o'clock. Just before midnight she awoke, experiencing a peculiarly cold feeling. As she awoke she saw a man standing a few feet from her bed, with his back toward her. It was the male ghost of No. 131 West Fourteenth-street. The girl gave one scream and fainted. When she recovered the figure was still in the room, but it had moved to a corner and stood there eyeing her. She fainted again and again recovered. The ghost was now at the foot of the bed, but he seemed to have diminished in height about one-half. He gradually grew smaller and smaller, until finally he disappeared altogether. The girl jumped from the bed and ran screaming down the stairs to her mistress, to whom she told her story. The whole house was aroused, and people in the streets, attracted by the girl's cries, congregated around the door. Officer Chapman was on post at the time, and Mrs. Carr called him into the house. He says that the excitement was tremendous. The chamber-maid sat in the basement, trembling with fright, and rocking herself to and fro. The cook, who is a Catholic, was sprinkling holy water on the floor and every article of furniture in the room. Accompanied by Mrs. Carr, who is a woman of extraordinary nerve, the policeman searched the house from the top floor to the basement, but found no man answering to the description of the ghost.

The New York Times
October 11, 1885

THE GREAT MINE SPRUNG

A girl's hand unlocking the mighty force

THE GRAND SPECTACLE WHICH A CITY TURNED OUT TO SEE—A SOLID WALL OF WATER HANGING TREMBLING IN MID-AIR—A SHOCK WHICH WAS FELT FOR MILES IN EVERY DIRECTION—THE SUCCESSFUL CONCLUSION OF NINE YEARS OF WORK

Three hundred thousand pounds of rackarock and dynamite, the greatest single charge of explosives ever used, thundered yesterday morning in the depths of the East River, and Flood Rock, the great barrier that stood at the entrance of Long Island Sound, was shattered into fragments. The long labor and thoughtful study of Gen. John Newton and his corps of assistants culminated in a momentary but magnificent display of upheaved waters, and another triumph of human skill over the resistance of nature was recorded.

Those who wanted to see the explosion sought the various

points from which a good view could be obtained. Before 9 o'clock crowds began to move up town. The cross streets east of the upper end of Central Park were full of people moving toward the East River. Down town great numbers of people were climbing to the tops of high buildings. The bulk of the crowd, however, assembled opposite the scene of the explosion. Men, women, children, dogs, and goats mingled in one broad, variegated mass. Hundreds of people gathered on the tops of the big breweries and other tall buildings that loom one above another on the easterly decline of the city. Away up on the tops of chimneys and on the outermost pinnacles of roofs could be seen the irrepressible, never-to-be-left small boy, filled with the American instinct for getting to the top and looking down on the whole business. Trees had their usual load of sightseers and lamp posts were opportunities to be embraced with avidity.

People held their breath.

Eyes were strained and riveted on the bare brown rock. There was a deathlike silence.

Away it flew, that viewless spark, to loose three hundred thousand chained demons buried in darkness and the cold, salt waves under the iron rocks. A deep rumble, then a dull boom, like the smothered bursting of a hundred mighty guns far away beyond the blue horizon, rolled across the yellow river. Up, up, and still up into the frightened air soared a great, ghastly, writhing wall of white and silver and gray. Fifty gigantic geysers, linked together like shivering, twisting masses of spray, soared upward, their shining pinnacles, with dome-like summits, looming like shattered floods of molten silver against the azure sky. Three magnificent monuments of solid water sprang far above the rest of the mass, the most westerly of them still rising after all else had begun to fall, till it towered nearly 200 feet in air. To east and west the waters rose, a long blinding sheet of white. Far and wide the great wall spread, defying the human eye to take in its breadth and height and thickness. The contortion of the wreathed waters was like the dumb agony of some stricken thing.

For a trembling moment the sublime spectacle stood sharp against the sky, like a mighty vision of distant snow-capped mountains. Then down, down, and still down the enormous mass rushed with a wild hissing, as if ten thousand huge steam valves had been opened. The yellow waters of the river were riven and torn into immense boiling masses of white foam. . . . And when the spray had sunk down and the waters of the river filled with brown mud lay boiling around the site of the great explosion, there lay the old rock, torn into myriads of pieces and scatted with débris, a ragged, smoking dun-brown mass.